LOVE ALL
A ROMANCE

RACHEL SPANGLER

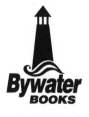

Bywater
BOOKS

Ann Arbor
2018

Bywater Books

Print ISBN: 978-1-61294-137-0

Bywater Books First Edition: October 2018

Printed in the United States of America on acid-free paper.

Cover designer: Ann McMan, TreeHouse Studio

Bywater Books
PO Box 3671
Ann Arbor MI 48106-3671
www.bywaterbooks.com

To Susie, best of wives and best of women…
this is still all your fault.

Prologue

"Sadie, you can't do this all by yourself." Tad echoed the refrain of her parents, her brother, and every one of their friends. The only difference was, he held a golden ring between his trembling fingers. "I enlisted. I'm going to have insurance and housing and a steady paycheck. I'll be able to take care of you both."

Both.

She glanced down, surveying the face so small it was nearly lost in the sea of pink swaddling blankets and the oversized hospital gown obscuring her own features. The two of them were a unit, a package deal, tethered together now every bit as much as they'd been when connected by a cord. She didn't need him to tell her. She felt the tie tugging at her core the same way she'd felt every kick, every shift, every hiccup.

"A baby needs a dad." He pressed, the anguish making his voice raw.

"She's got a dad." She cupped one hand gently around his cheek, marveling at the contrast of her dark skin stark against the paleness of his.

Black and white. That's how he saw the world. Right and wrong. So clear-cut. He would make a good soldier. His righteousness would give him strength, but so would hers. She held the sleeping baby closer in the crook of her arm, noticing for the first time that her eyes were the same shape as his. Would they hold her color? Retain the proud bridge of her nose? The little dimple of her chin mirrored his, but the shape of her tiny mouth clearly came from Sadie. She inspected the strangely familiar face, then looked back up at his, unable to tell which of them seemed more vulnerable in that moment. "I'm glad you're her father, but I don't want a husband."

A little muscle in his jaw twitched under her fingers. "You don't want a husband, or you don't want me for a husband?"

She sighed softly. That was the question on which all their futures hung. She could add it to the long list of ones she couldn't answer. "Tad, I don't know how to explain, much less make anyone understand, but I have to do this on my own."

"You're sixteen." Emotion cracked in his voice.

"I'm almost seventeen."

"You haven't finished high school."

"I will."

"You don't have a job."

"I'll find one," she said matter-of-factly, partly because this wasn't the first time she'd had this conversation, and partly because each time she said the words, her certainty grew.

"And who's going to take care of her?" He nodded toward the sleeping infant, his smooth face contorted with a worry so discordant with her youthful features. "You can't be everything she needs."

She let her hand fall from his cheek as the final break between them was cemented. "I will be."

He rose, tears shimmering over the cobalt eyes she'd been so drawn to so many months ago. She'd never seen eyes like his, not on anyone who'd ever looked at her the way he had.

"I'm trying to do the right thing, Sadie."

"So am I," she said resolutely.

He stared down at them for a long, heavy moment before bending to place the lightest of kisses across the baby's smooth brow, but he made no attempt to repeat the gesture with her. She could feel the grief radiate off of him in waves with each exhale, but she managed to feel only relief as he straightened.

"I left my enlistment details with your mom. I'll send my address as soon as I get to basic training in case you change your mind." He sighed. "Or maybe if you want to send me pictures at least."

She nodded. "Be safe."

A strangled sound escaped his throat. "You too."

She didn't want him to go, but she didn't want him to stay either. She didn't feel anything at all from his absence, except maybe a hint of finality. Perhaps she should've felt scared, but she couldn't summon any fear. Did that make her unrealistic? With all the doctors and nurses and social workers gone, had he been the only sensible one left in the room? When it came to her prospects as an unwed teenage mother, everyone she knew agreed with his assessment of her fitness.

Everyone but her.

She lifted her sleeping daughter to her chest, gently easing back the blanket to drop a kiss atop the wispy black curls. The scent of baby shampoo and fresh powder overtook the antiseptic tinge of the hospital air, and peace settled through her aching body. She didn't know why she couldn't share everyone else's concern. She didn't have answers to all their questions, but she knew with the same certainty she had had since the moment she'd first felt life growing inside her that she would find a way. This was her life, her child, her destiny.

"Destiny," she whispered, and the baby's eyes fluttered open, so big and round and beautifully full of awe.

A smile built in Sadie's chest and spread slowly until it stretched her cheeks.

"Do you like that?" she cooed softly.

The little girl blinked up at her, then furrowed her brow as if trying to focus on something complex.

"I think you do," Sadie continued. "I think it's going to stick."

Sadie cradled the baby's head in the palm of her hand and

stared into the wonderment reflected there. "Everything's going to work out. I don't know how yet, but I know it will. You're just going to have to trust me on that, because I'm your mama, and you are my Destiny."

The baby blinked, and Sadie grinned. "Just me and you, kid. From here on out, everything I do, it's going to be for you."

Chapter One

Seventeen years later.
Melbourne, Australia

Even if Jay Pierce hadn't felt the racket frame give way when it crashed against the mockingly cheerful blue of the court, the sharp crack of carbon fiber snapping in two gave her away.

She could barely make out the chair umpire's swift judgment of a fine above the wild cheering of the crowd, but she did the math quickly in her head. It didn't take advanced calculus to realize another five grand added to the hefty damages she'd had levied against her in the last match would put a dent in her spending money for a few weeks.

"No, no, no," she called, jogging over to the chair. "I didn't break it."

The umpire rolled her eyes, and Peggy Hamilton snorted her amusement from the other side of the court.

"The strings were too tight for this heat." She glared up at the sun as if it were the real culprit. "I had to loosen them up."

The chair pursed her lips, green eyes impassive, and her white Keds-clad toes tapped the foot-rail of her elevated seat.

"I made a legal adjustment to my equipment, and I didn't use any profanity while doing it."

The corner of the chair's mouth turned up, and she covered

the mic with her hand. "Jay, your racket is broken. Swap it out to finish the match."

"What? Broken?" she said, loudly enough for the TV and audio folks to hear, then winked up at Heather. "It's perfect. I'm going to play next point with it."

"You have to *win* the next point in order to force a changeover."

Jay smiled broadly now. "Challenge accepted."

She strode back to her baseline as Heather's voice echoed through the loudspeaker of Margaret Court Arena. "40-30, third set point, Ms. Pierce."

"Come on," she mumbled to herself, as she mopped the sweat off her brow with the back of her equally sweaty forearm. "Just like back home, Grandma's racket, hot asphalt, Bobby Thompson's stupid, pimply face across the net."

She closed her eyes and could see it all again, bouncing the ball, one, two, three times, until it popped back up perfectly into the middle of her calloused palm. She opened her eyes and in one fluid motion tossed the ball high into the air. She arched her body back like a bow pulled taut. Every muscle coiled in anticipation, as years of practice and conditioning strained to be unleashed. But as the ball peaked in the midday sun and started its descent, Jay restrained herself for a fraction of a second before snapping forward. With a subtle flick of her wrist, she brushed a glancing stroke along the top of it.

The racket gave slightly, but the ball spun wildly, causing it to career like a drunken sailor on stormy seas. If she'd been a pitcher, the commentators would've called the result a slurve ball as it arced from two to six on the clock face. She had no idea what Mary Carillo would label the shot in the booth above her, and she didn't have time to wonder as she charged the net. The ball dropped into the service box opposite her and kicked dramatically toward the sideline. The decreased tempo and heavy spin prevented her opponent from timing a powerful return stroke. Peggy managed only to bounce the ball on its upward track for a high lob, but Jay reached toward the sky with her entire wingspan and pushed off the court with both feet. She barely managed to get high enough to bring her racket head down with all the force its broken frame still had left in it. As she finished the motion, she flipped her right hand outward and sent the ball skittering off the far sideline into the wall.

Peggy didn't even try to dive for it. She merely shook her head, causing her blond ponytail to sway, before wordlessly turning toward her bench. Jay followed at a more leisurely pace, taking great pains not to make eye contact with either of the women ahead of her as Heather leaned toward the mic and declared, "Game and set, Ms. Pierce. One set all."

Jay kept her head low as she dropped onto her bench and dug out a fresh racket from her bag. Careful to move her lips as little as possible so none of the on-court cameras would catch the comment, she asked, "So, no fine?"

Heather cleared her throat as if to make sure the mic wasn't live before confirming. "Well played."

She grabbed a thick, white towel and tossed it over her head, both to dry the sweat dripping from her hair and to hide the smile tugging at her lips. She might not possess all the tools she'd once had at her disposal, but her bag o' tricks wasn't completely empty. Besides, now, no matter what happened with the match, she'd have something to talk about in the press conference afterward, something other than her temper, or her personal life, or the faint strands of gray she kept plucking from around her temples. Plus, even if she didn't win any money today, she'd at least stopped herself from losing any more of it.

She pulled the towel from her head, trying not to think about how much her goals had shifted over the last few years. She wouldn't exactly say she'd lowered her standards, but everyone else around the wide world of tennis would.

"How do you feel about your first major tournament?" someone called from among the many rows of reporters.

"I feel like I should've played better."

A smattering of laughter filtered through the room. Sadie

fought a grimace. She knew the comment hadn't been made for comic effect, but rather as a blunt statement of fact.

"Now that you're knocked out of contention, do you have a favorite to win?"

"I don't really follow anyone else's play unless I'm preparing to face them."

A few murmurs passed through the crowd, and Hank shifted in his seat beside her. Sadie kept her eyes trained on the young woman in front of the room. Over the years she'd learned to keep her facial expressions neutral—a benign smile, eyes open, chin up—no matter what happened, in the view of cameras or kids.

"A lot of pundits say you turned pro too soon. Does a second-round exit in your first Australian Open make you worry you should've stayed on the junior tour for another year?"

"No."

Silence reigned for a few seconds, save for the scattered click of flashbulbs, but if the press were waiting for her to elaborate, they'd all be here for a long time.

"Dead air time," Hank whispered. "It makes her seem dumb or spoiled."

"She's stoic. She gets that from her father."

He snorted softly.

Finally, another reporter asked, "Have you received a warm welcome from the other Americans in the field?"

"I haven't met any of them yet. Honestly, I don't know that there are that many of them left to meet here." This time the murmurs weren't as quiet.

Hank began to rise, but Sadie clamped a hand on his knee and pushed firmly. "She didn't mean any offense."

"I know that, and you know that, but no one else in the room does."

"She knows it," Sadie said confidently. "She just hasn't figured out how to convey her ideas clearly yet."

"Well, she needs to learn," Hank grumbled. "This isn't the YMCA anymore, Sadie. If she doesn't learn to—"

"She'll learn what she's taught," Sadie said, the steel in her voice causing a few heads around them to turn.

"Destiny," a reporter called from the row behind them, "do you see yourself as the future of American tennis?"

She shrugged, looking more like the teenager she rarely had time to be. "Not really. I see myself as the future of tennis, period."

"And our time is up," Hank said, hopping up so fast Sadie didn't have the reflexes to stop him. "Destiny's got two weeks off-tour to train; then we'll be in Qatar, followed by Dubai in February before heading back stateside."

The reporters all talked over themselves, but no one in particular seemed intent on pushing for more with Destiny. Some of the tension slipped from Sadie's shoulders as she watched her daughter thread her way through the crowd with a duffel bag thrown over her shoulder.

"Can we go now?" Destiny asked, her jaw tight and her voice strained.

"Of course, baby."

"Actually," Hank cut in, as cameras flashed around them once more, "I'd like to stay for the next conference, and I think you should, too."

Sadie turned back toward the stage to see what all the fuss was about. She had to sway from side to side to catch a glimpse of the player taking a seat.

She had golden brown hair, streaked with sweat and sun, and her skin was tan enough to make her biceps stand out against the white of her tank top, but every other color faded from the room as soon as Sadie saw her eyes. Even from several rows back, the azure sparkled like sapphires flecked with light and mischief.

"Good afternoon, everyone," the woman said in a voice so steady and confident she hardly needed the mic. "I'm Jay Pierce, and I'll be your tour guide for today, as we take a walk through the museum of how not to win tennis matches."

Everyone laughed, and Sadie eased back into her seat with a gentle tug on her daughter's arm.

Hank leaned over her to whisper to Destiny. "Watch and learn."

"Are you disappointed with your finish, Jay?" a voice called out from one of the front rows.

"Of course I'm disappointed, Chuck. My day finished without a single dinner invitation."

Everyone laughed again as Chuck added, "I meant about your play."

"Oh well, my play wasn't nearly as dismal as my social prospects, but still not up to snuff."

"Why is that?" someone else called.

"Probably I got dropped on the head as a child," Jay said with a magnetic smile. "Oh wait, you were talking about the tennis again, weren't you? Well, no, actually same answer."

"You were neck and neck going into the third set," a reporter prompted.

"That's generally what a third set means, isn't it? It'd be hard for a woman to go into a third set when she'd already lost two of them."

Sadie wasn't sure if she was watching a press conference or a sports comedian, but either way, the results were entertaining, with none of the awkward silences that had punctuated the previous interview session.

"Did you break your racket in the final game of the second set?"

"No!" she declared loudly, even as she nodded the affirmative. "The racket was too uptight."

"Too tight, or uptight?"

"Yes," Jay said emphatically. "I loosened it."

"Did you loosen it by cracking the frame?"

"Look, Terry," Jay said, leaning forward conspiratorially. "I could tell you my secrets, but then all the tennis stars would use them, and I'd lose my edge."

Terry shook his head. "You want me to write that in my column?"

"How about you write that after taking a 40-love lead in the game, I dropped three set points in a row, and I knew all you jaboneys in the press corps were going to start speculating about my mental fortitude, or whatever you like to call it, so I used my superior knowledge of tennising and fixed my racket. Then I played the best point of the tournament to the wild adulation of my massive fan base."

By now it was abundantly clear that everyone in the room could be included in the fan base she spoke of. Sadie's smile stretched so wide her cheeks strained, until Destiny elbowed her in the side. She glanced at her daughter's furrowed brow and questioning eyes.

"She's not even talking about tennis strategy or craft," Destiny whispered.

"Exactly," Hank said out of the corner of his mouth. "She's holding court. She does it better than anyone in the business."

"I'm not an entertainer. I'm a gamer."

Hank nodded toward the stage. "She's both."

Sadie lifted her index finger to her lips, not wanting to miss a word this woman uttered.

"Any more questions?" Jay started to rise.

"What happened in the third set?" someone called out, with a bitter edge to her voice.

Jay's smile twisted slightly but didn't disappear. "What? You didn't see it? I'm disappointed in you, Haley. I wouldn't think a journalist of your caliber would spend an entire set asleep at the wheel."

"I saw, Jay." The words sounded clipped, and Sadie craned her neck to see the woman who'd spoken them. She had pale skin and a severe, dark updo. Her cheekbones seemed impossibly high, but maybe she'd merely accentuated them by pursing her lips. "I wanted your take on why you fell apart after your self-proclaimed glorious rally in the second set."

The room fell silent, and Jay's smile faded only to the point where it didn't crinkle the edges of her amazing eyes. "I suppose that's a question we'll all spend the next few hours pondering, but for me, I suspect I'll settle on the explanation that Peggy Hamilton had a great rally of her own. I'll raise a glass of wine to her fine play as I dine alone tonight."

The tone of the room had shifted as reporters bowed their heads over notepads and tape recorders.

"Now, if there are no other questions, comments, or endorsement offers," Jay said, her voice once again light, "I'll let you all get back to your thesauruses, as you'll no doubt want to look up a few synonyms for charming, charismatic, and humble in order to write your stories about me."

"Just one more, Jay," a reporter down front called.

"Shoot," Jay said, kicking her feet up on the table. "I've got nothing else going on for the next week."

"After her loss today, rookie Destiny Larsen said she didn't know of any other American tennis stars left to meet in Melbourne this week. How do you feel about that?"

Destiny stiffened beside her, and Sadie placed a hand on her arm, trying not to tighten her fingers with the same torque twisting in her chest.

"Well," Jay drew out the word, then grinned. "I think the kid and I have a few things in common."

"How so?" the reporter pushed.

"We both lost in the second round, and I don't know who she is, either." With that, Jay hopped up and waved for all the cameras. "Thanks all. You've been great. No need to applaud. I'll see myself out."

With that she bounded off the stage and out a side door to the players only area, leaving the room abuzz with energy. Everywhere reporters stood, chatted, and compared notes, leaving only Sadie, Destiny, and Hank sitting silently.

"Well," Sadie finally said, "I think it's probably a good time to call it a day. We've all got plenty to think about before we discuss anything."

"Did she just call me a nobody?" Destiny asked softly.

"No," Sadie said quickly.

"Little bit," Hank corrected, as he rose and stretched. "Sort of like you did to her."

Destiny hopped up. "I didn't mean it the way the reporter said. They put words in my mouth."

"That's what happens when you don't give them anything else for their columns."

Sadie stood between them, placing a hand flatly on each of their chests. "This is an important conversation that can happen over the course of the next several weeks, not in the middle of the press corps."

Both of them glanced around and seemed to notice they'd begun to attract a bit of attention.

"You're probably right," Hank said. Sadie raised an eyebrow at him, and he smiled before adding, "As usual."

Then she turned to her daughter, who just shrugged. "Fine. Let's get out of here."

Sadie didn't argue. She'd seen and heard and defused enough for one day, or week. She would've given anything to sink into her own bed with a good book and a mug of tea, but she would settle for a quiet hotel couch and room service. The thought made her flash back to Jay's jokes about her plans to eat alone, and her stomach tightened unexpectedly. She glanced over her shoulder toward the door Jay had fled through, as a pang she didn't recognize settled in her chest.

"Mom."

The word cut through her haze and instantly sharpened her focus, the way it always did. Destiny stood before her, one hand on an open door. "Come on."

She smiled broadly at the center of her universe. "I'm right behind you."

No one paid much attention to Jay once she got back to the locker room. Players came and went with their entourages in tow. Staff scurried about trying to look busy, or maybe they actually were busy. This early in the tournament, there were still roughly sixty-four women in the main draw, and even more when you counted the doubles and junior fields. Just because she had never been one to place excessive demands on the locker room attendants didn't mean her fellow tour members had the same mentality. Still, she couldn't help but wonder why everyone had to do everything in such a rush. Did they really all have somewhere better to be and something more important to do? The thought might have been more depressing if it didn't also give her the freedom to come and go unnoticed and unquestioned.

Jay slung a bag full of rackets over her shoulder and pushed through the door labeled "players only." She remembered when access to the room behind it had felt like a privilege instead of a burden. She shook her head. Not a burden. Maybe a responsibility, though. Press conferences, fines, twenty-hour flights, nights alone in unfamiliar beds—they all added up. The good still outweighed the bad, though, and they both outweighed any other options she currently had on the table.

With that happy thought, she headed down a long hallway adorned with the smiling portraits of past champions, purposefully averting her eyes from her own, albeit much younger, likeness. She kept her head down so long she didn't notice the person standing in front of her until she nearly slammed into him.

"Hey, Jay. Didn't anyone ever tell you to look ahead every now and then?"

She grinned as the familiar voice cascaded over her.

"Someone might have mentioned it, many years ago, back before his hair started to thin and turn gray."

Hank laughed so loudly the roll of it echoed down the long corridor. "Says the woman with arthritic knees."

"Hey now, tendonitis, not arthritis."

"How's it feeling?" Hank nodded to her right leg.

"It's been worse."

"You've still got a way with words. Maybe I'll have you write my biography someday."

She winced as a slew of unbidden memories made her stomach lurch. "Yeah, no thanks. I've had enough people telling stories about me to last a lifetime."

His face softened. "I'm sorry. I didn't mean it that way."

"It's fine." She shrugged. "We've all moved on."

"Really?" he asked quietly.

14

"Yeah." She forced a smile to let him off the hook. "Water under the bridge."

"Good." He clapped a meaty palm on her shoulder and gave a little shake.

The easy affection of the contact felt better than it should have, and she forced herself not to lean into the sturdiness of him. "It's really great to see you again, Hank."

He smiled. "I'm glad you think so, 'cause I've found a new doubles partner for you."

She stepped back with a sharp inhale. Unable to find a voice that wouldn't betray the panic gripping her chest, she shook her head forcefully.

"Come on. You don't have to commit. Just come meet with the girl."

"No." The single word offered the entirety of her thoughts on the subject.

"I need your help, as a favor to me, for old times' sake."

She clenched her jaw. He, of all people, knew better than to play the "old times" card. The old times were exactly why she wouldn't even entertain the request. Resentment bubbled up at him for even making it. Tilting her shoulder at him she muscled her way past.

"Jay," he called after her. "I'm sorry. Please come back. I should have said it differently. I didn't mean to hurt you . . . again."

The pain in his voice was the same one spreading through her chest, and she couldn't face either, not now, not after she'd come so far. But something else inside her wouldn't let her turn her back on him completely. She hated that instinct more than the one to run. Gritting her teeth and clenching her fists, she planted her feet until the urge to bolt subsided enough for her to turn and face him once more.

"Look," she said, her voice raspier than she would've liked. "You didn't hurt me, okay? I just don't play doubles anymore." With that, she hoisted the strap of her bag a little higher, lowered her head, and trudged off down the hall.

Trying in vain not to listen for his footsteps, she didn't know if she should feel relieved or betrayed that he didn't come after her. Maybe a little bit of both. She hated that. She'd spent so much time feeling so many things, but she would gladly have taken any one of them over the mix of emotions warring inside her now. Sadness, anger, regret, happiness—they each came with their own social cues. She knew how to express them or bury them as needed, but she had no protocol for being ripped in half as comfort and pain collided again. She had no recourse but to bury them both in equal measure.

At least she'd had plenty of practice in that arena.

Chapter Two

Indian Wells, California

Sadie sat in the shade created by a cluster of palm trees while Hank put Destiny through her paces. Forehand, backhand, overhead, lob—they all looked flawless to her. Then again, they'd all looked flawless to her since around the time of Destiny's eighth birthday. She'd been a marvel even then, so naturally gifted she made every swing appear effortless. Not that Sadie was biased, but if it'd been up to her, Destiny would've been handed every major tennis award in existence the moment she first picked up a racket. She smiled at the only slight hyperbole.

Thankfully, Hank had no hint of a mother's disposition. He was one hundred percent bear, grizzly when it came to all things tennis, and teddy when it came to everything else.

"Lean into it, Des," he called from the baseline of the practice court nearest to where Sadie sat. "You have to use your body weight to maximize your forward momentum. Some of these women serve a hundred and twenty miles per hour. You can't let your wrist take the brunt of that force."

Destiny knew that; even Sadie knew it, but she supposed sometimes everyone needed a reminder. She couldn't imagine all the things Destiny had to remember in the second between when a ball left an opposing player's racket and when she had to decide how to play it. Footwork, angle, bounce, speed, spin. Even after nearly a decade of following the game closely, Sadie couldn't imagine taking center court herself. Not under the kind of pressure her daughter now faced. Just keeping up with her travel schedule and court times and vitamin regimen consumed Sadie's entire life. She thought she'd finally gotten the hang of everything last year, but as soon as she'd settled in, the conversations about going pro began in earnest. Now her baby girl was leaning into shots in the middle of the desert, a mere two practice courts away from Novak Djokovic.

"Sadie," Hank called, jolting her out of her thoughts, "come give us a hand. We need a line judge."

"Fine, unless by 'line judge,' you mean 'target.'"

He and Destiny both laughed, but neither one of them refuted the charge. Still, she'd never been able to deny her daughter help with anything from a science project to playing the role of human bull's-eye. She pushed out of the chair and strode onto the court, shading her eyes from the sun hanging low over the mountain horizon. "Where should I stand, and do you want me to put on a blindfold so I don't flinch as the knives are thrown?"

"No target practice . . . yet," Hank said matter-of-factly. "I want Des to work on her baseline rally shot."

"Her baseline or your baseline?"

"Both," he said. "She got burned last week by power players pushing her back, then rushing to the net to take balls out of the air and dumping them toward the sidelines. She can't let them manhandle her if she wants to get past the second round here."

Sadie stifled the urge to rush to Destiny's defense. She'd gotten better about not getting upset by every criticism, but habits formed in the early years of parenthood turned out to be hardest to shake. "So, you want me to stand on the baseline and see if the ball goes in or out?"

"Exactly," Hank said, choking up on his white-rimmed racket. "I'll serve, then rush forward, Destiny. Every time your return gets within arm's reach of me, you lose the point whether I make the shot or not. And every time it goes out, you lose the point."

"Sure seems like a lot of ways for me to lose the point."

"That's not even close to how many ways you've found to lose them in real matches."

Sadie's fists tightened at the comment, but she bit her tongue and took her place at the corner.

Taking her line judge job very seriously, she didn't watch Hank, or Destiny. She looked up only when she got to flash a thumbs up to show the ball was in or on the line. At all times during the actual drill, she kept her eyes glued to the line and prayed neither of them shanked an errant shot in her direction, though at least if she got hit, it would be with a lob and not a serve.

The exercise went on for several minutes. Sadie fell into an easy rhythm of giving both player and coach the thumbs-up signal they all three wanted, but about five minutes in, one index finger became three in a row, then four. On the fifth miss, she heard a racket clatter to the court, and checked to see which one had dropped it.

"Good God," Hank called. "What's the problem now? And don't say the heat, 'cause this is nothing compared to the cavernous toaster oven you played in during the Australian."

"No." Destiny shot back, racket at her feet. "It's all the fluids you've forced on me since then."

"Hydrate or die." Hank bellowed one of his many mantras.

"I'm hyper-hydrated, to the point where I can't last an hour practice session without having to pee."

"Then how are you going to last a long set against one of the toughest players in the league? Do you think Azarenka's going to give you a mid-set potty break?"

"Maybe I'll have to invest in some Depends."

"Maybe you should've had that brilliant idea before we came on court, 'cause time is money out here."

"Hank!" Sadie finally scolded. "The sooner she runs to the bathroom, the sooner you get back to practice. The more you argue with her, the more she's just going to dig her heels in."

"Sadie, I'm her coach."

"And I potty-trained the child," Sadie snapped back. "Trust me. She's got a weak bladder and an iron will."

He cracked a smile, but tried to hide it by bending over to check his shoestrings. "Fine, go. But hustle."

Destiny didn't have to be told twice as she scurried off the court.

"And drink some more water while you're at it!" he called after her.

He turned to Sadie, his voice softening. "You too, Line Judge."

She didn't have to be told twice. While Indian Wells didn't compare to Dubai in the heat department, 87 degrees was still entirely too hot for mid-March if you asked her. She grabbed Destiny's racket as she walked off the court and carried it over to the player's bench.

"Is she really doing as bad as you made her out to be?" Sadie asked when Hank joined her.

"Nah," he said. "I mean, in practice today, yes, but overall she's making the transition as well as anyone could expect."

"As well as, or better?" Sadie twirled the racket in one hand and lifted the water bottle to her lips with the other.

He sighed. "As well as, Sadie. She can't be perfect at everything." She raised an eyebrow at him and he laughed. "Down, Mama Bear. It's not a bad thing to struggle every now and then. It builds character. She's not going to win her first major this year. It'll be a long journey, but she's going to grow up quickly along the way."

"Yesterday I was baby-proofing our first apartment. Today we're talking about winning majors. Growing up," Sadie scoffed. "You can't even imagine how fast it all happens."

A fence gate clanked shut behind them, and they both turned to see a lone woman enter the practice area carrying a bag and ball hopper filled to the brim. She glanced their way with a hopeful smile that faded quickly as she lowered her head.

Hank turned back to Sadie, his jovial expression gone. "Sorry, what were you saying?"

"Kids, growing up," she offered to jog his memory, while wondering about the change she'd just witnessed in both of them.

"Yeah," he nodded solemnly. "Faster than you can ever expect."

The woman took the court next to them, wordlessly dropping her bag several feet away from their shared seating area.

Hank looked over again and opened his mouth like he wanted to say something, but stopped himself.

The woman tipped back her white ball cap, and her eyes emerged from the shadows, strikingly blue in an almost unnatural shade that sent a shot of recognition up Sadie's spine. "That's Jay Pierce, right?"

Hank's mouth curled up in a half smile. "The one and only."

"Do you know her?"

"It's been a while."

Sadie tried to decipher the unspoken behind the comment. Hank was never overly gregarious, but his usual straightforward tone had grown guarded. Jay, too, seemed to be working hard at polite but distantly nonchalant as she stretched with her back to them. She didn't seem like a loner, or at least she hadn't at the press conference, but Sadie had heard plenty of horror stories about temperamental athletes. Maybe Jay didn't play well with others. Still, when Jay twisted her midsection in an obliques stretch, Sadie couldn't resist flashing her a smile. Jay immediately returned the expression or, more accurately, escalated it, because her smile was more brilliant than any Sadie could've offered. She had perfect white teeth and pink cheeks that pushed all the way up to crinkle her mischievous eyes.

"Hi," Sadie said dumbly. She didn't know why the word spilled out, but she also didn't know how she could keep from responding to someone with a smile like Jay's. "I'm Sadie Larsen."

"Jay." She extended her hand, the calluses on her palms causing a pleasant grate across Sadie's smoother skin.

"I know." She internally chastised herself for not saying something more, or better, but the simple acknowledgment seemed sufficient for Jay, whose cheeks flushed a little deeper.

"Hi, Jay," Hank said.

Her expression shifted subtly, but didn't exactly darken, as she nodded to him. "Hank."

He shuffled his feet. "Sorry . . . 'bout Melbourne."

21

She shrugged. "No worries. It's nothing."

Her smile didn't fade, but the sparkle left her eyes, and a twinge of something protective twisted in Sadie's chest. She wanted to ask what had happened in Melbourne, but more than that, she wanted to erase it, to wipe it away the way she used to wipe Destiny's tears. The thought was so disconcerting she took a step back.

"Who you working out with these days?" Hank asked, seemingly oblivious to Sadie's discomfort.

"I hit with Peggy Hamilton at the Australian, till she knocked me out. So, you know, for two days."

He laughed. "Quite a streak there."

Jay shrugged. "I never have trouble finding a pickup game."

"Probably because of your winning smile," Sadie offered without thinking.

Hank turned to look at her, his eyes wide, but Jay laughed. "You know, I think I'm going to use that next time a reporter asks me the same question."

Hank turned to her, his eyes now narrowing.

"I'm doing some serve work today," Jay said, turning her whole body toward Sadie now. She wasn't insanely tall for a tennis player, a few inches taller than Sadie's five feet seven, but her broad shoulders and lanky limbs made her seem bigger. Perhaps her personality contributed a bit as well. "If you want to hit a few returns, I wouldn't mind."

Hank made a small choking sound, but Sadie managed to form actual words. "Oh, no. I couldn't return your serves. I'm—"

"We're done for today," Hank cut in quickly. "What about tomorrow? When's your practice time?"

"You know me. No set plans."

He laughed. "Glad some things never change, but we've got the court at three. If you want to hit a few balls with Ms. Larsen I could plan a session on returns."

Jay pretended to think about the idea, but while she did, Sadie noticed her eyes wandering over to her once more. Jay's smile shifted to something a little more playful before she said, "Sure, I'd love to see what you've got."

"Oh, I'm not—" Sadie started as soon as she realized Jay had mistakenly pegged her for a player, but before she could finish the statement, Hank quickly threw his arm around her shoulder and tugged her close.

"Great. We'll see you tomorrow."

Jay raised an eyebrow, but Hank steered her away before she could say anything else.

"Just one return session, Hank," Jay called nervously after them, but Hank kept right on walking.

"Grab Destiny's bag on the way off the court," he whispered, as they neared the security fence.

"I thought Des had more work to do today, and why didn't you tell her I'm not—"

"Just go with it. I'll explain everything later," Hank said.

"And by 'everything' and 'later,' you mean only as much as I need to know and only when I absolutely need to know it?"

He stifled a laugh, causing his chest to shake. "Exactly."

Sadie sighed, scooped up Destiny's bag, and slung it over her shoulder, trying not to stagger under the bulk of it or the weight of the million questions filling her mind. "You're lucky I trust you as much as I do."

"Yeah," he said, with a grin, "but you'll thank me for this one later."

Jay was early. She couldn't remember the last time she'd been early for a workout on purpose. She didn't want to overthink why she'd chosen today to break her streak, but it didn't take a ton of analysis to realize Sadie Larsen's smile had been a primary factor. Every time she pictured Sadie, something she'd done frequently over the last twenty hours or so, she felt a little thud under her rib cage. Then again, when she thought of Hank and his allusion to "a new doubles partner," she felt the thud somewhere lower in her stomach. She wasn't great at math, but even she could add two and two together. She'd realized as soon as she'd seen them both standing on the court holding rackets yesterday that Sadie must be the woman he'd mentioned, and she'd had every intention of keeping her distance. But something about the smile made her forget her resolve for a moment.

"Just one return session," she said aloud. That's the note she'd ended on yesterday and the refrain she'd woken up echoing this morning. She'd remember the mantra no matter how many times Sadie smiled at her this afternoon, and she hoped it was a lot.

Did that make her pathetic? Wanting a pretty woman to smile at her while also dodging playing tennis with her, because last time she'd combined those two things . . .

"You're here." Hank sounded so shocked you'd have thought she'd teleported onto the court.

"Did you think she was going to stand us up?"

"She's never on time," he said to the woman pushing through the gate behind him.

Jay leaned slightly to the left, trying to see around his hulking shoulders, her so-called winning smile already stretching her cheeks, but as soon as the woman stepped out of Hank's shadow, her expression changed. Confusion? Surprise? Disappointment? All of the above wrinkled her brow and tightened her chest.

"Jay, I'd like you to meet Ms. Larsen," Hank said, in his clipped business tone. "Destiny Larsen."

Jay stared, trying to process what she'd just heard. Larsen. Ms. Larsen. That's the name Hank had used two times now, and yet the woman he'd seemingly referred to had changed drastically between then and now. Not that there wasn't a striking resemblance between the two. The nose was the same, broad and proud, and the mouth carried a remarkably similar pout. The oval shape of her face carried more than a hint of familiarity as well, but this woman's skin tone was more tawny than mocha, her hair longer, her eyes flecked with hazel rather than the smooth mahogany she'd been drawn to yesterday. Most importantly, though, her smile was tight and guarded, not the heart-thudding, open expression that had made Jay forget her past and her promises. Also, the girl before her now was just that, a girl, maybe sixteen or seventeen, whereas Sadie Larsen was most definitely all woman.

Jay glanced over her shoulder and under the bench before laughing. "Is there a camera here somewhere? A practical joke? Punk the tennis pro?"

Destiny scrunched up her youthful face. "Excuse me?"

"Jay," Hank said, "I can explain."

"Sure, but can you tap dance?" Jay's cheeks warmed with the realization he'd played her. "Because I think you'll need to in order to distract me while you pull another bait and switch."

Hank frowned and opened his mouth, but before the words came out, the gate opened again, and this time the woman who entered the court caused Jay's temperature to rise for a different reason.

"Sadie," Hank called, his voice registering a notch higher than his regular baritone. "What great timing you have."

Sadie looked from one of them to the other before rolling her dark eyes. "So much for her always being late."

Jay laughed in spite of her lingering confusion. "You talk about me at home, don't you, Hank? What else did you tell them? How gullible I am? How dense? How I'm so oblivious that you could just show up with a different Ms. Larsen and I'd never notice?"

"A different Ms. Larsen?" Destiny asked, her tone suggesting she hadn't been in on the little charade. "I thought Hank set up a hitting session for you and me."

"Oh, he did," Jay explained. "Only when he did, he led me to believe I'd be hitting with . . . with your . . . what, sister?"

"My sister?" Destiny's eyebrows knitted together, then shot up. "You mean my mom?"

Now it was Jay's turn to feel confused again. Apparently, they were all playing a game where they passed the emotion around like a hot potato. "Your mom? No, Sadie, right?"

She turned from Destiny to Sadie, nodding for her to explain that they'd made the tennis date, or even that Sadie was actually her name and she hadn't just imagined the whole encounter.

Destiny sighed with all the drama of teenage-girldom and said, "Sadie is my *mom*, and she doesn't even play tennis."

She didn't know what part of that statement to try to process

25

first. She knew the second half was the only one that really affected her personally, but somehow, she couldn't make it past the first. "Mom? As in like, 'mother'? I mean, like adoptive, right, 'cause you're so . . . but you also look alike, eyes and . . ."

"And mouth." Destiny finished for her, clearly having gone through this before. "We look alike because she is, in fact, my mother. As in, she gave birth to me and hasn't let me out of her sight for more than ten minutes since then."

Jay turned back to Sadie, her mouth wide open.

Sadie smiled sweetly. "Guilty on all counts."

"Were you, like, ten years old?" Jay finally stammered.

"Sixteen, but thank you again," Sadie said. "I think."

"Wow." Jay knew she should say something else. She was likely verging on impolite, but she couldn't help doing the math in her head. If Sadie was sixteen when she'd given birth to Destiny, and Destiny wasn't much older than that herself, then Sadie must be . . . two carry the one . . . thirty-two? Thirty-three? Or in other words, a year younger than Jay herself.

"Jay?" Hank finally said. "Are you okay?"

She nodded.

"Are you doing math in your head?"

She nodded again.

"And?"

She blurted, "I'm old enough to be her mother!"

He burst out laughing, a deep belly roar she hadn't heard in over a decade. "Yes, yes you are."

"You wanted me to play tennis with a kid young enough to be my daughter?"

"Why not?" he asked plainly. "She's exactly the type of person you're going to face if you want to make a comeback."

"She's a teenager."

"So were you when you broke onto the tour," he answered, without raising his voice to match hers. "And so are your opponents."

"Name one person I'll face in this tournament who's as young as she is."

"Me," Destiny said flatly.

"What?"

"You'll face me in the third round," she said, then added, "if you make it that far."

Jay clenched her jaw, then slowly shook her head. The kid was already on the tour. Why hadn't she realized that? Oh, right, because it never occurred to her that someone she could've given birth to might be a professional fucking athlete. She sighed and rubbed her forehead.

"I'm sorry." A soft voice cut in. "I don't know why Hank felt the need to let you think I was a tennis player."

Jay snorted, but when she looked up and met Sadie's warm mahogany eyes, all the bite faded from the retort she'd planned. Her voice came out sounding little more than a whisper. "Because he knew if he told me the truth I'd say no."

Sadie shook her head. "I don't understand. Why wouldn't you want to practice with Destiny?"

"It's not Destiny," she said quickly, then turning to the girl added, "I mean it. I'm sure you're a fine tennis player, but Hank and I go back a long way, and we both learned our lesson about these little pairings a long time ago. Trust me, it's just not a good idea."

Destiny folded her arms across her chest. "It wasn't my idea in the first place."

The muscles along the top of Jay's shoulders knotted at the little dig, but she kept her mouth shut and shouldered her bag. Then looking apologetically to Sadie once more, she said, "Sorry I wasted your time."

Sadie shrugged. "I won't say I'm not disappointed. I'd looked forward to seeing you two hit together, but I respect someone who refuses to be played, and I'm sorry for any part I had in misleading you."

Jay nodded. It was such a nice thing to say, she almost didn't want to go. Everyone always argued with her, told her she was wrong or unreasonable. She had to work so hard to remind herself that only she knew what was right, that having someone suddenly agree with her made her want to be wrong.

27

But she wasn't.

Sadie laid a hand on her arm, long fingers curling so softly around her biceps and they sent a tingle all the way to her core. "Could I ask just one question before you go, though?"

"Um, yes," she said, staring helplessly into Sadie's sympathetic eyes and hoping she wasn't about to ask for a kidney, because in that moment Jay might have answered in the affirmative.

"Why were you willing to practice with one of Hank's students when you thought it was me?"

Her chest constricted and her mouth opened, but no words came out, so she closed it again. She knew the answer, but she didn't care for it, and she sure as hell couldn't speak the words right now. Not to Sadie, and not in front of her daughter, the one she might face on the court in a matter of days. She glanced over at Hank, who was doing a piss-poor job of hiding his smile. He'd clearly known the truth all along. What's worse, he knew why the truth would be so unsettling, and he'd still let her paint herself into this corner.

She'd either have to fabricate a lie on the spot, something she wasn't great at, or tell Sadie she'd only agreed to the hitting session because she was too attracted to her to say no. That fact had been embarrassing enough when she'd imagined Sadie as an aspiring pro. It was damn near laughable now that she was the mother of an actual member of the tour.

Also, probably straight. That added another layer she hadn't even had a chance to peel back yet. Once again, stereotypes be damned, an up-and-coming women's sports star had respectable odds of being gay, but a shockingly young tennis mom had considerably less probability of the same. She wasn't about to take any more chances of playing the role of predatory lesbian. Her jaw tightened again at that thought.

"Jay?" Sadie said softly, reminding her three people were still waiting for an explanation.

"I . . . well, you see, when I thought I'd be playing with you, I kind of felt like we had . . . um, I mean, I'd never met you before."

"And?" Sadie prodded gently.

"So, I figured you weren't on the tour yet. But Destiny is."

"Right," Hank cut in, "she's a tour member just like Peggy Hamilton, who you hit with in Melbourne."

"Exactly," Jay said, rubbing the wrinkles out of her forehead.

"So?" Hank asked.

She sighed. "So I wouldn't want to get too close to a competitor."

"Which is why we agreed to just one session," Hank offered.

"Just one session." She repeated the mantra she'd walked in with, then allowed her bag strap to slip off her shoulder. Maybe the easiest way out of the situation was to plunge right through. "Yeah, sure. Fine."

"Fine?" Destiny asked suspiciously.

"One session." She nodded. One session to get out of here gracefully, one session to save her from an awkward explanation, and one session to remind herself why she needed to keep her guard up.

Sadie gave her arm a little squeeze and flashed an appreciative smile.

One session to make Sadie smile at her one more time.

Fair trade.

Sadie wasn't sure what had just happened, but whatever it was ended with Jay and Destiny on the court, so she supposed all was well that ended well. Still, Jay had seemed more upset than a moment of confusion warranted. She'd seemed frustrated and irritated, but also almost hurt. That's the emotion that had caused Sadie to reach out to her, to connect, to touch. She wanted to know about the shadows of pain she'd seen flicker over the blue eyes that refused to dance today. All the rest had seemed secondary. She was used to being mistaken for Destiny's sister, even if she didn't enjoy the misconception, and she couldn't have cared less about a tennis practice if it came at the expense of someone else's feelings. Even Destiny's pouty temper hadn't registered above the hurt in Jay's eyes.

The thought made her frown. She didn't even know this woman. Why should she care about her practice habits or the reasons behind them? Jay had turned up her nose at a chance to work out with Destiny, to compete against her, to help her grow as a player. And why? The stonewalling of her daughter should've made her furious; it always had before, and the more Sadie thought about it, the more Jay's reluctance bothered her.

"Easy, Mama Bear," Hank said, from his position at the side of the net.

"I didn't say anything."

"You didn't have to," Hank said, without taking his eyes off the court. "I can hear your toes tapping on the concrete."

"So?"

"You tap 'em when you're trying not to let anyone see how torqued off you are."

She frowned, but didn't argue.

"They're out there now," Hank continued, as the two women warmed up with short, easy strokes. "It doesn't matter how they got there."

"I'm not sure I agree," Sadie said. "Your job is to prepare my daughter to be the best competitor possible. My job is to prepare her to be the best human being possible. You might have done your job, but I'm not sure I did mine."

He turned to her, his face solemn. "Maybe my job is to do both, but maybe I'm only doing the first part with Destiny and the second part with Jay."

She considered the comment for a minute. "Does making them good players have to detract from making them good humans?"

He jammed his hands into the pockets of his cargo shorts and watched as both players switched to harder ground strokes before saying, "I hope not."

They watched in silence for a few more minutes until both Destiny and Jay broke for water. Destiny barely looked as if she'd been moving, not a hair out of its perfect place, and her skin carrying not even a hint of flush. Jay, on the other hand, had a clear sheen of sweat across her brow, and her sandy hair stuck to her neck in a few places. If you'd asked Sadie which one looked more the part of professional athlete, she would've said her daughter. The thought pleased her.

"What's next?" She attempted to make conversation as Destiny sat next to her on the bench, but when her pride and joy merely shrugged off the question, it was Jay who answered.

"I need to work on my serve, and Hank apparently wants Larsen Junior over here to work on some return strokes, so we'll go out there, and I'll do a poor impression of Serena while she'll undoubtedly prove herself to be Andre Agassi with hair."

Sadie laughed, then glanced at Destiny, who hadn't cracked a smile. "I thought it was funny."

"It's okay," Jay said with a shrug. "She's just not old enough to get my mom-aged jokes."

Destiny pursed her lips and rose. "Oh, I got it. I just don't joke until the work is done."

Jay grinned as they watched her walk back onto the court. "Are you sure she's not the mom and you're the daughter?"

Sadie stifled another laugh. "She's very serious about her job. She gets that from her father."

"Right." Jay said dryly. "Father. So she didn't spring from your forehead fully formed?

"Sadly, no. I remember the twelve-hour labor very clearly, and my head was about the only part of my body that didn't hurt."

All the color drained from Jay's face. "Right, well, okay then. Back to work."

She jogged onto the court and unceremoniously let fly one of the sharpest serves Sadie had ever seen up close. The ball jumped off her racket and flattened right along the T-line before exploding back up with a sharp kick to the right. Destiny didn't even manage to get a racket on the ball as it whirred past her.

Sadie leaned back and let out a low whistle.

Hank turned toward her, one eyebrow raised. "Surprised?"

She nodded. "She was just over here joking around about hair and childbirth, and then—bam."

"Bam," Hank agreed giddily. "It's not the fastest serve in tennis, but it's a live wire."

"I've never seen any ball move like that."

He shook his head. "And it's not random. She knows exactly where it's going, but she's the only person who does."

Jay let fly with another serve that, this time, hit the center of the service box and jumped high into the air. Destiny managed to clock it back on the upswing, but the ball had so much spin, it arced right into Jay's wheelhouse. If she'd wanted to crank it back down Des's throat, she'd have had no problem doing so. Instead she cradled the ball softly onto her racket as if it had been tossed by a child. Then she tapped it back into her hand before setting up to serve again.

"Why isn't she the top player in the game?" Sadie asked, nearly breathless from the display of skill.

"That is the million-dollar question," Hank said, without much inflection.

"You don't even have a hunch?"

"It's not physical. I can tell you that much."

"What then?" Sadie asked, suddenly fascinated. "Mental? Emotional? Not enough drive, not enough heart?"

He turned and met her eyes, revealing the same sad reflection she'd seen in Jay's earlier. "No. Maybe the opposite. She's got too much heart."

Despite a few early aces, practicing with Destiny wasn't totally an ego boost. The kid caught on quickly, and Jay couldn't ever hit the same serve more than twice before the ball came back at her head with brutal force. A time or two, it'd been all she could do to deflect the return before it blackened one of her eyes, but at least the girl kept her moving, which was more than half her hitting partners did. Jay had to work hard mentally and physically to mix things up, choosing her spots and her spin deliberately instead of running through a rote workout. Half an hour in, sweat poured down her neck, gnats buzzed around her hair, muscles ached down her sides, and her thighs burned from lateral movement, but she couldn't say she wasn't having fun.

Destiny grooved another return down the line, and Jay didn't even try to reach for it. Clapping her freehand against her racket string, she laughed.

"What?" Destiny frowned.

"Nice shot."

"Why's that funny?"

Jay shrugged. "I don't know that it's funny, but it's fun, right?"

"Fun?" Destiny sounded almost suspicious. "You call getting burned up the line fun?"

"I played a great serve. You struck an even better return," Jay said, then looked at Hank, who nodded in confirmation. "That's good tennis, and good tennis is fun."

Destiny scrunched down her eyebrows, but didn't reply.

Jay turned to Sadie. "Was she born with that furrowed brow, or has it taken her seventeen years to perfect the expression?"

Sadie's shoulders went rigid, but then she tilted her head slightly to the side as if pondering the question before answering, "Born with it."

"So, a child prodigy on and off the courts," Jay said with a grin, as she let herself be pulled toward Sadie once more. She didn't really need a water break, but took one anyway.

As she lowered herself gingerly onto the bench, Sadie's eyes wandered to her legs, but not in the appreciative way she would've preferred.

"No worries. They won't give out on me," Jay said reassuringly. "I just sit and stand up like an old woman out of habit."

"You have a bad knee, though?" Sadie asked, then shook her head. "I'm sorry. That was rude. I didn't mean to pry."

"Oh no, pry away. Everyone else does. I'll give you the same answer I give the press, not because it's PC, but because it's true. I'm playing at full strength again."

"Good," Sadie said, "because if those serves aren't full strength, I'd hate to see the ones that are."

Jay threw back her head and laughed. "Wow, a compliment from a tennis mom. Hank, where did you find this woman?"

"Buffalo," Hank responded dryly.

"Are you sure she's not a plant? She doesn't talk like any tennis moms I know, and she doesn't look like one, either. I mean where's her white visor? Where's her sensible, short haircut? Where's her Lexus crossover vehicle with the stick figure family stickers on the back and a tennis ball on the antenna?"

Sadie's smile widened at the gentle ribbing, and she opened her mouth as if she intended to give a little bit back, but she was cut off.

"Are we going to practice any more, or what?" Destiny called from her baseline, the irritation in her voice serving only to make Jay want to move more slowly.

"I don't know," she called, lounging back on the bench and crossing one leg lazily over the other before turning to Sadie. "What do you think? Have we done enough for one day, or do we need to battle the heat and the bugs a little longer?"

"Oh, I think you should ask Hank," Sadie said quickly.

"Why? I already know what he's going to say. He votes for more practice. Sounds like your daughter does, too. I vote for being done for the day. You have the vote that can deadlock us and force a game of rock, paper, scissors to break the tie. Who do you side with?"

Sadie's smile went from genuine interest to politely tight in an instant, as a steely glint flashed in her dark eyes. "I always side with my daughter."

Jay let out a low whistle in an attempt to cover the icy chill that ran the length of her spine. Standing up, she glanced at Hank and dryly said, "Never mind. She's a total tennis mom."

Hank didn't argue. "Don't take it personal."

Jay forced a smile. "Me? Personal? Never."

Hank sighed, but she didn't want to hear whatever words he had on the other side of it, so she tossed a ball quickly in the air and knocked a flat rocket right at Destiny's backhand. The kid sent it screaming back, and Jay sliced it hard and away, enjoying the squeak of the girl's shoes as she pushed off futilely toward the opposite sideline.

"What was that?" Sadie asked Hank.

But Jay answered, "That was an exercise in control."

Sadie frowned, her eyes still laced with intensity. "For whose benefit?"

"Mine," Jay said flatly. "All mine."

"Can you do it again?" Destiny called, her racket ready as she balanced on the balls of her feet, her eyes carrying a challenge not completely unlike her mother's.

Jay sighed and fished another ball from her pocket before saying, "All day long."

Chapter Three

Miami, Florida

Destiny chucked her racket to the floor with a clatter, causing heads to turn all around the locker room. Sadie bent to pick it up and slipped it neatly into the bag alongside the others. If Destiny had been five or ten, she'd have doled out a few minutes on the naughty seat for such a temper tantrum, but given the pressure the girl was under these days, she found the reaction rather mild. At least her daughter hadn't broken the racket on the court like Jay had earlier in the day. Not that Sadie had witnessed the meltdown. She hadn't seen Jay in person since the practice session in Indian Wells. Neither she nor Destiny had made it to their third-round match and therefore hadn't faced each other when they'd ended up on opposite sides of the draw in Miami. Still, the outburst had been the talk of the tournament for the last couple hours.

Destiny slammed the door to her locker. "I got blanked in the second set."

"Yes," Sadie said. She'd been there for every excruciating point. "By the number three player in the world."

Destiny rolled her eyes. The move made her seem younger than the loss had, and once again, Sadie wondered if they'd made the right choice allowing her to go pro. She knew that losing was a big part of tennis. Roughly a hundred women had entered this tournament, and only one of them would end on a win. Still,

Destiny seemed to have taken more than her fair share of drubbings over the last few weeks. Hank kept saying that struggling was a normal part of growing up, but nothing about life felt normal to Sadie right now. How many other teenagers lived in hotels? How many of them had their struggles broadcast on national television? How many of them had to go explain their bad days to a room full of reporters, mere minutes after being embarrassed in front of a live stadium audience?

Sadie would've given anything to take her place in the interview room, to stand before the flashbulbs and microphones and tell them Destiny was a kid, and she was doing better than any other kid in the country, maybe even the world. Her daughter was doing something most of them would never have the guts or the talent or the drive to do. Who were they to sit in judgment of her?

Fire raced through her veins and tinged her vision as every motherly instinct to protect and defend clawed to the surface, but Destiny's heavy sigh brought her back into the moment.

"How can I help?" Sadie asked softly.

"Just sit somewhere I can see you, okay?" Destiny asked, the quaver in her voice nearly breaking Sadie's heart.

"Of course." Sadie fought the urge to wrap her in the kind of public embrace that would only humiliate her further.

Destiny nodded, and her mouth straightened. "Fine. Then let's get this part over with."

Sadie nodded, marveling once again at her daughter's fortitude, and followed her to the interview room.

She saw Hank waiting for them near the back and motioned him closer to the front as they waited their turn.

"How much were you fined for the racket smashing?" a reporter asked the woman currently sitting on the hot seat.

"A cool five grand," a familiar voice said lightly, "so I'm going to pass this hat around the room before I leave, and you all can make a gratitude offering to show your appreciation for all the entertainment and column inches I've given you over the years."

Several reporters laughed, but Destiny grumbled, "Why is she still here? Her match ended before mine began."

37

"She had to meet with some tour officials," Hank whispered.

Destiny's eyes widened. "Because she smashed a racket?"

"I'd imagine there was more to it than that," Hank said, without going into detail.

Sadie was still tense about Destiny's upcoming trial by fire, but she did wonder about the "more" Hank mentioned. He wasn't generally a circumspect guy.

"What's next for you?" a reporter called then added, "and don't say dinner. I mean on the court."

Jay laughed. "You cut me off at the knees there, Wally, but if you must know, I'm going to take a few days to limp on up to Charleston and try not to get my ass—er, butt kicked. Then I have to take a week off to wash dishes or bus tables so I can afford the airfare to Europe for the start of clay court season, 'cause you all know how much I love clay court season."

Several reporters laughed in a way that made Sadie suspect Jay did not, in fact, love clay court season.

"All right," Jay said, pushing back from the table. "Since I didn't play any tennis worth talking about today, why don't we wrap this up and let you guys move on to lovely contestant number whoever's after me. Bueller? Bueller?"

"Destiny Larsen," someone offered.

The smile faded from Jay's face only for a second, but it was enough to make Sadie's heart pulse faster. What had caused the momentary lapse? Should she feel offended that the mere mention of her daughter's name shook this woman's joy more than a room full of reporters? Or did the flash of something genuine in her practiced facade mean more than Jay liked to show in public? Either way, she recovered quickly.

"Well, by all means, will the younger Ms. Larsen step right up. You're the next contestant on the price is probably not right."

Sadie glanced at Destiny, whose jaw had tightened so much, she must've already worn a layer of enamel off her teeth.

"She's just lightening the mood," Sadie whispered and gave Destiny's hand a little squeeze.

Destiny rolled her eyes and shook off the touch before rising and heading to the front of the room.

As Destiny reached the table, Jay pulled out the chair even farther, and Destiny gave her a steely glare before accepting the chair. Everywhere, flashbulbs exploded, with Jay smiling broadly and Destiny glaring up at her.

Hank groaned loudly enough to be heard all over the room, had it not been for the rapid-fire questions.

"Do you two know each other?"

"We've met," Destiny said into the mic.

"Jay, what do you think of Destiny's play?"

"I think I told someone once, when it comes to returns, she's like Agassi with hair."

Everyone but Destiny laughed.

"What do you have to say to people who argue the future of American tennis is on the rocks?"

Jay stood back and nodded to Destiny. "It's your show now, kid."

Destiny seemed to ponder the question. "I guess I'd tell those people to keep watching."

"Keep watching a tournament you've both been knocked out of?"

Jay winced and Destiny's face flushed.

"Believe it or not," Jay cut in, "we don't sit around thinking about our master plans to revive the game or its ties to our country of origin. I mean, who would put that kind of pressure on a kid? Oh wait, just you guys!"

Sadie fought the urge to cheer. Jay had just said for Destiny what she'd ached to be able to, and she'd done it in a way that didn't reflect badly on either of them.

A ripple of laugher spread through the room.

"So, you don't feel any sense of camaraderie about being the only American women who qualified for this tournament?"

"I feel a sense of camaraderie with all the women on the tour," Jay said, then shook her head. "You're going to twist that until it sounds risqué, aren't you?"

x

A few more laughs made Sadie wonder again what inside joke she'd missed.

"What about you, Destiny? Any sense of patriotism tying you to Jay?"

Destiny leaned in close to the mic, a strand of her long curls falling forward over her shoulder, and said, "No."

The room grew still and quiet once more, as everyone waited for more. Sadie held her breath as Jay stepped back, looking bemused, then began a slow clap, her smile growing as she picked up pace until she was a one-person applause section. "Ladies and gentlemen of the press, you just got D-jacked. That's right. I said, D-jacked, a new nickname coming at you, trademarked by Jay, all rights reserved, and I'm going to do you one more and give you the slogan to boot. You ready? Wait for it. D-jack, hashtag, just say no."

Destiny turned to stare at her as if she'd lost her mind, and quite frankly, Sadie couldn't blame her anymore. Jay had gone off topic and possibly off her rocker. She wasn't answering any question she'd been asked. She wasn't even talking about tennis anymore, but she just kept going.

"Try to out-serve her, she just says 'no.' Try to beat her from the baseline, she just says 'no.' Try to ask her annoying questions, she just says 'no.' Cross a line and you get D-jacked."

"What is she doing?" Sadie asked out of the side of her mouth, unsure as to whether she was watching a train wreck or a sideshow.

"She's saving Destiny's ass," Hank replied, his eyes sparkling with something akin to pride.

"Did you write that down, Wally?" Jay asked.

"All of it," Wally said.

"You're welcome," she said to the reporters, then took a dramatic bow, before turning to Destiny. "And so are you." Then she hopped off the riser and headed for the back exit, but as she walked past their row, Hank reached out and caught her arm, pulling her into the seat Destiny had vacated.

Jay didn't argue. She sank into the chair and tilted back her head so her sandy brown hair fell away from her face. Closing her eyes and parting her lips slightly, every crease faded from her forehead and around her mouth. For the first time, Sadie noticed how young she looked, and how exhausted. That kind of tired didn't come from the court, and it couldn't be undone by a few days off.

"I obviously didn't play as well as I hoped," Destiny said into the mic, and Sadie nearly jumped out of her seat. She'd been so absorbed in watching Jay, she hadn't heard the question, only the answer and the clipped tone in which it had been delivered.

"Are you feeling the grind of the tour already?"

"No," Destiny said again, and several reporters shifted awkwardly in the seats until she added, "I feel fine."

"You won the French Open last year as a junior. Are you looking forward to clay court season?"

Jay raised one eyebrow without actually opening an eye. The expression made Sadie smile, but then she immediately chided herself for allowing her attention to be diverted again.

"I don't have a favorite season," Destiny said.

"Do you have a least favorite surface?"

Destiny tilted her head to the side as if considering some deep, philosophical issue, and everyone waited for an answer profound enough to warrant such introspection, but when she finally leaned forward again, she merely said, "No."

Jay snorted softly, and this time Hank joined her. Sadie's shoulders tensed as her mothering instincts kicked in again.

"Any more questions?" Destiny asked. Thankfully, no one seemed eager to try to drag another monosyllabic response out of her, so they mercifully sat in silence long enough for her to nod her conclusion and walk off the stage. She hadn't even hit the bottom step before the reporters moved on in their own conversations.

Sadie jumped up, and Hank followed suit, but Jay remained slouched in her chair, her long legs stretched out so they blocked the aisle. Sadie had to reach over them to give Destiny a little hug.

"Let's go," Destiny said coldly, as she shot some side-eye toward Jay.

Hank kicked Jay's feet. "Come on, rock star. You're coming to dinner with us."

Jay cracked open an eye at him, then smiled up at Destiny. "You want me to come to dinner with you, D-jack?"

"No," Destiny said quickly, causing Jay to laugh a deep, hearty belly laugh.

Sadie scooted past her, not even caring if she stepped on her toes, but when Jay flashed those blue eyes all the way open, she had a harder time remembering her frustration.

"Was Nancy Reagan her nanny or something?" Jay pushed herself up to her feet with a small groan. "'Cause that 'just say no' business is endearing for only so long."

"What's that supposed to mean?" Destiny snapped.

"Hey, let's take this somewhere more private," Hank suggested.

Destiny planted her feet on the well-worn maroon carpet. "No, I want an answer."

"And you're going to get one," Hank said more firmly, "but trust me, you don't want to hear it here." He gave her shoulder a little nudge and put a hand on Jay's back, pushing them both toward the door like a dad who'd had enough lip for one night.

They both dutifully followed his command, but Destiny's mouth twisted in a frown while Jay's curled up smugly. Sadie followed behind, feeling out of her league once more. There was entirely too much going on beneath the surface here, and she suspected at least part of it was about to come bubbling up. What she didn't know was how she felt about that. Releasing the pressure valve was one thing, but she had a feeling that if Destiny cut loose right now, she'd blow off a lot more than steam.

The heavy metal door had no sooner slammed behind them when Destiny Larsen whirled on her. "What the hell's your problem?"

"Wow, language," Jay said, as she leaned her back against the wall. "Do you let her talk like that, Mom?"

Sadie shook her head, but before she could answer, Destiny

shoved an index finger in Jay's face. "I'm not a kid. Why do you keep looking at her when I'm talking to you?"

"Maybe because she knows words other than 'no,' or maybe because you are legally still a kid, or maybe it's because you've got a big ole chip on your shoulder that's no fun to engage with. She, on the other hand, has one of the nicest smiles I've had leveled at me in a very long time, okay?"

All three of them stared at her with their jaws dropped to varying degrees, causing Jay to wonder belatedly if she might have been a bit too honest on the last count. She'd had a long day, between losing a match she should've won and getting a fine she couldn't afford and taking a meeting with people she didn't like to discuss problems that she couldn't fix. Maybe she'd used up all of her professionalism or worn down all her guard.

"Look," Hank finally said, "I understand why you're frustrated, Destiny. You and Jay could not be more different in temperament, but that's a good thing. She saved your press conference there."

"She turned it into a sideshow. I didn't get a single question about today's match."

"Did you really want to answer questions about how you melted down in the second set?" Jay folded her arms across her chest and basked in the glow of Hank's defense.

"I wanted to talk about tennis," Destiny said. "I always want to talk about tennis."

"And I want to be able to teleport," Jay retorted, then noticed Sadie wince and changed her course, if not her tone. "Tell me, out of every ten questions, how many of them are good, solid inquiries about the nuts and bolts of your game right now?"

Destiny pursed her lips and seemed to be flipping through a mental catalogue of recent press encounters. "Probably one. Maybe."

"And how many of them are about your age? Or your mental makeup? Or your relationship with other players?"

Destiny didn't answer right away, so Jay, picking up steam again, filled in the blank for her. "Probably eight, right? And when they ask you those questions, how many times do you manage to give them an answer longer than one sentence or, hell, even one syllable?"

"All right," Sadie cut in. "That's enough. She's had a long day. I'm not going to stand here and let anyone badger her."

"I'm sorry," Jay snapped back. She'd had enough of the forward and back routine with both of the Larsen women. "Did I sound like I was badgering her? Because if I'd intended to, I would've said I'd like a cut of every advertising dollar you ever earn with the phrase 'D-jacked,' or 'just say no,' because you sure as hell weren't coming up with that on your own."

"I don't think—" Destiny started.

"About anything other than tennis," Jay finished for her. "But maybe you should start, because the way you're playing right now, you're not going to make enough money to keep playing tennis for very long."

Destiny rolled her eyes, but Jay was on a roll of a different kind. "I get it, kid. You were a champ last year, but guess what? Everyone on this tour was one of the top players of their grade at one point. They've all got the talent, they've all got the drive, but not all of them have the strength or the knees or the sheer luck to go two full weeks without dropping a match. And if you can't do that at least a couple times a year, it gets really expensive to pay for flights to Europe for you and your crew, and hotel rooms in China, and meals in New York City, and rackets professionally restrung in Morocco."

Destiny glanced at Sadie, who shook her head almost imperceptibly, but Jay recognized the subtle worry lines around her eyes. She saw the same ones in the mirror every morning.

"The hard truth is that nothing lasts forever, no one gets paid to play this game at sixty-two, and everybody struggles on the court at some point, which is why you have to learn to be good in the other arenas as well."

Hank nodded. "She's right, Des. The press game is part of the game, too, no matter how much you hate it."

"And most of us hate it," Jay said softly, "but we need the reporters as much as they need us."

"Jay," Hank said quietly, "come on. Let's go get something to eat. My treat."

She managed a half smile. "Thanks, but things aren't so bleak that I can't afford some Holiday Inn room service . . . yet."

He nodded again, his expression somber. "Thank you for what you did for Destiny back there."

"What did she do?" Destiny asked, more confused than angry now.

"I helped you kick-start a brand," Jay said, wearily, "and a good brand attracts better brands if you wield them correctly. But that's up to you."

"Up to her how?" Sadie sounded genuinely interested now that she was sure her daughter wasn't under attack.

"She's got to learn to play a different kind of game."

"And if I don't?" Destiny asked.

Jay shrugged and pushed off the wall, her heart aching in a way not even Sadie's smile could soothe. "Then you'll have to pray your time doesn't run out before the money does."

Hank clasped a hand on her shoulder. "You've still got my number?"

She forced a smile. "I'm sure I do somewhere."

"We'll see you in Charleston?" Sadie asked, her voice cautiously optimistic.

"I'll be there . . . I don't know for how long, but I'll be there."

"Good," Sadie said, her smile warmer than Jay had seen it all day. "I hope we cross paths."

"Yeah," Jay said, feeling inexplicably lighter as she realized she did too. "We probably will."

She thought she heard Hank give a little chuckle, but she kept right on walking. She'd had enough to mull over for one day, and she'd undoubtedly keep doing so for days to come. If she wanted to enjoy the pinprick of hope Sadie's smile sparked in her chest, she wasn't going to let whatever Hank was thinking undercut the last bit of joy she had left.

★ ★ ★

Sadie quietly closed her laptop and shuffled some receipts into a file folder marked "Taxes." She needed to hire a CPA to manage all of Destiny's business expenses, but even with her limited financial experience, she could tell they really couldn't afford one.

Destiny had lost in the first round this time, though the defeat could hardly be pinned squarely on her young shoulders. She'd had a terrible draw and ended up facing the number two player in the world right out of the gate. By all accounts, the match was one of her better ones so far. She'd held serve through much of the first set and even broken her opponent once in the second before dropping four games in a row. She'd played a stronger first match than half the women in the field, but at the end of the day, none of those facts mattered on paper.

They would get a check for about $2,500, and enough per diem to cover one hotel room and one of their flights. Nothing for Hank's salary, nothing for Destiny's rackets or shoes or the trip to the chiropractor this afternoon. And then, with the money left over after those bills were paid, they needed to buy plane tickets to Germany.

A soft knock sounded on the door to the adjoining room, and she heard Hank whisper, "Sadie, you up?"

She padded over to unlatch the deadbolt. "What's wrong?"

"Nothing a good stiff drink can't fix," he said, working a bottle of Fireball Whiskey through the door as soon as she opened it enough for him to do so.

She sighed but didn't argue. "Okay, but Des is sleeping."

"My place it is." He swung his own door wider. She smiled at the sight of his bright green pajama pants covered in hot pink tennis rackets. They'd been a Christmas present from Destiny two years ago, and she wouldn't have expected him to keep them, much less wear them.

He set two coffee mugs on the standard hotel desk and unscrewed the top to the whiskey bottle. "I'll make yours a double."

"What makes you think I need it?"

"Your light's still on at midnight after the day we had, so I can only assume you're trying to balance the budget," he said matter-of-factly.

She sighed and took the mug he offered. "We're going to be fine."

"Of course we are."

"I've been through worse."

"Yes, you have."

"I finished school and worked and paid the bills as a teenager," she reminded herself aloud.

"And you raised a happy, healthy, well-rounded kid in the process."

That, she was less sure about. Not the happy part. There had been happy times even during the hardships. Now, not so much. "I can't remember the last time I heard her laugh, Hank."

"She will again, though."

"I don't know. She's not my tiny little princess anymore. I can't just give her a quarter to ride the mechanical horse at the mall these days."

He smiled. "You could try."

She laughed, then hung her head. "She asked about the money tonight."

"What'd you tell her?"

"Same thing I've always told her, that we have enough. At least this time she didn't suggest we call her dad."

Hank looked at the floor.

"What, you think I should call Tad?"

He held up his hands. "I didn't say that."

"Oh God, you don't have to. She doesn't have to. I think about it every time the worry lines cross her forehead. Am I doing enough? Can I give her what she needs? Is she happy? Is she growing into the kind of woman she deserves to be? Can I teach her what she needs to know on my own?"

"Hey," Hank whispered, "she's doing fine."

"That's the thing though, she's always done so much better

47

than fine. She excelled at everything she ever tried. Math, dance, reading, tennis. Everything she touched turned to gold."

"Not the guitar," Hank said with a chuckle.

Sadie grimaced and sipped her drink, enjoying the way it warmed her core. "Thank God we started flying more, so she had to leave that damn thing at home."

"Yeah, who'd ever think I'd be so grateful for excess baggage fees."

She appreciated his attempt to lighten the mood, but every subject seemed to lead back to money. "Speaking of airlines, we've got enough money to get to Stuttgart, but if she loses in the first round there, I'm not sure we'll have enough to get home."

"Oh, we'll get home." He waved his hand. "Eventually our visas will run out, and they'll deport us. We wouldn't be allowed back in the European Union for several years, but we'd get home."

She stared at him.

"Not helpful?"

"Not really. And don't you dare repeat the suggestion to Destiny. She's under enough pressure without you making her think she's got to violate her visa and become an international criminal."

Hank sipped his whiskey. "It's just one option, but there's an easier one. Well, not easier, but more legal."

Sadie shook her head and took another hard swallow of Fireball. "I know Europe has more lax laws than we do, but if you're going to suggest anything that involves drugs or prostitution, just don't."

"Wait, prostitution for you or me?"

She started to get up, but he just laughed. "I'm kidding. I intended to suggest Destiny play some doubles."

Sadie shook her head. "On second thought, I'll go research the drug laws in Germany."

"Listen, I know she doesn't enjoy doubles as much as singles."

"Understatement of the year."

"But she likes winning, and she needs money. Doubles can offer her both," Hank said, then raised his large hand to cut off Sadie's retort. "I get that she's an only child who doesn't always play well with others, but the women's doubles game isn't as competitive as the singles pool right now, and there aren't as many teams in the field at most of the smaller tournaments. She has a chance to go much further in the draw."

"But won't doubles matches and training sessions take away from the work she needs to do to stay competitive in singles?" Sadie asked. "I worry about diverting attention from the main draw right now."

"You worry about it because Destiny has taught you to, but neither of you are her coach. I am, and I say mixing things up could be exactly what she needs."

"I'm all for letting you make the tennis calls, but if you want to convince her, you're going to need a stronger argument than just wanting to shake her up. She's too driven to give up on her primary goal because she's facing a rough patch."

"It's more than a rough patch, Sadie," he said seriously.

"You said her game is getting stronger."

"Physically, maybe, but mentally, emotionally, she's too susceptible to the stress, and she's losing, which makes her press harder, which makes her lose more."

She stared down at her own hands, stark against the pure white of the mug. She couldn't argue, no matter how much she wanted to defend her daughter. She knew Destiny well enough to understand the pressure she put on herself. "How do we break the cycle?"

"Nothing breeds winning like winning. Maybe if we could get her some wins on the doubles side, she'd loosen up a little bit in singles, too."

"I don't know," she said skeptically, meaning she didn't know about any of it. Destiny had never had much interest in doubles, and Sadie had never had any reason to push the issue. Trying to do so now seemed about like making it all the way through med school, then trying to become a mechanic. Both jobs might be about tools and hands and fixing, but the commonalities were very surface level. "Doesn't doubles have a different space, and pace, and skill set?"

"Definitely." Excitement sparked in Hank's eyes. "It's not just two-person tennis. There's more strategy, quicker thinking, and fast—oh you can't even believe how fast the game moves, but those are all plus attributes for Des. They're all things she could bring back into singles with her. Especially if we pair her with someone who will balance her out in more than just the physical arena. She needs someone older, with more experience. Someone who can mentor her on and off the court."

"I take it you're not talking about a hypothetical person." She leaned forward, holding up her mug. "I'm also starting to suspect you got me liquored up to drop a very specific name on me. Should I go ahead and down the rest of this?"

"Maybe one more sip."

She did as instructed, then braced herself on the arm of the desk chair.

"I already asked Jay Pierce."

Sadie choked on the whiskey and somehow managed not to spit it back into her mug despite the fact that the devil's brew burned considerably more on the way back up than it had on the way down. Jay of the dancing blue eyes. Jay of the infectious laugh. Jay of the easygoing smile. She shook the images and echoes from her mind to focus on the only thing that would really matter. "Destiny will kill you."

"Don't worry. Jay said no."

"Oh." Sadie frowned. Disappointment flooded her chest in a rush. She'd barely had time to consider the possibility in the first place, but hearing the potential had been undercut before she'd had a chance to warm to the idea made her disproportionately sad. "I guess that's probably for the best."

"I don't think so."

"Destiny doesn't like her."

"Destiny's seventeen. You're the mom. Stubborn or not, you can bring her around."

Sadie had her doubts but decided to work with the premise anyway. "Can Jay be brought around?"

Hank's smile faded. "It's not impossible, but once again, you'd have to do the bringing."

"Me?" Sadie rose and paced in front of him. "I barely know her. She probably couldn't pick me out of a lineup."

"Oh no," Hank said, "she totally could."

She paused, uncertain what to make of the comment, or the little tinge of pleasure it caused in her stomach. "But you know her so much better than I do."

"Which is why it has to be you. Just trust me."

"I trust you have your reasons, but I also think you're putting way too much trust in me. I've had, like, two real conversations with her, and neither was profound. Now you want me to go ask her to play tennis with my kid?"

"Honestly, I don't think it'll be all that different than talking to Des. They're in the same predicament with the same few options left on the table. I suspect Jay is broke and hurt and feeling pretty insecure."

Her stomach clenched even tighter. "Insecure about what?"

"Sorry, that's not my story to tell. I'm probably already pushing into territory I shouldn't have." Hank shook his head. "I hope you can respect that I'd say the same thing to anyone asking about you and Des. There's a kind of confidence that goes with coaching as much as counseling."

She sighed. How could she argue with something so noble? And yet he'd still asked her to take a shot in the dark based on a cryptic endorsement. She and he could take their own risks, but Destiny's career, and maybe even her happiness, was at stake here, too.

"Jay seems like she's got some baggage, and I'm not sure I want my daughter mixed up with someone you can't fully vouch for."

"I can," he said quickly. "I do. Jay's got her history, but she's a good person. She just needs to be reminded there are other good people out there who still care."

"And what makes you think I'm the right person for the job?"

"Just a hunch," he said, but one corner of his mouth curled up in a wistful sort of expression she'd never seen on him. "Think about it."

She didn't hate the idea. In fact, she sort of liked the prospect of spending more time with Jay, from a business standpoint, of course, because she really did think the doubles connection could help financially. From a parenting standpoint, Jay also appealed to her as a role model for Destiny, who had a lot to learn from Jay's easygoing attitude and off-court acumen. Sadie could probably learn a thing or two about brands and marketing and making a dollar stretch, too.

Still, no matter how she tried to justify her logic, she couldn't stop coming back to those blue eyes, the way they filled with mirth, the way they crinkled at the corners, the way they could swirl from pensive to playful in a blink. Their image weighed on her mind as much as the finances, but couldn't do anything to sway the odds in their favor. If anything, the fact that she was considering a player's physical attributes only highlighted the absurdity of Hank's request.

"You want me to go to a professional athlete I've barely talked to and ask her to play doubles with my daughter because you have a hunch she'll think I'm a good person?"

Hank downed the rest of his whiskey and set the mug on the desk. "Does that sound like a terrible plan?"

"It really does," Sadie admitted, feeling more than a little disappointed.

"Hey," Hank said, sitting up a little taller, "you could mention that Des is good on clay."

"You think that'd really make the difference?" Sadie asked hopefully.

He laughed. "I doubt it, but right now, it's all we've got."

A knock on Jay's door roused her long before she actually wanted to be aware of her surroundings, or her right knee, or the outcome of yesterday's match. Another second-round loss. Another morning with nothing to do but rearrange travel plans. Another five days to sit around and worry before the next tournament began. She would rather have slept away a few more of those empty hours, but whoever was knocking wouldn't allow her to do so.

She sat up and looked at the clock. Nine a.m. seemed a little early for housekeeping, but the knock came again. If she didn't answer, they'd likely let themselves in and get a visual of her naked in bed. Not even the most intrusive of tabloid reporters had seen quite that much, so she rolled off the bed and pulled on a pair of shorts she found on the floor. Then, groaning only a little, she straightened and glanced around for a shirt.

Another knock sounded on the door a few feet away.

"Just a second," she called, her heart rate accelerating at the thought of a hotel employee letting themselves in. She grabbed frantically for the nearest covering, snapped a sports bra tightly into place, and dove for the doorknob.

She cracked open the door slightly and said, "I don't need any shampoo or towels or . . . Sadie?"

"Hi."

She was so surprised, she dropped her hand, allowing the door to open more. She didn't even realize what she'd done until Sadie's eyes flickered down over her torso.

"I, um." Sadie looked back up, then away before lifting two Starbucks travel cups. "I brought coffee."

Jay bit her lip at the adorableness of the offer. "Thanks. Want to come in?"

Sadie seemed torn between wanting to accept and wanting to run as she looked anywhere but at Jay's body. "I hoped you and I could talk before I leave for Germany, but I think I may have woken you."

"You did," Jay said cheerfully, "but you brought coffee, so all is forgiven."

"Oh good." She wore khaki-colored linen pants and a gauzy turquoise top that flowed loosely around her waist as she shifted awkwardly from side to side. "I just had a proposition for you."

Jay smiled. "I don't know what you've read about me in the press, but propositions from beautiful women generally don't come around before noon in my world."

Sadie's mouth formed the most perfect "o" to match her wide

eyes. "I didn't mean, that's not the kind of proposition, I didn't even think about you being . . ."

"Gay?" Jay leaned against the doorjamb, the cool metal pressing along the length of her bare arm. "It's not a secret in the sports world, or any world for that matter."

"Right, no. I guess I knew." Sadie frowned slightly, as if maybe she hadn't, actually.

The reaction caused something to clench in Jay's chest. Was it possible that Sadie hadn't considered her sexual orientation until this moment? She probably should've felt let down, but she actually liked the idea of her past not being on the forefront of someone's mind. She decided to let Sadie off the hook.

"I'm just teasing you. Come in. We'll have some coffee and discuss this purely platonic proposition of yours."

Sadie smiled gratefully. "Thank you. I can wait if you want to change clothes or anything."

"I'm good," Jay said, then turned to walk back toward the bed, enjoying the idea of her body flustering Sadie, regardless of the reason. Either she didn't want to be alone with a half-dressed lesbian because she didn't trust Jay, or she didn't want to be alone with a half-dressed lesbian because she didn't trust herself. And while Jay would prefer the latter, she'd also learned the best way to deal with the former was by proving that the only person who'd make any passes this morning would be Sadie.

Sadie set the coffee on the desk and glanced around the room. Jay wondered if she and Destiny were staying somewhere a little nicer than the Days Inn. Then again, maybe she was simply trying to find a place to sit down, but Jay's tennis bag took up the only chair in the room, and the rumpled bed probably didn't seem like a valid option either.

"Feel free to move the rackets if you want the chair," Jay said, hopping back onto the bed and propping herself up against the headboard.

Sadie's dark eyes took her in once more before she shook her head. "I'll stand, thanks."

"All business—got it. But if you're going to ask me any serious questions, I suggest you pass the caffeine."

Sadie obliged, her fingers grazing Jay's as she handed her the cup. She didn't jerk away from the touch, but neither did she let it linger, and Jay wondered if Sadie was warring with her instincts or merely tap dancing around whatever she'd come here to say. Part of Jay would've enjoyed drawing out the tension if only to spend time together, but she'd lost her stomach for games years ago. She took a sip of the java and laid her cards on the table.

"I don't play doubles."

Sadie sighed. "Well, there it is then. I suppose I should thank you for putting me out of my misery quickly."

"Yeah," Jay said, pleased by how easily Sadie had accepted her verdict. "Thanks for the coffee, though."

"No problem. I was at Starbucks already." She yawned, and Jay noticed faint circles under her eyes. "It's been a long few days paired with too-short nights."

"I know the feeling. You're headed to Germany now?"

"Yes and no. We leave Charleston today to drive to Atlanta to take a flight tomorrow to Germany, overnight of course."

"The cheapest airport paired with an overnight flight to save you a hotel stay. I know the drill."

Sadie sipped her coffee slowly, her full lips leaving a faint press of maroon lipstick against the white lid. "Glad to know I'm not the only one working the system. Sometimes I think everyone else is better at it than I am, though."

"No," Jay said, the warmth of the coffee doing little to loosen the tightness in her chest. "We all jump through the hoops to make ends meet at some point in our careers, but they're rarely the same hoops. Some people do bad Japanese commercials. Others take out loans or offer private lessons. Some of us sleep in hostels or even rental cars."

"Some of you play doubles," Sadie said lightly.

"Touché," Jay said. "I take it that's the rub of the visit, then? Sad story about finances, you figure I'm in the same boat, we can

55

both row together to try to fight the tide of money slipping out to sea?"

Sadie nodded slowly. "That was the plan of attack, but it doesn't seem to have much chance of working, so would you mind if I just took a few minutes to drink my cappuccino and collect myself before I go face my daughter?"

"Take all the time you need." Jay shifted on the bed to take the pressure off her lower back. "I get the sense Destiny's a little intense."

"Little bit," Sadie said, as if that were a massive understatement.

"She really does have a great return. She'll hit her stride eventually."

"Thank you, but it's not the tennis stride I worry about most," Sadie admitted, sounding almost embarrassed.

"No?"

"You don't have kids, do you?"

Jay's laughed came so fast and sharp she had to cover her mouth.

"I'll take that as a no," Sadie said, dryly. "So, you'll just have to trust me when I say the money worries are piddly compared with the emotional responsibilities that come with throwing a seventeen-year-old girl into the shark tank of professional sports."

"No, actually, I don't need to have kids to get it. I lived it," Jay said, trying to keep the bitterness out of her voice.

"That's right," Sadie said. "I keep forgetting you've been around this business as long as you have. I didn't really follow the sport until Des got serious, and even then, I really only watched the level she played. I'm sorry I don't know more about your career."

"I'm not," Jay said, honestly. "It's kind of refreshing."

"Why's that?"

"It's an unforgiving game, and I'm not just talking about my knees. Sometimes I think people in the stands and the front offices watch me on the court and still see my seventeen-year-old self." She shook her head. "That's not true. They see my twenty-two-year-old self, as painted by someone else."

"I don't know what that means," Sadie admitted. "I've always sort of liked how tennis players change over the years. From what I'm told, Agassi went from an angry young kid to such a thoughtful sportsman. And Serena used to be so divided in her attention, but she became such a steady force. I want that for Destiny. I want to watch her grow into a better person as she becomes a better player, not that there's anything wrong with who she is now, but she's young and stressed out, and she's struggling so much with the transition."

Jay shifted on the bed again, only this time her back had nothing to do with her discomfort. "I'm sure she'll be fine. She's got good people by her side."

"I wish I could be so certain. I don't know this game. I don't know the agents or the officials. I don't even know the other players. I thought we'd spend these years taking driver's ed and arguing about curfews and dishing about boys. I never expected to be the mother of a professional athlete."

Jay's heart ached for all the fear and the love pleading through Sadie's voice. "That's why you're going to do right by her. You never set out to make her a star. You just wanted to raise a good, kind, well-rounded human. That's really rare in this sport. Tennis parents can be a terrible breed, pushy, angry, backbiting, jealous and manipulative, so their kids learn those lessons about life. You're none of those things."

Sadie smiled wearily. "Maybe not most of them, but I did track down your hotel room and your favorite coffee order to try to catch you off guard in the hopes that you'd play doubles with my daughter."

Jay laughed. "Wow, it was too early in the morning for me to process through that chain of events. I should've been way more creeped out to see you at my door this morning, shouldn't I?"

"You really should have!" Sadie exclaimed, her face lighting up again as humor lines softened the ones from worry. "Why did you even let me in here?"

"I am very gullible," Jay said, without a hint of teasing. "And while we're being completely honest, I have a soft spot for your smile."

"Oh." Sadie did a poor job hiding her pleasure. "I didn't know."

"Well, now you do," Jay said, "but don't let it go to your pushy tennis-mom head that you can use my weakness against me. And for the love of all things holy, don't tell Hank I told you that, or he's going to get all smug."

"Hank? Why?"

"Because he thinks he knows me so well, and he thinks he knows what's best."

Sadie's eyes went wide again. "Doesn't he? I mean not about you, but about tennis, because he's Destiny's coach, and I lean on him for everything. If he doesn't know how to do his job—"

"Oh no, I mean he does know everything about tennis," Jay said quickly, trying to soothe both Sadie's worries and her own sense of betrayal. "He's a tennis genius. You can trust his instincts about all aspects of the game."

Sadie's smile returned, this time slightly more superior as she took her time pulling another long sip from her Starbucks cup. The expression took Sadie's appeal from sweet to sexy in .02 seconds.

"What?" Jay swung her feet off the bed as her heartbeat kicked up a few notches.

"It's just that you said I should trust Hank's instincts about all aspects of the game."

"Yeah, I was there for that part of the conversation."

Sadie's smile widened. "But his instincts said that the best thing for both you and Destiny would be to play doubles together. So, by your own logic, shouldn't you listen to him?"

Jay flopped back onto the bed and pulled a pillow over her face as the genius of that play rolled over her. Sadie had painted her into the perfect corner, or rather, she'd let Jay do the painting. She probably should have been angry, but all she felt was a mixture of admiration and amusement with a hint of foreboding. It had been a long time since anyone had been able to tie her in knots. Her laughter subsided; then she tossed the pillow in Sadie's direction. "I take back everything I said."

"About Hank?"

"No, about you," Jay said, not knowing if she should smile or cry. "You are a total tennis mom. You set me up like a ball on a tee."

"Who, me?" Sadie didn't look the least bit chagrined. "I'd given up on you the moment I walked in here. You're the one who talked yourself right back around to the point I wanted to make."

"Did not."

"You did. It was beautiful." Sadie pushed off the desk and strode toward the door. "You laid out the argument better than I ever could have."

"I didn't agree to play doubles with your daughter."

"Not yet," Sadie admitted gleefully.

"Then what makes you think I will?"

"Because you're smart and thoughtful, and you know it's the right thing to do, even if it's not what you want to do."

"I have just as many reasons to say no as I do to say yes." Jay pouted.

Sadie smiled at her from the doorway. "I believe you."

"You don't even know me."

"Sure I do," she said, her tone maddeningly calm. "I know all the important things now, anyway."

"How?" she asked, her heart beating painfully in her throat as the room closed in around her.

"I'm a mom. I know things," Sadie said lightly.

"Why do I get the feeling you've used that line before?"

Sadie pushed open the door with a laugh. "I'll see you in Germany."

Jay didn't respond. She merely rolled over onto her stomach and listened for the door to click shut. When the sound finally came, she let out a muffled scream right into the sheets.

She couldn't believe she was going here again, after all the years and all the pain and all the lessons learned the hard way. She couldn't believe any of it, but she knew herself well enough to realize she couldn't fight it either.

Chapter Four

They were over international waters by the time Hank tapped Destiny on the shoulder. "I've got an empty seat by me. Go get some sleep."

"Really?" She looked up at him, her dark eyes flecked with gold and gratitude. "But you're bigger than me."

He smiled lovingly down at her cramped form folded awkwardly into the window seat. "You need it more than I do. Go on, row 23."

She didn't protest again. Grabbing her phone and travel pillow, she climbed over Sadie, then scooted off down the narrow aisle.

"That was nice of you," Sadie said, after she'd gone.

"Yeah, it was," he said with a grin, "but now you gotta move over, because there's no way I can squeeze past you into her seat."

"Fair enough." She unclasped her seatbelt and slid over. She didn't mind getting bumped from her aisle seat if it meant Des could get some sleep. In fact, she hadn't minded anything all day. Not the car ride with a sullen teenager, not the extra pat-down from airport security, not even the four-hour delay on an already late-night flight. She couldn't explain her newfound impervious attitude, but if pressed, she'd have to say she felt almost smug since leaving Jay's hotel room.

Hank dropped down next to her, his body so heavy it shook her own seat as he settled in, pushing her closer to the cool, double-pane window. "So, how did it go?"

She bit the inside of her cheek to keep from grinning. They hadn't had a chance to talk alone all day, and she'd been anticipating this moment since she left Jay's room. "She'll do it."

"What?" Hank practically yelled, and then caught himself before continuing in a whisper. "She agreed?"

"No," Sadie said. "She said she doesn't play doubles, but she didn't mean it, or maybe she meant it at the time, but she was wrong."

Hank stared at her blankly.

"Don't worry. The bottom line is she'll play doubles soon enough."

"How do you know? Did she concede any of your points?"

"No, but she conceded a few of her own."

Confusion creased his brow. "She made her own points about why she should play doubles?"

"Yes, rather unintentionally." Even now the memory of Jay's flustered expression almost made her giggle.

"But she still didn't agree to play with Des?"

"No. When I left she remained adamant she didn't play doubles, but she'll come around. She's just got to do so on her own terms."

His eyes narrowed. "This morning you didn't want to talk to a near stranger, and now you're talking like you know her inner workings. Why are you so sure of yourself all of a sudden?"

She considered the question seriously. What had changed? Her hand had been shaking so badly she'd nearly spilled the coffee even before knocking on Jay's door. When had she gone from nervous wreck to confident? When Jay had opened the door wearing athletic shorts and a bra? No, the sight of Jay's body, toned and lean, had shifted something in her, but it hadn't made her feel self-assured. Maybe the change had come when the two of them had settled into an easy conversation about the ins and outs of tennis travel? Jay's assurance that she wasn't alone in juggling schedules certainly helped put her at ease, but it hadn't triggered the kind of difference she felt now. Perhaps the moment had come when Jay had admitted she had a soft spot for Sadie's smile.

Her heart gave a little hiccup, and she suspected she'd hit her mark. How had one simple comment changed their whole dynamic? Surely she wasn't so susceptible to flattery. Then again, the compliment had seemed like so much more than a simple come-on. In fact, it hadn't felt like a come-on at all, so much as a genuine statement of fact. It felt like the first moment between them that had been about just the two of them.

Her breath grew shallow as she pictured Jay in bed, her arms folded behind her head, long legs stretched atop a knot of rumpled sheets. If she'd been engaging on the court or on the stage, she was downright alluring off of it. Stripped of pretense and playacting, she retained all her best qualities but lost the showmanship that gave them distance. Sadie had more than enjoyed her openness. She pulled strength from it. She could read Jay's emotions, see the subtle flush of her arousal even if it never overtook her more caring nature or stubborn resolve. The combination had made Sadie feel powerful, possessed, both known and knowing.

More than twelve hours later, she still carried herself with the same certainty she had when they'd parted. What would it be like for her to have someone like Jay around more often, and in more ways than one?

Her breath caught tightly in her throat, and she shook her head.

"What?" Hank asked.

She blinked back into focus and noticed the confusion on his face had shifted to concern. "Nothing."

"Are you sure?" he asked, "because you look . . . different."

She shook her head. "No. I'm not different."

She might have felt that way for a while, but she couldn't stay in Jay's hotel room forever. She didn't even want to. She was thirty thousand feet above the Atlantic Ocean on an overnight flight to Europe, talking to a tennis coach about the future of her daughter, the professional athlete. Surreal as those facts may have seemed, this was her life, and it was a good one.

Maybe someday she would have the luxury of daydreaming about celebrity romances, but not today. She hadn't gone to Jay's room to ask for a date, or even friendship. She'd been there to ask the woman to enter a professional relationship with her teenage daughter. She couldn't think of anything more complicated and less sexy than that. Even Jay had admitted Sadie played the role of tennis mom perfectly. How could she ever expect Jay to see her as anything else when she didn't even see herself as anything else? And she didn't want to. She was Destiny Larsen's mom, and that was more than enough for her.

Or at least it had been for the last seventeen years.

Jay slid across the red clay, or at least that's what she intended to do. Instead she sort of slipped and then stopped abruptly, her racket waving fruitlessly in the general direction of the ball Peggy Hamilton sent skipping off the sideline.

"Game. Ms. Hamilton leads 5- 2," the chair umpire called, as if there had been any doubt.

"Fuck fuckity fuck," she muttered under her breath as she tried to wrench her groin muscles back out of the unintentional split they'd nearly sent her into. Then the panic seized her chest at the fear that one of the cameras had caught the muttering and broadcast it to a lip-reading official who would fine her for yet another grievous offense. Then she laughed, remembering she was playing a 10 a.m. match, in Germany, during the first round of a minor tournament, against another player whose rank barely broke the top fifty and yet still managed to best her own by a solid twenty spots. All of those facts should've depressed the living shit out of her, but on the bright side, it meant no one was televising this match, much less watching the damn thing.

No one except Sadie Larsen, of course, who sat in the second row behind the chair umpire, alone. Which was bad, very bad, for a multitude of reasons.

Her presence had inspired a mix of emotions throughout the match, none of which had helped her play any better. Annoyance, confusion, a hint of pleasure, anger at herself for the hint of happiness that someone had come to watch her play. What she wanted to feel was nothing, but that hadn't been an option for her ever since Sadie had breezed out of her hotel room in Charleston. Nearly ten days had passed, and not one of them had gone by without Jay replaying their conversation. She kept rolling their words over in her mind, wondering how she'd managed to tie herself in a knot. They had been talking about tennis, and then they weren't, and then all of a sudden Jay had all but agreed to the point Sadie had been trying to make about tennis.

Which was bad, because not only couldn't she figure out how that had happened, she'd also spent the last week and a half wondering if she'd been right. "She" being herself, but also Sadie, because somehow they'd both ended up at the same damn conclusion.

She strode back to the baseline and assumed her ready position, feet shoulder width apart, knees bent, racket out in front, not even glancing at the stands. But not looking and not seeing were two very different things, because she couldn't stop thinking about the smug smile on Sadie's face as she assured Jay she'd come around.

Where had that come from? Certainly not from the timid woman who hadn't been able to look her in the eye when she'd first arrived. Jay had spent a fair share of her waking hours marveling at the woman Sadie had become as her confidence had risen, and the implications the shift had had on her own emotions. A little playful banter with a stressed-out tennis mom was one thing. Flirting with a confident, knowing, satisfied woman ratcheted the danger quotient up several degrees, especially when she considered the possibility of them spending more time together, which of course she wasn't, because that also would be very bad.

A ball pounded the clay right at the service line and sprang back up just to her right. Jay lunged but didn't get her racket up in time to ward off an ace that wouldn't have been one if she hadn't been standing flat-footed thinking about Sadie. Somewhere in her musing about the woman in the stands, she'd forgotten the fact that she was losing, again, which should bother her a lot more than seeing Sadie. But it didn't, which was also very bad.

So much bad, and not nearly enough good. The downward trend weighed on her so heavily she barely had the strength to return the next two serves, much less score winners with them.

"40-love," the chair called, then to rub salt in the wound added, "Ms. Hamilton has three match points."

"Thanks for clearing that up," Jay whispered, and held her racket at the ready again. She wouldn't win. She wasn't naive, but she had one more crack at the ball, and if she couldn't afford to slam her racket or scream any profanity, she intended to land her blows where she could. As Peggy served, Jay turned her feet toward her forehand side and drew back her racket, then clamping both hands on the hilt swung it forward like a baseball bat and laced a line drive right at her opponent's body. All Peggy could do was jump out of the way as the ball screamed past her to hit the back wall of the court.

"Out!" a line judge called unnecessarily.

"Game, set, match. Ms. Hamilton wins 6-4, 6-2."

Jay jogged to the net, her racket clenched tightly in her left fist as she extended her other hand. Peggy accepted and pulled her into a hug.

"Sorry about the last one," Jay muttered.

"No worries," Peggy said calmly. "We've all been there. Now who's the woman?"

Jay stepped back and shook her head. "Trouble."

Peggy laughed as they walked toward their respective benches. "Then she's right up your alley."

"Who?" Heather switched off her mic and climbed down from the umpire's chair.

Peggy nodded to Sadie, and Heather turned to look before grinning back to Jay. "Nice."

"Come on, don't encourage her," Jay complained. "It's nothing."

"Doesn't seem like nothing," Heather said. "You played like shit, even for clay."

"She's totally in your head," Peggy said gleefully, as she swung her bag onto her shoulder. "Is she local?"

"No," Jay said flatly.

"A reporter?" Heather asked.

"No. God, no."

"She's not a player," Heather said. "She looks familiar though."

"She kind of does. I think I've seen her around," Peggy said. "Is she a groupie?"

"God, no, just stop."

"Is she—"

"She's Destiny Larsen's mom," Jay blurted.

Both mouths fell open as they stared at her, then at each other, and then fell into giggle fits.

"Nice, guys." Jay jammed her racket into her bag and yanked the zipper up. "Real nice."

Heather recovered first. "I'm sorry. It's just . . . is she really a tennis mom? You're dating *a tennis mom?*"

"No!" Jay exploded, then lowered her voice again. "We're not dating, not even close."

"You're blushing," Peggy teased. "Oh my God, Heather. Jay Pierce's cheeks are turning pink. I didn't think there was anything left in the whole world that could make her blush."

"It's hot in here. I just got my ass kicked, and I'm pissed about it. Exertion and anger are all you see here."

"Tennis Mom is totally under your skin," Heather said.

"She's not. Or maybe she is, but not the way you think." Jay sighed, then surrendered. "She wants me to play doubles with her daughter."

Both of them stopped laughing immediately. Jay shifted awkwardly as they once again stared at her. She sort of preferred their teasing to their serious concern.

"You're going to do it, right?" Heather asked.

"No," she practically shouted, "of course not."

"Jay," Heather said sharply, "the doubles game needs you as much as you need it. And now someone with talent and promise and a bright future is begging you to join forces. You have to play."

"I don't have to do anything, and I don't play doubles."

"Good," Peggy said, causing Heather to shoot her a stern look.

"What? She was unstoppable at doubles. She and Larsen together would kill us all."

"And you like being able to waltz to an easy payday," Heather filled in.

"Damn right I do," Peggy said. "I got a split of forty grand two weeks ago."

Jay dropped onto the bench, feeling light-headed. Twenty thousand dollars, and Peggy wasn't even great at doubles. She hated to play the net, whereas Jay had used to love it. She snatched up a towel and mopped up some of the sweat beading along the back of her neck. *Used to* was the operative phrase there, she reminded herself internally.

"Hey," Heather said, her voice soft with worry, "I didn't mean to pressure you. I just thought it sounded like a great chance to get your groove back."

"And I didn't mean to be insensitive," Peggy added, patting her shoulder, then laughed. "I'm just worried it'd be a great chance for you to get your groove back."

She snorted. "It's fine. I'm fine."

"Good," Heather said. "You know you can call me if you need to talk."

"Yeah, me too," Peggy said quickly. "And I mean that, 'cause I think you're going to need someone to vent to soon."

"Why's that?"

"'Cause Tennis Mom is sitting next to the locker room tunnel now."

Jay craned her neck to see the exit. Sure enough, Sadie had switched seats. Jay would have to pass almost within arm's reach in order to leave the arena. She sighed as she took in Sadie's full lips and bare shoulders under a white silk shell.

"You want me to call security?" Heather asked.

She shook her head. "Nah, just give me some time, okay?"

"Of course," Heather said.

Peggy gave her shoulder a little squeeze, and they both exited the court. Jay hung her head for a moment, her chest tight, her throat dry. She'd just lost a match, and that stung, but she worried she was about to lose a piece of her dignity as well. She knew all the reasons she would use to justify the decision. She needed the money. She wanted to win. Destiny could use her help. Hank was always right. She wasn't ready to let go of this game. Every one of them made sense, and clearly no one would argue against her.

She rose, threw a towel over her shoulder and grabbed her bag, but as she locked eyes with Sadie, she understood all the reasons to say *yes* were counterbalanced by one reason to say *no*.

Still, she walked toward her, chin up, eyes level, until she got close enough to say one word. "Fine."

Sadie's brilliant smile told Jay she'd gotten the message, and the way her heart gave a little thud against her ribs said her concerns were not in any way unfounded.

Prague, Czech Republic

"Late flight?" Hank asked, clearly trying to hide a grin and doing a poor job of it.

Jay stared at him over the rim of her Ray-Bans, a leftover from a time when she hadn't had to pay for her own accessories. "I took the train."

He grimaced, and her defenses rose. "I like the trains in Europe. They're nice, the seats are bigger than planes, and you see more."

"They're cheaper," he added.

She sighed and dropped her gear at his feet.

He clasped a beefy hand on her shoulder and squeezed. "It's okay, Jay. It's going to start getting better now."

She shook her head. "Clay courts."

"Des is good on clay. Besides, most of the field went to Morocco. There's only sixteen teams in double draw here."

"The purse is bigger there," she said matter-of-factly.

"You'd never see a tenth of it."

"Thanks." She didn't argue, but she didn't appreciate him stating the obvious.

"You've got a shot to get to the middle rounds here, Jay."

She shrugged.

"Fine," he said, "you don't have to be happy about everything. You're here. That's half the battle won."

"Nothing's won," she grumbled, "and I'm only half the team. I would've thought the Larsen women would beat me to the court this morning."

Hank nodded grimly. "Me too."

"Please tell me this kid isn't a diva."

"She's not," he said quickly. "Don't get me wrong. She's stubborn and driven, and she's got very high standards. Also a bit of a temper."

"Yeah, doesn't sound like a diva at all," Jay agreed facetiously. She still had time to run, to pull the plug on this whole little experience. She could still withdraw from the doubles field with no penalty. While the idea helped her feel a little more in control, it was a false hope. She needed the money. It was as simple as that.

She heard the gate open behind her and turned to see Sadie smiling brightly at her. Today she wore a white polo and navy shorts that didn't cover even a quarter of her shapely legs. Her dark curls fell down across her shoulders, but not one of them dared obscure her perfect face. She seemed smooth, classy, and classically beautiful. Jay's chest tightened pleasantly, and she had to admit, if only to herself, maybe things weren't quite as simple as her budget might suggest.

"What's she doing here?" Destiny asked.

Both the question and the incredulous tone in which it was delivered jolted Jay out of her stupor.

"I told you I wanted you to work out with an old doubles player of mine," Hank said casually.

Des wheeled on her mom. "Did you know about this?"

"Well, yes," Sadie said guiltily.

"Wait a second," Jay cut in. "You didn't know about this little plan?"

"No," Destiny said flatly, then turned to her mother. "What the fuck?"

69

"Language," Sadie said sharply.

"No. I'm actually with her on this," Jay said. "What the actual fuck? You came to my hotel room asking me to play doubles with her and—"

"You went to her hotel room?" Destiny jumped back in. "God, Mom, did anyone see you?"

"No," Sadie said.

"Wait. You're more upset about her being seen with me than about her lying to you?"

"Yes," Destiny said, folding her arms across her chest. "I don't want her alone with you."

Jay stepped into Destiny's personal space, their chests almost touching, and stared up into eyes so much colder than her mother's. "What's that supposed to mean?"

"Hey," Hank shouted, thrusting a shoulder between them. "Knock it off. Both of you. You're professional athletes, not a pair of middle school girls."

"She's not far off from being a middle school girl," Jay grumbled, but she stepped back.

"Look," Hank said more calmly. "You two don't have to like each other. You don't have to hang out together. You don't have to talk about anything other than tennis, but you need each other right now. There's no use pretending otherwise."

Destiny shook her head. "I don't need this. I'm not working out with her again."

"No," Sadie said firmly. "You're not. You're playing doubles with her starting in three days."

"Mom," Destiny said, eyes wide with disbelief, "I'm not."

"You are. Hank got you a wild card entry. It's already decided."

"You can't make me play with someone I don't want to play with," Destiny said through clenched teeth. "I'm a professional tennis player."

"And I'm still your mother. It's still my job to make sure you're on the right track, and not throwing away opportunities. It's my job to make sure you don't let a temper tantrum get in the way of your future. And it's my job to put your rusty ass back on a

70

plane to the United States if, for one minute, you make me believe you're not mature enough to handle the conflicts inherent in the path you've chosen."

"Whoa," Jay said, not sure if she should be terrified or turned on by the display of force.

"And *you.*" Sadie wheeled on her, and Jay's internal warning scales tipped heavily toward the side of terrified. "I did not ask you to play with her so that you could antagonize my child. There are plenty of other pros out there, and a lot of them are faring much better in the standings right now. I chose you because I thought you'd be a role model, a leader, a calming influence for a young woman who's struggling on and off the court."

Sadie stepped closer, the smell of sunscreen and tangerine filling Jay's senses. "I came to you because of the sensitivity and understanding you showed us in Charleston. I trusted you with the most precious thing in my life because I thought you were a better person than a player. It would break my heart to find out you aren't."

"Ouch," Jay said, all the teasing gone out of her voice. She would've given a kidney to trade disappointed Sadie for angry tennis mom. Her chest couldn't handle the pressure crushing it right now. She barely knew this woman. Sadie had no right to push her around. Jay didn't owe her or her daughter anything. Maybe a stronger person would've told her so, but whether it was a weakness, or the sneaking suspicion that Sadie's assessment of her behavior might be accurate, she didn't want to ever again be the cause of the sadness clouding those espresso eyes. "Okay."

"Okay what?" Sadie asked.

"Okay, I'll try," Jay said with a nod, as she tried to regain some hint of professionalism amid her swirling emotions. "Point taken. I'm committed to one tournament. I'm ready to practice whenever Destiny is."

They all turned to the girl, whose jaw remained clenched so tightly even her ears appeared tense. Jay felt torn between wanting her to blow her top so they could all just go home, and wishing she would pull her shit together so they could get to work.

Finally, Destiny rolled her eyes. "Sure, whatever."

Sadie opened her mouth, but Hank raised a hand. "I'll take it from here. Why don't you go relax, or shop, or drink some hard liquor."

Jay forced a smile. "If you choose option three, save some for me."

Sadie shook her head, but Jay thought she might have seen the corners of her mouth turn up slightly as she walked away.

Jay turned to Destiny and shrugged. "Looks like we're in this together. Might as well make the best of it, right?"

"I've never played doubles before," Destiny said flatly. "And I don't want to do so now."

Jay laughed. "Well, at least we can agree on that last part."

"Guys," Hank pleaded.

She slapped him on the shoulder as she turned toward the court. "No worries, big guy. Des and I just found some common ground. We're bonding. Consider our mutual displeasure the first aspect of team-building."

"Oh, this is not going well," Sadie said, fighting the urge to cover her eyes.

"They aren't losing . . . yet," Hank said, not managing to hide a grimace. "They had a rough start, but they're back on serve."

"They just ran into each other." Sadie whimpered as she watched Jay limp across the clay, dragging the foot that Destiny had just landed on after going up for a high lob.

"They're in the second round."

"Only because their first-round team had to forfeit."

"Sometimes you catch a break," Hank said, then added, "and sometimes your partner breaks your foot. You just hope it all comes out in the wash."

Sadie sat on her hands to keep from biting her nails as Jay and Destiny dropped another game. "Did we make the right call?"

"Do you want $3,000?" Hank asked dryly.

She elbowed him in the side. "I didn't mean financially. I mean for Des mentally, emotionally. I wanted to push her out of her comfort zone a little, but I didn't want to embarrass her in front of the whole tennis world."

He made a big show of looking around slowly. "What's that? I can hardly hear you over the crowd."

She sighed. So maybe they were two of only ten people in the stands, which appeared to be the metal bleachers cast off when the local high school went out of business. "You know what I mean. I wanted playing doubles to build her confidence instead of knocking her down another notch."

"Maybe she needs to be knocked down a few pegs," Hank said, as he applauded the first point they'd scored in a while. "You know I'd never want to do anything to kill her drive, but she's not Superwoman. She needs to make adjustments, and she can't control everything. The sooner she learns that, the happier she'll be."

"I don't know," Sadie worried aloud.

"Of course you don't. You're just like her."

"What?" She turned to stare at him, but his eyes remained focused on the court.

"Watch this," he muttered, as Jay surged so close to the net she almost fell over it, then holding her racket straight up and down, waited for the ball to strike before she flipped her wrist to the side. The ball struck the court in the doubles alley and spun like a dreidel. "Atta girl, Jay."

"Can we go back to the part where I'm controlling?"

He grinned. "It's not always a bad thing. You got them both on the court. The whole mom meltdown during practice was glorious."

"I didn't melt down."

"You threatened to put your daughter's rusty ass back on a plane." He chuckled. "Then you almost made Jay cry. Seriously, I've only ever seen her cry once."

Sadie's throat tightened. "Who made her cry?"

He shifted from one butt cheek to the other on the aluminum bench and cleared his throat. "It was a long time ago, but the point is, you're used to getting what you want every bit as much

73

as Des, and that's why they're out there, but you can't control the game for them."

Another shot lobbed over Destiny's head and dropped right on the baseline while both Destiny and Jay stood at the net watching it.

"That was Des's ball," Hank said, but Jay didn't so much as look at her. She just fished another ball from under the hem of her black lycra shorts and bounced it back to Des.

"Des is trying to play full court tennis. She doesn't trust Jay yet, so she's still playing singles in her mind."

"They've only been playing together for four days," Sadie said defensively. "I'm sure Jay hasn't been flawless in the transition either."

"She was born to play doubles," Hank replied almost wistfully. "She's a little rusty with her lateral movements, but her only real mistake so far has been expecting Des to be where she's supposed to be."

Sadie's shoulders tightened. "Well, Des made it to the second round in the singles, and Jay didn't. Maybe she's fresher. Maybe I should talk to the scheduler."

He nudged her shoulder with his own. "Yeah, you're not controlling at all."

"I'm not. I just want Destiny to have a fair shot." Another ball whizzed past Destiny, who was standing too close to the middle of the court to cover the extra ground the doubles court offered.

"Tennis is as fair as anything else in life," Hank said. "You have to let her experience all of it. She might learn some lessons about letting go and trusting the people around her. Hell, you might, too."

She bristled at the comment. "I don't think—"

"Shhh," he scolded. "Des is about to get broken."

"I'm watching," Sadie said, not at all appreciative of being shushed like a child. "I can do that and talk at the same time."

"Well, stop and watch Jay instead of Des."

She clamped down her instinct to argue. As Des reached the baseline and tossed a ball in the air, Sadie turned her attention to Jay. Her muscles flexed, from her biceps all the way to her calves. Sweat glistened on her skin as a subtle shift of her feet stirred a cloud of red dust. She went up on her toes, then pivoted to the forehand side, slid a half step back and rocked forward as the ball came back to her. She laced a forehand down the line, but before it had even landed she'd backpedaled two steps, then planting her feet, pushed up into the air, racket arm extended to catch a high lob. She came down with the force of a volleyball player spiking the ball so hard it smashed into the court and then bounced completely into the stands.

Sadie applauded the play instinctually, but Jay didn't even give so much as a fist pump. Sadie looked back at her daughter to see her still standing on the baseline, racket lowered, her mouth pressed into a tight line.

Her chest constricted. Jay was carrying Destiny, and now they all knew it. She'd become almost superhuman, her feet moving as constantly as a tap dancer's, while Destiny sank further into her frustration. What's more, she didn't seem to appreciate Jay's caliber of play so much as resent it. No high fives, no huddling together between plays, not even a smile. Sadie sighed. Whatever was bothering her daughter clearly went beyond her Herculean desire to win.

Jay rolled out her stiff shoulders under the warm spray of the locker room showers. Adding doubles matches and practices to her singles load had started to take a toll on her muscles a few days ago, but now she worried the cost of that extra exertion showed to the people in the crowd. And there had been a bit of a crowd at their match today, at least relatively speaking. Doubles never drew the attention singles did, but after they'd scraped out their last match to reach the quarterfinals, a few more people took notice. Amid the handful of local fans, she'd also seen a few players and coaches in the bleachers today. She'd noticed a handful of reporters, too.

She'd managed to keep from obsessing about them during the

match because she'd had her hands full trying to cover her ground and half of Destiny's without making it clear she had to carry the kid, but had her forced casualness fooled the press? Had they taken note of the chill between the two of them? Maybe the contrast wouldn't have been so stark if they hadn't been playing Peggy and Carla today. Those two felt like a sorority and a cheer-leading squad gave birth to twins and handed them tennis rackets. Between the high fives and hand signals and calling out secret code words, Jay couldn't tell if they were playing tennis or running a covert, synchronized dance squad.

She blew a spray of water away from her mouth and rolled her neck. Good thing she didn't want to play doubles long-term, or she might find herself wishing for a connection like that. Instead she appreciated Destiny's cold shoulder to a certain extent because it meant there'd be no risk of falling into that sort of camaraderie accidently. She didn't even mind that her hug with Peggy at the net after the match offered more affection than she'd gotten from her own partner all afternoon. She would've welcomed a bit more communication from Des when the tide had turned against them in the third set, but if they were striking a delicate balance between winning and professional distance, they hadn't done a terrible job in their first tournament.

Quarterfinalist.

She tried not to let the semantics warm her as she turned off the shower and stepped out of the steam. Still, she hadn't had that word used to describe her in years. Sure, they'd been lucky in the first round, but in the second, she'd played her ass off. And even today they'd forced a third set. But then again, it was a weak field.

She laughed aloud at the war raging inside her between hope and realism. She didn't want to get too excited, but she hadn't had anything to be proud of in a long time, and at least this little accomplishment came with a nice paycheck. Even when she and Destiny split the pot, she'd have an extra two grand to help her get through to the French Open. There was nothing wrong with feeling a little relief about that.

Wrapping a towel around her waist, she wandered back to her locker, only to find Sadie leaning against it, in capri pants and a carob-colored sweater that almost exactly matched her eyes. Her eyebrows shot up as they fell on Jay, then trained on the floor, making Jay immediately wish she'd fastened the towel a little higher.

"Jay," Sadie said, her voice a little higher than usual. "I didn't expect you to still be, umm, well . . ."

"Naked?" Jay offered.

"I was going to go with 'in the shower,' but yes. That, too."

"I like long showers," Jay said, then felt kind of stupid for not having a better comeback.

"You certainly earned one this week. You worked double time on an already frantic practice schedule. I hope you know I appreciate your commitment."

Jay shrugged and pulled on the first T-shirt she grabbed, not even bothering with a bra. "It's part of the job."

"Hank assures me everything will get easier once you two get used to playing with each other."

She snorted. "Well played, Tennis Mom. I see what you did there."

"What?" Sadie asked innocently.

"I agreed to one tournament. To earn one check. I made good on my word."

"You did," Sadie said, clasping a hand gently around her right biceps. "Thank you."

The touch sent Jay's nerve endings into overdrive. "You're welcome."

"I know you probably have other offers, and you only played with Destiny as a favor to me. I also know she's been a little slower to come around than you have."

Jay smiled. "Ya think?"

Sadie squeezed her arm, and her dark eyes flickered up to meet Jay's. "Okay, a lot slower, but she's not good with change, and she's had a lot of it lately. If she had more time . . ."

Jay shook her head. "We're all in Madrid next week. It's a primary tournament. She's going to be under a lot of pressure to do well in the singles in order to make it into the main draw at the French."

"Exactly. There's so much pressure in the singles. Wouldn't it be nice to play a little doubles, where no one expects anything from you?" Sadie leaned close enough to whisper. "And the first-round payout is $9,000? Even if you lose in the second round, you still win."

Jay's head felt like she was hanging upside down, and while she wanted to pretend the numbers had sparked the blood rush, she suspected Sadie's proximity had more to do with it.

She nodded mutely. "Yeah, I—"

"Mom?"

The word was like a bucket of ice water right under her towel, and they both jumped back to stare at Destiny.

"What's going on?" Destiny asked, as if she feared the answer. "Hank and I have been waiting for you."

"I'm sorry," Sadie said. "Jay and I were just talking about Madrid."

Her eyes narrowed. "What about it?"

Jay cleared her throat. "We're going to see if we can get a wild card for the doubles."

"No," Destiny said flatly.

Jay shrugged. "Okay then."

But Sadie didn't fold so easily. "I understand you're not in love with the idea, but—"

Destiny clenched her jaw and shook her head.

Jay looked awkwardly into her locker, trying not to be caught in the middle of another family disagreement. The last time that had happened, she'd been roped into playing big sister.

"It's a good opportunity for you, Des. After how far you went this time—"

"We got the money we needed to get to Madrid," the girl said coolly. "It's the last major tournament before the French Open."

"Exactly," Sadie said, so emphatically her curls gave a little bounce. "If you and Jay do well there, you could qualify for doubles in the French Open."

"Whoa," Jay said, peeking out from behind the locker door. "Did you just commit me to playing doubles for four more weeks?"

Sadie rolled her eyes. "It's clay court season. You got better plans?"

"Zing." Jay laughed. "Your sassy side comes with a sharp edge."

"No," Destiny said again. "Stop it, both of you. You can't just decide things for me."

"Don't look at me," Jay muttered, then ducked back behind the locker door again. "Your tennis mom is steering the ship."

"Hank had a say in the plan, too," Sadie defended. "He thinks playing doubles at a larger event will be good for you. More practice under pressure, and more opportunity to quicken your footwork on clay. He's the coach. What he says, goes. I happen to agree with him, but even if I didn't, I'd suggest you listen to him."

Destiny folded her arms across her chest. "What about Nuremburg? Let's skip Madrid and play doubles when we get to Germany."

"Why not both?"

"Madrid's too important. The press will be there in force, along with all the best players. I don't want to be seen with her."

Jay closed the locker door with a metallic thud. "You mean you won't *play* with me, right? Not that you won't be *seen* with me, 'cause they mean two different things."

"And I meant both of them," Destiny said, still looking at her mother. "If we have to, we'll make money a different way."

"It's not about the money," Sadie said, her own voice showcasing where her daughter's had inherited its steely bent.

"Then we'll practice another time," Des shot back.

"It's not about the practice, not after that comment," Sadie said, looking over her shoulder at Jay. "I'm sorry for my daughter's behavior. If you don't want to play with a rude child, I'll forgive you, because apparently in addition to more footwork, she also needs an attitude adjustment."

"Mom," Destiny snapped, but Sadie held up a palm right in her face.

"Jay, if you're still willing to help us out, I'd be honored if you'd travel with us to Madrid. Then we'll make sure we get hotel rooms nearby, so Destiny can have plenty of opportunity to work on her manners. If you want, she'll do her penance by carrying your bags."

Jay laughed, but Destiny's eyes darkened even further, and the sound died in her throat. God, this kid really hated her. Initially Jay had just pegged her for scared and overwhelmed with a strong dose of parental-based spoiling, but now the hair on the back of her neck stood on end. The disgust on Destiny's face wasn't self-centered. It was pointed right at Jay.

Her stomach tightened as the bile started to churn. It'd been a long time since she'd recognized that undisguised repulsion in someone opposite her, but her body hadn't forgotten its standard reaction. Shame burned her cheeks as the whispers rushed back through her ears. She felt the hot stares against her back and the twisted knots in her shoulders. She'd been through enough to know she had to let the emotions run their course. Bottling them up only allowed the acid to burn longer or bubble up later. Allowing them to rush over her and fade away offered the only quick relief. Only this time the feelings didn't subside, so much as shift. Something hotter than humiliation baked beneath the surface now.

Who the hell was Destiny Larsen to judge her? The kid had barely been born when she'd met Katia. She would've been in elementary school when their worlds crashed down. Any of the lies she'd heard wouldn't have just been secondhand. They'd have been filtered through a decade of hazy innuendo and snarky backchannels. Jay had done the work of a lifetime to rebuild her credibility with people who actually mattered, people she'd legitimately disappointed or hurt no matter how involuntarily, but she owed nothing to a kid who cut her teeth on someone else's personal tragedy.

"Jay," Sadie whispered. "I'm sorry."

"What?" She blinked, her eyes focusing away from the past and onto the woman before her.

"I'm sorry for Destiny's bad behavior. She's never spoken to anyone like that in my presence, not in seventeen years. I don't know what I did to let her think that level of rudeness would be tolerated."

"You didn't," Jay said softly. "Plenty of other people did that work for you."

Sadie seemed genuinely confused. "I don't understand."

Jay smiled slightly, believing her. Sadie had no idea what they were talking about. They'd had a fresh start. She knew Jay only for the woman she'd become, and she liked her enough to want her around. Would the same hold true after she heard more? Because she undoubtedly would. Which version of Jay would she accept then? The one she knew, or the one so many others thought they did? For the first time in a long time, Jay wanted to stick around long enough to find out, or maybe even try to tip the scales in her favor. After years of hiding, of throwing up walls and keeping a healthy distance between herself and anyone who looked at her the way Destiny did, had Jay's impulse to run finally run out?

Or had Sadie somehow done something to override it?

"I don't want to hear it," Sadie snapped at Destiny, as she wheeled their suitcases into a row at the hotel room door.

"You have to listen," Destiny pleaded. "She's not a good person, like, ten years ago she started a huge scandal by—"

"I don't care if she shot someone on the court," Sadie said. "She's been nothing but polite and reasonable with you. Hank swears she's trustworthy. She bailed you out on the court last week, and she didn't throttle you for speaking to her with blatant disrespect. As far as I'm concerned, she's been infinitely more patient than she should've been."

"So, you don't even care about the girl whose life she ruined?"

"No." She didn't. She honestly didn't want to hear whatever horrific tale Destiny had dredged up about Jay. Maybe if she'd seen anything suspicious in Jay over the last few weeks, or maybe if Hank's endorsement hadn't been quite so ringing, or maybe if she hadn't seen the hurt and shame pass so heartbreakingly over Jay's jubilant features, she would've worried, but Sadie trusted her gut. She always made her own decisions, and she wouldn't let Jay be an exception to the rule. She didn't know why she felt such a strong urge to protect her, but she didn't ignore those impulses. Then again, her mothering instincts were equally strong, and the discordance between her assessment of Jay's character and the need to be there for her daughter was tearing her apart.

"You can't trust people like her. She's doesn't have any self-control—"

"Destiny," Sadie shouted loud enough to be heard several rooms over, "stop!"

Destiny's chest heaved under a magenta tank top, but she heeded the warning. Without another word, she hoisted her carry-on and marched it into the hallway.

"Not another word about Jay," Sadie said more softly. "You do not have to like her. You don't have to trust her. You do have to show her some basic level of respect. You need to extend her at least the common courtesies you would give a stranger on the street. Is that clear?"

"Yes," Destiny said tersely, then let the door fall shut behind her.

Sadie sighed. It wasn't the answer she would've liked, but Destiny hadn't argued, so she'd take it. A hug would've been nice though. When Destiny was little and had done something rude or just wrong, Sadie would sit her down and explain the consequences of her actions, a time-out, a grounding, no dessert, but no matter what, she would always hug her and tell her she loved her unconditionally. When had the tradition stopped?

She was still pondering the question as they all shuffled through airport security and Destiny jammed her headphones back in her ears. She'd taken them out only long enough to go through the metal detector, thus cutting off all hope of small talk, much less a meaningful conversation.

"Hey," a gentle voice said from just over her left shoulder.

Sadie turned to see Jay standing beside her, one hand jammed in the pocket of her dark jeans. Her button-down shirt was cuffed at her sleeves and open at her throat, giving a rakish appeal to business casual, and the cerulean color made her eyes seem even more entrancing than usual.

"Hi," Sadie said with a smile. Not the most brilliant greeting in the world, but it seemed to suffice, because Jay returned her expression.

"You ready for sunny Spain?"

Sadie hadn't thought about Spain until that moment, not the tournament, not the weather, not the country at all. Tennis travel had long ago lost its luster. She rarely had time to see things other than courts, locker rooms, and hotels. Still, something about the way Jay asked the question gave her a little thrill of anticipation. "You know? I think I'm ready for a change of latitude if it helps with a change of attitude."

"You and me both," Jay said, only a slight hint of exhaustion in her voice.

"I don't know," Hank said, coming up behind them. "We didn't do too bad in Prague."

"We'll do better in Madrid," Jay said amicably. "Right, Destiny?"

They all turned to look at Des, who merely stared straight ahead.

"She's got her headphones in," Sadie explained, tension returning to her jaw.

"Oh, in that case, we can talk about her freely," Jay said, then went on to mouth several soundless words until Destiny finally rolled her eyes.

"I know you're not really talking."

"Ah, the ol' headphones-in, iPod-off trick," Jay said with a grin. "I know it well."

Sadie's stomach dropped. "You're not listening to any music?"

"Not at the moment," Destiny mumbled.

"I see." Sadie didn't elaborate for fear her hurt and insecurity would be evident to everyone.

Destiny had picked up the habit of using earphones almost

constantly when she'd started traveling for tennis tournaments around the age of thirteen. Sadie initially wrote the disconnect off as a way for Des to unwind after busy, loud, stressful competitions, though now she wondered if the coinciding timing with her entry into the teenage years had been connected. Maybe she hadn't wanted a break from the outside hustle and bustle so much as she'd needed time off from talking to Sadie.

Hank cleared his throat. "Our gate's right there. Why don't you get settled in? I'll go find us some coffee."

"I'll go, too," Destiny offered, then, as if trying to force the words painfully from her mouth, added, "Can I, um, get something for you? I mean, Jay."

Jay held up a blue refillable water bottle. "I filled up when I got through security. Thanks though."

Destiny nodded, then turned back to Sadie as if she wanted to say more, then shrugged and walked away.

Sadie wove her way through a group of American high schoolers with matching backpacks, clearly on a school spring break trip, until she found some empty seats near a floor-to-ceiling window. Dropping her purse with a thud, she landed in the chair in similar fashion, then sighed heavily.

"Rough morning?" Jay settled a little more gingerly beside her.
Sadie hung her head. "You could say that."

"My fault?" Jay asked softly.

"No." Sadie met her alluring eyes. "We're all under a lot of pressure. Des is tense and defensive. I'm tense and insecure. Hank is tense and overcompensating. None of that is your fault. Honestly, I'm not even sure why you're here when we've offered you nothing but stress and awkwardness and bad manners."

"You also helped me earn an extra paycheck last week," Jay offered.

"Is that it?" Sadie asked, her limbs heavy as the logic of the answer settled over her. "Do you really need the money badly enough to put up with us all?"

Jay smiled and shook her head, her sandy hair skimming across her shoulders and curling unevenly along her starched shirt collar. "I should say yes, and don't get me wrong, the money helps, but it's not the primary reason."

"Is it because Hank guilted you?"

She laughed. "Hank is good at many things. Emotional appeals are not among them. You, on the other hand, are like, ninja level with the mom guilt. Seriously, the force is strong with you, but not even the dressing-down you gave me about being a good role model weighed as much as you probably would have liked."

"No?" Sadie asked, turning in her seat so that her body angled toward Jay's. "What tipped the scales then?"

"You seem to like me."

Sadie waited for more of an explanation, but none came.

"I like you? Really? You've played a game you don't want to play, put up with a surly teen, added hours of practice to your schedule, and rearranged travel plans simply because *I* seem to like you?"

"Pretty pathetic, huh?" Jay asked, her cheeks coloring.

"No," Sadie said quickly. "Not pathetic. Everyone wants to be liked. I'd just think that almost everyone would find you likable."

Jay's smile returned, this time with a hint of shyness, "Well, you'd be wrong. For one, a lot of people don't ever take the chance, and for two, I don't often give people the chance."

"Why?"

"What's the saying? Once bitten, twice shy? Or, fool me once something something shame on me? It's part of growing up." Her blue eyes darkened slightly, causing Sadie to wonder what undercurrent of seriousness or pain ran beneath the casualness of the comment. "But either way, I don't trust the press, and I don't travel with a coach anymore, so it's nice to see a friendly face on the road, even if that face is attached to a tennis mom who sometimes yells at me to be a better person."

"Thank you . . . I think," Sadie said, struck by the sweetness laced with humor. Was Jay naturally prone to the combination, or had she learned to weave the two together as a sort of survival instinct?

"You're welcome," Jay said, a slight frown tugging at her lips, "for now, anyway. I'll let you reserve full judgment until after Madrid. The stakes are about to go up, and the pressure will, too, along with scrutiny from the press and the officials and, well, the world at large."

"I know Des is worried about it, but I don't understand all the fuss. You've still got a couple weeks until the French Open. Madrid is a clay court, which she's good on. And I don't see any reason for the press to behave any differently than they have until now."

"Let's put it this way. You know how Des and I are practicing in progressively bigger venues and against tougher opponents as a way of ramping up for the big show ahead? Well, the press is, too."

"How so?"

"Basically, no one in the American public has cared about tennis a bit since the Australian Open, and even that's the least compelling of the majors for a viewing public coming off the holidays and gearing up for the Superbowl. The reporters following us had their stories filed in the back of newspapers or tucked away on obscure websites, but in a few weeks, they'll be catapulted back onto the front page."

"So what, they need to start practicing more detailed stories?"

"Oh, how we all wish they would focus more on craft or technical aspects of the game." Jay shook her head. "More likely, though, they'll be laying the groundwork for human interest stories, trying to get the scoop on anything that will hook casual tennis followers on their column or news reports for the duration of the summer."

"Well, I happen to find Destiny very interesting and appealing, but so far the press hasn't shown much interest in her as a person. I can't imagine why they'd start now."

Jay shifted in her chair, putting her hands on the armrests as if she were about to push herself up, then sighed and settled back in. "Look, remember how I said I don't let a lot of people get close?"

Sadie nodded.

"It hasn't always been about protecting myself. And when Des said she didn't want to be seen with me, like people might get the wrong idea . . ."

"Jay, I don't know what came over her."

"I do," Jay said quickly, "and for the record, the stories that sparked her concerns were wrong, but her fears about added press coverage aren't baseless. People will talk. Eventually someone will say something stupid, or make unfair assumptions, or stereotypes."

Sadie's breath shallowed, as if she couldn't get air all the way to her lungs due to the pressure building in her chest. Her urge to protect her daughter collided with her natural defiance against being pushed around by other people's ideals. "Why do I get the feeling the whole world knows something I don't?"

"Because they do," Jay said matter-of-factly. "You've got a smartphone, you can use Google, you can talk to Des or any reporter or player you come across this week, and they'd bring you up to speed."

"Why don't you bring me up to speed?" She wondered why Jay would be so willing to let someone else tell her story when Sadie had spent so much of her life fighting against that very prospect.

"It doesn't matter what I say." Jay shrugged again, but this time she stared out the window as a plane pulled up to the gate. "The story was agreed upon a long time ago. There's no changing it now."

"It's never too late to change the ending," Sadie said, not even quite sure if the comment was for Jay or herself.

"Yeah." Jay's throat visibly tightened, as if she were trying to force down a ball of emotions. "I'm not sure I'm ready to get to the ending yet, but maybe I wouldn't mind adding a few footnotes to my career."

"Footnotes?" Hank asked from behind them. They both jumped, and Jay leaned away from her.

"I didn't sign on for footnotes. I want highlights," Hank said.

Jay's smile returned, but it didn't reach her eyes. "I suppose stranger things have happened, but either way, I've been meaning to ask you to help set up some footwork drills for us in Madrid. Maybe some ladder work."

Hank nodded. "We could do that easily. Des would benefit from those exercises, too, both in doubles and singles. As the pace of your last game sped up, she tried to replace finesse with power, which is one of the reasons why I wanted her to work with you instead of a baseline striker."

He turned to Destiny, who had stopped farther down along the window. "Des, come here. We need to go over some schedule additions."

Destiny edged closer, her earlier anger replaced, or maybe simply tempered, by a more childlike need to please both coach and mother as she got close enough to be included in their circle. Once Sadie felt certain her daughter wouldn't cause any more trouble, she glanced back to Jay, who nodded slightly as Hank ran through some workout options. Her brow had smoothed, her expression studiously neutral, her shoulders relaxed, and she'd propped one long leg atop the other, ankle over knee.

Nothing in her demeanor spoke of the tension that had accompanied their conversation minutes ago, leaving Sadie to wonder whether she'd misread the emotions she'd seen in Jay's eyes then, or if the transition back to tennis topics was one she'd perfected over years of practicing self-preservation.

Madrid, Spain

Jay backed up a few steps and rocked forward with a backhand right at the opposing net player's feet. She didn't even wait to see the ball come off her racket. The only play would be straight up. She charged up to the net as if her feet intuited the dance even before the music began to play. Then with the push of a basketball player going for the easy layup, she spiked the ball into the service box a good six feet in front of her Austrian opponent. She gave a fist pump as it bounced into the first row of the stands.

God, it felt good to be in command again.

Then, without thinking, she wheeled to smile at Destiny, who stood stone-faced as usual.

"Game, and set Pierce/Larsen," the chair umpire called. "6-3."

Another jolt of exhilaration raced through her, like the blood being pushed along by her rapidly beating heart. Turning away from Destiny, she looked up into the players' box to see both Hank and Sadie on their feet applauding the shot and the set. Her stomach gave a pleasing little lurch like one might get on a carnival ride. There were people rooting for her. Well, her and Destiny, but still, even a half-share of Sadie's smile was better than a full portion of anyone else's.

She jogged to her bench and snatched a towel from atop her bag, then snagged another and tossed it to Destiny, who caught it wordlessly.

"You're welcome," Jay said cheerfully as she dropped onto the bench.

Destiny snorted and remained standing.

She thought about telling the kid she couldn't catch gayness from sweating in close proximity, but she didn't want to get into that conversation now, or maybe ever. They'd reached a politely distant sort of stasis over the last four days, and that had led to a quarterfinalist berth. Destiny hadn't warmed to her so much as resigned herself to a sort of business relationship. She at least answered direct questions from Hank or Jay. She'd also worked her ass off on the practice courts, even while keeping up with a full slate of singles matches. Maybe the singles matches had even helped the doubles, or vice versa, because they'd each made it to the third round individually, a fact that would help both their rankings and their wallets. Even if they somehow managed to blow the next two sets, they'd exceeded all expectations for their time in Madrid.

"Plus, the sun is nice," Jay said aloud before taking a big swig from her water bottle.

"What?" Destiny asked tersely.

"I was just mentally listing all the good things about today,"

Jay said breezily. "We've made enough money to cover our travel all the way through the French, we've bumped up our rankings both together and separately, we're killing it out there on the court so far, and the weather is nice. I might get a tan."

"I don't need a tan," Destiny said flatly.

"Yeah, well, not all of us were born with your fabulously bronze skin tone and teen-model good looks," Jay said, as she tossed the water back onto her bag and pushed off the bench.

"Was that some kind of a come-on?"

Jay rolled her eyes. "Don't flatter yourself, kiddo. You're not my type."

"That's not what I heard," Des muttered as she brushed past her, heading toward the court.

"Seriously?" Jay asked in a harsh whisper. "You want to do this now?"

Destiny said nothing as she accepted three tennis balls from a ball boy and took turns bouncing them.

"You're going to say something like that to me in the middle of a match? A match where I am carrying you, by the way." Jay pushed. "What the fuck is wrong with you?"

A muscle twitched in the girl's jaw as she palmed one of the balls and tossed the other one back to the ball kid. "Get back in position."

"Or what?"

"I'll serve with you standing right here."

"No, you won't," Jay said as she reached her boiling point. "You don't have it in you."

She narrowed her eyes. "You don't know me."

"Yeah, I do," Jay snapped, barely bothering to whisper now. "I've known women like you my whole career. You want to win, and you want to do it on your terms, but you don't want it bad enough to make a scene. If you serve with me standing here, you'll catch the attention of every reporter from here to Paris. Then everyone would know we got into a tiff on the court, and they'll start to wonder why you're having passionate debates with a known lesbian."

"You think I care that you're a lesbian?" Destiny asked. "You really think that's the issue here?"

"I do," Jay said, her face growing hot despite the cool breeze. "That and the prospect of your guilt by association. Wouldn't want the young suitors and hot sponsors to get the wrong idea . . . or the right one."

Destiny waved her away dismissively. "Go back to your position."

"No," Jay said adamantly, "I will not be bossed around by a baby bigot."

"Time," the chair called.

"We're about to get fined for delay of game," Destiny said.

"Look at my face," Jay instructed. "Do I really seem concerned about the score right now?"

"I couldn't care less about your concerns," Destiny said. "Just like I couldn't care less about what the press thinks of my sexual orientation. I care about their opinion of me about as much as I care about yours."

"Fault," called the chair umpire. "Time violation, Pierce/Larsen."

"That's one," Destiny said. "One more and we lose the point."

"I know the rules, damn it."

She couldn't figure out what Destiny was trying to play at, but she wanted it to end right now. If she had to walk off the court to teach the kid a lesson, she would. She'd thought they were past all the snarking and tantrums, but maybe Destiny had only been waiting to lob her insults out of earshot of her mother. Jay had plenty of familiarity with that two-faced bullying tactic, but she wasn't in high school, and she wouldn't let Destiny act like she was either. "I'm not going to roll over just because we're in the middle of a match. I won't be held hostage by a set point, or by you. I know more than I care to about dealing with run-of-the-mill mean girls."

"Then you know nothing about me," Destiny said. She tossed the ball high into the air and brought her racket down with a whip and a crack. Jay didn't turn to see where the serve landed, but she heard the murmurs flutter through the small crowd, followed by the chair umpire's score call.

"15-Love."

91

Any other time she would've been amused by scoring a point with her back to the court, but Destiny had already ruined her good vibes from the first set, and right now the second set seemed secondary to drawing a hard line with the person who was supposed to be her partner.

"I'm not some prima donna," Destiny said flatly. "And whether you believe it or not, I'm certainly not a homophobe."

"Yeah," Jay scoffed. "Have you looked in the mirror lately?"

"Every morning. I know who I am and what I stand for." She tossed her frizzy ponytail over her shoulder and met Jay's eyes with a steely glint in her own. "I'm the daughter of a single black woman who never took one ounce of crap from anyone and who gave me everything she had. I'm the product of a woman who never wavered, and never compromised, and never once put her needs over mine."

Jay took a step back, unsure of where this conversation had taken its latest bizarre turn.

"If you think for one second, I'm going to sell out my mother to some playgirl predator in order to further my career, you've severely underestimated me." Destiny grabbed another ball and tossed it up without so much as a bounce. Jay watched, transfixed, as she crushed her serve, then heard the ball clunk off someone else's racket, quickly followed by a shout of "out."

"Thirty-Love."

"When did this become about your mom?" Jay felt disoriented and a little stupid for needing to ask the question.

"The first time I saw you look at her, the morning she went to your hotel room, just a second ago when we walked off the court and you sought her out in the crowd before I did," Destiny said as the ball boy approached once more. She took a ball and started to lift it toward the sky.

"Wait." Jay held up her free hand.

Destiny paused and arched a regally high eyebrow. "I'll go back to my spot. Just gimme a second to catch my breath."

"Why? You haven't moved in five minutes. I'm pulling all the weight here."

Jay chuckled in spite of her clenched stomach. Who the hell was this girl? She'd been nothing but a complete shit for weeks, and then she went and dropped a bomb in the middle of a quarterfinal match. Now she followed up her overprotective daughter routine with more shit. Jay should snatch the ball and shove it down her throat, or at least walk off the court. Instead she wandered back to her spot at the net and tucked low to offer Destiny a better serve angle.

The ball whizzed past her head, and she had only a flash of time to feel grateful the sizzling shot hadn't hit her between the shoulder blades before it arched back over to her right. She watched out of the corner of her eye while jogging backward as Destiny sent a crosscourt laser smacking into the baseline.

"40-Love."

Jay turned to see they were standing only a few feet apart and thought now was as good a time as any to ask for clarification. "So, this whole bullshit attitude of yours since, like, day one wasn't about your image at all? It's because you don't want me to hit on your mom?"

"I don't want you near my mom."

"But not because I'm gay?"

Destiny rolled her eyes. "Because she's better than you. I know all the stories about you. I've heard what you did and, more importantly, how you ran."

Jay winced, but years of practice kept her from responding to the charge.

"My mom is a queen. She deserves better. She deserves better than you," Destiny shot back. "Man, woman, gay or straight, I don't care, but she deserves the best."

All the air left Jay's lungs. Without thinking, she turned to seek Sadie in the stands once more. She had her hair pulled back under a white cap. Her dark eyes peeking out from the shadow of the bill were filled with concern, but she managed to force a smile anyway. Even her worry was more beautiful than anything Jay had let herself look at in years. Her heart constricted, but she managed to say, "Yeah, she does."

Destiny lowered her racket. "What?"

"You're right."

Destiny's light brown eyes narrowed suspiciously.

"Your mom is special. And she deserves the best in every way," Jay admitted.

"And you can't give her that."

Jay frowned at the bluntness of the statement. She wanted to argue, wanted to feel some of the fire or anger that had burned her up minutes ago, but she couldn't. What could she possibly offer a woman like Sadie other than a little light flirting? Some company on the road? A role model for her daughter, who clearly already had the best anyone could ever hope for in that arena? And in return she'd expose Sadie to a firestorm of innuendo and insane scrutiny. She would obscure a bright future with the cloud of her past, and eventually Sadie would have no choice but to cut ties. She'd made it clear the first time they'd met she would always do what was best for Destiny, and eventually that wouldn't be Jay anymore. Why run the risk of putting any of them through that kind of trauma when they all knew how it had to end?

"Time." The chair umpire called again, pulling Jay out of her musings.

"Fine, if that's really your worry, let's end it now," Jay said quickly. "I like your mom a lot. I like to talk to her and travel with her, and yeah, I adore her smile, but I know the score. I always know the score. I won't do anything to drop trouble on her doorstep."

"It's not her doorstep I'm worried about," Destiny said, clearly not satisfied. "It's her heart. I won't let you hurt her, even if it means losing this match, or every match for the rest of my life."

Jay nodded solemnly. At least they could agree on that point. Neither one of them wanted Sadie to get hurt. "I don't know what else to say. You can believe my promises or not, but you have my word. I won't do anything to put her heart or her reputation in jeopardy."

With that, Des tossed the ball and aced a corker down the middle of the court.

"Game, Ms. Pierce and Ms. Larsen."

Destiny stuck out her fist in Jay's direction.

She stared at the peace offering, knowing she should accept. They'd crossed a bridge today, and it was the right call to make, but even as Jay tapped her own knuckles against Destiny's, she feared she'd paid a heavy price for the tentative peace she'd won.

Chapter Five

Sadie wondered if body snatchers had to be physically present, or if they could just teleport into someone's skin mid-tennis match without anyone around them seeing the switch. She hadn't read a lot of science fiction, but she did know her daughter, and the woman sitting in front of the press corps right now wasn't her.

"How does it feel to be a semifinalist?" someone called out.

"Well," Destiny said with the quirk of a smile, "it feels a lot better than being knocked out in the first round."

"Was that a complete sentence?" Hank asked under his breath. "And kind of a joke?"

Sadie didn't answer. She was too busy sitting in awe.

"And you're the last Americans anywhere in the draw," another reporter added. "Did your shared nationality bring any sort of added connection or sense of national pride to your matches?"

"I can't speak for Jay, but I want to win no matter who else is in the draw. As to a connection, I think winning is a better uniting force than both being from the same country."

"What did you lace her Cheerios with this morning?" Hank asked.

"She wasn't like this after breakfast," said Sadie, recalling her daughter's surly mood before coming to the court. She'd written it off as a combination of mental hangover from Destiny's singles loss the evening before and her displeasure at playing doubles.

Still, she hadn't noticed anything out of the ordinary from her until the start of the second set. Clearly Destiny and Jay had had a sizable dispute, but about what? By the time they'd come off the court happy and sweaty and tired, but semifinalists, she hadn't had the heart to bring it up. The reporters didn't share her unwillingness to dampen the mood, though.

"What happened in the first game of the second set?" a man asked from the front row.

"We won," Jay said, the sound of her voice amplified by the mic as she leaned forward, her arms folded casually across the top of the table, making her biceps flex. "With no help from me."

"It looked like you guys might have been disagreeing, or that something was off about the play," the reporter pushed.

"We were winning going in, we won that game, and then we went on to win five more," Jay said, without her usual cocky smile or good-natured give and take. "We couldn't have been that far off, Terry."

"Come on, Jay, a time violation, and then she served with your back to the court three times?"

"We're still working out the details of our movements," Destiny offered. "I've never played doubles before, so I'm not used to considering anyone else's position or timing."

"So you served with someone standing right in front of you?"

"I did," Destiny said, without losing the hint of a smile that had graced her lips since the game in question. Sadie's heart seemed to beat out of rhythm for a second as pride clashed with skepticism. There was clearly more to the story, and the fact that they felt the need to lie to the press meant it probably wasn't pretty, yet neither one of them cracked or threw the other under the bus. They were presenting a unified front, which had to be a good sign.

"She didn't just serve," Jay added. "She aced."

"Because you said or did something to make her mad?" a different reporter asked.

"If I did, I'll be sure never to do it if I'm ever playing opposite her in singles."

The press corps laughed, and some of the tension left Sadie's chest. So far, all of her curiosity and worry had been focused on her daughter, but when Jay cracked a joke, she realized that her own uncharacteristic behavior had contributed to the disconcerting dynamic shift as much as Destiny's swing in the opposite direction. They hadn't quite traded personalities so much as each of them had slid a little closer to the other. Perhaps Hank had been right, and winning had gone a long way to smooth the roughness between them, but she suspected more had taken place, and she was glad neither of them had any intention of discussing the details with the press.

"Will you play together in Rome?" a woman asked.

Jay raised her eyebrow at Destiny. "What do you say?"

Destiny nodded and extended her hand. "I'm in if you are."

Jay shook, and then without a smile turned back to the mic. "I guess so."

The press seemed happy with the announcement and the photo op, so Jay and Destiny both took the chance to make their escapes. Hank intercepted them at the door to the restricted area. He slapped each woman on the back so hard they both rocked forward. "Well done. All around."

Destiny smiled at him, and then turned to Sadie, who wrapped her in a hug. "I'm so proud of you."

"For the match or the press conference?" Destiny asked, a humor in her voice Sadie hadn't heard in a long time.

"Both."

"I'm more proud of the press conference." Hank laughed. "You had a better bob-and-weave there than you did on the court."

"I don't know," Sadie said. "They were pretty dominant in the second set; 6-1 in the quarterfinals isn't nothing."

"Des still spent too much time behind the baseline," he said, then shook his head. "But it doesn't matter tonight. I feel like we had a breakthrough today. We need to celebrate."

"*We* still have another match to play," Destiny protested, then added, "at least one."

"Never miss a chance to bask in a little happiness," Sadie said, wanting to extend the joy in her daughter's eyes for as long as she could.

"Your mother's right. Let's go out. Dinner's on me tonight," Hank said. He turned to Jay and asked, "What do you want, tapas, paella, some of the salty ham everyone likes around here?"

Jay smiled, but it didn't make her eyes sparkle. "Can I get a rain check? I'm beat."

"What? No," Hank said. "I've seen you so tired you can't stand up, but you've never turned down free food. Even when you were rich."

"I was also young," Jay said. "You guys go have fun. I'm going to ice my feet and go to bed early."

Sadie clutched her arm, feeling a cool sheen of sweat over the taut muscle of her triceps. "Are you sure?"

"Positive," Jay said without quite looking her in the eye. "I can't just expect Destiny to hit aces all the time, and if she wants me to cover my half of the court tomorrow, I need rest."

Sadie looked from Jay to Destiny and back again. They'd said exactly what everyone wanted to hear and done what they needed to do, but a mother had intuitions the press didn't, and something was off. But Des seemed better than she had in weeks, happier, more confident, more content, so if a mother's impulse mattered above all else, she shouldn't have any serious concerns. And yet Jay's subdued demeanor sent a jolt to the part of her heart usually held solely by her daughter. Surely she hadn't taken to mothering her, too. No, as she gave Jay's muscle another squeeze, she noted the feelings stirring in her chest might have come from the same spot, but they weren't the same.

"Mom, it's been a big day." Destiny cut in before Sadie could sort through the emotions stirring in her. "She's already done a lot for us over the last couple weeks. Let her have some time to herself."

Sadie frowned. She hadn't considered the possibility that Jay wanted time away from them. Maybe the problem wasn't with Jay, but with the constant contact. They'd needled her to play doubles, practiced her endlessly, traveled together, eaten together, won together, and held press conferences together. It made sense that the woman might need a night off, but even with such a logical explanation, the thought made her ribs feel tighter than ever. She stepped back and released her hold. "Destiny's right. We've asked a lot of you lately. If you need some space, I understand."

"It's not that. You haven't asked too much," Jay said quickly, then glanced at Destiny and sighed. "It's the job and commitments, and you guys go enjoy your dinner. I'll see you tomorrow."

"Great. Thanks," Des said with a genuine smile. "See you tomorrow."

"Works for me," Hank added with a shrug. Then he and Des pushed through the door, already talking about dinner options, but Sadie couldn't quite let go yet.

"Are you sure this isn't about whatever happened on the court today?"

Jay's face drained of all its color. "I don't know what you mean. Other than, you know, the playing, in which case, yes. I played hard. I need to rest."

Sadie nodded and just let her keep talking.

"I mean, I'm not as young as I used to be. And Des hits hard. I have to move a lot to keep up, which is fine, it's good, but you know, we work hard."

"And sometimes you get into arguments."

"No. I mean, yes. Well, disagreements, but that's part of working with someone new, and . . ." She sighed and hung her head. "I'm tired, okay?"

She did seem exhausted, more than just her sweaty hair and slumped shoulders revealed. Her eyes were dull and unfocused. "Okay. Just tell me one thing, though. Whatever caused the blowup in the second set, was it Destiny's fault?"

Jay opened her mouth as if she intended to deny there was a problem, but instead she shook her head. "No. She wasn't out of line. I was."

"You?"

"We just needed to lay some ground rules for our relationship," Jay said; then her smile perked up a little bit more. "And for what

100

it's worth, I think your worries about Destiny's adjusting to pro tennis are unfounded. She's smart and strong-willed, and she loves you very much."

Sadie wasn't at all sure how those things were connected with each other, much less a doubles match. "Why do I get the feeling there's a very big 'but' coming?"

"There's not," Jay said quickly. "You did a good job, Tennis Mom. She's got her priorities in line, maybe better than I did for a while, but we're sorted out now."

"And this agreement," Sadie asked skeptically, "you're both happy with the terms?"

"Happy might not be the best word," Jay admitted, "but it's in agreement with our values and how we want to go about our business, which is winning tennis games, so I'm going to go back to the hotel now and focus on doing what I can to help us win tomorrow."

"Okay." Sadie acquiesced.

What more could she say? She couldn't force Jay to go to dinner with them, and she couldn't needle her anymore in the pressroom. Honestly, Jay would've been well within her bounds to tell her to butt out several minutes ago, or even several weeks ago, but she hadn't. She'd been polite and clearly more forthcoming than she really wanted to be. To ask for more of her time or energy or trust would have been unfair, but that didn't mean Sadie didn't want more of all of them.

Rome

"Pierce and Larsen continue to make a steady run up the doubles ladder. After reaching the semifinals last week in Madrid, they've served and sliced their way through the competition here in Rome to find themselves on the brink of their first tournament win as a team."

Jay bounced on the balls of her feet, trying to ignore the chatter on the locker room TV, but it wasn't easy to do when they kept saying her name. She'd never been one of those players who could tune out the crowd, so she'd learned to use their energy to feed her own. Only now she didn't have a crowd, and she didn't like the energy floating around the tense locker room.

"They have been impressive," another commentator said. "I actually got to see their first-round match on one of the back courts. I admit I only peeked in expecting a train wreck. I'd heard stories about them bumping into each other and bickering on the court, but it felt like I was watching a much more experienced duo."

She bent down and touched her toes, then crossed one leg over the other and tried again. No pain. At least not the physical kind. She glanced up at Sadie, sitting behind Destiny and braiding her long curls. She ran her fingers tenderly through strands the color of a perfectly toasted marshmallow, and Jay felt a twinge of regret over trimming her own mundane, sandy locks just off her shoulders earlier in the week. What would it feel like to have Sadie's tender touch—the line of thought would only lead down a dangerous dark alley, so she bent a little lower, forcing her lumbar muscles to stretch farther than they wanted to.

"Let's not forget Jay Pierce is plenty experienced," the first commentator droned on, clearly trying to fill airtime between matches few people stateside had any interest in. "People who are new to the sport might not remember how thrilling it was to watch her with Katia Vitrov. A lot of years have passed since then, but the two of them were absolutely electric."

"In more ways than one," the second commentator added with a suggestiveness in his voice that made Jay want to retch. Instead, she reached over her head and slapped the power button on the television.

Sadie and Destiny both stared at her. So did their opponents, who had been chatting quietly in Spanish across the room.

"Sorry," she grumbled. "Gotta focus."

Des and Sadie exchanged another quizzical look, probably wondering if one of them should talk to her, or ignore her odd behavior in the hopes that it would go away.

"I'm fine," Jay said in a completely unconvincing tone. "I'm going to run to the bathroom before we head out."

Without waiting for a response, she strode out of the room and around the corner. She thought briefly about sticking her head under a shower faucet, but settled instead for a handful of cool water from the sink. She splashed her face and stared at herself in the mirror while drops of water fell from her dark eyelashes.

They'd played brilliantly all week. It was like the dam of anger and fear holding Destiny back had cracked in Madrid, allowing a flow of talent to flood through. She still didn't move well on the doubles court, but what she lacked in footwork, she made up for with power and grit. She served like a beast and gutted out every point. And while she hadn't exactly warmed to anything resembling friendship with Jay, she did smile more, and even offered the occasional "nice shot" or fist bump. And they won. Steadily, handily, they mowed down the competition, and damned if the command didn't rejuvenate her. When Jay took the court with Destiny, she played like she was twenty years old again. Then she'd look into the stands for Sadie and feel like she was twenty years old again.

She couldn't even relax and enjoy the little moments. Everything good reminded her of everything bad, and if her own mind wasn't bad enough about dredging up the past, now the press was getting in on the act too. She'd reached the point where she almost feared the prospect of winning.

"Hey," Sadie said softly.

Jay blinked away the remaining water from her eyes and forced a smile. "Time to go?"

Sadie shook her head and leaned her shoulder against the wall so her body blocked much of the doorway. Her frame wasn't as long as Jay's, but the slow, languid movement made it seem as though she took up more space than she did. Or maybe she'd simply taken up a disproportionate amount of space in Jay's mind.

"I just wanted to tell you how much I appreciate you," Sadie said. "No matter what happens today."

"It's nothing," Jay said quickly, wishing Sadie wasn't quite so grateful. The heartfelt moments of thanks always set her emotions on edge, and the more she'd tried to pull away, the more Sadie seemed to try to connect.

"It is something," Sadie said, her voice low and soft. "You being here, being steady and confident, has helped Destiny so much over the last few weeks."

"Right, Destiny," she muttered. Every time Sadie said the name, with so much love, so much gravity, the heat building in Jay's chest and cheeks chilled more than any splash of water could provide. She'd learned to lean on the inevitability of that shift away from herself and toward Sadie's primary interest, because what she really meant when she said she appreciated Jay in their lives was that she appreciated what Jay did for Destiny. "She's coming right along. If she hadn't run up against Halep in the singles this week, she would've reached the quarterfinals here in singles, maybe even the semis. She'll get there."

"And what about you?" Sadie asked.

"I didn't play as well as last week," Jay said, grateful to be back on more neutral subjects. "I'm relying too much on my return, which has always been my strength, of course, but—"

"I didn't mean on the court," Sadie clarified. "Not when talking about Des, and not when asking about you."

"Oh," Jay said. So much for solid ground.

"She's blossoming, emotionally and socially. She smiles more and yells less, but you seem to be experiencing the opposite."

"I yell more?" Jay tried to deflect. "That's hard to imagine. I already yelled a lot before we met."

Sadie's smile flashed brighter than the overhead lights. "Okay, maybe you yell the same on the court, but I hate to think that Destiny only found her smile by stealing yours."

"No." The thought hurt her heart. She and Destiny had found their balance. The girl had been harsh, but for all the right reasons—reasons Jay respected and agreed with even if she hated that she'd needed to be reminded of them. She respected Des for her willingness to be blunt about a topic most people only alluded to, and she was happy to find out what she'd initially read as spoiled behavior actually covered a fierce loyalty. "Des and I are good. It's the pace, and the play, and the pressure . . ."

"It's not," Sadie said lightly. "It's something else, something that happened to you, something you still carry with you, that we've somehow tripped a trigger for."

Jay wanted to respond, to deny, to shake the tightness from her chest, but she couldn't speak for all the pressure building there.

"I'm not asking for an explanation," Sadie continued, stepping slowly closer now. "Your past, your memories are yours, and no one else has a right to try to tell you what to do with your demons. I know this as well as anyone can, but I want you to know I see them. I see the hurt in your eyes. I see the strain behind your smile. I know that whatever the last few weeks have given back, they're also taking a lot from you."

Jay hung her head. Even if her throat wasn't raw and her breath burning, how could she look Sadie in the eye and, do what? Explain? Apologize? She'd exerted so much energy and emotion trying not to let it show, giving everything she could to the game while offering no distractions or complications or any part of herself that might amplify anyone else's discomfort.

Sadie closed the gap between them, and cupping Jay's cheek in her hand, lifted her chin just enough for their eyes to meet. "I also see you choosing patience over frustration. I see you putting our needs above your own. I see your strength and your steadiness despite whatever's swirling inside you."

"You really don't know my history?" Jay asked, a little amazed that Sadie had seen so much of her and still hadn't gone looking for answers. They weren't hard to find.

"I know you. That's enough for me."

Jay tried to shake her head, but Sadie held her still.

"You're fighting an internal battle, and I won't tell you to stop. I only wanted to tell you how grateful I am that you haven't surrendered yet, and I hope you never do." Sadie arched up on tiptoe and placed a gentle kiss on her cheek, her scent forming an aura of sweetness around them. Then she stepped back, leaving Jay alone in the haze.

"Ms. Pierce?" A league official called from the waiting area of the locker room. "Time to take the court."

Jay sighed, but this time it came with a smile and a strange kind of peace. "Yes. Yes it is."

"You're a winner!" Sadie called as she pointed to her daughter, before turning to include Jay in the gesture, "and you're a winner. And Hank, where did Hank go? Oh, he's in the bathroom, but he's a winner."

Jay laughed. "And you're a winner, too."

"Damn right I am. You wouldn't even have been playing in this tournament, or playing doubles at all, without me." She spun back to Destiny so quickly her wine nearly sloshed out of the glass in her hand. "What did I always tell you when you were growing up?"

"Just trust Mommy," Destiny said, with a hint of a smirk.

"Why?"

Des rolled her eyes. "Because Mommy knows things."

"You bet she does." Sadie threw back her head and laughed. God, it felt good. The worry had weighed on her for so long. Every loss had caused the whispers to hiss through her ears. Maybe it was too soon. Maybe Des was too young. Maybe she wasn't mature enough or strong enough. Maybe Sadie hadn't prepared her well enough, or maybe Sadie couldn't possibly parent her through something so far out of her own experience. Well, perhaps the last part was still partially true, but the other shadows of doubt had been vanquished. Destiny did belong in the big leagues, and she'd proven herself worthy both on and off the court today. Parenting achievement unlocked.

"You guys were magnificent." She sighed happily as she sank onto the edge of the bed. "Your match, your press conference, all the hoopla afterwards. Perfect."

"They really were," Hank agreed, as he exited the bathroom.

"You unleashed a barrage of serve-and-volley that might have taken down Fort Knox. I never even worried."

Everyone laughed.

"What?" he asked.

"You totally worried," Destiny said. "I thought you might faint when we lost the second-set tiebreaker."

"No," he bellowed. "I knew you'd come back."

"Oh yeah?" Jay asked. "Let me see your fingernails."

He quickly jammed his hands into his pockets, and they all roared with laughter again.

"It's okay," Jay said kindly. "All's well that ends well."

"Exactly." Sadie sipped her wine, pleased to see Jay smiling and joking again. "And today ended very well."

"But today is only the beginning," Hank said.

"The beginning of my week off," Destiny said, as she flopped onto the bed next to Sadie.

"Are you sure you don't want to play in Strasbourg?" Hank asked. "Might be fun."

"No!" Both Jay and Destiny shouted at once.

Hank held up his hands. "Okay, don't shoot. I just thought we could keep rolling."

"You thought you could roll me to an early grave," Jay said, but her smile only grew brighter. "We both qualified for French in singles and doubles. What more could we ask for?"

"Better tournament seeds, more money, a chance to warm an old man's heart and—"

"Hank!" Sadie scolded. "This is a party, and I'm actually with them, on this point anyway. A week to recuperate in Paris will be good for all of us, body and soul."

"Fine." Hank pretended to pout, but even he couldn't stay down for long. "I guess they earned it."

They'd earned a lot, Sadie thought. About sixty grand each when it was all said and done. She could pay Hank's cut, their taxes, and still have plenty left over for two months' worth of travel and accommodations even with Destiny choosing to take her own hotel room. More importantly, though, both Des and

Jay had earned a great deal of respect. She could see it in the way other players approached them at dinner. So many of them seemed both genuinely pleased and concerned for Jay. They all wanted her to do well, just not too well against them.

The sponsors seemed to take notice too, and it hadn't just shown in the form of more requests for autographs and selfies. Several people had inquired about Destiny's advertising commitments, and a few of them had asked Sadie for her business card. She didn't even have business cards. A new set of doubts threatened to overtake her, but she washed them down with another generous swig of wine.

"Good vino?" Jay asked from her perch atop the hotel-style desk.

"We're in Italy, aren't we?" Sadie asked, noticing for the first time the subtle spread of heat from her chest up into her face. Had the alcohol taken hold to a greater extent than she realized, or was that the effect of Jay's proximity?

She looked so different than she had before the match. Some color had returned to her complexion, and her pale, parched lips had been smoothed over with a neutral shade of gloss. She'd combed back her hair so it flipped up ever so slightly at the curve of her neck and left her sparkling blue eyes completely unshadowed. She'd changed into more formal attire for the post-tournament reception, but even in a cream-colored suit over a lavender shell, she still managed to look more casual than she had in weeks. Sadie's heart beat faster, reminding her of the first time she'd seen Jay in the Australian Open press conference. Knowing what she now did about her personality only amplified her physical appeal.

Perhaps the combination should have worried her, but she preferred Jay's allure to the anguish she'd seen flare up in those expressive eyes when the reporters alluded to her past this morning. It had taken everything Sadie had in her not to beg Jay to share that pain, to let her help soothe it. Only her own experiences had given her the understanding and the faith necessary to respect that such hard truths couldn't be pried from someone. Still, she had reached out, desperate to make a connection that would allow Jay the freedom and the security to turn to her if she were ever ready.

"Mom," Destiny said. "Earth to Mom."

"What?" She looked around the room as everyone stared at her expectantly.

"Hank asked if the wine was cheaper here."

She glanced at the glass she'd forgotten she held. "Oh yes. Very much. Cheaper than tea, even, so who am I to waste hard-earned dollars on tea when there's a more economical alternative?"

Hank chuckled as he settled down on the floor, his long legs stretched out in front of him. "No one could ever accuse you of irresponsible accounting."

Destiny shook her head. "She's the budget police."

"Hey, I let you have your own room tonight, didn't I?"

Destiny laughed. "Yes, you did. At seventeen and a half, and months after making the professional tour, you finally let me sleep in my own hotel room only after winning my first tournament."

"If you're going to get sassy about having your own room," Sadie said playfully, "I still have the right to send you there for a time-out."

"No need," Destiny replied with a yawn. "I'll go willingly."

"To throw a wild party of your own?" Jay asked.

"Yes," Destiny said. "I'm going to jump on the bed for exactly two minutes to prove I can, then I'm going to fall down on all of the many pillows I get completely to myself. Then I'm going to sleep for two days."

"That does sound like the best party ever." Jay echoed Destiny's yawn.

"No," Sadie whined. "You can't leave me all alone while I'm so hyped up. Hank, you aren't fading, are you?"

They all turned to Hank, who was sitting on the floor with his back to the wall and his chin to his chest, a light snore rumbling through his throat.

"Oh, come on, guys," Sadie pleaded. "This is our first professional win."

"The first of many," Destiny said soothingly, as she collected her phone and purse. "We'll have lots more to celebrate down the road . . . after we sleep."

"Yeah," Jay added. "We have to pace ourselves. Besides, we're going to Paris. Think of all the parties we can have there. We have to rest up from this party to get ready for those."

Sadie shook her head and pointed at her. "Don't think I don't see right through you, Ms. Pierce."

Jay's smile softened. "I wouldn't dare. You've already proved you've got my number, well beyond what I'm comfortable with."

Destiny turned to looked at them, her usually smooth brow furrowed with something akin to worry, but Jay pulled her attention away by hopping off the desk. "And on that note, I'm going to make my break for it. Des, you create a diversion, and I'll grab Hank on my way out."

Destiny's expression softened, but she didn't quite smile. "Leave Hank. Save yourself."

"I like the way you think." Jay headed for the door. "I'll see you tomorrow."

"Sleep in," Destiny said. "No matter what my mother tells you, we do not have to be at the airport until three. You're in no way obligated to attend a celebratory brunch, or lunch, or tour of the Colosseum."

"Good to know," Jay called as she left the room.

Sadie watched her go, feeling a subtle drop in her stomach that she wrote off as a letdown at the night ending so soon. She turned to make another appeal to her daughter, only to find her trying to rouse Hank.

"Come on, big guy. Night's over, but I'm way too tired to lift you."

Sadie sighed. "Don't worry about him. I'll be up for a while. I'm sure he'll want to find his own bed eventually."

"Thanks. Are you sure you'll be okay alone tonight?"

She forced a smile. "I won't be alone. I'll have Hank."

He snorted out another snore as if offering his assent, and Destiny laughed, then turning suddenly serious, she threw her arms about Sadie's neck and squeezed tightly. "Thank you, Mom. For everything."

Sadie's chest filled with love almost to the point of overflowing. Destiny had always been able to spin her emotions on a dime. Even as an infant, she would push Sadie right up to the brink of tears with her crying and feeding schedule and squirming diaper changes. Then just at the point when Sadie felt like she couldn't get any lower, a tiny palm would caress her cheek, or wide eyes would look adoringly into her own, and she'd melt again. "You're welcome, baby."

"I love you," Destiny whispered.

"I love you, too," Sadie managed around the lump in her throat. Then, afraid she'd dissolve into a puddle of tears, she stepped back and took a shaky breath. "Now get out of here before I change my mind and make you watch sappy movies with me all night."

"You don't have to tell me twice," Destiny said with feigned terror. "I don't want to be subjected to *The Bodyguard* . . . again."

Sadie pointed to the door. "Then you better run."

Destiny took the threat seriously enough to flee, but her laughter followed her all the way down the hall.

Sadie listened to the beautiful sound for as long as she could, then sank back onto the bed, a wisp of wistfulness curling at her core. Her baby was growing up. It hadn't happened in the way she'd expected. She didn't have to drop her off at college and drive away, and in some ways she was grateful for that. But in others, she envied mothers who had such clear and culturally situated rites of passage to lean on. She was in uncharted territory, where a room down the hall felt a million miles away. She wouldn't have traded today for anything, but at least when Destiny was struggling both physically and emotionally, she'd known what her role was. She had to protect and guide and soothe. Those were familiar tasks, but what did her daughter need from her when she won, when her confidence soared, when possibility spread out endlessly before her? Did she even need her mother at all?

Her breath grew shallow at the thought. Wasn't that supposed to be every parent's goal? To give their child everything they needed to be completely independent? If so, she'd come pretty close to succeeding as a mother, and yet, without that sense of urgency or the constant need to put Destiny at the forefront, where did that leave her as a woman?

A light knock sounded at the door, and she sprang from her bed, gleeful at the thought of any distraction as she sent up a hurried prayer that Destiny had decided she wanted to stay with her a little longer.

"Did you decide you wanted a movie night after all?" She threw open the door to find Jay standing there, looking all tall and debonair in her suit with the silk shirt open one button past professional.

"Um, actually I just forgot my room key," she said apologetically.

"Oh," Sadie said, feeling a little silly.

"Sorry I'm not up for a movie tonight," Jay said. "Maybe a rain check?"

"Don't worry about it," Sadie said, trying to control the disappointment in her voice. "I was only teasing Destiny—well, I mean, I thought you were Destiny, and I had been teasing her, but she left and—"

"And I came back," Jay finished for her.

"For your key."

"Which is right there." Jay reached past her to snatch the little plastic card off a table near the door. The move put their bodies so close Sadie could smell her sea salt and sandalwood cologne. Without thinking, she leaned in so their bodies brushed lightly against each other. Her face flushed hot.

"I'm, uh, well . . . thanks," Jay stammered. "For the key, and tonight, and you know . . . all the things."

"All the things?" Sadie stared into Jay's endless blue eyes. God, what was wrong with her? Was this some holdover from her earlier musing about her place in the world? Or was the heat building in her now some sort of answer?

"You know, today. The stuff you said in the locker room before the match." Jay's eyes flicked down to her lips, and Sadie felt their proximity even more acutely than before.

It would be so easy to lean forward and kiss her.

The thought startled her, and she stepped back. "What?"

"Um, when you told me I could talk to you, and you . . . well, you touched my face." Jay's complexion flushed pink.

"And I kissed your cheek," Sadie said. She remembered the moment clearly. The kiss had seemed so natural at the time, she hadn't even given it a second thought, but now she wondered if Jay had.

Her heart throbbed heavily in her chest. Had Jay considered the move a come-on? Had she welcomed it? She'd given no indication she wanted that kind of attention from Sadie. Well, aside from the comment early on about not being able to resist her smile, but since then she'd been kind and sweet and professional, but distant. Until now. Now, Jay felt anything but distant. Sadie could clearly feel the heat radiating off her.

Jay cleared her throat. "Right. Well, you were nice, and you said nice things, and you didn't push me. I guess I'm just saying I appreciate you, too. For, you know, respecting my boundaries."

"We've all got them, Jay," Sadie said, meaning the words even as she considered blurring every boundary between them. "I've had plenty over the last seventeen years. They were hard and fast, and they kept me going."

"Were?" Jay asked, her voice an octave higher, as her eyes wandered to Sadie's lips again. "Past tense?"

"I don't know," Sadie admitted. "Everything's changing. I feel, I don't know, different."

"Really?" Jay asked, a plaintiveness in her voice that only drew Sadie closer. "Because I'm starting to feel something very familiar."

"Good. Maybe you can explain this to me," Sadie said, arching up onto her toes.

"That might not be the best idea ever," Jay whispered even as she swayed forward.

Sadie slid her palm along the smoothness of Jay's cheek until her fingers curled around the base of her neck. Then, as Jay bent to her will, Sadie muttered, "Let's find out," and pressed their lips together.

A shot of energy surged through her, and she whimpered as electricity crackled across her skin. How could a kiss be so tender and so raw at once? Their mouths moved together flawlessly, fearlessly, asking and granting all at once. Sinking her fingers into Jay's hair, she held her close, but she didn't need to. All of the misgivings between them seemed to have vanished the moment they connected. Jay melted into her, easing her back until her body pressed firmly against the open door, then clasping both hands on Sadie's hips, urged her forward once more in the most deliriously sexy push and pull.

Breath escaped sharply, only to be snatched away once more as the kiss sped from slow to searing in a matter of seconds. She fleetingly worried about the possibility of willfully suffocating, but before she had the chance to ponder the pros and cons of surrendering to the desire to kiss Jay for all eternity, it ended so abruptly she let out a little gasp.

"Sadie." Jay spoke her name with so much anguish, she froze.

"What? What is it?"

"I can't," Jay practically panted. "I promised."

She blinked and shook her head. "You what?"

"I promised," Jay repeated on a shaky breath. "I gave my word."

"I don't understand." She couldn't make sense of anything but the way her body screamed to take hold of Jay again. "Did I do something wrong?"

"No," Jay said quickly. "God, no. You are amazing."

Sadie eyed her skeptically, dark doubts swirling inside her again. What if she'd allowed her own mounting desire to make her misread Jay's, or what if Jay hadn't enjoyed the kiss? What if it hadn't caused her world to tilt the way it had Sadie's?

Jay seemed to read her worries and rushed to soothe them. "I mean it, Sadie. You're too good."

"I don't have a lot of experience," Sadie whispered. "Maybe you're used to—"

Jay cut her off with another kiss, this one so quick and hard it almost lifted her off the ground, but like the other, it ended entirely too soon.

"Stop, please," Jay begged. "You don't have any idea what you're doing to me."

Sadie didn't let go, but her hand slipped from Jay's neck to her shoulder, feeling the knot of tension there. "What am I doing?"

"Tearing me apart," Jay nearly sobbed. She lowered her head and kissed Sadie once more, this time more soulfully. The need poured out of her, putting Sadie's initial concerns to rest, but stirring a new set as her lips parted to welcome Jay's tongue in a broad, sweeping stroke. She wanted more, she wanted all of her, but not this way, not at the cost she'd seen reflected in those amazing eyes. This time she pulled away.

Jay's breath flooded out in a hot rush against her skin; then she drew back with a sharp inhale. "I'm sorry."

"For what?" Sadie asked softly. "For starting, or stopping?"

"Both." Jay rubbed her face and then took a step back, like she didn't trust herself to be in arm's reach. "I tried so hard. God, you won't believe me. No one will, but I wanted to be better this time. I wanted better for you."

"Better?" Sadie couldn't process anything as the haze of arousal still clouded her mind. "Jay, you were wonderful. You *are* wonderful. I haven't felt like this since . . . never."

"I can't," Jay said, her hands clenching into tight fists.

"You can't what?" Sadie stepped forward again, but Jay shook her head violently.

"Please." Jay sounded nearly frantic. "If you care about me at all, you won't push me."

"Okay." Sadie held up her hands and eased back.

"I'm sorry," Jay said.

"Can you at least tell me why?"

Jay shook her head again, then said, "For putting you in this position."

The answer did nothing to clear up her confusion, but the pain contorting Jay's beautiful mouth stopped her from pushing for more. "You didn't put me in any position I didn't want to be in. I kissed you."

"Thank you." Jay sagged. "Thank you for saying that."

"Why wouldn't I?" Sadie asked. "It's the truth."

Jay nodded. "Thank you for saying that, too."

"I don't understand," Sadie said again. She didn't know what else she could say until she got some answers.

Jay straightened her shoulders slightly. "Good. I know that probably seems cold, but for both of our sakes, I hope you never do."

Sadie stared at her, uncertain what to say or do next. She'd waited so long for this moment, dreamed of so many details, but none of them had prepared her for Jay's reaction. Her heart felt like her ribs were too small to contain its fullness.

"I have to go," Jay finally said, then added again, "I'm so sorry."

Sadie wanted to say something more, to call her back, to hold her, or kiss her again, if only to ease the pain, but she doubted she could. So she did the most merciful thing she could and let her go.

Chapter Six

Jay awoke with a start and looked frantically around the non-descript hotel room. Nothing seemed out of place. Relief surged through her as she thought for one glorious second she might've been dreaming, but as she pushed herself up to sitting, she noticed she was still in her suit from the night before. She'd never changed, or even crawled under the covers. She'd merely crashed into a pile of anguish and fear atop the comforter last night after kissing Sadie.

She hung her head in her hands and stifled a scream for what most certainly had not been a dream.

She'd kissed Sadie.

No. Sadie had kissed her first. Then, of course, Jay had kissed her back, and then she kissed her again, and maybe another time. She couldn't be sure, and she doubted anyone would care about the order of events if they ever found out, but still she clung to the fact that Sadie had kissed her first.

She groaned and flopped back onto the bed. Who was she kidding? No one else had seen any of the kisses, which, of course, was good, because maybe she wouldn't have to explain herself to anyone. But if she ever did, there'd also be no one to back her up, which would be bad.

So very bad.

Her phone buzzed, and she about shot out of her skin, jumping to standing position.

"Calm the fuck down," she said aloud, her voice sounding raw and harsh in the silence. She had to pull herself together. Despite her ingrained association between pleasure and guilt, the world was not falling down around her, at least not yet. Sadie had been as kind and understanding as anyone could ever ask. They'd stopped things before they went very far. They'd both admitted Jay hadn't instigated the encounter, and she had most certainly ended it. Not a bad recap, when she thought of things in that order.

A little voice whispered that no one else would ever stop to consider any of those things if word got out.

"Word won't get out," she told herself aloud once more. Sadie wasn't the kind of person to tell anyone, and Hank had been snoring softly the whole time. Not that he would run to the press either, but he'd probably have a few choice words for her, given their previous trials. Would he believe Sadie had initiated? She doubted it. He'd seen her attraction early on. Hell, he'd played it to his own advantage. He'd thrown them together in the first place. Maybe she could use that defense.

"You don't need a defense," she said louder. "He doesn't know."

No one knew. And no one was even paying attention. The press conference after their win yesterday had gone so smoothly. No one had even hinted at her past. She'd almost felt like a normal player. Maybe that's why she'd let her guard down. Still, it didn't mean anyone else had to find out. Hell, if anything, the press would be digging for dirt between her and Destiny, and they wouldn't find anything there.

Her phone buzzed again, and she looked at the screen to see a text message that said, "We're going to brunch. Save yourself."

It was from Destiny.

Destiny.

"Fuck."

She would know. They'd come so far on and off the court, but Jay still caught Destiny watching her more closely around Sadie. She hadn't wanted to leave her mom's room last night until Jay did, and now it turned out her worst fears were totally warranted.

The minute the two of them were alone, Jay had done exactly what she'd promised she wouldn't.

Did she not take her promises seriously, or could she simply not control her own actions? Neither option said anything good about her honesty or her fortitude. What if the accusations and criticism were warranted all along? The questions burned through her chest like a hot lance, and she pressed her hand to her sternum, trying to stem the pain.

She paced around the room and struggled to take deep, even breaths. This wasn't catastrophic. Just because she'd made mistakes in the past didn't mean she had to make them again. She'd hoped she'd learned her lesson by now, but even if her heart did seem to revel in risky behavior, she had other ways to exert control. If she couldn't be trusted enough to keep her word for whatever reason, she could keep her distance.

She shook that line of thinking from her mind. One day at a time.

"Still beat." She texted Destiny back. "Meet you at the airport."

She dropped the phone to stave off the unreasonable fear that somehow her guilt could be detected wirelessly. Even that technological connection felt too close.

Close, that's where she'd gone wrong. Her downward slide had started yesterday morning. She'd let Sadie get too close, physically and emotionally. Exhaustion and worry combined to make her let down her walls. Well, that and her gross misunderstanding of Sadie's feelings for her, since she hadn't realized Sadie even really wanted to kiss her until she'd done it. Jay had done an admirable job of convincing herself she was alone in her attraction. She'd painted Sadie as a stereotypical tennis mom, and the labeling game had helped her quite a bit, right up until the point when Sadie had cupped her face in her soft palm. By then, it was too late to turn back. She'd yearned for the touch and fallen into her midnight eyes. And then came the kiss.

She let out an involuntary moan at the memory. It had been so long, she thought her memories would've taken on mythic proportions in the intervening years, but nothing in the recesses of her mind could compare to the electric press of Sadie's mouth against her own. Everything about her set Jay's body alight, from the ample curve of her hip under eager fingers to the lingering taste of wine on her lips. Jay was powerless to resist. She knew that for certain now. Which was why she couldn't ever let herself get close enough to fall again.

It was just that simple. She couldn't ever be alone with Sadie again. She'd stay busy. She'd work. She'd travel with the whole group. She would eat alone. She would redouble her efforts to keep a healthy, professional distance. She could do this. She had to.

She shed her suitcoat and pants, but couldn't be bothered with the shirt as sadness settled over her. Crawling under the covers this time, she let her limbs go heavy. Just because she knew what she needed to do didn't mean she had to be happy in her resolve. She tried not to remember a time when she'd been young enough and naive enough to think love could make her strong. It didn't do any good to dwell on "what ifs." She had a good life, one most people could only dream of, and even if she were ready to throw it all away, it wasn't just her career or her heart on the line anymore. Destiny and Sadie and Hank, they all deserved better. As the quiet darkness of her sorrow lulled her back to sleep, her only solace came from knowing that at least maybe this time she could take pride in knowing she was doing the right things, for the right people.

"She's not joining us for dinner?" Sadie tried not to sound disappointed.

"She's got plans with Peggy Hamilton again."

Sadie frowned. She wasn't surprised. Jay had had plans for each of the last five nights. The excuse was rarely the same, meetings with tour officials, a video session, a late appointment with a tour trainer, and now dinner with a friendly rival. She didn't doubt the stories were genuine, but she did find it suspicious that Jay was suddenly busier than ever the week after they'd kissed. She also felt a little pinprick of something unpleasant at the fact that, for two nights this week, Jay had chosen Peggy as her distraction of choice.

"Good," Hank said. "She and Peggy used to pal around when they were younger."

Sadie didn't know what to make of the comment. She wasn't so full of herself to assume Jay sat around thinking about her all the time, but surely a trauma like she'd seen on her face after they'd kissed couldn't be buried inside forever. Did she need someone to talk to, or had she turned to Peggy for a different kind of solace?

Her chest tightened again, and this time she recognized the mix of hurt and envy. She'd felt both emotions before, but this was the first time she'd ever experienced them simultaneously, and she didn't care for the combination.

"What do you want for dinner?" Destiny scrolled through something on her phone, oblivious to the struggle occurring inside Sadie. "There's tons of stuff around here. There's sushi, and down the block there's sushi, two-tenths of a mile, and there's a Japanese place with, well, more sushi."

Hank groaned. "Did we really come all the way to Paris to eat sushi?"

"I think we might be in some sort of Asian district. Wait, here's an Italian place less than half a mile away."

"We just left Italy."

"Well, I for one can eat only so many baguettes and cheeses," Des said, then laughed. "Actually, that's not true. I *should* eat only so many baguettes and cheeses, but I will eat a lot more of them if you insist."

"If I wasn't your coach I would, but somehow asking a player to eat extra carbs when she wants fish doesn't seem right."

"Two halfhearted votes for sushi," Destiny said. "What do you say, Mom?"

At the sound of the word "mom," some deep-grained instinct kicked in, and Sadie made herself fully present in the room. "I'm fine with whatever you want."

Destiny frowned. "Really? I know you don't love sushi."

"I don't mind," she said, when what she really meant was she didn't care. She hadn't had the mental space required to form strong opinions since Jay's lips had left her own. When they were kissing, a part of her she'd never known existed had blown wide open. Her every sense had heightened, and then imprinted, those cues on her mind, from the vivid blue of Jay's eyes, to the clutch of Jay's strong hands on her waist, to the thunderous echo of her own pulse. Everything since then had seemed dull and muted. She felt like someone who'd seen TV in color for one glorious show and now had to go back to viewing the world in black and white. She found it hard to get too excited about any shade of gray.

"Sushi it is," said Des with a shrug.

They strolled through the streets of Paris down to the banks of the Seine. In the distance, across the river, the Eiffel Tower peaked dark and proud against the orange evening sky, but the iconic view only helped to amplify her melancholy. Paris in the springtime was supposed to be the trip of a lifetime, and having her daughter smiling by her side should have been more than enough.

It always had been before.

They entered the restaurant, and Hank made a valiant attempt at speaking just enough French to get them seated. The young maître d', dressed head to toe in black, turned up his nose but clearly understood the request enough to motion for them to follow him up a spiraling set of stairs for what felt like ages.

"Are they tucking us away in the attic?" Hank asked between heavy breaths.

"Do you think we're underdressed?" Destiny whispered, glancing down at her jeans and red tank top. "I'm still not used to all the dress codes in all these different countries."

"You look beautiful," Sadie said from the back of the line.

"Maybe it was my French," Hank said.

"Was that French?" Destiny teased. "I thought you were having a seizure."

"Very fun—" Hank's reply fell short as he reached the top of the stairs. "Whoa."

"Whoa," Destiny repeated, coming to a halt right in front of her.

"What?" Sadie asked. "Did they dump us in some sort of crime scene or public restroom?"

"The opposite." Des stepped out of the doorway to reveal a rooftop deck with an expansive view of the City of Lights. Below, the river curved in a lazy arc around the gardens surrounding the Eiffel Tower in lush green. Beyond it, the city spread out in a maze of stone and concrete showered golden by the glow of street lamps just flickering to life. Sadie's heart clenched at the beauty of the sight before her, so bittersweet in its sweeping splendor, and yet all of it merely backdrop to the striking sight of Jay Pierce standing casually at the railing.

A slight breeze stirred her hair, and she shook it out of her face, her smile bright as she took in the view, but a shadow crossed over the joyous expression at the sight of them watching her.

"Oh. Hello," Jay said, after the second it took for her to replace her surprise with a forced smile. "Great minds must think alike."

The comment was on par with the last few days. Every time they'd been forced to interact, starting from the plane ride to Paris and going right up through today's hitting session, Jay had walked a pleasantly benign conversational line. She'd resorted to clichés and sound bites at every turn. Sadie had been impressed with Jay's ability to skirt heavy topics in press conferences, but she found the skill less endearing on a personal level. Hank didn't seem bothered by the banality though.

"Hey, look who's here." He strode over, arms wide in exuberant greeting.

"Hank." Peggy laughed as she kissed him on each cheek. "You haven't changed a bit."

He patted his protruding stomach. "You're nice to say that, but I've got access to mirrors."

"Will you be dining together?" the waiter asked, his English only slightly accented.

Everyone glanced around at each other awkwardly, but Jay spoke first. "We don't want to intrude on your dinner."

"Don't be silly," Hank said. "This feels like a family reunion."

Peggy turned to Jay, questions in her eyes. The unspoken communication caused another twinge of jealousy in Sadie. Why should this Peggy woman understand Jay better simply because they'd known each other years ago? Sadie was the one who'd been there for months. She'd been the one who'd held her and kissed her. And why should Jay get to share the awkwardness with someone else when Sadie had to deal with her emotions alone?

"Hi, I'm Destiny Larsen," Des said, stepping forward with her hand extended. "If we're having a family reunion, I suppose I should at least introduce myself."

Peggy took her hand and smiled brightly. "I'm Peggy Hamilton."

"Yeah, I know," Des said with a dopey grin.

"Sorry. I always forget to do the formal introduction thing. This is my doubles partner. As she mentioned, her name is Destiny," Jay said, sounding chagrined. Then gesturing hastily toward Sadie, added, "And this is her mom."

Peggy turned, her smile widening so far it might have actually made her blond ponytail bob. "So wonderful to meet you, Ms. Larsen."

"Please, call me Sadie," she replied, trying not to overthink the fact that Jay hadn't used her name and had instead identified her by her relationship to Destiny.

"Great." Hank clapped his hands together and turned back toward the maître d'. "Now that we got the formalities out of the way and figured out you speak English better than I speak French, can we get a table for five?"

The maître d' waved his hand toward a circular table in the corner of the rooftop, as if leading them there would be entirely too tedious for him, and then walked away in the opposite direction.

"Oh, don't you just love that French hospitality?" Peggy joked. Then pulling out two chairs, she said, "Destiny, come sit by me and tell me all your secrets, because we're bound to face each other on the court sooner rather than later."

"Careful," Jay warned, her tone light as she hung back. "You and Peggy are in the same quarter of the draw next week."

"Yeah, and don't let those dimples fool you," Hank said. "She'd sell her own mother to earn a few extra points."

"I don't deny it," Peggy said, as Sadie took the seat on the other side of Destiny, "but if you met my mother, you'd hardly blame me. Jay can vouch."

"It's true. She's horrible." Jay sat down on the other side of Peggy, leaving a chair for Hank right between her and Sadie. Another subtle move that could easily be explained away, but the total of all of them put together added up to something more than coincidence.

"How's your mom horrible?" Destiny leaned forward like a kid at story time.

"Total tennis mom," Peggy said lightly, but the term bore none of the humor it had when Jay had used it with Sadie. "Complete micromanager, from my clothes down to the guys she wanted me to date. And don't even get me started on the money. I can't begin to estimate how many of my paychecks went to cover her manicures or massages."

"Whoa," Des said, then glanced at Sadie, "and I was mad at you for making us share a room for so long."

"Yeah, well, just remember that next time you get sulky with me after a loss. I might not have all the answers, but at least I'm not a tennis mom."

Jay chuckled. "You're totally a tennis mom."

"Excuse me?" Sadie's eyebrows shot up in surprise, more at the fact that Jay had addressed her without having to, rather than at the comment itself.

"You're a total tennis mom," Jay repeated, then rushed to add, "not the nightmare variety like Peggy's mom, but you're still one hundred percent in the game, on the tour, at the practices."

Hank made a sound like he had something stuck in his throat.

"Not that it's a bad thing," Peggy said quickly. "It's just, um, a newer thing. People as old as Jay aren't totally used to having so many parents around."

"Oh, yes," Sadie said, shifting uncomfortably in her seat. "I'm sure that's probably what she meant."

"I've never even heard you mention your parents," Des said, as if she she'd never considered the thought before, then with a teasing lilt in her voice added, "Do you even have a family, or were you raised by wolves?"

"Wolves," Jay said dryly, then looked over her shoulder at the city without elaborating.

"Where did that waiter get to?" Hank asked impatiently. "I'm all for this relaxed European time schedule, but not until after the wine arrives."

"I hear you." Peggy picked up a menu as if she might use it to shield herself from the awkwardness around her. "I'm on a self-imposed training curfew. Maybe we can all be ready to order whenever he deigns to come back up here."

"I always liked you," Hank said, picking up his menu and burying his face between the folds.

Everyone else at the table joined in, everyone but Jay. Sadie watched her surreptitiously over the edge of her laminated sushi list. She seemed to have drifted off as her eyes stared off toward the horizon. Only the faintest hints of orange remained from the setting sun, but it cast her face in a warm aura. The image would have been serenely beautiful if not for the undercurrent of pain in Jay's eyes. It wasn't as plainly visible as the moment when she'd practically run from Sadie's embrace, but she could see the uncertainty there now, more than she had over the past few days.

She wanted almost desperately to reach across Hank and take Jay's hand in her own, to give it a squeeze or lead her away and beg her to open up, but even if she had felt comfortable doing so in front of the others, Jay had made it clear she didn't want that. Sadie didn't understand her decision, or the anguish that came with it, but she'd had to ward off more than a few advances over the years for reasons she didn't want to explain, so she respected those boundaries. The thought bothered her though. Did Jay see her the same way Sadie saw the men who tried to angle their way into her and Destiny's lives?

126

The kiss hadn't seemed unwelcomed at first. Jay had melted into her with the most amazing mix of surrender and command. Her face grew hot again at the memory of Jay's body, so long and strong, providing a contrast to the softness of her lips. She hadn't kissed like a conflicted woman. Her struggle only emerged after they broke apart, and even then, it hadn't fully taken hold until they'd gotten several more scorching kisses out of their systems. Still, Jay had pulled away, and she had stayed away, at least emotionally. Sadie didn't know how to reconcile the woman who'd poured so much passion into a few heated moments with the disconnect she felt watching Jay now.

Mercifully a waiter appeared, and everyone ordered uneventfully before Peggy turned to Destiny and made another attempt at polite conversation. "Who do you have first in the draw?"

"Maria Cruz," Des said with a grimace. "She knocked me out of the Australian open."

"She's got a wicked forehand slice," Peggy commiserated. "She took me out at the knees in Cincinnati last year, but she hates clay."

"Really?" Hank leaned forward. "Why's that?"

"Probably because it messes with her flawless skin tone," Peggy said, then grinned. "Was that catty of me?"

"Not at all," Jay said drolly. "You merely put down a woman's professional shortcomings to her appearance. Any speculation as to why I underperform on clay?"

Peggy snorted but didn't miss a beat. "Because you, my dear, don't like to play dirty."

Jay stared at her for a moment, then threw back her head and laughed. "Well played."

"It's the truth," Hank said. "I mean, maybe not about the clay, but the playing dirty part. If you were willing to pull half the shit people have pulled on you over the years, you'd have made a lot more money."

"But then I'd have a lot fewer friends," Jay shot back quickly, her eyes regaining some of their usual mischief. "And you all know I'm extremely popular. I mean, like, you don't even know how many people invited me to dinner tonight."

"What? You had other dinner options?" Peggy gave her a friendly shove. "I only came out with you tonight because I felt bad for your lonely-ass self."

"We invited her," Hank said with a little frown. "We invite her every night."

"Oh, Hank," Peggy laughed. "You do love yourself some hopeless cases, don't you?"

"Des, I think she might have implied something about you there," Jay said quickly. "You better beat her in your quarter of the draw so I don't have to face her in the semis."

"No, then you'd have to face me. Are you saying that'd be an easier road for you?"

"Ouch," Jay said, rubbing her jaw. "I walked right into that one, didn't I?"

Peggy wrapped her arm around Destiny's shoulders. "I like you, kid. Stick with your Auntie Peggy here, and we'll gang up on Jay together."

"Oh, I'm throwing in the towel." Jay tossed her napkin dramatically on the table. "Two against one. What is this, Canadian doubles?"

The conversation spun on around her, as everyone seemed to talk at once. Destiny had jumped in with the joking, and normally that would've been enough for Sadie, but as she watched Jay come back to life before her eyes, she couldn't help but feel another twinge of disappointment. She'd hated to see her hurt, but at least when she'd been withdrawn Sadie had been able to tell herself Jay must be dealing with something dark and painful, deep inside of her. Now, watching her laugh and touch and joke with every other person at the table, Sadie had to wonder if Jay's conflict wasn't internal, but rather something specific to her.

"I almost crapped my pants when I turned around and saw them standing there," Peggy said, laughter still ringing in her voice as she flopped onto Jay's hotel bed.

Jay didn't find the memory quite so amusing, but she didn't

have to say so. Peggy had kept the conversation going all night. She didn't want to seem ungrateful for her help, but she didn't want to keep reliving or rehashing the evening now that it had finally ended.

"You looked like you were going to be seasick. Your skin even went a little greenish-gray. I thought I might have to hold your hair while you heaved over the side of the building."

"Come on." Jay leaned up against the dresser and folded her arms across her chest. "I wasn't that bad."

"Maybe not to someone who hasn't seen you melt down before, but I could tell you were close."

"First of all, I recovered quickly. Second of all, this is nothing like the last time. I won't let it get as far as last time."

Peggy sat up. "Of course not, which is why you've gone out with me two nights in one week after dodging every one of my invitations for, like, five years."

"Not five years. I went through hell, and I was off the tour because of the hell, and then I was playing basically in the bush leagues to get points, then I was off the tour for my knees and then—"

"You had a phone." Peggy drolly cut in. "Did you use it?"

"We're talking about going out, and I've only been back for, like, a year."

"A year in which we had drinks outside official functions what, once?" Peggy raised her hand, cutting off Jay's protest before she could give it voice. "I get it. I'm not complaining. I'm glad to have you back for any reason, but let's not pretend you're not using me to jock block Tennis Mom, okay?"

"Tennis mom," Jay repeated. "Tennis mom, tennis mom, tennis mom."

Peggy rolled onto her side and stared at her. "Does that help?"

"What?"

"Tucking her into a nice little box labeled, 'my doubles partner's mom'?" She practically giggled when she said the words. "Sorry. I mean, it's not funny, but it's kind of funny."

"Not even a little funny. I'm in the middle of my comeback

here. I worked years to get to a good place, first emotionally, then physically. I'm finally feeling good about myself. I don't want to backslide."

"I don't want you to either, but I also don't want you to be alone forever. Hermit is not a good look on you."

"I'm not a hermit, and I'm not talking about forever. I've got a couple years at most to secure my legacy as something other than a scandal. I want to spend that time focused on tennis."

"Also, you promised Destiny you wouldn't sleep with her tennis mom."

Jay tried in vain to roll some of the tension from her neck. "Yes, I did."

"And that promise means a lot to you. I get it. I'm not saying it shouldn't. God knows, in this business, someone who keeps their word even when it goes against their own self-interest, well, it's a rare quality, but—" Peggy got to her feet and placed a hand on each of Jay's shoulders. "It was an unfair promise to ask of someone."

Jay let her head fall forward until her chin touched her chest to avoid her own troubled reflection in Peggy's green eyes. "Normally I'd agree with you."

"Normally? Under what circumstances does a teenager get to tell a business associate or her mother who they can or cannot date?" Peggy gave her a shake. "Hell, my mother picked my partners both on and off the court for years after I became of legal age, and I'm not saying you need to go that far, but if two consenting adults want to make out in the privacy of a hotel room, I don't see why the kid gets a vote on the issue."

"You know it's not that simple. She's not some typical high school senior, and nothing on this tour stays private for long. She's protecting herself, her brand, and her mother all at once. It's smart, and it's admirable."

"It's controlling."

"Do you honestly think, given my past, that her concerns are unfounded?"

"Maybe not unfounded, but a lot of her assumptions are based on lies. If you told her the truth—"

"The truth doesn't matter to the press!" Jay exploded, as a week's worth of frustration boiled to the surface. "It doesn't matter to players who want to gain the upper hand. It doesn't matter to the fans. I hate that, but I know my reputation, and I know how hard it is to change it. Do you really think it's fair to put Destiny in the same position as she tries to get her career off the ground? You saw her tonight. Do you really think she deserves to be subjected to that kind of circus?"

Peggy frowned, and Jay took the opportunity to shake her off. "At first, I pegged her for a spoiled brat, but she's every bit as strong as Sadie, and her heart's in the right place. She'd willingly forgo doubles completely to take care of someone who's always taken care of her."

"Sadie doesn't strike me as someone who needs protecting. She's a grown-ass woman, a smart, resilient, and damn good-looking woman. She didn't get a kid this far on her own without learning to make her own choices and assess her own risks."

"It wouldn't be an informed decision or a calculated risk. She doesn't know about what happened."

"Then tell her!"

"And what?" Jay paced the room despite the tweak of tightness in her knee. "Make her choose between me and her daughter? What a terrible position to be in for all of us. And to what end? Maybe we have some fun, maybe we make a good match for a while, but then what? There's no happily ever after in this business."

"There could be."

Jay shook her head

"Agassi and Graf."

"What?"

"Andre Agassi and Steffi Graf," Peggy said triumphantly. "They got a happily ever after."

"*After* she retired," Jay said, quickly tamping down the little flutter of hope in her chest. "And they're just one example. You know how the odds are stacked against a pairing like them. Hell, how many of your mixed doubles partners have you dated?"

Peggy shrugged. "A few."

"And how many of them did you manage to keep playing with after you split?"

Peggy mumbled something unintelligible.

"How many?"

"None."

"Exactly," Jay said emphatically. "Business romances don't end well even under the best of circumstances. They sure as hell won't work if you pile all my excess baggage on top of an already fraught situation."

"So, you ignore all your feelings, and hers, and hope they go away? Because that ended so well last week. You can't hide from her forever."

Jay shook her head. "No, and I don't have to. I survived dinner tonight."

"Barely."

"I needed some time to pull myself together. My emotions were raw, and I had too much downtime, but once the tournament starts on Monday, I'll go into business mode, and it'll be fine. Destiny's a crucial part of my career at the moment, and I won't do anything to screw up our chances."

"And what about Sadie? What about what she wants?"

"She wants what's best for her daughter, no matter what." Jay's jaw tightened, but she managed to force out the next few words. "She made it clear the day we met. She doesn't love anything as much as she loves Destiny."

There, she'd said it. Destiny came first for Sadie, and Sadie came first for Destiny. She would never be on the inside of their circle. Now she just needed to remember that fact, no matter how good Sadie smelled or felt or tasted or looked. Jay had to pack Sadie back into a tiny box labeled Tennis Mom, and then do everything in her power to keep her there.

Chapter Seven

Paris

"Yes!" Sadie shouted loudly. Her own fist pump mirrored Destiny's and Jay's as the ball clipped the baseline two feet to the right of their back-court opponent. She turned to hug Hank. "Quarter-finals here we come!"

"That's three wins down, three more to go," he said, as he turned to applaud Jay and Destiny with the rest of the crowd.

"Let's just enjoy this one for a minute, okay?" Sadie said. Her heart needed some time to recuperate from the thumping it'd taken during the last hour and a half.

Everyone had tried to warn her that a major would be a whole different experience, but she thought she'd been prepared. She'd been to the Australian Open, so she'd expected the bigger stadium and thicker crowds. What she hadn't taken into account, though, was Destiny and Jay's rise in popularity. Even in the third round, they'd been given a priority time slot right before a headline match in men's singles on court N1, which was the first court outside the mammoth stadiums reserved for marquee events. The circular arena had over 800 seats, and glancing around, Sadie estimated more than half of them were full. In a matter of weeks, they'd gone from fourteen spectators to four hundred, and that number was likely to double for the next round, which would be played on the biggest court of the complex, Philippe-Chatrier.

Sadie shook her head and smiled. So much for staying in the moment. Even she couldn't help but get swept away by the excitement of it all. They were still playing in the second week of a major tournament. At least in the doubles. Destiny had been knocked out of singles the day before in a tight fourth-round match, but even she hadn't seemed devastated about the loss, perhaps because she'd played well enough to exceed most people's expectations, but Sadie suspected having a doubles match to prepare for had gone a long way toward warding off her depression and keeping her focused on something positive. Instead of sinking into a funk and waiting for the next tournament to start, she hit the practice courts with a determination to keep her French Open alive. And now her smile was back in full as she collected her things and headed for the exit, stopping only to sign a few autographs along the way.

Jay trailed behind her, with a slightly more subdued expression. She hadn't been quite as exuberant in her play, but then again, she'd also seemed more focused, so maybe the trade-off was warranted. She'd remained steadfastly professional despite taking a beating in the third round of singles. In fact, she hadn't broken a racket or been fined in weeks. Sadie couldn't help but notice that the time frame coincided with her and Destiny's doubles pairing. Was that why Jay hadn't wanted to kiss her? Because she didn't want to jeopardize her relationship with Destiny? The logic added up, but not enough to explain the emotional turmoil Sadie had seen in her that night, or her ensuing distance when she could've easily explained herself to everyone involved and worked something out.

"What's wrong?" Hank nudged her toward the end of the row.

"Nothing. Why?"

"You're blocking the aisle and scowling like someone asked Des a stupid question. Are you already dreading the press conference?"

"No," she said quickly. "They've been much better lately."

"Jay's been good for her on a lot of levels," Hank agreed. "The pressroom still isn't her natural habitat, but she's learning to sidestep well enough to avoid the traps and snares."

They wound through the stands and waited patiently to be checked through security before being allowed entry into the restricted area. By the time they finally arrived outside the locker rooms, Destiny had freshened up and met them with a huge grin and equally big hugs.

"Great work out there. Those two aces in the second set broke their backs." Hank lifted her off the ground as he squeezed. Then, setting her down, he turned right back to work mode. "You'll face Harris and Cruz tomorrow. I want to go over a few videos of Harris's serve tonight because she's a lefty, so I expect they'll want her to match up against you as much as possible to try to neutralize your power and make Jay play the finesse game against Cruz's slice."

"Hank!" Sadie scolded. "They haven't even finished their press conference for this match. Do we really need to strategize for the next one right here?"

He mumbled something that sounded like "short turnaround," but after she raised her eyebrows at him mom-style, he nodded. "Right. Go on in there and talk about your brilliance."

"Just waiting on Jay," Destiny said. "She hopped in the shower."

"Oh Lord," Hank groaned. "We're at the French Open, not a day spa. She needs to stay on schedule."

"I'm sure it'll be fine," Sadie said.

"Jay has never taken a short shower in her life." Hank put his hand on the locker room door, dwarfing the knob. "I'm going to get her."

"No," Sadie protested. "You can't go into the women's locker room."

"Fine. You get her then."

Sadie froze as memories of other locker room encounters with Jay flashed through her mind. Jay in a towel, Jay pushing her away, Jay's face in her hands.

"Mom?" Destiny asked.

"Hmm?"

"You okay? You look a little lightheaded."

She felt a little lightheaded, too, but she didn't want to explain why. "No, I'm fine. Just coming down from your exciting match. I may need to call it an early night."

"Then go call Jay to the pressroom so we can go home," Hank said matter-of-factly.

"I'll go," Destiny said quickly, her eyes wide with worry.

"Don't be silly." Sadie pushed open the door. "You've got to get in there, too. I'll be right back."

Before they could argue further, she let the door close quickly behind her. Taking a deep breath, she plowed forward past a group of attendants between two tall rows of wooden lockers. She threaded her way around some junior players giggling over something on a cell phone and skirted a wall filled with TVs showing various matches taking place across the grounds. She told herself that no one paid her any attention, because she wasn't doing anything out of the ordinary. She just needed to tell a player to get to the pressroom. Happened all the time. There was no need for her heart to start beating all the way up in her throat.

She could do this. She could face Jay with the same polite professionalism with which Jay had faced her over the last two weeks. The fact that they were seeing each other for the first time without Des or Hank shouldn't change anything. The fact that Jay might be naked with hot water sluicing across her tight muscles shouldn't change anything either. But that didn't keep Sadie's stride from faltering as she neared the showers.

She stopped right on the line where concrete met tile and called out, "Jay, are you in here?"

"Who?" an unfamiliar voice asked.

"Jay," Sadie called, a little louder. "Jay Pierce."

"Hey," someone said softly behind her, causing her to jump.

"Sorry," Jay said, with a crooked smile that caused Sadie's breath to catch in her chest. Jay stood a few feet away, her back against one of the banks of oak-paneled lockers. She wore low-slung jeans with a plain black V-neck sweater and held a white towel to the ends of her damp hair. "Didn't mean to startle you."

For a moment Sadie could only stare. She'd spent so much energy bracing herself to see Jay half-dressed, she hadn't prepared herself to simply see her casual beauty.

Jay lowered the towel. "What's wrong?"

Sadie sighed. "Why do people keep asking me that?"

"Sorry," Jay said again.

"No, it's fine. Just . . . you have a press conference."

"I know."

"Well, good." Sadie looked down at the floor, only to notice Jay was barefoot. For some reason that felt intimate, and Sadie's eyes shot up to the ceiling. God, this wasn't even a serious test. Why couldn't she just look Jay in the eye?

"I'll be right out," Jay said, turning back to the locker.

"I will too," Sadie said as she turned to go, then added, "I mean, I'll be in the press conference."

"Of course you will," Jay said, a hint of frustration in her voice.

Sadie froze. "Excuse me?"

"Of course you'll be in the press conference," Jay said flatly, "just like you're at the matches and at the practices."

"What's that supposed to mean?" Sadie asked, her ribs squeezing her lungs.

"Just what I said." Jay sat down on a wooden bench and pulled on a fresh pair of black socks. "I didn't mean any offense. I just meant, you're all over the place."

Sadie's throat tightened with emotion at the unspoken parts of the comments. Jay didn't want her there. The admission shouldn't have surprised her given the way Jay had avoided her since the kiss, but it still hurt.

Even if they couldn't share in the passion they'd exchanged the night of the kiss, Sadie had held out some hope that once the awkwardness wore off they could go back to being friends. Up until two weeks ago, she would've sworn Jay liked her on a fundamental level, and she'd enjoyed having someone to travel with, to talk to, and to confide in. Had she really been such a terrible kisser to undo that connection entirely? Or had the kiss itself been such a grievous offense that it couldn't be overcome?

"I'm sorry if my presence is a burden for you."

Jay pulled on a pair of red high-top sneakers and didn't bother to lace them up before standing. "I didn't mean that. I just meant . . . I don't know. I guess I just meant, of course you'll be around. It's what you do. You're a tennis mom."

Tennis mom.

Jay had used the term with such affectionate teasing early on. Sadie hadn't realized it could also be derisive. Which version did Jay pin on her? And was that the reason she'd been so withdrawn? Sadie was a tennis mom, and Jay was a tennis star. Was that reason enough to keep her from wanting to explore their attraction? Jay had alluded to her own reputation more than once. Did she fear Sadie would bring down her social stock? She wouldn't have thought Jay capable of such shallow thinking two weeks ago, but after facing her cold shoulder and now her dismissive remarks, she wondered if the Jay she'd let herself fall for was the real Jay, or if the pressure of the last few weeks had revealed her true nature.

Sadie was still pondering the question after the press conference when they got back to the hotel. She hadn't heard a word anyone had said. She was too hurt and confused to focus. She supposed everything had gone well because Destiny was still smiling, but she felt guilty for zoning out. This was the biggest tournament of her daughter's life so far, and she'd spent the last forty-five minutes in a haze, trying to figure out what she should do about Jay.

"Can we just order room service while we go over video tonight?" Des asked. "I don't want to put on real pants."

"I vote for that option," Hank said quickly. "Can you get pizza in Paris?"

Sadie's stomach roiled at the thought of putting food into it. "Would you two mind doing the video in one of your rooms tonight? I'm wiped out."

"Are you okay?" Des put her hand on Sadie's forehead like Sadie had used to do for her when she was little. "Are you getting sick?"

The tenderness of her concern almost caused Sadie's emotional dam to burst, but she forced the tears not to fall just yet and said, "I'm fine. I think the travel and excitement have finally caught up with me though. Would you mind terribly if I went to bed early?"

"No, of course not," Des said.

"You've earned more than a few nights off," Hank agreed. "And tomorrow's another big day followed by more sponsor events in the evening. Go get all the sleep you can while you've got the chance."

"Thank you," she said, as the relief threatened to buckle her knees. "I'm sure a solid ten hours of shut-eye will fix me right up."

Destiny hugged her extra tightly but didn't press for more, and she ducked into her room as quickly as possible to hide the tears that wouldn't be held at bay any longer.

Dropping her purse on the table, she kicked off her shoes and collapsed onto the bed. She hadn't been lying when she'd claimed exhaustion. She was weary almost to the point of collapse, but the cause wasn't physical. After weeks of trying desperately to understand and respect Jay's boundaries, then make peace with the new disconnect between them, and now battle her own hurt and confusion at Jay's apparent distaste for her, she didn't know how much longer she could go on alone. And yet she couldn't burden Destiny or Hank with such a trivial matter amid a major tournament. Her love life, or lack thereof, and subsequent loneliness shouldn't rank on their radar right now. Honestly, those issues shouldn't be on hers, either. They never had been before. She didn't need anyone else in her life. She was a strong, independent woman.

A knock on the door interrupted her internal pep talk. She hopped up and quickly wiped her tears, for fear Destiny would notice and worry. "Hey, what did—" Her question died at the sight of Jay standing in the doorway, and all the consequent memories rushing back to her.

"You thought I was Des again?" Jay's mouth twisted into something that didn't quite qualify as a smile.

"I guess I'd better learn to use the peephole if I want to stop opening my door to strangers."

"Ouch," Jay said, her cheeks reddening slightly. "Stranger. All right then. Fair enough."

"Really?" Myriad emotions warred for prominence within her. "Fair? Is it?"

Jay shifted awkwardly from one foot to the other. "So, I take it Destiny's not here?"

Sadie snorted at the quick redirect. "She and Hank are going to study video in her room tonight."

"Oh. Change of plans." Then with a grimace, she added, "I suppose I'll see you there?"

"No," Sadie said, anger rising up as the winner of the emotional tug of war. "You won't. I hope you're relieved, but I need a night off from all of this."

"All of this," Jay repeated.

"Everything," Sadie managed to say. She knew she hadn't actually conveyed any new information, but she didn't know what to call the problems weighing on her right now, and honestly that was a huge part of the problem. "Whatever happened between us, or whatever's happened since then. Whatever I did to offend you so badly that you now feel the need to treat me like some social pariah."

"Sadie," Jay said softly.

"No, don't say my name like you know me, like you care about me."

"I do," Jay mumbled, still staring at her feet.

"You don't. You don't want me, or you don't want me bad enough to deal with whatever it is you don't want to deal with, and that's fine. I've been rejected before, by more people than you can even imagine, but I cannot, for the life of me, understand why you can't stand to even look me in the eye anymore." Her voice cracked, but the words were rushing out now, and she couldn't stop. "Maybe you don't want to be seen with a tennis mom. Maybe I embarrass you, the way I sometimes embarrass Des."

"No," Jay said.

"Or maybe I'm not your type. I'm sure younger, fitter, skinnier, prettier women throw themselves at you all the time. Maybe I made a fool of myself by thinking you were attracted to me."

"Sadie—"

"Or maybe you don't want to risk your career on someone like me, someone who doesn't have much of a life or a future of her own. I'm just a tennis mom—where's the excitement there?"

"You've got this all wrong," Jay pleaded.

"Maybe I do," Sadie shot back. "Maybe I don't understand you. I don't understand the world you live in. I'm trying to figure it all out, and I thought you were someone I could trust to help me, to be honest with me. Do you have any idea how bad it hurts to find out I was wrong? That you don't even like to be around me?"

Jay shook her head, but made no attempt at either an excuse or an explanation.

Sadie threw up her hands. "Just go. You're obviously not going to tell me what I did, so the least you can do is let me face my embarrassment in peace."

Jay opened her mouth as if she finally had something to say, but Sadie had passed the point where she cared to hear it, and slammed the door in her face.

Jay stepped back as the door nearly struck her in the open mouth. She stood blinking at the solid slate of wood, trying to figure out what had just happened. She'd gotten told off, that was for sure. She deserved it. Sadie's assertions about her shitty comments were on point, and she'd had every right to say them. Jay'd also been let off the hook socially, which probably should've pleased her. Sadie didn't want to talk to her anymore. That should help with the temptation to slip and end up in another lip-lock. She'd struggled all week to keep her distance emotionally and physically, and she hadn't always trusted her own resolve, but Sadie's now seemed so much stronger.

Sadie's fortitude also seemed laced with sadness though, and that's why Jay couldn't force her feet to move backward. Or to the side. Or anywhere, really, because where they really ached to go was through the door blocking her way. No matter how convenient it might be to let Sadie hold onto her anger, Jay couldn't walk away without soothing the pain she'd seen behind it. She'd known as soon as she'd seen her that Sadie had been crying. Then all of her pain spilled out in a million different theories as to why Jay had pulled away, and none of them had come anywhere near the truth. Instead of placing the blame on Jay's shoulders where it belonged, Sadie had assumed she'd done something wrong or, even worse, that she was somehow deficient.

It was ultimately that last point that made Jay knock again.

"Go away," Sadie said, her voice sounding as though she hadn't moved any farther from the door than Jay had.

"Can't we talk?"

No answer.

She knocked again. "Please."

She thought she heard Sadie moving around, but she didn't open the door, so Jay knocked again, and called, "Housekeeping."

Sadie sighed. "Jay, just leave."

"Oh sure, now you use the peephole," Jay said, then rested her forehead on the door. "I'm sorry, Sadie."

"You should be," Sadie called, "but I deserve more than that."

"I agree. You deserve so much better than me. That's what I wanted to explain." She let out a shuddering breath. "I'm not good, Sadie. I didn't want you to end up like, like . . . can I please come in?"

She waited what seemed like an eternity, with her heart clenched painfully in her chest, but just when her hopes had started to sink, she heard the metallic click of a lock turning. Sadie opened the door just a crack.

"I shouldn't do this," Sadie said.

"You really shouldn't," Jay agreed. "I have nothing good to offer you."

"How about an explanation? Can you offer me that?"

Jay couldn't find the words right away, but she knew she would have to, so she nodded.

Sadie swung the door open wide. "All right then."

The relief surging through her at Sadie's guarded welcome was followed quickly by a sense of dread that made each step feel like a thousand. The room seemed stiflingly small and hot, or maybe that was her own skin. God, where was she even going to start? Maybe she should tell Sadie to just Google her. That would probably get the job done. She'd get the bare bones of the story and then enough conjecture to keep her away for a lifetime. What she wouldn't get was much of the truth. Not that the truth had ever mattered to anyone, but for some reason she wanted desperately for it to matter to Sadie. Maybe that's what scared her most right now. Sadie's opinion mattered more than anyone's had for years.

"Well," Sadie prodded, folding her arms across her chest in a way that accentuated the hint of cleavage visible beneath her red V-neck T-shirt. Jay stared for a second, then smiled at the realization she'd been distracted by Sadie's figure at a moment like this. Then she chuckled.

"What's funny?" Sadie did not sound amused.

"I was just trying to figure out where to start, and I lost of my train of thought because you're so damn beautiful."

Sadie's lips parted in surprise.

"And I figure that's as good a place to start as any when it comes to clearing up a few misunderstandings, because I am attracted to you. You are exactly my type. Kissing you was the most wonderfully fulfilling thing I have done in years, and whatever concerns you have about not exciting me, or not stacking up to some image you have in your mind, just lay them to rest right now, because you're the first woman I've let touch me in roughly five years."

"What?" Sadie asked. "I mean, why? You are . . . well look at you. You're stunning, and you're fit, and you're funny. You're a professional athlete, and you have everything going for you that goes with that."

"Yeah, and not everything that goes with that is a good thing. Some of it's actually pretty horrible, and some of it leads to people getting hurt." Her voice cracked. "Some of it leads to *me* getting hurt, and maybe I could take that, but I wanted to do better this time. I wanted to do better for you."

Sadie's expression softened, and she reached for her hand. With a little tug, she pulled Jay over to an overstuffed loveseat. "Who was she?"

Jay sank onto the sofa and said a name that sounded too much like a sob. "Katia."

"Katia," Sadie repeated the name, and it didn't sound nearly as jagged leaving her beautiful lips. "Katia Vitrov, I've heard her name."

"She was my doubles partner," Jay said, a little more steadily. "She trained with Hank."

"And the two of you were in love?"

She shook her head and waited for the sharp pain in her heart to subside. "I loved her. She didn't love me."

Sadie sank down beside her, her body so close and warm, her dark eyes filled with sympathy and tenderness. Something inside Jay broke, and all the hurt and pain and embarrassment she'd kept locked away for nearly a decade burst forth in a single rush of anguish. "She never loved me."

Sadie stared in awe, feeling as if her own heart were tethered to Jay's, as the waves of pain radiated from her. She'd asked for this. She'd demanded an explanation. For two weeks she'd wanted nothing more than to understand what had ripped Jay apart that night in the hallway. If only she could've understood then that giving her those answers would take so much more than words, from both of them.

Jay sat hunched forward on the couch, elbows on her jeans-clad knees and face in her hands. Sadie placed a palm on her back and rubbed in slow, soothing circles, her fingers skimming over the ridge of knotted muscles. She didn't say anything. She didn't have the words to end the torment. Like a virus, the agony would have to work its way painfully out of Jay's system, but Sadie vowed internally to stay here, to stay present and close, so Jay wouldn't have to face any of what came next alone.

"I went pro on my eighteenth birthday," Jay finally said, her voice rough. "And I didn't do badly. I didn't do amazing, but I loved the game so much, and I made enough money to keep playing, which was all I ever really wanted, you know, just more time on the court. I didn't have any cohesive aspirations until I met Hank, right after I turned twenty. You should have seen him then. He was ripped, and he had a pornstache."

Sadie smiled, not just at the idea of Hank with a creepy mustache, but at the hint of humor in Jay's memory.

"He said he thought I was built for doubles because of the live spin on my strokes and my quick feet. He also said he had a new, young player ready to be a star, so he introduced me to Katia."

Oh Hank, Sadie thought as her chest tightened. She didn't even know the story yet, but she understood so much more of the sadness she'd seen in him in those early days of working with Jay again.

"It took all of two practices to see we'd struck gold," Jay continued, her voice steadier now. "Katia and I were magic together. We had this unspoken connection on the court. We burned up the tour. People who'd never watched doubles came out to see us. Fans, reporters, other players, and sponsors, man, they wanted us to sell everything for them. And we worked together on camera. We flowed together so naturally, it only seemed natural when that spilled over, off the court and into the bedroom."

Sadie's face warmed with a mix of feelings she didn't want to examine too closely, but jealousy ranked high among them. She knew the story wouldn't end well, but she hated the thought of Jay in bed with someone else almost as much as she hated that that person had hurt her.

"It was my twenty-first birthday. We'd just won the Australian Open. We sipped champagne and talked about the future. I felt on top of the world, and I kissed her. I didn't even stop to think. Everything else was perfect. The move felt seamless to me, and the first time we made love, I don't know, I just thought the final piece of the puzzle had snapped into place."

"You were young and in love," Sadie summed up.

"Yeah," Jay said, looking up, but her eyes were far away, as if she could see things Sadie could only imagine. "I wanted to shout it into every microphone after every match. I wanted the world to know we were a couple."

"But she didn't?"

Jay shook her head.

"She'd been in the U.S. since she was, like, five, but her family was still culturally very Russian. She played for the Russian Federation in the Davis Cup and during the Olympics. A lot of her sponsors came from there. It made sense for her to stay closeted. I didn't like hiding the best part of me, but I never doubted her intentions. I never suspected anything. Not for years."

"Years?" Sadie asked. Of course, she knew better than most how people could go their whole lives without acknowledging their sexual orientation, but somehow Jay didn't strike her as the kind to hide her joy. "How many years?"

"Too many. Looking back, I should have seen, I should've realized the relationship was the only part of my life not progressing, but when you're twenty-three and most of the people your age are drowning in debt or working entry-level jobs, it's hard to get any sort of perspective on the kind of life we were living." Jay explained as best she could, but Sadie couldn't imagine what her life had been like then. "It's hard to ask yourself to answer tough questions when you're winning and everyone loves you. Things took off for me. Not just in doubles, but singles, too. Playing with Katia, or loving her, or maybe the combination, made me feel invincible. By the time I turned twenty-four, we were the number one team in the world together, and a few months later I broke the top ten in singles, too."

"Wow." Sadie felt both impressed and a little chagrined that she didn't know Jay had ever achieved that kind of success. "I had no idea you two owned so much of the tennis world."

"We didn't," Jay said flatly. "I owned a lot. She owned only her share of the doubles. The higher I climbed in the singles, the further she fell. The week I landed at number nine, she dropped out of the top one hundred. I'm not saying that was the end of things, because I'm still not sure what we ever really had, but the disparity in our careers didn't do us any favors."

"You know that's not your fault, right?"

Jay shrugged. "Knowing something and believing it are two different things."

"If she'd loved you the way you loved her, she would've been happy for you, no matter who you were beating."

"Well, she wasn't. First she got cold. She turned away from my kisses and started sleeping in her own hotel room again. Then she got mean. She made snide remarks about me being more coarse and clumsy than anyone would guess, both in private and in the press. And she clearly wasn't talking about my style of play."

Sadie's face flamed. What a horrible little jab on any level, but particularly in a press setting. "She actually made thinly disguised accusations about your personal life to reporters?"

Jay snorted softly, then buried her face in her hands again, before mumbling, "She did so much more. And I tried to stop it. I really did. I even offered to quit singles altogether."

"When you were in the top ten?"

"The ranking never mattered to me as much as she did," Jay said quickly, "but I think she must have been addicted to the limelight more than I ever understood. She loved attention, and eventually all the attention was on me. Even after a doubles win, the press and the fans flocked to my side. I started getting offers for solo endorsements and special interviews without her. That's when she snapped."

"Snapped?" Sadie asked, a quiver in her voice.

"She went to the tabloids," Jay said with a resigned sigh.

"Why?"

Jay shrugged again. "I lay awake asking myself that for years. I think maybe she wanted to end things between us. Maybe she'd never wanted to start with me. Maybe she felt trapped, but either way I think she knew once we broke up it would be the end of her career, so she panicked."

Sadie couldn't make sense of that explanation. What could make a closeted woman talk to the press? "So she came out?"

"No. She just outed me."

"Wait, how could she out you without outing herself in the process? Wouldn't that be like blowing a hole in her own boat?"

"She told them I seduced her," Jay said, then in a whisper added, "more than that, really. She said I coerced her, that she wasn't gay, but I pursued her so hard, when she was so young, she didn't know how to tell me no."

"What?"

"She never accused me of rape," Jay said, as the first tear fell atop her bright red shoes. Sadie watched the spot spread and darken, and she felt as though Jay were actually bleeding in front of her as she reopened the old wound. "But the picture she painted was a pretty clear one of me as the brash, charismatic, older predator who led a younger, more demure girl astray."

Sadie could barely process the unfairness of what she was hearing, much less believe anyone who'd been around Jay would sit idly by and listen to someone assassinate her character. "I can't imagine what a betrayal of that magnitude must've felt like on a personal level, but please tell me no one who knew you believed her."

"Almost everyone believed her," Jay said. Taking a ragged breath as if she couldn't get quite enough air for the force of the words, she continued. "A few of the players who had been around us realized her story didn't add up, but we'd been so closeted, very few people had really gotten to see our personal dynamic. The fans, the press, even the league officials were all willing to buy into the drama. I was a big story in our circles."

"But you told them she was lying, right?"

"At first I was just too stunned. And I was heartbroken. The loss crippled me. It was like I forgot how to function as a human for a while. Any day that I managed to eat and shower felt like a win at first."

Sadie fought the urge to jump up and pace as the anger surged through her, but she didn't want to put any distance between Jay and herself right now as Jay's emotion poured out with each anguished syllable.

"I had been so in love, I'd been willing to throw my entire

career away for her, and now every time I turned on the TV or stumbled across a newspaper, there was Katia talking about how she'd never wanted to be anything more than my tennis partner. Nothing made sense anymore. I didn't know who I was without her. I spent weeks second-guessing every memory, scrutinizing every moment that had mattered to me."

Sadie rubbed Jay's back in slow, soothing circles as she fought her own tears now. How could someone hurt another human being that badly? How could you make love with someone one night and then betray them the next?

Her heart gave a painful little hiccup, but she pushed her own insecurities away as Jay began to speak again.

"Eventually I started to feel something other than pain again, and when I did, I realized I was the one who'd gotten played. But then I almost drowned in the crushing embarrassment of how wrong I'd been to give her so much of myself. By then, she had a book deal with some freakish Russian ex-gay group. She was releasing excerpts. She shared intimate details of our lives together, and some of them were close enough to the truth that even I started to believe her version of them, so you can hardly blame other people for buying into it."

"I do," Sadie said, a fire spreading in her chest. "I blame each and every one of them."

"I didn't. I didn't even blame her. She was scared or maybe she really was confused or felt trapped."

"Anyone can be confused for a night or for a short while, but not for years, Jay."

"She was young."

"So were you!"

"I don't know," Jay said, sounding utterly dejected.

"I do," Sadie said emphatically. "I *know*."

Jay met her eyes for the first time in what felt like weeks, and Sadie's breath caught as the beauty of that gaze peered into hers. The connection seemed to have some effect on Jay as well, because she didn't push her line of reasoning any further.

"Anyway, by the time I found the strength to get angry, most of the damage was done. My lawyers managed to stop the book from coming out, but all the excerpts were already online. We couldn't chase all those feathers in the wind. My lawyers wanted me to sue her for libel, but I didn't have it in me to try to hurt her."

"You still loved her, after everything?"

"She was my first." Jay hung her head again. "And part of me still worried she might have been right about me, or maybe that she'd had her reasons at least. I think I needed to believe it at the time, because it was easier than the alternative. Somehow it seemed worse to admit I'd given my heart and soul to someone who disdained me. I certainly couldn't bring myself to say so in court."

"Wait, she got away with everything?" Sadie asked, unable to temper her incredulous tone. "No one believed the truth?"

"Truth doesn't sell newspapers or bump ratings, but I thought it would all go away soon enough if I stopped talking about it. Americans don't really follow tennis the way they do other sports, and I had just barely made the top ten. I didn't see why anyone else would care about me long-term, but I misjudged the public's attention span and their bloodthirstiness."

"It didn't go away?" Sadie already knew the answer.

"No." Jay wrung her hands now. "I lost all my sponsors. Fans turned on me. They booed and screamed horrible things at me. The press followed me everywhere. Even the gay community didn't know what to do with me. I mean, they liked having a new celebrity, but they didn't want one that perpetuated the lesbian-predator myth."

"Didn't anyone stand by you?"

"Hank tried," Jay said. "He saw right through Katia. So did Peggy and a handful of other players, but anyone who defended me came under fire or at least under suspicion. Guilty by association. Eventually I stopped going out with anyone I really cared about."

"You faced it all alone?"

She grimaced. "No, that would have been better in the long

run, but I was so desperately insecure, and all of a sudden there were all of these women slipping me numbers and sneaking into my hotel. They wanted me, they made their desires abundantly clear, and I wanted so badly to feel wanted that I didn't tell them *no* nearly as much as I should have. I'm not sure I slept alone two nights in a row for at least a year."

"Got it," Sadie managed, her voice tighter than she would have liked.

Jay looked up again, this time her cheeks scarlet with embarrassment. "I'm not proud. I never felt proud, but you deserve to know. You have to know, I wasn't some helpless victim the whole time. I played into the press and the public's image of me for way too long. I became the womanizer they all wanted to see. It didn't matter why, and it didn't matter that those women got way more out of me than I ever got out of them."

"You had your reasons."

"Reasons don't excuse actions," she said, so emphatically that Sadie believed her. "I humiliated myself, my parents, my friends, the tour. I couldn't give a teenage fan an autograph without someone raising an eyebrow, and I didn't even fight back. I hated myself, and it showed on the court. I lost constantly, and within two years, I had dropped from ninth to ninetieth."

"But somehow you turned it all around," Sadie said, desperate to find the happy ending Jay deserved.

"It was a long, slow process, but it started when I stopped with the women. What I had with them was all flash and no substance, which is what people were saying about me by then, and I didn't want that to be true. So, I buckled down and focused exclusively on tennis, but in an attempt to find something, anything good left in me, I pushed too hard and hurt my knee."

All the air left Sadie in a rush. "Oh my God, Jay, how have you not just curled into a ball and given up?"

Her mouth curled up slightly. "I kind of did for a while, but eventually self-pity got boring, and I started bouncing a ball off my bedroom wall. Then I started hitting against my garage. Before I knew it, I was having fun again. I started to feel like me again. I didn't want to lose that feeling, and I didn't want to be the person Katia had made me out to be. I didn't want her to have the last word on my career or my life story."

Sadie squeezed Jay's shoulder, grateful to hear a hint of passion in her voice again.

"I told myself I could do things differently this time. I believed I could play my style of tennis on my own terms and just stay away from the rest of it."

"And you have," Sadie interjected, feeling almost triumphant on her behalf. "You're back."

"I was," Jay said. "I had clawed and crawled my way back to a place I could feel proud of, and I'd managed to do so without dragging anyone else into my drama. I was just to the point where I really thought I could trust myself again, and then . . ."

Sadie waited, the slow realization causing her stomach to sink. "And then I kissed you."

Jay nodded. "It's my fault. I got too close."

"No," Sadie said quickly. "I can't stand for you to blame yourself. Please, Jay, if I was the person who shook you off the foundation you worked so hard to build, I couldn't live with myself."

"Well, I couldn't stand to see you blame yourself, either," Jay said, turning to face her. "You are perfect to me, Sadie. You are beautiful and tenacious and kind, and I would rather die than put you through what I went through before."

Now it was Sadie's turn to nod numbly. None of this had ever occurred to her before. Not just Jay's past, but the implications for her future. She could never date again without causing a field day for the paparazzi. "I feel like I'm living on another planet. Normally I would just say forget everything and everyone. I do what I want. I have always gone with my gut, but it's not just about what I want, is it?"

Jay shook her head sadly. "And as reluctant as I am to go through the trauma again, it's not even about me, either. We have Destiny to think about. If anyone knew I had feelings for you, she'd have to face some very real consequences too."

"But you do have feelings for me?" Sadie asked, suddenly unable to focus on consequences.

"I do. I have from the moment I saw you standing on that tennis court in Indian Wells. You sparked things in me I never imagined I could feel after everything I've gone through."

"Indian Wells?" Sadie's heart tapped along her ribs as if they were a xylophone. "It took me till Charleston. Good Lord, that morning in your hotel room. I've never had such a hard time getting an image out of my mind as I did with you, in bed that morning."

Jay's smile grew so broad it crinkled the corners of her eyes once more. "And then you kissed me, and I shattered."

Sadie cupped Jay's face in her hands. "I never wanted to hurt you, and I hate that you've been hurt in the past."

"I know," Jay said, her voice low and raspy once more. "And I never meant to hurt you by pulling away. I only wanted to protect you from what I've seen."

"I have no desire to take you back there."

"And I don't know any way to go forward together."

Sadie tilted her head until their foreheads touched. "I don't do well with bending to other people's wills."

"No. But you are very good at taking care of Des, which means no one can know what happened."

"Yes," Sadie sighed, her lips so close to Jay's she could hardly stand it. "But does it mean it can't happen again?"

Jay closed her eyes and whispered, "I can't do it, Sadie. I can't risk what happened before. I can't live in shadows worrying and wondering and waiting for the other shoe to kick me in the teeth."

"No." Sadie sat back. "I don't suppose you can."

"The doubt would eat me alive."

"I understand, and I don't want that for you. I don't want you to ever doubt my feelings for you." She tried to say the right thing, because she wanted nothing more than to soothe Jay, but coming a close second to that primary desire was a pulsing need she desperately wanted to have filled, despite all her better impulses. Even knowing what she knew now about the risks, she couldn't shake the memory of Jay's mouth, hot and commanding, against her own.

She glanced around the hotel room, trying to ground herself by putting her focus anywhere but those alluring blue eyes. Finally, her gaze landed on a stack of papers. Entry forms, releases, contracts. Hopping up, she grabbed a pen from the desk and sifted through the paperwork until she found one she didn't need and began to scrawl across the back of it, reading aloud as she wrote. "I, Sadie Larsen, being of legal age and sound mind, willingly and gleefully affirm that I enjoy kissing Jay Pierce, and I would joyfully continue to do so, discreetly, as often and for as long as she would let me."

Then she signed and dated the document.

When she turned around, Jay was no longer sitting on the couch, but had risen to read over her shoulder. The heat of her body so close made Sadie a little dizzy with anticipation. With trembling fingers, she pressed the paper into Jay's hands. "I know it's not perfect, but I'm not a child. I am not Katia. I'm not going to hurt you. And that might not be enough to make you kiss me again, but I hope it at least helps ease some of your fears about the first time." Then in one final rush, she added, "Also, I hope you do want to kiss me again. There, I said it, and I'll repeat it every day if—"

The end of the confession died on Jay's lips as they pressed beautifully against her own.

Chapter Eight

"Jay, over here."

"Destiny, this way."

"Ladies, can I get a smile?"

The two of them bumped into each other multiple times as they turned different directions, trying to accommodate all the requests. Having a large silver cup suspended between them didn't make the posing any easier. Not that she was complaining, because without the cup they wouldn't be posing at all.

"Can you lift the trophy a little higher?" someone asked.

Jay turned to Destiny with a smile. "Lift with your knees, not your back."

Destiny laughed, and Jay's core warmed with the realization she had her mother's laugh. Not exactly the same, but close enough to remind Jay of the sound she loved most in the world.

What a difference a few days had made. She'd spent the first half of this tournament trying to avoid those thoughts, but now she reveled in them. Of course, the title of French Open Champion didn't hurt her spirits, but it didn't really compare to the high she got every time Sadie's lips caressed hers.

As discreetly as possible, she shot a sideways glance to where Sadie and Hank stood watching the whole show. Hank had his hands in the pockets of his khakis and his chest puffed out like a proud papa, while Sadie held her phone at a level that indicated she must be shooting video.

Her smiled widened. There were at least fifty cameras in the room, but she loved that Sadie couldn't resist getting her own shots to savor. And why shouldn't she? Winning a first major was a big deal. Hell, winning any major was a big deal, but somehow getting to experience the thrills with Destiny and Sadie allowed her to see it all again through new eyes.

As the shutter clicks slowed, they were led, once again, to the pressroom, and someone held the trophy while they took their seats.

"They'll give it back," Jay whispered. "Well, not really. That's the display trophy, but they'll give you one of your own."

Destiny grinned. "I'm going to sleep with it tonight."

"I'm going to eat Cheerios out of it tomorrow morning."

They both laughed as the press corps settled into their seats.

"You two seem to have found your stride as doubles partners," someone said. "Would you say that winning on court has helped your friendship off the court?"

"It doesn't hurt," Destiny said, causing everyone to laugh.

"Does the age difference cause any issues?"

"Not for me," Jay said quickly. "I mean, her eight o'clock bedtime is actually beneficial for someone of my advanced age."

"Today Adam Martin of the USTA listed you as the most exciting prospect for American tennis in years. How does that feel?"

Destiny and Jay exchanged a look as if asking which one wanted to take it, but Jay sat back, wanting to give Destiny the chance to shine on the big stage.

"It's a great compliment, of course, but there are plenty of fantastic junior players and"—she nodded to Jay—"veteran players still out there. I don't want to take away from what they're doing. Also, it's just a lot of pressure to put on us while we're celebrating a win here, guys."

"Beautiful," Jay muttered, catching Hank's eye. He nodded in approval, and Jay felt some of his pride working its way into her own chest. She'd been more to Des than a playing partner, and she liked that, more than she would've expected a few weeks ago.

"Do you feel like this is a part of your redemption story, Jay? Or perhaps penance for your youthful transgressions?" a woman in the back of the room asked. Everyone shifted uncomfortably in their seats, trying to see who'd asked the question without making it obvious they were trying to see.

Jay didn't need to guess. She recognized the voice from many a nightmare. "No, Haley. I see our win today as part of our French Open, but if you want to write it up some other way, I'm sure you won't hesitate to draw your own conclusions."

The woman stared her down, dark eyebrows rising almost to the line where black hair met her pale skin, but she didn't push the topic any further. Jay unclenched her jaw and used every ounce of fortitude she had left in her not to look at Sadie. She didn't want to give away any hint of the emotions stirring in her now. "Any other questions?"

"Next up, you move to grass court season," another reporter called out. "Have you decided which tournaments you'll play?"

She and Des exchanged another look before Des decided to field that land mine. "No, Terry, we're going to enjoy this win for a while before we announce our future plans."

"Announce your plans or make plans?" Terry prodded.

Jay smiled broadly. "Terry, did you ever get an *A* on a test when you were in school?"

"A time or two," he managed, over the laughter in the room.

"And tell me," Jay teased, "that night, did you sit in your room studying, or did you go out with your friends? Maybe have a drink and try and pick up a girl who would invariably turn you down?"

"All right, all right," Terry said.

"I notice you didn't answer the questions," Jay joked, "which is fine, because I'm not going to answer yours, either. This young woman next to me just won her first major. How about you just let her bask in the warm glow of your admiration for a moment?"

"Fair enough," Terry said, "and congratulations."

"Thank you," Jay and Des said in unison.

The rest of the conference went more smoothly as they rehashed their highlight reel from the tournament. Then they were whisked away to more sponsor meetings, a cocktail party, and a dinner filled with sponsors, sponsors, and more sponsors.

At one point, hours in, Jay looked down and wondered when she'd changed clothes. She knew she'd left the court in navy shorts and a red tank top, but now she wore gray slacks and a black blouse with subtle beadwork down the low-cut collar. She had forgotten she even owned that top, much less packed it. Had it really been so long since she'd needed to dress up that she'd forgotten what was in her wardrobe?

"What's funny?" a familiar voice asked.

Jay turned to gaze on Sadie in all her glory. Her sleeveless black dress dipped just to the top of her ample cleavage before covering everything below in a shimmery sort of midnight, before flaring out again at her waist and ending above her knees. The ensemble was both classy and classic, but the woman wearing it made the look nothing short of sexy.

"I don't remember," Jay finally said. "Something about my outfit, I think, but yours is so much better to focus on."

Sadie's smile turned shy. "I disagree. I didn't even know you owned a top like that."

"Well, if we're being honest, neither did I," Jay admitted. "Do you know when I put it on?"

"Sometime before the dinner. We got separated for a while there. What did they do to you guys?"

"It's all a blur, but it involved pictures, lots and lots of pictures. What did you do?"

"I shook so many hands, and my clutch"—she lifted a tiny black handbag—"is full of business cards. It's going to take weeks to field all the calls I promised to make."

"We'll get you a second cell phone."

"I might have two ears, but I'm not sure I can conduct two conversations at once."

Jay laughed. "One for business, one for personal use. It'll help you set some boundaries and guard your time."

"Oh, that's a good idea," Sadie said, but she looked more than a little overwhelmed as she used a now-empty wine glass to gesture around the room. "I'm in over my head here. I need all the good ideas you can give me."

"Well, I didn't want to tell a woman her business, but since you asked, I do have one more idea."

"Please share."

"Let's get out of here."

"Can we do that?" Sadie asked, eyes wide with hope.

"I just won the French Open. I can do what I want."

"Really?"

Jay shook her head. "No, but I saw a side exit. Let's make a break for it."

"What about Des and Hank?"

Jay scanned the room before she finally found Destiny talking to one of the men's doubles finalists with Hank standing right behind him, arms across his massive chest and a parental glint in his eyes. Jay's stomach clenched as the echo of a promise floated through her mind. She hadn't exactly lied. She'd sworn not to endanger Sadie's heart, and she still had no intention of doing so, but she suspected Destiny wouldn't appreciate the finer points of that argument. Maybe she needed to slow down, think things through. Then Sadie brushed her hand across the small of Jay's back, and the guilt faded, or maybe it just got overshadowed by something more powerful. "I think they're going to be fine."

"I'll send Des a text and say I don't want to spoil her fun, but I'm ready for bed."

"I'll wait a few minutes, then text Hank that I've got a headache, and I'm heading out too."

Sadie smiled weakly. "It's not a total lie. I am tired."

"And all those flashbulbs did strain my eyes," Jay said. "So, not a total lie on my end either."

Sadie nodded solemnly. "Is it so wrong to just want a few minutes with you?"

"Some people in this room would think so."

"Are you one of them?"

She shook her head. "No."

"Then, follow me."

★ ★ ★

She led Jay out of the ballroom and down an ornate staircase through an opulent lobby. A man in a bellboy cap swung wide a door and bade them good night, or at least that's what Sadie assumed, because she didn't speak much French.

"Shall I hail us a cab?" Jay stepped onto the sidewalk, still bathed in golden light, eyes dancing with mirth and mischief. Sadie had the urge to simultaneously freeze the image of her and hold it forever, and the desire to drag her home as quickly as possible. She chose a middle path.

"It's only a few blocks to our hotel. Would you mind walking with me?"

"I'd love to."

Jay's acceptance put Sadie at ease as they started off through the streets of Paris, walking in amiable silence. She could hardly believe this was her life, such a long way from Buffalo, with her financial worries at an even greater distance. Not that other worries hadn't taken their place, but even they seemed duller and dimmer than the amber outline of the Eiffel Tower against the distant, darkened horizon.

"What are you thinking?" Jay asked softly, as if almost reluctant to interrupt her musings.

"I just can't believe any of this is real."

Jay didn't ask any more questions, and Sadie stole a sideways glance as they strolled along. She wore a similar mask of reflection across her beautiful features.

"You've been here before, haven't you?"

"Not exactly here," Jay said, "or maybe I wasn't exactly who I am now the last time I was here. It doesn't feel like that was me, anyway. Does that make sense?"

"Yes," Sadie said thoughtfully, flashing back to so many moments, like a movie of her life. That's what they felt like now, a movie, one she loved, one that still pulled at her heart, but not quite real life. Is this what she'd known that day in the hospital with Tad? When she'd been unable to explain to him the intuition

160

that had arrived with Destiny? Or maybe she'd always had it, but she hadn't needed to use it until then.

"Once upon a time," Sadie started, then laughed, "a boy asked me to marry him."

Jay made a strangled little sound that made Sadie's mouth twitch up just a little.

"I told him no, but I couldn't tell him why. I didn't even know why. I, *we*, were just kids, and everyone wanted us to do the conventional thing, the right thing by everyone's standards."

"Everyone but yours."

"I just knew something I couldn't even imagine—" She stopped and bit her lip, realizing she probably sounded insane, or at the very least silly. But then Jay's fingers brushed tenderly against hers, and the words spilled out again. "I just had this moment right now, with you beside me, where I thought, maybe this is it. Maybe this is what I knew was out here for me. Maybe this was the why."

Jay slowed to a stop. "That might be the most beautiful thing I've ever heard in my life."

"Really?" Sadie's face grew warm. "You're not just saying that to make me feel better about my life choices?"

Jay laughed. "No, that was the most beautiful thought coming from the most beautiful woman."

"Now I know you're teasing," Sadie said quickly. "You've known so many women."

Jay's jaw tightened. "I suppose I deserve that kind of doubt. I've certainly earned it."

"No." Sadie rushed to correct herself. "I didn't mean it that way. I didn't mean to hurt you. I just, I don't know. It's been so long since I've let myself just be complimented, since I've let myself relax and enjoy something purely mine. It's hard to believe I've arrived here, on the banks of the Seine, with someone so gorgeous looking at me the way you do, like maybe you could be mine."

"I can be," Jay said, her voice low. "I am, if you want."

Sadie stepped closer, her own voice trembling now. "I do want. Very much."

★ ★ ★

Jay cupped Sadie's face in her hands before the door slammed shut behind them. Taking a second to imprint the image in her mind, she allowed her gaze to travel from the smooth skin of Sadie's forehead over her perfectly arched eyebrows to her deliciously deep eyes. She made it as far down as her satin lips before she lost the ability to focus for the desire to have them pressed against her own. Closing her eyes, she allowed her other senses to guide her as they collided.

Running her tongue along the place where their lips met, she reveled in the subtle surrender as Sadie opened to her. Her mouth was a refuge from everything that had haunted Jay for years. When they kissed, all the regret and insecurity of the past were swallowed whole. Sadie clasped her hips, pulling them together so tightly, all the work and worry of the day were crushed to dust. Perfection only existed in the spaces between them now.

They had kissed like this in every stolen moment all week, and yet none of those kisses had yet carried the heady sense of urgency around them tonight. Something had shifted in Sadie on the walk home. Jay had been with enough women to recognize the certainty as it settled across stunning features, but she'd never been so moved by any declaration as she had been when Sadie spoke of knowing something like what they shared had been waiting for them. She felt as if her heart might break at the beauty and the bravery of the sentiment. Now, with an equally beautiful body pressed tightly against her, she felt as if nothing could ever break again.

Running her hands along the sides of Sadie's dress, she skimmed her fingers over satiny seams, suspecting their smoothness couldn't rival the skin beneath. Pulling her lips slowly from Sadie's, she slid the kiss across her cheek and up to her earlobe. Tugging and nibbling around the single diamond stud, she threaded her fingers through thick, dark curls.

"Sadie," Jay whispered, as she swept the curls aside.

Sadie tilted her head, exposing the graceful curve of her neck for adoration. Jay obliged the unspoken request and kissed her way downward once more until she reached the place where dress and shoulder met. Then turning Sadie slowly, she kissed along the silky neckline to the zipper running the length of her back.

"May I?" she asked quietly.

"Please," Sadie said between the rise and fall of shallow breath.

Jay lowered the zipper slowly as Sadie reached one skillful hand up behind her. She slipped her fingers into Jay's hair and urged her back to the spot where the dress had clasped. Wrapping her arms loosely around Sadie's waist, Jay pulled her close, back to chest, and kissed her neck and shoulders.

"You smell so good. I just want to breathe you in," Jay whispered, as she inhaled the subtle scent of tangerines.

"I want . . ." Sadie's voice caught, and she turned in Jay's embrace. "I want . . ."

Jay nodded, afraid she wouldn't be able to find the words for what Sadie had only hinted at with her simple statement.

Sadie kissed her again, then, pulling back, said, "I want all of you."

"Yes." Jay gently eased the straps of Sadie's dress off her shoulders and watched in awe as it fluttered to the floor, revealing more beauty than Jay had even imagined, soft curves and smooth planes. Hints of black lace hugged full hips and breasts that made Jay's vision swim. "Wow."

Sadie's thick eyelashes fluttered as she glanced down shyly, but Jay caught her chin softly and lifted. "You are the most gorgeous thing I have ever seen."

Sadie tried to shake her head, but Jay held it still and kissed her again. This time Jay allowed her hands to wander across the soft expanse of Sadie's body from curve to swell and back again, hoping to stroke away every unwarranted insecurity as she went. Then as Sadie relaxed into her once again, she urged her slowly backward across the room to the bed, stopping only when Sadie's legs bumped against the mattress. Breaking the kiss, she asked, "Are you sure you want this?"

"Yes," Sadie said in a rush of delayed breath.

"Tell me," Jay said, but even she could hear the words pulsing with need.

"I want you," Sadie said, running her hands up Jay's side, pushing her shirt up and over her head as she went. "I want to feel you all over me. I want to be all over you."

Jay unclasped Sadie's bra with trembling fingers and watched it join the dress on the floor. Then she followed them both by peeling lace over the magical curve of Sadie's hips. Her breath grew so quick at the unencumbered perfection before her, she worried fleetingly that she might pass out. Then she laughed softly.

"What is it?"

"I stood on one of the most hallowed courts in the world today, before thousands of people, and I maintained professional-grade command, but the sight of you so perfect and close has turned every joint in my body to marshmallows."

Sadie's smile dazzled her, only amplifying the effects she'd just put into words. "Then we'd better lie down."

She eased back onto the bed, grabbing hold of Jay's hips and pulling her along.

Once horizontal, some of the blood returned to Jay's brain, or maybe her baser instincts took over as she kissed her way along the rise of firm breasts, running her lips in slow spirals. Sadie arched up off the bed, urging Jay forward until she captured a taut nipple in her mouth.

Sadie released a groan and sank back into the bed, clutching Jay's head in her hands to hold her steady.

Jay lifted the other breast in her palm before kissing her way down along Sadie's ribs and over her stomach. She had the brief realization that she might be rushing, but it had been so long, she didn't trust restraint. Something primal churned at her core, and she needed, more than wanted, to be inside Sadie, to possess her, to fill her in the way she'd taken over every corner of Jay's mind and body.

Easing between the legs Sadie opened for her, she glanced up once again to see dark eyes, nearly all pupil now, encompassing her entirely, and yet only her.

"Please." Jay practically gasped the request.

"Yes," Sadie managed, between heavy breaths that caused her breasts to rise tantalizingly, but Jay couldn't be distracted from the promise before her. Dipping her head, she used her tongue to part delicate folds and run the length of her desire.

Sadie's hips rocked up with each pass as she reached out, near frantic to take hold of whatever parts of Jay she could reach—shoulder, arm, hair—trying to hold her ever closer.

Sensing the urgency mounting between them, Jay wasted no time pushing inside, as she circled her tongue in ever more focused patterns.

"God. Jay. Please. Yes." The words ran together, both incoherent and utterly complete, as Sadie's thighs tightened around her.

She relished every uneven thrust, every ridge of muscle and nerve tightening around her, every cue from Sadie's body urging her forward.

Using the flat of her tongue now and drowning in Sadie's need as it mingled with her own, Jay rode the writhing rhythm of her hips. As Sadie's breath grew erratic, Jay warred between the intrinsic drive toward satisfaction and the clutching compulsion to prolong. She didn't want to leave this moment and the thrilling sense of wholeness it inspired in her.

And yet, as Sadie pushed her both emotionally and physically deeper, she couldn't imagine giving her anything less than everything.

"Please," Sadie called again, her voice high and thin as Jay pulled back then slid forward again, nearly delirious with the friction between them.

She answered the request with her final reserve of energy, and Sadie went rigid beneath her. Muscles constricted and shook. Her own breath caught tightly in her throat at the flawlessness of it all. Sadie twisted around her, breath and fists caught in a tangled knot of body and emotion.

They rode out the waves of release together, slowing but refusing to subside completely until Sadie went lax, her thighs sinking to the sheets and her fingernails slipping from their grip on Jay's shoulder.

Jay kissed her way back up the glorious length of Sadie's body and fell as gracefully as she could to the pillow beside her.

"It has never been like this before." Sadie's voice was filled with a wonder that made Jay's heart flutter. "I always hoped, but I didn't know."

Jay rolled onto her side to face Sadie as she did the same.

"No, that's not true." Sadie corrected herself. "I didn't let myself hope. I think if I had, I would have gone crazy trying to find you sooner."

"I wish you had," Jay said dreamily. "You could've saved me years of doubt and deprivation."

"I don't know what's worse. Having been with a woman and knowing what you were missing, or never having had the chance to find out in the first place."

"Hmm." Jay didn't really have the energy or focus for such heavy questions or in-depth responses. "Yeah. I don't—wait, did you say never?"

"Yes."

She sat up. "As in, never never?"

Sadie laughed. "Is there another kind of never?"

Jay's heartbeat pounded for a very different reason than it had before. "Did I just take your virginity?"

"Whoa." Sadie sat up, too. "First of all, you didn't take anything I didn't give. Second of all, I have a seventeen-year-old daughter, so I think the virginity ship sailed a long time ago."

Jay frowned. "But, you said *never*."

Sadie leaned forward to kiss her, and for a moment every other thought faded from Jay's mind, but when she pulled back, she said, "You're just the first *woman* I've ever slept with."

"Oh, okay." Jay made her very best attempt at not outwardly freaking, but she must have done a poor job.

Sadie cupped her face in her hands. "Hey there, Champ. Stay with me."

She wondered if the wild fear glinted in her eyes, or if the sheen of cold sweat could be seen on her forehead. Or maybe all the blood had left her face, making the tan she'd started to get appear pallid and jaundiced? "So, you weren't really a lesbian until I came on to you. Or . . . or . . . um maybe you're not really a lesbian at all . . . maybe you identify as bisexual, or just curious, or maybe you didn't really want—"

Sadie silenced her babbling with another kiss. Jay wished she'd stop doing that so Jay could think more clearly, and then again she wished she'd never stop doing that, because with those amazing lips against hers, she felt certain thinking was highly overrated.

When she pulled back once more, Jay opened her mouth, but Sadie pressed her index finger to her lips. "I am a lesbian. I started to suspect I was a lesbian when I was fifteen."

Jay cocked her head to the side as she pondered that math.

"Then Tad came along—and listen closely, because I don't ever want to talk about him in bed again—but he was kind, and he was fundamentally good."

"Was?" Jay managed to get out.

"Is," Sadie amended. "He's an exceptional human and a loving, hardworking father, and there was a time when he looked at me like I was the most wonderful thing in the world."

Jay's stomach tightened. She knew the feeling and felt torn between jealousy that Sadie had seen the emotion in someone else, and gratitude that Destiny's father had at least given her the care she deserved.

"And when he made love to me for the first time, I felt loved and desired, but I couldn't return any of those feelings for him. I remember looking at him, watching his face change and his gaze intensify, and I could tell how much it meant to him, how much the physical melded with the emotional to make something bigger than I could even comprehend."

"You didn't feel anything for him?"

"I felt a general sort of affection, and until that moment I thought that could be enough, but the contrast between the magnitude of what he seemed to be experiencing and the mundanity of my own feelings made me realize something wasn't right." She smiled, then added, "And if I couldn't feel something for Tad, the odds of me feeling something for any other guys were slim."

"Okay," Jay managed, her heart rate decelerating to something below a constant thrum. "But you had Destiny seventeen years ago. And still you used the word *never*."

"Well, you might find this hard to believe," Sadie said, her smile seeming more tired than before. "But good-quality, single women don't generally hit on teenage mothers who are attending nighttime GED classes. And they don't hang out at children's dance classes, and they don't generally attend PTA nights. That was my life for ten years."

"Fair enough," Jay conceded once again, marveling at how different their lives had been. While she was running through supermodels, Sadie had been running errands for an active elementary school kid. Had she felt as lonely then as Jay had?

"By the time Des got into tennis and we actually got to know a wider circle of people, I didn't want to get involved with anyone. We were a team, me and her. We'd spent years defying the odds and battling expectations. I didn't want anyone to mess with that dynamic and, once again, sex and love had never meant to me what they did to other people. Maybe if I'd known then what I learned tonight, I would've felt differently."

Jay's heart rate kicked up a notch again, and she suspected falling for Sadie did more for her cardiovascular health than any interval workout she'd ever done. "So, I guess I'm sorry."

"For?" Sadie prodded playfully as she trailed her fingers up Jay's bare arm.

"For letting my fears of the past get in the way of seeing you clearly."

"And?"

"And for underestimating your ability to know your own mind."

"Oh, that's a good one."

"And for not realizing it was your first time, and maybe making it . . . I don't know . . . more special."

"Well, yes, I can see where making love with a beautiful, funny, professional athlete with the lights from the Eiffel Tower illuminating the windows of my four-star hotel room might feel like a letdown."

Jay snorted. "You're teasing me now."

"I am, because you're being silly. If that had been any more special, I might have spontaneously combusted and left you in bed with a pile of ashes."

"Well, in that case, I'm glad I stopped when I did." She flopped back onto the bed. "I just have some baggage, you know."

"I do." Sadie lay down beside her more gracefully.

"I need to know that you'll be open and honest about what you want, and what you don't want. No matter what."

"I can do that." Sadie scooted close enough to rest her head on Jay's shoulder. "But I have to warn you, now that I know what I've been missing all these years, I'm going to want to make up for a lot of lost time."

Warmth began to burn at her core. "Makes total sense."

"For instance, right now, I want to get on top of you so I can feel as much of you against as much of me as possible. Then I want to kiss you all over, until I memorize your taste and your scent, and learn which spots drive you crazy."

"I have a feeling that might be all the spots," Jay murmured, her nerve endings alight as Sadie traced her fingers lazily down her chest.

"And then I want you to teach me how to do what you did to me with your mouth." Sadie lowered her head to flick her tongue across one hard nipple. "Does that work for you?"

"Yeah," Jay managed to squeak before clearing her throat. "I think we can manage that."

Chapter Nine

Mallorca, Spain

"We should get up," Sadie said, as she slipped her hand between Jay's legs.

Jay rocked her firm ass off the bed to meet the stroke. "We really should. Someone's bound to come looking soon."

"I know you don't want anyone to know about us yet." Sadie coated her fingers with the wetness she thrilled at inspiring. "But at this point I wouldn't stop if the pope walked through the door."

"And I love that, but I want to protect you."

"That turns me on," Sadie whispered in her ear, then sucked the lobe between her teeth.

"Everything turns you on," Jay said, more in wonder than teasing.

"Everything about *you*." Sadie threw a leg over one of Jay's, relishing the way the hard muscles flexed and rippled beneath her. The muscles turned her on. So did the way Jay's eyes flashed open so breathtakingly blue even before they'd lost the sheen of sleep. Mostly though, she got turned on by the way Jay responded to her every touch as if she held some magic in the tips of her fingers.

Jay's head pressed hard into the pillow as her hips rocked up, seeking firmer contact. Sadie might have been tempted to make her wait, but they really didn't have a ton of time, and Jay had both a singles and doubles practice later in the day, so she decided to show a little mercy and tighten her circles where they'd do the most good.

Jay groaned and closed her eyes, her lips parting slightly to allow for her increasingly heavy breath. The sight reminded Sadie that her gift of a quick release wasn't a completely selfless act. The thing she'd come to crave most over the last week was the way Jay surrendered completely under her touch.

"Yes," Jay mumbled. "Sade, I'm so close."

Sadie smiled as Jay's smooth brow wrinkled in concentration as she poured every bit of her attention into the mounting pressure inside her. Sadie knew the feeling. It had knotted her insides in the most excruciatingly pleasurable way so many times, she could hardly imagine how she'd lived so long without the sensation. She craved the connection so fiercely now, it sometimes scared her. Yesterday she'd had the urge to pull Jay right from the court and push inside her. The thought made her own breath catch, and she slid her fingers low enough to work two of them inside while keeping her thumb where Jay needed it most.

Jay's entire body grew taut from the added stimulation, and Sadie's vision tinged white around the edges as anticipation clutched her chest. They raced toward release with steady pressure, and she gasped when Jay arched off the bed, one strangled cry escaping her lips before she crashed back down. Her muscles contracted around Sadie, holding her in place until every shudder had passed, and Jay went limp against the stark, white sheets.

Doing her best to memorize the feeling in hopes it would hold her over at least until that night, Sadie withdrew and lay down beside her.

"Well, that's an awesome way to wake up," Jay said with a contented sigh.

"I love the way you go from asleep to orgasm in under five minutes."

"I don't do it on my own."

Sadie smiled. "I'm happy to help."

Jay rolled onto her side and pushed a strand of curls from

171

Sadie's face. "You know the feeling is mutual, and I'd love nothing more than to repay the favor."

"I do." Sadie kissed her just long enough to keep from losing focus again. "But we really do need to go."

"And, by we, you mean me."

"I'm not the one who wants to hide our relationship."

Jay's smile tightened. "I know, and I appreciate that, really more than you can imagine. And for the record I don't want to hide us either, but if we tell Des and Hank, it puts them in a terrible position of lying to the press or, worse, defending us to the press."

"I understand," Sadie said, and she did. As much as she wanted the whole world to know she was sleeping with Jay on a regular basis, that impulse was selfish. A revelation of that magnitude, three weeks before Wimbledon, would put everything at risk, right when everything was going exceedingly well. "Which is why you've got to go."

Jay looked past her at the clock on the bedside table. "Oh, shit. It's after seven."

"I told Des to come down at eight."

"Right. Des, your daughter." Jay tossed back the sheet. "And Des, my doubles partner."

"Yes, we've met."

Jay snorted as she pulled her jeans from the floor. "I don't want to meet under these particular circumstances."

Sadie smiled at her bare back, visually tracing the line up her spine to the place where white skin met the tan neckline both she and the sun kissed frequently. "No, I admit. When the time comes for her to find out, I want all of us to be fully dressed."

"And in neutral territory," Jay added. She stood and zipped up her pants. "Rather than your bed."

"Hmm, I do so like you in my bed, but I agree it's not the place for a discussion with my daughter."

Jay gave a little shudder as she walked around the bed, eyes fixed on the floor. "Have you seen my sports bra?"

"On the desk." Sadie giggled. "Remember you had me up there for a while last night?"

"How could I forget?" She extracted the bra from a disheveled pile of paperwork. "Sorry about your travel vouchers."

"Totally worth the extra work. I think I'll try to get those done today, though, in case we want a repeat performance tonight."

Jay found her shirt on the dresser and pulled it over her head before turning back to smile at her. "I like the sound of that, but I'll see you before then, right?"

"I'm not going down to singles practice today, but I'll meet you before the photo shoot on the beach."

"Oh yeah, it's advertising day. What are we selling again?"

"Double Dutch chewing gum."

"Right," Jay said, then laughed. "I'm glad we just have to play some beach tennis and say our lines. 'Double the flavor, double the power' is a much better slogan than I would have written for them if I'd had to do the concept work, too."

"Dare I even ask what catch phrase you would have chosen?"

"Probably something along the lines of, 'smells like an air freshener, and tastes like one too.'"

Sadie shook her head.

"Or maybe 'try one piece and give the other one to your worst enemy.'"

Sadie threw a pillow at her. "Come on, it's not that bad."

Jay walked back over to the bed. "No, I'm only teasing because I know it's Destiny's first big ad campaign."

"It's my first one, too, you know."

Jay kissed her atop the head. "I do, and you did a great job, for her and for me. I promise to show my gratitude as soon as we get back here tonight."

She hummed contentedly. "Promises, promises. Any idea what time that might be?"

Jay frowned. "I thought you had a handle on all the schedules."

"You've got practice, then the shoot at eleven. Then doubles practice at four, followed by dinner with some kids from Nadal's academy."

"Want to come with me? You know, in a purely business sense."

"We've got a pretty good cover to travel together, but if I show up to things Des isn't invited to, we'll probably raise eyebrows." She hated the flash of sadness in Jay's eyes, so she rushed forward to finish the statement on a high note. "Besides, you love working with the kids, and they deserve your full attention."

"I see your point." Jay eased down onto the side of the bed. "If you're there, I won't be able to look at anyone else."

"And that's why you've got to go." Sadie shoved her away for fear if she didn't, they'd both end up back under the sheets.

"Okay, okay," Jay said, heading for the door, but just as she reached it she turned and said, "I love—" Her face flamed red, and she quickly finished, "waking up with you."

Sadie's breath hitched, and she nodded mutely several times before managing to say, "Me too."

As soon as the door clicked quietly closed behind Jay, she fell back to the bed, resting her hand above her beating heart. For a second, she'd been sure Jay had intended to drop the L-word on her, and she had—in a way. And yet not in *the* way she'd . . . what? Feared? Hoped? Reciprocated?

She sighed exasperatedly and got out of bed. Why couldn't she just relax? She was having the best time of her entire life. Why did she always have to worry about where they were headed or what would happen next, or what would happen in response to whatever happened next?

She snatched her oversized nightshirt off the floor and slipped it on before drawing back the curtain to her room. Sliding back a glass door, she stepped onto her balcony and stared out over the glittering Mediterranean horizon. She was in one of the most beautiful places she'd ever seen. She had a gorgeous, kind woman in her bed every night. Her daughter was happy and successful. Money was no longer a pressing issue for the foreseeable future. It didn't really matter what anyone else knew or thought. She had everything she could reasonably dream of, and then some. The few wishes she had left outstanding would come in time. Or they wouldn't, and that would be okay, too. Sure, she would like to hear Jay say the word to her, maybe even in front of the other most important people in their lives, but for now she knew what she felt, and that was good enough.

"Por favor, Miss Pierce. *Por favor. Peeese I can have you signat . . . signa . . . sign the ball?"*

Jay glanced apologetically at Sadie. "I'm sorry, but how can I pass up a request like that?"

"If you did, I would think less of you," Sadie admitted.

Jay fought down the urge to kiss her on the cheek before she jogged off toward the little girl holding an oversized tennis ball against the railing to the players-only entrance. She had dark hair and fair skin. When she grinned, Jay noticed two missing teeth right up front, making her even more adorable than she would've been with them.

"Hola," Jay said, taking a marker from the child's tightly squeezed fingers. "What's your name?"

A man standing beside her leaned down to whisper in her ear.

"Maite," the little girl said excitedly.

"Nice to meet you, Maite," Jay said, as she scribbled her name across the fluffy yellow ball.

"Thank you," the little girl blurted out, as if the phrase had taken a great deal of effort.

"She's still learning the English," the man explained.

"Your daughter?"

He nodded. "She just started playing tennis. I wanted her to see you and Ms. Larsen play, to give her something to aspire to."

Jay's face warmed even more than the sun overhead warranted. She'd been so focused on winning their semifinal match that she hadn't given much thought to the crowd, beyond noticing it was bigger than usual. "I hope we lived up to that tall order."

"You did," he said seriously. "I think she fell in love with both of you today."

Jay looked at the little girl again, her eyes watering slightly. "I'm glad."

"Thank you," he said again, before nudging the girl off down the line.

Jay shouldered her bag once more and headed for the car Hank had already secured to take them back to the hotel.

They rode the short way in silence, the little girl's dark eyes still in the forefront of her mind, but as soon as they hopped out, a young man rushed up to them.

"Hi, Ms. Pierce. I'm Billy Thomas. I work for an English language paper here on the island. Sorry to bother you, but could I get a quick quote?" He was young and lanky in a dress shirt and khakis, but his tie was askew, his face flushed. The disheveled qualities endeared him to her more than any amount of professionalism could have.

"I've got an event to get ready for, but if you work fast, I might be able to come up with something brilliant."

"I'm doing a piece on you and Destiny Larsen as a multigenerational team."

She fought an eye roll. The story angle wasn't exactly original, but people had kept coming back to it over the last month, so it must sell papers. She tried not to look too deeply into the implied surprise that Destiny would play with someone so much older, or that her value on the court came mostly in the form of her past experience.

"Do you see yourself as a sort of bridge to the next generation of women's tennis players?"

Jay pictured the little girl with the missing teeth, and her scrawny arms that barely reached around her souvenir. "No. Not in the way you mean. Not with Des. She's not what's next. She's a big part of what's now. She's here. She's thriving, and I'm happy to be part of that present with her."

"I notice you said, 'not with Des.' Does that mean maybe you do see yourself in that role of mentor or torchbearer in other circumstances?"

She shifted from one foot to the other. She had a standard answer to the question and all the pressure it implied. She generally said she could barely decide what to wear most mornings.

How was she supposed to think about sending messages to tennis stars of the future? It's what she'd told reporters for years, ever since the press and Katia had worked so hard to paint her as a terrible role model and she'd decided she didn't want to be a role model at all.

"Um, yeah, I guess so," she started haltingly. "I love the game of tennis, and I want girls to grow up knowing that, on the court, they can be judged for what they do between the lines, for their skills and their drive, not their age or race or the language they speak."

"Or who they love?" the man asked sympathetically.

Jay stiffened slightly, then forced herself to exhale. "Yeah. That too."

"Thank you," he said, with so much sincerity she suspected someone somewhere had judged Billy for who he loved.

The remaining tension slipped from her shoulders. "You're welcome."

As they got into the elevator, Hank gave her shoulder a little squeeze. "Well done."

Sadie nodded in silent agreement, and Jay quickly changed the subject in order to hold her emotions at bay. "So, Destiny's having dinner with Viktor again? Is that a thing now?"

"No. Not a thing," Sadie said lightly. "He came by to do an event at Nadal's academy."

"I thought Nadal's place was on the other side of the island."

"It is," Hank said flatly.

"Isn't this the fourth time they've gone out in two weeks?"

"The fifth," Hank practically growled.

Jay laughed. "Yeah, totally not a thing."

They both gave her a glare that said they'd forgotten about her emotional interview, and she grinned contentedly until the elevator dinged on Hank's floor.

"Dinner in or out tonight?" he asked.

"In." They said in unison, and perhaps a bit too emphatically.

He raised his eyebrows, but the door closed, saving them from having to make their usual excuses. Jay turned to Sadie, intending to make a joke, but no sooner had she opened her mouth than their lips were pressed together. They kissed feverishly, bouncing off the elevator like a pinball as they clutched and swayed around each other.

Jay couldn't breathe and she didn't care. God, this woman set her on fire, and she wanted nothing more than to burn for her. Running her fingers through dark locks, she tugged hard enough to pull Sadie's head back, exposing her throat. She kissed along the curve and down across her shoulder before the elevator pinged again. They jumped guiltily apart as the door slid open, then giggled like schoolgirls as they surveyed the empty hallway.

"I know people always say to take the stairs because it's good for heart health, but I'm pretty sure none of them have ever taken an elevator with someone like you."

Sadie shook her head. "I've never been someone like the woman I am with you. It's not fair, really."

"Not fair?" Jay put the keycard into her door.

"You're this together, professional athlete who wins tennis matches like most people fold laundry."

"Most matches aren't as easy as the one we played today."

"And you make little girls stare at you with stars in their eyes."

"She's, what, like, seven? She doesn't know good tennis yet."

"She knows good people, and you were very good with her. You're good with everyone, really. Kids, the press, you even won over Destiny. You have a gift."

Jay's chest ached, and she tamped down the urge to run. "You want to order some paella? Maybe some sangria from room service? We could eat on the balcony tonight."

"Sounds lovely, but don't think I don't realize you changed the subject."

Jay didn't respond. Instead she picked up the room phone and dialed down to the hotel restaurant. She took her time placing her order while she watched Sadie kick off her shoes and unfasten her earrings. She was stunning in so many situations, but Jay preferred these moments over all the others. Her life had been so complicated, so fraught and lonely for so long. The simplicity of watching a beautiful woman unwind after a busy day satisfied a longing she hadn't acknowledged for years. Then again, once she opened the door to one kind of fulfillment, she worried her heart might try to assert itself more fully in other areas as well.

"Please charge it to my room," Jay said, as Sadie came up behind her and wrapped her arms around her waist. "*Gracias.*"

"You're welcome," Sadie murmured, as Jay dropped the phone back onto its cradle.

Jay turned in the circle of her arms, and Sadie snuggled closer. Jay breathed in the now familiar scent of tangerine and talc that always encircled Sadie, even after a full day of sitting in the hot sun.

"It's okay, you know?" Sadie said, resting her cheek on Jay's chest.

"What is?"

"Being nervous about the attention you're getting."

"I'm not nervous."

Sadie squeezed tighter. "I used to think you dodged questions in the press conferences because they annoyed you, or because they were dumb, or because you didn't want to have to explain your bad play on any given point."

"All of the above," Jay said, not sure she liked where this was going.

"Then when I found out about Katia, I realized you were also protecting yourself from people who had hurt you before, and that made sense, too."

"Um, good?" Jay said, feeling certain there was a but on the end of that sentence.

"Lately, though, I've noticed you also dodge a lot of people who want to adore you."

"I let you adore me."

Sadie chuckled. "And I appreciate that greatly, but other people want to be close to you, too."

"Are you saying you want me to date other people?"

Sadie pushed her away. "Only if you want me to cut a bitch."

"Whoa." Jay raised her hands. "I'm kidding."

"I know," Sadie said with a smile.

"And you're kidding, too?"

Sadie pursed her lips. "Not really."

"Okay, cutting a bitch is a great relationship policy."

"You're doing it again." Sadie sounded exasperated now. "People want to know you. They like you. They look up to you. There's nothing wrong with embracing their goodwill. You're asking people to give your career a second chance. Maybe you should think about giving the public a second chance, too. You don't have to panic every time a kid asks for an autograph anymore."

Tears stung her eyes again. Sadie saw her, and saw through her. The realization both comforted and terrified her.

"Hey." Sadie ran the back of her fingers down Jay's cheek. "It's okay. It's not going to happen overnight, but your strength, your love, your kindness make you special. I don't think you should shy away from letting other people see that specialness, too."

She kissed her again, this time more slowly, soaking up the intimacy between them in the way that not only curled her toes, but also wrapped around her heart. Sadie cared about her. She thought she was good and beautiful and strong. She didn't dare let herself believe that might last forever, but knowing it now, in this moment, was enough.

Sadie held a shrimp on the end of her fork, just out of the reach of Jay's mouth. "Say it again."

"*Camarónes*," Jay repeated, her voice carrying a low, seductive timbre.

"I didn't know you spoke Spanish."

"I don't," Jay said, surging forward and snatching the shrimp with her perfect teeth. "But when I was younger, I decided to make sure I learned a few words in the languages of each of the countries I visited on tour."

Sadie laughed. "And you thought, of all the words in the Spanish language, 'shrimp' was one of the most important ones."

"Yeah. 'Hello, thank you, bathroom, and shrimp.' You'd be surprised how many times those have covered all my most pressing needs in Spain."

Sadie felt so light and free, she might have worried about drifting away into the endless blue sky if not for the equally azure eyes holding her right where she wanted to be. Staring out over the balcony railing to where the coral sun dipped into the Mediterranean Sea, she said, "This is my first trip to Mallorca, but if it's always like this, I think I'll want to come back often."

"It's never been like this before," Jay said almost wistfully. "I see the world differently with you. I was alone so long I got locked up in myself. I always felt alone, even in public with Katia because she was so guarded. On the court she was all business, and I'd always loved her intensity, but it never quite included me. Then, at our events or clubs or restaurants, she worked hard to appear neutral, or maybe what I'd read as self-protection was honestly neutrality toward me. I don't think I'll ever know."

Sadie reached across the tiny wrought-iron patio table and ran her fingers through Jay's thick, sandy locks. "I'm not neutral toward you. If it were up to me, I would stand up on this balcony railing and shout to all of Mallorca how proud I am of you."

Jay smiled sweetly, but not exuberantly. "For now, it's enough that I get to celebrate a win with you. I know you're in our player's box for Des, but I love being able to make eye contact after a good point, or see your smile even when I miss a shot. It's like I know that no matter what the score, I'm going to be in bed with you that night, and that's really all the win I need."

Sadie's heart filled to capacity and pressed on her ribs as if trying to grow enough to accommodate all the emotions Jay inspired. No one had said anything so unabashedly sweet to her in, perhaps, ever. She wanted to give it all back and then some. "I love being there for you at the matches, and I love being able to stand in the back of your press conferences with Des. And with Des having more sponsor events, and tour clinics, and people bending her ear in different directions, it's been nice to hover in the background just watching you two do your thing."

"Her having her own room these days has been helpful too,"

Jay admitted, "but as much as I love having you on the road with us, I don't want you in the background. Every day, even today when I'd won a tournament, I started counting down the hours until it would be just the two of us. The whole time the organizers were taking pictures and giving speeches, I was thinking of things I wanted to talk to you about."

"Like what?"

"Like, I know Des trained in Buffalo, but did you grow up there? What do your parents do? Any siblings? What jobs did you work before she went out on tour? Do you like cats or dogs? I want to know everything about you, not just as a tennis mom, but as a whole person."

Sadie's face flushed. She'd been just a tennis mom for so long, she barely remembered what it felt like to be a whole person, much less share those parts of herself with someone else. Jay had gone a long way toward opening up new parts of her sense of self, but it still baffled her that anyone would care about her past or interests, much less someone as wonderful as Jay.

She scooped up another bite of rice and shrimp *al ajillo* while she let the questions sink in.

"Well, I did grow up in Buffalo with a pretty close family. I'm named after my mother's mother. One older brother, Ty, still lives in the area. My parents are a lot older now. They can't travel much, but my mom was a special education teacher and my dad is a retired American Baptist preacher."

Jay's eyes went wide. "A Baptist preacher?"

"Indeed." Sadie laughed. "I was a walking stereotype at seventeen. Preacher's daughter, unwed pregnant teen. I know it sounds awful, like some after-school special, but it really wasn't. My parents are the kindest, most loving people. Not a judgmental bone in their bodies. I know they worried a lot about me. I think they wanted better for me than the choices I made early on, but I never doubted they loved me, and they adored Des from day one. I think that's why I never worried about staying a stereotype, no matter what people on the outside assumed about me. They instilled so much hope and drive in me."

"And strength," Jay added, taking Sadie's hand in her calloused palm and bringing it to her lips. "You are the strongest woman I've ever known."

She rolled her eyes playfully. "What I went through is nothing compared to what you've faced. Sure, people said and believed hurtful things about me, but I always had love and support, and I've never once thought of Destiny as a mistake. You had to face the doubts and venom of strangers and friends and lovers along with your own insecurities about the path you took. I would take a string of dead-end jobs and night school classes over trial by the press any day."

Jay didn't argue. Instead, she raised her glass of sangria. "And yet here we both are. So, to us."

Sadie clinked her glass against Jay's. "To us, and to a glorious night alone in a beautiful place with a bea—"

A knock sounded on the door.

Both of them froze, Sadie's heart beating so loudly she could barely hear her own voice as she called, "Who is it?"

"Your favorite daughter," Des called.

Panic registered on Jay's face, causing an ache to settle in Sadie's chest. Taking a deep breath, she said, "It's okay. We're not doing anything wrong. Pull out your phone."

"Coming." On her way to the door, she picked up a stack of receipts and travel vouchers off the dresser. Throwing open the door she said, "Hi, Baby Girl."

Des's smile flashed brightly at the welcome, sparking a similar reaction in her. No matter what she'd interrupted, Sadie had never been anything but thrilled to see her daughter happy.

"Whatcha doin?" Des hugged her, but midway through the embrace the muscles in her back and shoulders stiffened, and Sadie knew she'd spotted Jay.

"We were just going over some travel vouchers and trying to make arrangements for the next few weeks."

Destiny didn't quite relax as she stepped back and surveyed the room, as if scanning for more context clues.

"Hi, Des," Jay called from the balcony, her voice more casual than Sadie would have expected. "You want some paella? We've got plenty."

"Um, no. I ate with Viktor back at the venue."

"Good, as long as he didn't stick you with the bill."

Des grinned slightly. "No, we pawned it off on the organizers."

Jay laughed lightly. "Well done, you."

"What did you have planned for your big celebration tonight?"

"You're looking at it." Jay made an encompassing gesture with the phone in her hand. "A glamorous dinner of hotel paella, making flight and hotel arrangements for England, paying bills. If I'm really feeling frisky, I might treat myself to my third hot shower of the day."

Des nodded slowly, as if she couldn't find any fault in the individual aspects of the plan, but still didn't know if she liked the sum total. Sadie didn't think she'd put anything together yet, but her apparent unease stemmed from somewhere as she asked, "Where'd Hank go?"

"Some USTA officials took him out to dinner with the junior champions. He grumbled about having to put on a dress shirt, but honestly, I think he was pretty proud to have been invited."

"That's nice," Des said, as if she'd already moved on from the topic after the completely benign response. Her eyes kept wandering from Jay to the papers in Sadie's hands and back to the food on the balcony table. Then finally, she nodded once, hard enough to make her ponytail sway. "Okay then, I guess I'll let you guys get back to your planning and whatnot."

"You're welcome to stay," Jay said, and Sadie could have kissed her for the offer. "If we old people aren't too boring for you."

"No," Des said quickly. "I just, well, actually maybe since you're doing travel stuff for England, I should go ahead and tell you now that I talked to Dad earlier this evening."

Now it was Sadie's turn to tense, but years of practice in this area had given her the same skills Jay and Des had developed to appear calm on the court even when facing a superior player. "Oh? What did he have to say?"

Des glanced over her shoulder at Jay quickly before saying,

"He's going to use his leave time to come to Wimbledon. He wanted to know if he could still get tickets, but I told him he could sit in my player's box."

"Of course," Sadie said quickly. "I'll send him passes."

"Great. And can you let him know what hotel we're staying at, so he can stay there too?"

Sadie nodded and shifted some of the papers she'd clutched a little too tightly to buy time, afraid her voice would relay her tension. She glanced at Jay with a look that she hoped relayed more apology than panic. Jay thankfully seemed to get both messages and ambled casually back into the room.

"We're at the Rose and Crown in Wimbledon," she said, with one swipe across her phone screen. "They're sold out."

Des frowned. "Maybe the tour has some rooms set aside."

"You could always ask," Jay said noncommittally, "or I think there are some houses for rent in the area."

"Maybe we could all stay in a house together," Des said, eyes wide with childlike excitement.

A little squeak escaped Sadie's throat, but the sound was drowned out by her daughter's effusive praise. "Oh Jay, you'll love my Dad. He's like the perfect man. He's so handsome and strong, and he's an army officer, so he's also chivalrous."

"Hmm," Jay managed even as the color began to rise in her face.

"His name is Tad. Isn't that cute?"

"Yeah," Jay said, her smile strained. "Tad. Go figure."

"And he's kind of a war hero. He got a bunch of medals in Afghanistan, and he even met President Obama. That's why he can't come to many of my matches. He works all over, sometimes at embassies, sometimes even at the Pentagon. This is his first official leave since I turned pro," Des continued as she flopped onto Sadie's bed with a dreamy expression. "Oh, and he's got the most amazing blue eyes in the world, like a model."

"Sounds like Prince Charming," Jay managed, but her blush faded as if someone were slowly draining the blood from her complexion.

Sadie wanted to take her hand to connect them in any tangible way. Instead, she stood frozen in mutual awkwardness as Destiny rattled on.

"Everyone adores him. Just watch, the press will take, like, a thousand pictures of him and my mom together in our box. Even the tabloids love him."

"And he spoils her." Sadie finally cut in as Jay swayed slightly, her face now completely pallid. "So she might be a little biased in her assessment."

"Daddies are supposed to spoil their daughters," Destiny said, with a happy little laugh that made her seem so much younger and lighter than she had in months. Even when she'd started winning and smiling more, she'd still acted so much older than her age. Sadie's mood lightened at the reminder that her daughter could still feel like a teenager.

Still, as was too often the case, Destiny's joy came with a boatload of tangential insecurities for Jay. Sadie had more than a few complex emotions on the subject as well, but she would've preferred for them to discuss it privately, so she could soothe the fear and doubt she saw filling the blue eyes she found so much more appealing than Tad's. How deeply would those fears and self-recriminations take root before she had a chance to kiss them away?

"Hey, I have an idea," Des said, sitting up quickly. "Let's have a mother-daughter movie night!"

"What?" Sadie asked, not sure she'd heard correctly.

"We haven't hung out in weeks. We can get a movie online and get under the covers in our PJs and use all the pillows and eat popcorn from the vending machines, just like we used to do at my junior tournaments. Those trips were the best."

Sadie smiled broadly, both at Destiny's assessment of the memories she, too, cherished, and the hope that those days weren't over. Her daughter, the beautiful, driven French Open champion, still wanted to spend time cuddling and watching movies with her. Could any parent ever hope for anything more?

Even Jay seemed to understand the answer to that question, because she cleared her throat and said, "Sounds like the perfect night. Why don't we table our, um, travel planning?"

"Oh, Jay." Sadie's heart felt like it was being torn in two. How could the two most precious people in her life need the same thing from her at the same time, and yet so separately? She wanted to be with them both, to live a life where she could hold them close simultaneously. Surely that could be a possibility someday. And yet, standing there frozen between two halves of her heart, no hopes for the future would save her from the choice of the moment.

Jay rescued her by putting her choice into reasons she couldn't deny. "Life is busy, Destiny's only getting older; the rest of it will all be there later. Enjoy nights like these while you've got them."

Destiny's eyes narrowed at Jay, either out of suspicion or perhaps surprise that her normally playful friend had said something so uncharacteristically sentimental.

Sadie at least managed to cast Jay an apologetic look, and what she hoped sounded like a sincere, "thank you."

"Don't mention it." Jay turned her back on them, either to hide her emotion or to gather her things on the balcony. "But I'm taking my paella with me, 'cause, you know, food is kind of like company."

Destiny laughed. "Sometimes food is better than certain company."

"True words, young Padawan," Jay agreed, with a hint of wistfulness in her voice. Once again Sadie had to stifle the urge to cup Jay's face in her hands and kiss away the underlying sadness she saw so clearly there. As much as she loved her time with Jay, she was a mother first, and she hadn't had nearly enough time or opportunity to devote to that role lately.

Chapter Ten

London

"Des and Hank are meeting with the massage therapist at three if you want to join them," Sadie said, as she folded her arms across the top of the green half-wall separating her from Jay's practice court.

"Nah." Jay used a white towel to mop the sweat from her face. "I'm good."

Sadie sighed and whispered, "Yes, you are."

Jay's pulse radiated through her chest and to points farther south as she watched Sadie's espresso eyes sweep across her body. "I mean, my muscles are feeling good, but whatever compliment you just tossed out there, I gladly accept."

"All the compliments," Sadie said, her voice low enough that only Jay could hear, but she still leaned forward, offering a tantalizing peek of her cleavage disappearing under the sexy V-neck of the olive-colored shirt that hugged everything from her neck to her waist the way Jay wanted to.

"Hey, Pierce," a voice called across the court.

Jay jumped back and spun around guiltily, then wiped the back of her hand across her mouth in case she'd been caught drooling. She spotted one of the men's players entering through a cutout in the opposite wall.

"You done with the court?" he asked.

"I guess."

"You sure?" he asked amicably. "No rush."

She glanced back to Sadie and the shirt she wanted so much to be, and realized she wasn't going to focus on anything remotely close to tennis for the rest of the day. Then without even turning around to face him, she called, "No worries. My work here is done for today."

Sadie smiled seductively, and Jay barely had the strength in her knees to crouch down and collect her rackets.

"I'm sorry if I interrupted your workout," Sadie said, as they strolled toward the exit of the All England Lawn Tennis club.

"No you're not," Jay said, "but neither am I."

"I just thought that if Hank and Des were going to be busy until almost five . . ." She let the sentence dangle for Jay's imagination to fill in the unspoken.

"I like the way you think. Maybe we should hail a cab."

Sadie brushed her shoulder against Jay's slightly, then put a few more inches between them. "No, I cut out part of your workout. The least I can do is make sure you get a cooldown."

"A cooldown? Nothing about me is ever cool with you around. I might combust before we make it halfway back to the inn."

"It's only a mile," Sadie said, even though she sounded concerned as she drew in a shaky breath. "Come on, let's talk about something else."

"What else?" Jay asked, as they passed through metal gates and onto an asphalt sidewalk that skirted a lush, green park.

"Tennis. Tennis seems safe. How are you really feeling about the tournament?"

"Honestly?"

Sadie nodded.

"I don't want to jinx anything, but I feel fantastic. I don't know if it's the cool weather or the grass or just the gravity of Wimbledon, but I've always had an extra bounce in my step here." She felt more than a little bit of that bounce now. "And when I'm with you, all the good is magnified. It's not a technical answer, but I just kind of like everything right now."

"I know what you mean. Des played here as a junior last year, and I enjoyed it, but this trip is so much better. It's like everything good before now seems amplified by sharing it with you," Sadie said thoughtfully, as they turned down a residential street lined with tidy white homes. Then she chuckled. "Or maybe it's just that skirt you're wearing."

Jay glanced down at the short white skirt stretched tight over her upper thighs. "Really?"

Sadie bit her lower lip and nodded. "I never really pictured you as a skirt woman."

"I don't know that I am, or that I'm not." Her cheeks warmed. "I usually wear shorts because they have pockets, but you know Wimbledon is more traditional, and I don't know, I kind of like looking like I'm part of it all. And I mean, I'm not opposed to skirts, but this is kind of more of a skort."

"Don't cheapen the experience for me." Sadie bumped Jay's shoulder. "I've been over here fantasizing about the way that spandex stretches so tightly across your glutes when you lunge, and how I'd like to get back to the room and push it up, and . . ."

Jay held her breath waiting for more, but Sadie shook her head. "Sorry, it appears tennis is not actually a safe topic."

Jay blew out the air she'd been holding in a dramatic rush. "You're going to be the death of me if you keep teasing."

"I'm not teasing," Sadie said, with mock affront. "I fully intend to elaborate on all my skirt-based desires as soon as we get back to the hotel, but this lovely British neighborhood might not be the best place to get hot and bothered."

"Too late," Jay muttered, looking around furtively for a secluded place to drag Sadie where they wouldn't be seen. Some of the brick houses ahead had nice dividing walls between them and the street. If she could've been assured no one would pull into any of the driveways, she would've put one of them to good use.

"We're halfway there, Champ," Sadie said encouragingly, "then we're going to take everything but the skirt off."

Jay walked a little faster as she grumbled. "This is the worst cooldown ever."

"Patience, baby. Patience."

Jay didn't say that she'd been patient enough already. She didn't want to do anything to remind them of their last weekend in Mallorca, even in joking. The low thrum of panic she'd felt that night had finally subsided as Sadie had spent the week since then being just as loving and attentive and aroused as ever.

Logic had also had time to assert itself over her more emotional reactions. Sure, having their celebratory date night interrupted was disappointing, but things like that happened all the time, especially for parents. And while it might have felt similar to previous experiences, the more reasonable aspects of her brain repeatedly argued that Sadie's choice hadn't been a rejection. She and Des were not in competition. They both cared about Sadie, and Sadie cared about both of them. That's the way it should be. That was healthy and normal. It was only Jay's residual fears and bad relationship habits that made her feel otherwise.

The better parts of herself knew all those things, and still she couldn't quite shake the sting of doubt that came from knowing that, if there was a choice to make, she would always come in second.

"One more block," Sadie said, "then we've got an hour and a half for just the three of us."

"Three?" Jay blinked out of her haze at the word that didn't add up.

"Me, you, and your skirt."

Jay laughed, perhaps a bit harder than the joke warranted, but it felt so good to feel so great.

Turning into the stone front of the Crown and Rose, Jay swung the door to the inn open wide for Sadie to lead the way. Instead she stopped short so quickly, Jay nearly bumped into her.

"What's wrong?" she asked, but she didn't have to wait for an answer, because as soon as she followed the line of Sadie's eyes, she saw an American soldier in a green dress uniform decked out with so many bars and pins and stripes, she couldn't even begin to process them all. Instead, she let her gaze trail up past the man's perfect chin, strong jaw, and insanely blue eyes.

"Tad," Sadie finally said, in a rush of air.

He smiled to the point that his clean-shaven cheeks pushed his ears a little closer to his close-cut, blond hair. Then he spread his arms wide, as if he expected her to fall into them, and honestly, why wouldn't he? A man who looked like that in a uniform probably had women waiting in line for the privilege.

Sadie did hug him, but with more tentativeness than he seemed to expect, and as she stepped quickly back, he caught her by the shoulders, his fingers pressing their indent into the green cotton Jay had longed to run her hands over moments earlier. Her jaw clenched at the easy contact so obviously born of familiarity and public privilege.

"Our girl's in Wimbledon," he exclaimed, giving her a squeeze. "You did that, Sade! That tiny little pink bundle that we could hold in the palms of our hands, can you believe it?"

Jay noticed the corners of Sadie's mouth curl even in profile, and she couldn't blame her. This man certainly knew how to get to a mother's heart, or anyone who had a heart, really. His joy and pride in his daughter were infectious, and yet he laid all the credit where it belonged, at Sadie's feet.

Sadie brushed off the compliment. "She did all the work."

"No, come on. You did all the work and gave her all the opportunities. You moved mountains." He stopped and laughed. "Who am I kidding? You've never been able to take a compliment, not even when you were seventeen."

Jay's stomach tightened again at the intimacy of the comment, but before she could process her emotions, Tad noticed her presence. Releasing Sadie quickly, he stuck out one strong hand to grasp her own, and shaking vigorously said, "You must be Jay Pierce. It's such a pleasure to meet you."

Heads around the lobby turned at the exuberant greeting, but Tad didn't seem bothered as he continued to shake her hand about four pumps longer than a standard greeting required. "I'm Destiny's dad."

"Yes," Sadie said, more quietly. "Jay, this is Captain Tad Thompson."

"Oh please, no ranks needed here," he said, finally releasing her. "Call me Tad."

"Good to meet you, Tad." Jay rubbed her own hand where he'd gripped it, reminding herself that while his joviality might seem a bit overpowering, she certainly didn't want to make Captain Muscles angry.

"Can I buy you ladies a drink? I want to hear about everything that's going on with you and Des and the tour."

"Actually," Jay said, shooting a quick look to Sadie, who seemed frozen in place. "I had plans for the next hour, maybe hour and a half. Could we catch up later?"

"Oh, of course. I'm sure you've got a lot on your plate this week. I don't want to throw you off your game, especially since you're playing with my daughter. Why don't you go on ahead." Then he nodded at Sadie. "Don't mind if I steal this one from you, though, do you?"

The question felt like a kick to the stomach with his perfectly polished shoes. "Um, well. I'm sure I really . . ."

"Why don't you get settled into your room," Sadie suggested. "We can all meet up for dinner tonight? Say six?"

His smile dimmed, but his eyes still sparkled. "Okay, Sadie. You go do your thing. I'll meet you right here when you're ready."

Once again, the multiple meanings of the statement left a bitter taste in Jay's mouth, or maybe it was the completely unnerving ease with which Tad seemed to accept everything.

"You can regale us with tales of your brave adventures," Sadie said, her smile softening.

He shook his head. "I can't imagine anyone will want to hear a thing about me, with three powerful, engaging women at the table."

Jay pursed her lips as they headed for the stairs. There was no way the man standing behind her could possibly be a real human. Destiny hadn't been overstating how totally dreamy he was physically, but why couldn't she at least have been wrong about his personality? Someone who looked that good should have at least evened the playing field by being a bit of a jerk so Jay could find a reason to dislike him.

"So," Sadie said quietly, as Jay opened the door to her room, "we're going to dinner with Tad."

"Yeah. I got that," Jay said dryly. "You know, two minutes ago, when you volunteered me."

Sadie covered her face with her hands. "I'm sorry. I didn't think. I mean I did think, but I thought, I don't want to go to dinner with Tad by myself, so I—"

"Threw me under the bus?"

"I was thinking more along the lines of, I asked my girlfriend to help me out."

"Oh," Jay said, as her heart pounded in her ears so hard she wasn't sure she'd heard correctly. "Well, when you put it that way . . . girlfriend, huh?"

Sadie's hands fell, and her full lips formed the most perfect "o" as she started to stammer. "I, well, I thought, I mean, I didn't really think a lot about it. It's not like I've sat around trying to label us."

"Right, but if we did have a label . . ." Jay's smile stretched her cheeks now. "I would like for you to be my girlfriend."

Sadie sighed heavily. "Really?"

"Yes," Jay said emphatically. "And I suppose girlfriends do things like go to awkward dinners with their girlfriend's exes-slash-good-looking fathers of their children-slash-doubles partners."

Sadie laughed. "Do they? Even if no one else at the table will know they are girlfriends?"

"Totally," Jay said, her discomfort all but disappearing. With a woman as beautiful as Sadie on her arm, nothing else really mattered.

Jay wore white, just a plain, white, classic Tommy Hilfiger polo that accentuated the tan she'd gotten over the last few weeks of outdoor matches, paired with khaki capris. She left her sun-streaked hair down so it curled atop her shoulders. There was nothing outstanding or special about the outfit, but to Sadie, she outshone every medal pinned to Tad's chest as she sat between the two of them at dinner. It took everything Sadie had in her not to lean closer to Jay, to soak up the warmth of her body, to take her hand under the table. She wanted to run her tongue along the curve of her ear and . . .

"Bangers and mash?"

"Excuse me?" Sadie looked up at the young waiter towering over her with a tray full of food.

"You ordered the bangers and mash?"

"Right. Yes, I did."

He set a plate in front of her and then turned to Jay, saying, "And the fish and chips for Ms. Pierce."

Hank grimaced as he stared at a plate of greasy fried goodness. "For the love of Pete, Jay, which one of us are you trying to give a heart attack?"

"I'm at a pub in England." Jay stabbed a piece of fish with her fork. "Fish and chips is kind of a thing in these situations."

"You're also playing in Wimbledon in three days."

"Right. Three whole days to eat what I want without you grumbling."

"Does that mean on Monday you'll start eating healthier?"

"No," Jay said, as she picked up a steak fry and pointed it at Hank, "but on Monday you are allowed to start grumbling."

Tad laughed heartily and cut into his filet mignon. "I like you, Jay. After seventeen years of mess halls and MREs, I, too, am a fan of the eat-what-you-like-whenever-you-get-the-chance mentality."

"Daddy did three tours of duty in active war zones," Des said, in a way that made her seem younger than she had in months. "He earned his steak."

"Well, I don't know that I'd go that far. The last time I was in Afghanistan, I didn't do a full year there. I went back and forth between Kuwait and Qatar a lot," Tad said, as if that somehow made him less qualified to eat a slab of beef.

Sadie would have rolled her eyes if she hadn't understood his humility to be one hundred percent authentic.

"Wait, seventeen years?" Jay glanced from him to Des as if doing the math. "When did you enlist?"

Tad cast a quick glance at Sadie, and her heart tightened the way it had that day, the way it had every time she thought of him carrying a gun across a desert, the way it did every time she let herself remember he'd done it for their daughter, the one she didn't want to share with him. She stared down at her mashed potatoes.

"I enlisted the day after Des was born," he said evenly, and she could hear the smile in his voice as he continued. "Sadie clearly had all the day-to-day parenting duties down beyond my abilities, so I figured the best thing I could do to help my girls was to get out of her way and make a little money."

"And you made the world safer for us, too," Des said. "Don't forget that."

"I tried," he said seriously. "There's still a lot of stuff out there that scares me with you traveling as much as you do, but you're a strong, smart woman. Your mom saw to that, so I know you'll be okay."

Sadie forced a smile as she met his eyes. "Thank you." What else could she say?

"Well, I'm glad you get to be part of the travel this time," Des said. "It'll be so much fun having you right here over the next two weeks."

"Well." Tad drew out the word, then stuffed a bite of steak in his mouth and chewed slowly while everyone looked up, waiting to see what came next. "Maybe not right here the whole time, but close. Much closer than usual, so it's a win."

"What do you mean?" Hank asked. "Do you have to work?"

"No. I got the time off, but since my leave came through late, the hotels around here had all sold out. Apparently, there's a big tennis thing happening next week." He grinned. "But I got a place at the Union Jack. It's a hotel for military members staying in London."

"Where in London?" Destiny asked suspiciously.

"South Bank," he replied evenly, "a block from the Waterloo station, so I can just hop on the train every morning out to the Wimbledon area. Then it's only about a mile walk to the tennis courts."

"Dad!" Destiny exclaimed, in a register that made the hair on the back of Sadie's neck stand on end. "That'll take an hour."

He laughed. "I hoofed it today in under fifty minutes."

Des turned to Sadie with the unmistakable look of "do something" in her eyes. Sadie's stomach tightened with the mix of guilt and resentment she felt when these things fell to her. She wasn't Tad's keeper, but she was Destiny's, and Des loved her dad. God knows, Sadie'd kept her away from him enough over the years, probably too much, and he'd never complained, never threatened, never played Des against her. Still, she hated feeling like she owed him something, even if she did technically owe him for half of the person she loved most in life.

The silence stretched across the table as she tried to process not only what she should do, but the limits of what she actually *could* do at this point. She'd sent him the hotel listings close to the All England Club. He'd never said he couldn't get a room. Maybe if he'd mentioned the trouble earlier, she could've pulled strings. Maybe she wouldn't have, but none of that mattered this late in the game.

Thankfully Hank stepped in to cut the awkwardness. "I wish I'd gotten a double room. I wouldn't mind you bunking in, but I only have a single, and when I say single, I don't mean one bed. I mean like the bed barely feels big enough to hold me, and the room doesn't seem big enough for anything else."

"Mine too. The rooms over here aren't nearly as big as they are in the States." Des frowned, then turned hopefully back to Sadie. "Did you get a double?"

Sadie let out a shot of laughter, then recovered quickly, trying not to look overly thrilled as she said, "No, I did not. I got the same room you and Hank did, and since you wanted your own space, I didn't feel the need to get an extra bed in my room."

She sat back and popped another bite of sausage and gravy in her mouth to hide her smile at there being zero chance of Tad rooming with her. Then she realized everyone at the table had turned their attention to Jay, who in turn was looking at her.

"What?" Sadie swallowed her food.

197

"I . . . well, actually, you guys took the last of the single rooms." She shifted uncomfortably in her seat. "I have a double."

"There you go," Des said, brightening.

"Yeah." All the color had drained from Jay's face, but she managed to force out, "You're welcome to stay with me, man, but, um, be forewarned I sort of keep odd hours, and I, uh, I snore."

Sadie hid her smile behind a cloth napkin she picked quickly off her lap. Jay most certainly did not snore, but she couldn't blame her for lying to get out of rooming with Tad.

"Don't be silly," Tad said, ever the gentleman. "You're getting ready to play a major tennis tournament with my daughter. You cannot possibly room with a strange man during all that. I appreciate the offer, but I won't accept."

"You're right. That would be too weird," Des said, much to Sadie's surprise, but then she quickly added, "I'll room with Jay."

Sadie's mind immediately ran through a series of problematic scenarios that could arise from her girlfriend and daughter sharing a room while the two of them also shared the court in an international competition.

She opened her mouth to begin listing the more mundane complications when Jay said, "Yeah, sure. You're welcome to bunk in with me."

Sadie shot her a look of disbelief, but Jay wasn't watching her now. She had her attention focused solely on Des and the megawatt smile she was sending across the table.

"Thank you, thank you, thank you, Jay," Destiny gushed. "I promise I won't be in the way. I hope you know how much this means to me."

The little half-smile Jay gave as she tried to shrug off the comment suggested Jay did know what it meant to Des. She'd been thrown into the same situation Sadie had faced time and time again, and she'd responded in the same way. Jay had put Destiny's desires above her own wants and needs. Sadie both recognized the impulse and understood the cost. Her heart pressed against her chest as it swelled with pride, and something else. Something strong and powerful.

Love.

The realization struck with the force of one of Destiny's serves.

She was in love with Jay. Of course, she'd understood the attraction between them made her a little crazy. And the sex had been nothing short of life-changing. She also enjoyed traveling with Jay, talking to her for hours, or stealing hidden moments of unspoken connection, but until this second, it hadn't occurred to her that, amid all that, she'd fallen in love. Or maybe this was the exact moment she'd fallen in love, seeing the total package come together in the second in which Jay did something so caring and generous, something selfless, for Des. The act closed a circle or tied together the two outstanding threads in her life.

"Well, only if it's okay with your mother," Tad said hesitantly, but the word "mother" jolted Sadie back into the conversation, though she couldn't bring herself to look at anyone but Jay.

"Yeah," Jay added quickly, her eyes narrowing slightly as if she were having a hard time trying to read Sadie's expression. "Your mom's the boss. What she says, goes."

The comment made Sadie's lips curl up. She liked the sound of that. The idea of getting her way with Jay made her pulse pick up speed enough that she almost forgot she was supposed to be handing down judgment on Jay rooming with Destiny. "I don't think that's a great idea."

"What?" Des asked quickly. "Why not?"

"Well . . ." she drew out the word, trying to buy time. She could tell the truth and say that if the two of them roomed together it would be much harder for her to spontaneously rip Jay's clothes off or do all the things she wanted to do to that amazing body over the next two weeks, but she doubted that would win her points from anyone at the table. Instead, she fought to stay in mom-mode. "You're a light sleeper. You always have been."

"I didn't know that," Tad said, his voice laced with sadness.

She felt another flash of guilt, knowing it wasn't his fault he'd missed out on knowing such mundane details about his own daughter. He'd asked for so little and given her so much. And

Sadie loved him in a way, she really did, but not the same way Des did, and not the way she loved Jay, and she didn't want any of them sharing a room.

"Really, I don't mind commuting," he reiterated, "and I've certainly slept in worse places than the Union Jack hotel."

"No," Des said firmly. "This is my first pro event you've ever been to. It's important to spend time together, and I don't want to be worried about you coming back and forth every day. There has to be a way."

"I suppose," Sadie said slowly, then sighed heavily for extra effect, "if Jay doesn't mind, I could bunk in with her."

Jay's gasp sucked the end of a thick-cut French fry into her mouth, and then promptly coughed it back out. Destiny's reaction wasn't nearly as dramatic, but her expression rapidly shifted through a series of emotions from surprise, to frustration, to displeasure, and right back to frustration. Her dark eyebrows knit together, but so did her lips, as she held her objections in check.

Tad's blue eyes swiveled from one of them to the other, his baby face still open and patient.

"It makes the most sense," Sadie said. "I'm not training or competing, and I sleep like a log no matter where I am, so your snoring or odd hours won't matter, but it's not my choice to make. I don't mean to put you on the spot, Jay, but would you mind terribly? I promise to be as . . . unobtrusive as possible."

"Um, well, I mean, I'm not sure how much sleep you'll get with me in the room." Jay's face colored slightly, but she didn't crack a smile as she pretended to study her food and carefully consider the proposition. "But I guess if that doesn't bother you, it won't bother me."

Trying to keep the excitement stirring in her now from showing, Sadie glanced from Tad to Hank and then eventually to Destiny. No one seemed particularly thrilled with the plan, likely for different reasons, but since none of them spoke up with a better solution, she nodded resolutely. "Okay then, we'll have to make it work."

"We'll have to make it work." Jay did a breathless imitation of Sadie as she held her body up against the wall and thrust two fingers into her. "I didn't know you meant you'd make me work this hard."

"You complaining?" Sadie asked, but before Jay could answer, she kissed her hard. Their tongues danced in and out as hot breath escaped to run across flushed skin.

When they finally broke for air, Jay managed to growl, "No complaints." Then with each push deeper she added, "Not . . . a . . . single . . . one."

Sadie's whole body seemed to coil around Jay from the inside out. The strain of the physically strenuous position mingled with the thrill of anticipation caused Jay to sway, so she leaned the entirety of her body into Sadie's voluptuous curves, pinning them both against the wall. Sadie dropped her forehead against the tight mass of muscle along Jay's shoulder, giving it a sharp bite before exclaiming, "Heaven have mercy, you're too good at this."

"And you're a genius," Jay panted, as she once again marveled at Sadie's quick thinking during dinner. "I can't believe I get to do this every night."

Sadie sucked in a sharp breath, as if the mental image of things to come helped carry her closer to oblivion. "I want that, Jay. Every night. I want *you*."

"Good," Jay shot back, the desire lancing through her stomach, "because I need you."

"I . . . I . . . Jay . . ."

"Come on," Jay rasped in her ear, drunk with power and passion. As she pushed her thumb firmly against the pulsing center of Sadie's need, she coaxed her on. "Tell me, baby."

Sadie's body stiffened and she threw back her head as she shouted, "I love you."

The words rolled out of her with all the force of the release Jay had triggered.

The shudders subsided in silence, and the growing awareness of what she'd said seemed to hit Sadie like a powerful aftershock. She straightened, flattening herself against the wall as she groaned. "I said that out loud, didn't I?"

Jay eased back, slowly disentangling her legs from between Sadie's, then with one arm wrapped around her waist, eased them back toward the bed. "You did."

"Does that make you uncomfortable?"

"I suppose that depends," she answered slowly, as she perched on the edge of the mattress. "Was it one of those things that just came out in the moment, like a random exclamation, or something that's been on your mind before now?"

Sadie's dark eyes searched her own, as if seeking guidance or some sort of clue as to which option Jay preferred, but Jay kept her expression as neutral as possible. She knew the risks of taking the words of a moment to heart, and she also understood that her own hopes and desires could too easily color the intentions of another person. She desperately needed Sadie's answer to be her own, independent of pressure or circumstance.

"I've been thinking it ever since dinner," Sadie said, then with a heavy sigh added, "I'm sorry if that's too fast, or too much, or not romantic enough. It's not something I was ready to feel or not feel, or something I gave a lot of thought to when and how I'm supposed to say it. I don't know if I should've waited for you to say it first, but it's not like I can unsay it now, and I'm not sure if I want to, or if you want me to . . ."

"I don't," Jay said, a smile starting in her chest and curling its way up to her lips. "I don't want you to unsay it." Then giving a gentle squeeze, she pulled Sadie into the space between her knees. "If you really mean it."

Sadie cupped Jay's face in her hands and tilted it up until their eyes met. "I do mean it."

Jay's throat constricted with the same emotions that caused her eyes to water. "I mean it too."

Sadie raised an eyebrow, and Jay realized she wouldn't get away with a half-declaration. She'd have to say the words, and despite all the fear and pain that had held her in check for so long, sitting there cradled in the caring caress of Sadie's steady hands, she realized she didn't want to hold back. "I love you too, Sadie. I might be stupid or crazy, but I can't help it. And it's not like I didn't fight. I struggled and denied and tried to run, but I started falling the first time I saw you, and I haven't stopped since."

"This can't be my life." Sadie's brown eyes sparkled and danced in the dim light as she shook her head. "How is that even possible? How can you say something like that about someone like me?"

Jay laughed and in one swift motion pulled Sadie's naked body onto the bed, then straddled her waist and stared down at her breathtaking beauty. "What do you mean, someone like you? Someone stunningly beautiful? Someone who makes my heart beat faster than playing a third-set tie-break? Someone who makes me feel like I can face any foe, on or off court, and win? Someone who's singlehandedly bucked stereotypes and social norms with more strength and grace and fortitude and—"

Sadie surged up off the bed and captured her mouth in a searing kiss that stopped Jay's monologue, but not her train of thought. She mentally added the way Sadie's soft body molded against her hard, flat planes to the growing list of reasons she loved this woman.

Sadie eased back, pulling Jay down on top of her as the kiss turned slow and languid. Her muscle tension melted away, and her limbs grew heavy with contentment. She marveled once again at the ease with which Sadie could arouse her and comfort her all at once.

Breaking the kiss and rolling onto her side, she dragged the comforter over them both and murmured, "You're perfect."

"You're perfect. You're always perfect, you know that?"

She snorted softly as Sadie snuggled closer.

"You are," Sadie reiterated. "I kept thinking all through dinner how magnificent you are."

"Me? I think you mean Tad," Jay said, a little flash of insecurity trying to work its way through their postcoital haze. Knowing that Sadie had chosen her helped to stem the feelings, but the decision hardly seemed logical.

"No," Sadie said quickly. "I mean you, and I know you both pretty well."

"Thank you for not saying you know us both intimately."

"That too, but I meant more than knowing you both in the biblical sense. I've seen you both in a variety of different situations, seen how you face problems, how you carry yourselves, how you relate to the people you love and who love you."

"And?"

"And while Tad is an amazing person, he's almost too good to be real sometimes. It can be hard to be around such genuine valor constantly and not feel jaded or inferior."

"Right?" Jay laced her calloused fingers through Sadie's softer ones. "Like I kept waiting for him to blow his top or say something shitty to the waiter, but the man just never slips up. He's polite, and he defers to you and dotes on Des and, oh yeah, he's a fucking war hero."

"He is," Sadie said matter-of-factly. "He never pushed me to do anything out of my comfort zone. He never criticized or made demands. He never failed to support me one hundred percent, but—and here's the big thing—he's also never stirred my blood the way you do."

Jays heart rate revved again. "I win that category then?"

"Hands down," Sadie said, with a hint of laugher in her voice. "You win all the sexy categories, tens across the board, but more than that, you're also passionate in a way that sweeps me off my feet and makes me forget myself in the most amazing ways. Normally when Tad's in town, I'm a ball of tension."

"Why?"

"Because he is so damn wonderful all the time, and Des adores him so much, and he is too good to me."

"Sure, sounds terrible."

"I know. I'm terrible. Most single mothers would kill for someone like Tad. Hell, most women would've married him when he asked and never let him go."

Jay remembered Sadie's comments in Paris about passing up a proposal on the hope of something better. "When did he ask?"

"The day I had Destiny, the day he enlisted. He said all the right things, he'd done the right things, and he wanted to keep doing everything right. I hurt him so badly by refusing him that chance, but I wasn't in love with him." A hint of anguish tinged her voice. "I'd known it all along, and I felt so guilty about leading him on. I tried to tell myself maybe I could love him someday. I did care about him, and he looked at me like no other person ever had, with eyes so blue. I'd never seen anything like his eyes until I looked into yours. I wanted to love him the way he loved me, and for a few months I thought I might be able to, but then Destiny was born."

"And that made you love him less?"

"No, I don't think I loved him less. I think it was just that once I felt the love I had for her, I finally knew for sure what real love felt like, and the way I felt about him paled in comparison."

"Oh." Jay's stomach tightened.

"But more importantly, having Destiny changed the way I thought of my love for him, made it more complicated. On some level it made me love him more deeply because without him I wouldn't have Des, and I can see so many beautiful parts of her that come from him. She's got his honor, his unwavering sense of right and wrong."

"She's also got his chin cleft," Jay mused, "which was strange to see. I've always thought of her as being a mini you. It felt weird to see that the little dimple came from someone else."

"Yes, it does!" Sadie said, the exclamation laced with relief. "Which is where the complicated part comes in. I love what he gave me in her, but at the same time, I also resented the reminder that Des wasn't just mine. With him gone so much, it was easy to just believe Des was my baby only. I provided for her. I cared for her. I taught and comforted her. It's always so jarring when he shows up after so much time to remind me that half of her came from someone else."

Sadie covered her eyes with her hands and blew out an exasperated breath. "I don't want to share my grown daughter with her kind, patient, heroic father. Does that make me an awful person?"

"No." Jay wrapped an arm around her possessively. "You love her more than anything in the world, and there's nothing wrong with loving someone like that."

"For so long I felt like maybe Des would just be the love of my life. Not all women get to have a grand romance, you know. I know so many people who grow old, lonely, and sad about what they didn't have. I always felt blessed that we had our little family of two." Sadie placed a soft kiss on her cheek and whispered, "Until you came along and made me greedy."

"Greedy?" Jay asked, not sure what the comment meant, but she certainly enjoyed the low tone in which it had been delivered.

"Yes, now I want it all. I want my family, I want your body, I want Des to win all the tennis trophies, I want to wake up next to you every morning, and tonight at dinner, I realized that for the first time in my life, I actually *got* everything I wanted. You did that for me, Jay. You made me believe I could have it all, and I fell head over heart in love with you for it."

Jay's throat tightened, and she held Sadie tightly, hoping her proximity would cause more of Sadie's optimism to rub off on her. She wasn't unfamiliar with the process Sadie had described. If she had the words or the emotional fortitude, she would tell her so. She'd say that Sadie had done the same for her. She'd tell her that, when they met, she'd closed off parts of her heart and her hopes. She'd given up on anything more than cementing her legacy as a solid tennis player, and even after setting the bar so low, she worried she might not clear the hurdle. Then Sadie had come along and had seen parts of her she'd hidden, even from herself. Sadie'd refused to accept the narrative written by the press and demanded that Jay show her who she really wanted to be. She'd made Jay believe that not only could she have something more in her life, but also that she deserved it.

Jay's heart thrummed with the desire to tell her all that, but the words wouldn't come out through a knot of emotions clogging her throat, so instead she said the closest thing she could manage. "I love you too."

Sadie laid her palm flat on Jay's stomach and hooked a leg possessively over her thigh. Then, with a contented sigh, she murmured, "That's the best goodnight I've ever gotten."

Jay closed her eyes, content to stay ensconced in the utter perfection of the moment all night, but before she could drift off, her phone buzzed on the nightstand. She thought about ignoring it, but quickly realized that if someone was texting her, they probably wouldn't stop at one message. She didn't want to have to deal with interruptions all night. Grabbing the phone quickly, she lifted it to her face in the dim light, hoping only to switch the settings to nighttime mode, but Peggy's text appeared on the front screen.

"Got a sneak peek at the draw. You've got Des in the third round."

She stiffened slightly as she processed the news and raced through the implications. A sense of cold dread seeped into the haze of warmth she'd relished seconds earlier, and she fought to hold it at bay.

There was no need to freak out. They were all professionals. They were bound to play each other eventually. They could separate singles from doubles. Plenty of friendships survived healthy competition every day, in their world. Besides, what happened between her and Des on the court didn't have to affect her and Sadie. Her stomach clenched, as she wasn't quite sure she believed that last part. She scrambled to find another thread as she powered down the phone completely and tossed it back onto the nightstand. She had no guarantee she and Des would both make it to the third round. She tried to make herself stick to that argument, but it must not have been working, because Sadie finally muttered, "What's wrong?"

"Nothing." She kissed the top of Sadie's head and pulled her a little closer. "Just a tech alert. I'll deal with it later."

Chapter Eleven

"So, how many times did you end up in an actual battle?" Hank asked Tad, as they slipped into their seats in Destiny's box on court two.

Sadie slipped into her seat too, careful not to flash any of the TV cameras as she pulled her cream-colored skirt over her knees. Hank sort of flopped into his lightly padded green chair. Green, everything here was green, even Tad's uniform today, and he did no slipping or flopping and instead stood ramrod straight as he surveyed the grass court. "Well, it depends on what you mean by battles. I participated in a few direct assaults on Baghdad early in the second Gulf War, but those were rare there, and almost unheard of during my time in Afghanistan. There, the fighting always seemed to sneak up on you. I can't say I saw anything most people would consider glorious, mostly ambushed convoys, IEDs, that sort of thing."

Sadie closed her eyes and pinched the bridge of her nose. Part of her was thrilled Hank and Tad were getting on so well. It meant she didn't feel obligated to entertain Tad or have to feel guilty for avoiding him, but today her nerves were already frayed, and she feared one more male bonding moment about war or tanks or macho games might cause something to snap.

To be fair, Tad never glorified the fighting, but Hank was starting to sound a bit like a child with a mild case of hero worship. Between him and Des, she was subjected to a near constant fawning fest. And even after nearly a week, there'd been no sign of either of them wavering. All through breakfast this morning, they'd occupied themselves by asking him to list the meaning of every medal on his chest.

She glanced down at the court as the crowd began to stir with increased anticipation. The ball boys and girls scurried about, looking sufficiently busy as officials paced purposefully and mumbled into walkie-talkies. She'd learned to recognize these little flourishes in activities as a subtle signal that the players were expected on court soon. Her stomach jittered like it might when a rollercoaster begins to click up the first big hill, and you realize there is no turning back. Why hadn't she fully realized how hard this would be until right now? Probably because she'd found such lovely ways to distract herself all week.

The thought made her smile. She'd spent the last year traveling all over the world. She'd seen everything from Paris lights to the Shanghai skyline, but none of them held the appeal of the little double room without a view she was sharing with Jay. She'd spent hours lying in her arms, staring up at the ceiling, just breathing in the scent of her or basking in the heat of her body. She fanned herself with her program. How was she ever going to go back to sleeping alone?

The thought startled her.

She'd worked hard not to think too far ahead. She wanted to enjoy these two weeks for what they were and not get wrapped up in silly worries, and so far it hadn't been hard. She had enough to focus on here and now without trying to add the concerns of the future. Case in point, Jay and Des walked out of the tunnel below and onto the court.

The crowd erupted in hearty applause, and Sadie rose with them. The atmosphere felt more like a final than a third-round draw, and she didn't think that was just her own nerves kicking in. The clash had been heavily hyped even in the British press, as the top two Americans would now be pitted against each other. The fact that they were doubles partners shouldn't matter, or at least that's what all the professional commentators said, but as she watched Des start her warm-ups at fever pitch, she knew they were wrong.

Jay stayed calmer, as usual, but as she casually returned Destiny's blasts, Sadie suspected more than their temperaments came into play. Jay was on a tear. She hadn't dropped a set in her first two matches, whereas Des had to dig out two hard wins in a row. In doubles, they'd breezed through their first pairing, but Jay had been the stronger half in that arena as well, and she carried herself now with all the ease of someone who felt confident in her capabilities. The easy toss of her hair when she served, or the stretch of her white Lycra skirt when she lunged would have normally sent Sadie's libido into overdrive, but following a high lob across the court, her eyes fell on the one thing that could drop a bucket of ice water onto her hot hormones.

Destiny set up to crush the lob, but managed only to send a screecher into the net. She scowled, and Sadie's mothering instincts kicked in. Something wasn't right. Her daughter didn't feel her best. Maybe not in the physical sense, but certainly in the emotional sense, and that was worse. If her head hurt, Sadie had Advil. If she rolled an ankle, there would be icepacks, but there was nothing Sadie could do from the stands to ease her daughter's mind. The realization struck her where it always did, right in the center of her chest.

The umpire called for the coin toss, and Jay smiled for the cameras, then both players glanced up at Destiny's box as they headed for their respective baselines. Sadie smiled back, trying to encompass them both even as she struggled to tell herself they could both play well. It was just one match and, no matter who won, they'd still have doubles. They could go back to playing together even stronger and more fit if they played an epic match here. That's what she wanted, for them to leave the court proud of their accomplishments, but even in that "best of all worlds" scenario, only one of them would advance to the next round.

"Here we go," Hank muttered, as the blows began.

Des's serve careened to the corner, but Jay neutralized it with a subtle arc that allowed her to reset in the middle of the court, and from there she moved gracefully in all directions. Destiny tried to overpower Jay with her explosive swing, and occasionally she did, but Jay refused to get frazzled, and her softer touch sent a wide array of finesse shots around the court. It was as if her racket were a magic wand: All she had to do was point it in the direction she wanted the ball to land, and it would obey her command. She really was stunning to watch, and Sadie's breath caught in her chest over and over as she managed to repeatedly drop her shots right on the white lines. The urge to surge up and cheer with the spectators surrounding her was held in check only by the grave expression on the face of her only child.

"Game, Ms. Pierce," the chair umpire finally called. "Ms. Pierce leads two games to one."

Destiny headed for the bench on the changeover, head low, shoulders tight. Sadie wanted to go rub her back the way she had at bedtime when she'd been a child. That had always helped calm her down.

"She held her serve," Hank said, as if trying to find a silver lining. "Jay hasn't really taken anything from her."

"Which means she's not really losing?" Tad asked.

"Not in the conventional sense, and it's still early," Hank explained, but Sadie knew him well enough to hear the nervousness in his voice, just as much as she knew that if he had concerns, Destiny had likely come to the same conclusion. She was fighting to hold her head above water while Jay was doing the backstroke.

They switched sides, and once again Destiny came out swinging as if her life depended on it, and yet the harder she hit, the more Jay danced. She moved like some unearthly combination of a linebacker and a ballerina, and once again Sadie's heart would rise with each soaring point, only to crash against her ribcage as the ball skidded past a flailing Destiny. Back and forth they went, bash by bash, up and down, wide and right back, until it felt like Sadie's insides were being split down the middle.

At the next changeover, a strong hand on her shoulder gave a little squeeze, and she looked up to see Tad's eyes searching her own. She blinked a few times, as if trying to process his presence.

211

"How do you do it?" he finally asked.

"What?"

"How do you watch her out there every day, every match, and not feel totally helpless?"

"That's what being a parent is all about." Sadie sighed. "The old adage is true. Being a mom always involves walking around with half of your heart outside your body."

He nodded solemnly. "Every time I went into a fight, I knew I'd been trained. I knew I had the resources I needed, and whatever happened, I had a chance to bend the outcome at least a little."

"You have to have faith that no matter what the outcome, she will ultimately succeed."

His smile was weak. "But don't you want to mow down the rest of the world so that no one gets in her way?"

Sadie considered the question quietly as Jay and Des took the court again. Any other time, she would have had to answer in the affirmative. Despite all her talk about life lessons, her tiger-mom instincts were strong. The thought of someone, anyone, standing between Destiny and something she wanted badly enough to work tirelessly for made Sadie want to do more than growl.

Down below, Jay drew Des right up to the net with a drop shot, then whizzed a return hotly into the back corner. The crowd roared again, but this time Sadie didn't feel as strong a pull to join them. The combination had been beautifully brutal and broke her daughter's serve, giving Jay a five-three lead and the chance to serve for the first set.

Hank groaned as Destiny netted her first return. "She's in her head now."

"No," Sadie said, through the gritted teeth of an increasingly tight smile, as Des's second return went long. "She's not falling apart. Jay's just playing a wonderful game."

Hank didn't argue, which she took as a sort of grudging agreement, but she could have done without Jay illustrating her point quite so well by closing out the next two points with lasers down opposite sidelines.

Everyone breathed again, if only a for a moment. Tad took the opportunity to hop to his feet. "I had no idea it could feel this awful. The first two matches were so exciting, and the doubles were like a coronation parade. This is more like a gauntlet."

Sadie nodded. "Some days are like this."

"Doesn't it just tie your stomach in knots? She's so alone out there. We can't even go talk to her." He turned almost frantically to Hank. "Are you sure you can't go talk to her? You're her coach."

Hank shook his head. "Totally against the rules."

"The rules are terrible," Tad grumbled, in perhaps his most uncharacteristic comment ever. Mr. Military never chafed against any rule in his life as far as Sadie knew. Did his love for his daughter really eclipse every part of his nature?

Of course it did. The same had always been true for her. She'd simply had more practice putting these situations into perspective. Or at least that's what she told herself as the second set began, but as the battle renewed in another barrage of backhands, a little twinge of guilt wormed its way into her brain.

Why should Tad be more upset than she? He hadn't lost sleep and rearranged work to fit multiple practice slots into a single day. He hadn't sat outside in the heat and wind as junior tournaments stretched on for days. He hadn't bandaged bloody knees, or wiped away tired, dejected tears. She had worked nearly as hard as Destiny for years and invested every bit as much emotion to get to this point. Shouldn't she be at least as sick as Tad that Jay's forehand slice skimmed so unfairly off the top of the net before spinning to an abrupt stop without so much as a bounce?

"That was a lucky break for Jay," Hank said, as the umpire used her microphone to confirm that Jay had, in fact, gone up a break.

"It hit the net. That shouldn't be legal. Don't they have to take a do-over?" Tad asked.

"Only on a serve."

But Jay did not need any do-overs in her next service game, as she ran a clinic in precision placement. Blow by blow, her confidence magnified her skill as she assumed full command of one game, then another.

"She's going to lose," Tad whispered, as Jay took her fourth game in a row.

Sadie didn't respond, but slipped into her cool and controlled mom mask as Des's serve went long and her shoulders sagged.

Sadie wasn't even watching Jay now. Her gaze remained on her daughter. Maybe Tad's tensions had exacerbated her own, or maybe her mother instincts had been pushed to their natural limits, but she had to sit on her hands to keep from digging her fingernails into her own palms now.

Perhaps it only made sense that when one loved-one struggled and another thrived, she would be drawn toward the one in need. She wasn't rooting against Jay. She wasn't even aware of Jay anymore, or at least she hadn't been until she flicked a drop shot crosscourt so far that Destiny didn't even take a dejected step toward the ball.

Hank let out a low whistle, and Tad grumbled, "Was that really necessary?"

A little voice inside her head whispered that Jay didn't really have a good angle on another shot, but still, she could have just surrendered the point. She had an absurd lead. Would it have really been the end of the world to concede one point? Even if it led to dropping a game, it would hardly matter at this point.

"She's trying to end this as quickly as possible," Hank said matter-of-factly.

"Am I supposed to find that merciful?" Tad asked curtly.

"She wants to save her knees for the next round," Hank replied.

"She's saving her knees by crushing my daughter," Sadie shot back before Tad had the chance.

"Would you rather she toy with Des or give her false hope?" Hank asked.

"I'd rather she just lose," Sadie said flatly. Tears immediately sprang to her eyes as the rush of guilt surged through her once more. She didn't mean that. She didn't want Jay to fail, but damn it, why did she have to beat Destiny? Didn't Jay know what that would do to her? How it would twist her heart and split her insides? Didn't she understand that a mother had only one choice when backed into a corner?

The final shots were quick as Hank had predicted, but they were far from painless, and when Sadie rose with the rest of the crowd, it was to applaud Destiny's effort more than Jay's skill. Still, as the two women met at the net, she couldn't help but notice that Jay held her in an embrace longer than Destiny probably would have wanted. What had she said? Something gracious, no doubt, and from Destiny's sad attempt at a smile, Jay had probably also managed to be at least mildly amusing. But as her daughter dropped, demoralized, onto the bench and hung her head, Sadie began to worry that she wouldn't be able to muster the same level of grace that seemed to come so naturally to the victor.

"Tell us about the break in the first set," a reporter called as soon as Jay sank into the chair behind the long desk bearing the famous purple and green crossed rackets of the Wimbledon logo.

"I'd love to claim tactical brilliance, but it was a lucky shot that happened to skim off the back-corner line," Jay said, as she adjusted her microphone and tried not to notice the large image of the Championship trophy on the wall just over her shoulder. She wanted to enjoy this moment for what it was. She'd made it into the round of sixteen at a major tournament for the first time in years. There was a time, not all that long ago, she'd worried she'd never play again, much less play at this level. She'd worked so hard for so many years, but it wasn't until this moment that she really felt like she might succeed in being better than she was before.

"You seemed to have a lot of those shots today," the reporter pushed. "Were they all lucky?"

"Luck never hurts, but the grass court gives me a little more chance to dance. The grass is fast, which is harder to react to, especially against someone who has a superior return game like Destiny. But the slickness of the court also accelerates the kick and spin on the ball."

"Which plays to your strengths," the reporter concluded.

Jay smiled, almost as thrilled to be talking about tennis as she was about winning. She hadn't faced a question about her past in weeks, not even now, sitting under the bright white spotlights of a major win. "It certainly saved me from what could have just as easily been a loss today."

"The scoreboard didn't look like you were in danger of losing at any point," a different reporter called.

"Was there a question there, Terry?"

Everyone chuckled, even Terry. "Did you really think that you might lose, even in the second set?"

"I did," Jay said, not disingenuously. Maybe she hadn't felt any sort of fear in the last two games, but she hadn't counted Destiny out until then. "You forget, I practice with the formidable Ms. Larsen on a regular basis, and I've played alongside her in some pretty intense matches. You all may have underestimated her out there, but I never did."

"Did you have any concerns about knocking the only other remaining American out of the draw, especially since she's also your doubles partner?"

"None," Jay said flatly into the microphone, even as she refrained from seeking Sadie's eyes in the dimly lit crowd. "Destiny Larsen isn't a fragile child. She's a professional athlete. Playing at any level less than my best would be disrespectful. It would imply she isn't strong enough mentally or that she isn't mature enough to handle the ups and downs of this business."

"So, you don't think a loss of this magnitude will affect your doubles match tomorrow?"

"Absolutely not," Jay said, then quickly added, "and you all aren't giving her enough credit if you keep talking about this as some massive letdown for her. I know what the final line score said, but if a few of my shots had gone a millimeter farther outside, it would've ended the other way today. I wouldn't be surprised if, next time we play, it does go the other way."

"Is that what you told her at the net after the match?" a reporter asked from the back of the room.

Jay laughed again as she remembered the moment she'd pulled

216

Destiny's tense frame close. She'd seen her dejection take hold, watched those proud shoulders slump, and seen the fire in her eyes dim. In that moment she'd wanted to comfort her as much as she'd wanted to celebrate. "If you must know, I told her that someday I'd be sitting in an old folks' home watching her still playing on TV, and when I'd tell everyone that I'd beaten her once upon a time, they'd all write me off as another senile old woman."

Everyone in the audience laughed with her this time, everyone but Sadie.

Jay had finally dared to seek her eyes, hoping that she'd offered up enough self-deprecating humor to brave what she'd find there, but Sadie wasn't even looking at her. Instead, her eyes were trained on the doorway where Destiny waited for her turn on the stage.

A stab of loneliness cut through her reverie, and she fought to push it aside, but the longer it went on, the harder she found the task.

The feeling had started about halfway through the first set, right after she broke Des. Up until that point, their box had only been slightly biased toward Des, but they had politely applauded good plays on both sides. Everything felt friendly, almost like a side practice session in front of thousands of people. She had enjoyed the heightened jubilee, but as if the crowd took their cues from Destiny's body language, as soon as her demeanor changed, so did the atmosphere. The stadium shifted to Jay's favor, but the player's box leaned more heavily the other direction. The better Jay played, the worse their scrutiny felt.

She'd watched surreptitiously as first Tad, then Sadie, went rigid. She'd seen out of the corner of her eye how he leaned close to whisper in her ear, both their facial expressions and features reflecting those of their daughter's, until their united concern became too much to watch. She tried to tell herself they weren't rooting against her, they were cheering on their daughter.

Their daughter.

She'd finally had to break the habit of looking to Sadie after a good point, and in the cold, calculated moments on the court, her professional instincts had taken over and preserved her focus

217

with a sharp mix of endorphins and muscle memory. Now, however, as the press conference wore down, so did her defenses.

"If there are no more questions," she said, with a smile that took a little more effort than it had moments earlier, "I think I've earned one of my famously long showers."

No one objected, and she made a break for the side door, throwing a deliberately casual glance in Sadie's direction to see if she would make any move to intercept her. She shouldn't have bothered. As Des brushed past her wordlessly, Sadie remained fully ensconced between Tad and Hank, her attention clearly focused on what mattered most.

Jay sighed and pushed through the door to the locker room without another look back. There was no need to stick around and see what came next. Sadie, Tad, and Hank would rally around Des, and her better angels whispered that that's exactly how things should be. Des needed them more, and if it had been any other player on the other side of the equation, they'd be with Jay. By tomorrow, they'd all get back to work. At least that was the party line. She hoped if she kept repeating it often enough into enough microphones, it would become true.

Still, a twinge of fear that needled its way up from her chest whispered that she knew better. There was no logic to winning and losing. Those two entities carried animal emotions that kept a person up at night, twisting and gnawing until reason faded to darkness. She did her best to quiet that voice with simple, silent refrains. This wasn't like last time. Sadie wasn't Katia. Everything was different now. But as the high of winning butted up against Sadie's emotional withdrawal, the ensuing disconnect felt disconcertingly familiar.

"Hey, you did great up there," Sadie said. She threw an arm around Destiny's waist and gave a little squeeze as Hank ushered them out of the pressroom. "You were gracious and concise and—"

"A loveable loser."

"No." Sadie pulled her tighter to her hip. "You were professional."

"A professional would've played better."

"No, your mom's right," Tad cut in. "You fought hard. You took one on the chin and squared up and faced it. That's the epitome of professional."

"Come on." Hank nudged them down the hallway past the locker room toward the exit. "You two wait by the players' gate. Tad and I will get a car. Let's go have a dinner, get some sleep, and shake it off before we go back to work tomorrow."

Destiny looked up at him, her eyes wide with surprise. "Don't you want to go over some film and tell me what I did wrong?"

He shook his head. "You didn't do much wrong today. Jay was right in her assessment. The ball skipped and skidded her way, but on any given day, that match could have spun in your favor."

Then, grabbing Tad by the arm, Hank steered him out onto the grounds, leaving Sadie with Destiny, who wasn't buying the explanation he'd tried to sell her. "She moved me around the court like a puppet, and I let her. I had no control compared to her. I folded in the second set. It was like I didn't even deserve to be on the court with her."

"Hush," Sadie said, in the most soothing tone she could muster. "You're always your harshest critic. You didn't play poorly."

"She crushed me."

The shame in Destiny's voice caused a vise to squeeze around Sadie's heart. Not trusting herself to speak, she pressed her lips to Destiny's bare shoulder, wishing she could kiss away the hurt the way she had back when the pain had come from a skinned knee or elbow. But how could she put a Band-Aid on such a strong, brave young woman who had been crushed in more ways than the scoreboard could show?

"I know I'm going to lose," Destiny continued. "I'm used to it by now, but everything was going too well for us all. We had some money, we had some endorsements, I was winning more, and even when I lost, the matches were either close or against a top-three player. Everything made sense, and Dad was here for the first time ever."

Sadie nodded at the confirmation that losing in front of Tad added to the anguish. Even strong, powerful young women wanted to impress their fathers. Still, she got the feeling Destiny wasn't done venting yet, so she held her tongue.

"And it's Wimbledon, you know? I just felt like if I could make it here, it would finally be real. I could finally stop worrying about whether or not I really belonged at this level."

"You do!" Sadie said emphatically. "You're a French Open champion."

"Only with Jay by my side, and I think we saw today which one of us is the better player."

Sadie pursed her lips as Destiny peeled back the final layer to reveal Jay at the heart of all her seemingly disproportionate turmoil. It wasn't just a loss. It was a loss to the woman she'd felt dependent on. Jay was the one person left that could be credited with Destiny's successes, and of course that bothered someone as independent as Destiny. She had clearly wanted to prove to everyone—and more importantly to herself—that she was Jay's equal, if not her better. Instead, the matchup had confirmed her worst insecurities.

What could Sadie say now? No platitude would convince someone so concretely competitive that anything but the final score mattered. If she wouldn't listen to such logic from Hank or even Jay herself, there was no way Sadie could change her mind. And still, standing by helplessly while her daughter suffered was never an option. She pulled her into a full hug, wrapping her arms tightly around Destiny's body, until the muscles relaxed into her own, and she bore some fraction of the burden weighing on her daughter. But no sooner had Destiny folded her frame into the embrace than a door opened behind them and hurried footsteps skidded to a stop.

"Oh, sorry," Jay muttered, causing Destiny to jerk up to full height, rigid and tense once more.

"You're fine," Des said quickly, her expression hard and her voice flat.

"I can go back in." Jay shuffled back toward the door that had closed behind her.

"No," Destiny said, "we're leaving."

"Cool," Jay said, too quickly to be comfortable. Then, looking quickly from Des to Sadie, a thousand unspoken questions filling her eyes, she said, "Me too."

The vise grip around Sadie's heart tightened painfully as the three of them stood in a triangle of awkwardness. Jay was so perfectly golden, eyes bright, skin flushed, the ends of her hair still damp from the shower. She looked every bit the part of the victor, and that stirred something proud and powerfully possessive in Sadie. But those emotions were tempered by a protective instinct that ran deeper. Amplified by the tension radiating off Destiny, that baser imperative held her captive.

How could she reconcile what they both needed from her, or the feelings they inspired in her? She needed to be gracious and soothing and fair and loving to both of them; she wanted that more than anything. But everything she thought to say put one of them above the other. Finally, swallowing hard, she managed to choke out a quiet, "Good match, Jay."

Instead of sounding like a compliment, the words came out strangled and clipped. Jay's lips parted as if she needed extra air to take the blow, but she forced a smile that hurt worse than a frown. "Thanks."

The silence stretched between them once more as Sadie wordlessly pleaded for Jay to understand. If only she could explain, if only she could tell her what she knew about her daughter in this moment, about the crushing blow to her sense of self and the insecurities it had exposed, about how none of this was about a tennis score, but she couldn't say so in front of Destiny. Even if Destiny hadn't been there, how could she explain the most intangible aspects of motherhood to someone who had never felt another human being walk away with half their heart beat?

"I think I'll catch a cab on my own," Jay finally said, "let you guys have some family time tonight."

Destiny didn't argue with this break from their normal routine, but the clamp around Sadie's heart felt more like a knife now. Family time. Hadn't it been just a few days ago when that term would have included Jay? She still wanted it to. No tennis match could ever change that. The tug-of-war taking place inside her shifted slightly toward Jay's side.

"Actually, I just want to have dinner in." Destiny turned to Sadie, her caramel eyes soft and pleading.

"Of course." Sadie patted the clammy skin of her bare shoulder.

"Do you think Hank and Dad would mind if we just had some girl time?"

We? Sadie's heart struggled to break the grip that held it so tightly.

Destiny shrugged with her best attempt at casualness, then relenting, nodded. "Please?"

"Of course." Sadie said, without so much as looking at Jay. The pain and divide hadn't disappeared, but Destiny needed her, and only her. She didn't revert to work mode and seek out Hank. She hadn't reached for her dad. She wanted Sadie. "Whatever you want."

The corners of Destiny's mouth twitched up only slightly, but it was the first hint of a smile Sadie'd seen in hours. "I want to eat pizza in bed and watch *The Wiz* until I fall asleep."

Sadie beamed, and the final tightness in her chest shattered. Finally, something she knew how to do. The medicine she'd doled out so many times throughout the years was needed once more, and she was elated to be in a position to administer it once more. "That can definitely be arranged."

Destiny's grin widened, then faltered again as she looked past Sadie once more to Jay. "See you tomorrow."

Sadie turned to see that, as Destiny's smile had grown, what was left of Jay's had faded. The urge to reach out to her was swift and strong as she felt herself dragged back over the chasm of roiled emotions, but before she had a chance to even lift a hand, Jay straightened her shoulders and stepped back.

"You guys have fun," Jay croaked, her voice thick and scratchy. "I'll see you later."

Then she fled, not quite at a sprint, but close enough that Sadie didn't dare attempt to follow. Everything she had to say to Jay couldn't be said here. All she could do was have faith in Jay to understand, and try to have faith in her own ability to make it up to her. The former came easily. Sadly, she felt much less certain about the latter.

Jay lay awake, alone in the room she was supposed to share with Sadie. She watched the gray light as shadows from the street below danced across the ceiling. They seemed to sway to a song she couldn't hear over the refrain of doubts echoing through her brain. She'd heard the chorus a thousand times already, but still it pounded onward, rising, falling, and looping back around to start again, like some demented version of "It's a Small World After All." Only this rendition wasn't sung in the happy array of international voices. It came on the whispers of her past and in a language she understood all too well.

This time was not like before, though. Despite the swell of emotions that had surged in her when Sadie had barely been able to compliment her win today, she understood that it wasn't her success Sadie resented. In that moment, Sadie'd barely been able to see her through Destiny's pain. Jay had spent hours trying to understand what that must have felt like for a mother to witness, and to some small extent she did. She cared about Destiny, too, and what's more, she loved Sadie. Seeing them hurt for any reason caused her to hurt, too. In that sense, all their reactions had been reasonable, understandable, even logical.

What wasn't logical were Jay's feelings about what had caused the pain in the first place, namely, herself. No matter how many times she told herself she'd done the right thing by playing her best, she couldn't escape the fact that she was responsible for the turmoil she'd seen in Sadie's beautiful features. She couldn't stop envisioning the way her forehead had furrowed when Jay had taken the lead. Sadie had been rooting for Des. They hadn't talked about it, but deep down she'd always known that. Des was still young, and even when she grew older, Sadie wouldn't lose those protective instincts.

It had stung when her compassionate gaze had focused on Des to Jay's exclusion during the press conference, when she could easily have encompassed them both, but it made sense that Sadie would put her attention where it was needed most. Worse still was the way her beautiful smile had flattened into a tight line when Sadie tried to force herself to even speak to her before they parted ways, and yet Jay had spent hours justifying the tension because Destiny was there, and she had obviously interrupted a personal moment. The emotions of the match had still been raw, she told herself over and over, but the one question she couldn't brush away was that if everything really was all right, why hadn't Sadie come back yet?

The clock on the bedside table flashed 12:44. She rolled over and tried not to let her mind wander down any dark alleyways, but the longer she tangled the sheets alone, the harder Sadie's absence became to justify. Destiny had lost before. Hell, she'd lost a lot, and while that always made her mad, she had usually wanted to be alone. Why hadn't she sent Sadie away yet? Or maybe she had, and did Sadie want to be alone too? Or maybe Sadie didn't mind company, like Des or Tad, but didn't want to see Jay.

That was ultimately the fear that had kept Jay awake long after her muscles had given out. What if Sadie's withdrawal wasn't about Des, so much as it was about her? What if the tension she'd heard in Sadie's voice actually had been anger, and she'd been trying to argue away the truth for hours? What if Sadie loved her winning only if that winning also served to help further Destiny's career rather than hinder it?

Sadie's own voice echoed from the night Jay had first told her about Katia. *If she'd loved you the way you loved her, she would've been happy for you, no matter who you were beating.*

Her breath came in raspy, shallow gulps, and she sat up, trying to use gravity to pull more oxygen into her lungs, but as she rose, so did memories of Katia's resentment. The punishments for winning had always involved both an emotional and physical withdrawal. She knew better than to think Sadie capable of such a calculated and cold response, or at least she thought she did, but what would happen if her career took off again and Des's didn't? Des was Sadie's top priority, and she'd made it clear that anything that stood in their way would be held at a distance. Hadn't that been Tad's sin, after all? He'd only wanted to be a small part of their circle, and still Sadie held him at bay. And at least Tad had never been much of a bother. He'd never stood in their way. Sadie had said her love for Tad suffered in comparison to her love for Des. Had she come to the same conclusion about Jay?

She covered her face and screamed into her hands as, once again, Katia's memory grabbed hold of her faith and shook it violently, until she no longer knew what was real and what had been conjured by ghosts.

Springing from bed now, she paced the room, frantic for any interaction, but everywhere she looked, she saw only reminders of Sadie. Her well-worn flannel pajama-pants sat neatly folded atop her suitcase. A brush that had stolen a few dark strands of hair lay beside the clock. Jay couldn't even escape the reminders of her in the bathroom, where Sadie's purple toothbrush stood upright in a hotel coffee mug. She stared at it longingly as an idea started to form.

Hank's earlier warning about not poking the bear played through her mind, but she heard it now about as well as she had then, and for the same reasons. She wanted desperately to be close to Sadie, and if that led to some sort of backlash, then she'd face it head-on.

Grabbing the toothbrush and a few of the other reminders that ripped at her heart, she padded down the hallway barefoot until she reached the only room she really wanted to enter.

Before she thought it through, she knocked lightly, then again with only a little more force, certainly not loud enough to be heard over the jackhammering of her heart. Maybe that's why she didn't hear anyone approaching on the other side of the door until Sadie opened it.

As soon as they saw each other, the air left both their lungs in a united rush. They stood frozen and staring for long seconds before Jay held up the pile of items in her arms as a panicky peace offering. "I brought pajamas, and a toothbrush, and a bottle of some, um, lotiony stuff from the bathroom because you might need it if you're not coming back." The last part caused her voice to crack, and she struggled to swallow the emotion behind the break. "I mean, if you're sleeping in here."

Sadie's surprise melted into an expression of pure, unadulterated love as the lines in her forehead melted away and her smile crinkled the corners of her eyes, but before she could speak Destiny called, "Who is it?"

"Jay brought over my pajamas so we could have a slumber party," Sadie said. "Go back to sleep."

"That's nice," Des mumbled, and Jay heard the sheet rustling as Sadie stepped into the hallway, leaving the door behind her open only a crack.

"Sorry to wake her up," Jay muttered, feeling silly and bashful all of a sudden.

"Don't apologize. Once she falls asleep, she sleeps harder than any person I know, and it was a taxing day. She'll be dead to the world again in two seconds flat."

Jay nodded, reassured. "I just thought, well, maybe I worried a little bit that you weren't going to come back to our room tonight." She sighed. "I'm sorry. I didn't mean to freak out. I know Des needs you, and I don't begrudge her that, but when you didn't come back, I started to worry that you were mad at me for winning, and ... well, you know, that felt like, sort of like—"

"Katia," Sadie finished for her.

She shrugged, even more embarrassed now, but Sadie cupped her face in her hands, and gently tugged her closer. "Listen to me.

Today was hard on all of us, but I am not mad at you. I am happy for you."

"But you're sad for Des."

"I am," Sadie admitted with a sigh, "and as hard as it is to feel both those things at once, it's even harder to show them. You're right. Tonight I had to go where I was needed more."

"I know. I don't ever want to come between you two. I care about Des, too," Jay said in a rush.

Sadie pulled her down and kissed her forehead. "I know you do. You're wonderful, which is why it breaks my heart that you thought for even a moment that I would love you less because of some tennis match."

"It was silly of me."

"It was." Sadie grinned at her. "But it was also insensitive of me not to realize where your mind would go. I didn't intend to stay away all night. I thought I'd be able to explain everything to you when we settled down and Des went to sleep, but we dozed off."

They'd dozed off. In all her hours of attempting to battle insecurity with logic, why hadn't that possibility even occurred to her?

"I'm so sorry for bringing up those horrible memories. I can imagine what you must have thought, and I hate myself for hurting you." Her eyes filled with tears, and Jay hated herself a little for putting Sadie through any fraction of the emotional turmoil she'd felt earlier.

"Stop. You didn't do anything wrong. I'm just a mess. It's been so long since I've trusted anyone. It feels so new again."

"And it *is* new for me. I've never had anyone but Des to worry about."

"Don't worry about me. I'm fine."

Sadie raised dark eyebrows questioningly.

"I promise. We'll get through this." Jay put her hands on the perfect curve of Sadie's hips, relishing the contact she'd craved all day. "We'll figure things out as we go, but you make me believe we can get through anything."

Sadie melted into her, pressing their bodies and lips together with a fervor Jay couldn't possibly question. As her lips parted in the most delicious surrender, Jay felt part of her heart slipping back into place. The tension drained from her body along with the fear, leaving a space that could be filled only with the love she felt. Within Sadie's arms she was whole again, and totally immersed to the point that she didn't even notice the door open behind them until Destiny spoke.

"What the hell?"

Chapter Twelve

Jay jumped back before Sadie could even process what had happened, but as she whirled around, she couldn't mistake the look of horror that played over her daughter's face. She reached out for her instinctively, but Destiny jerked away as if Sadie were a monster rather than the woman she'd leaned on mere hours before.

"Des, please," Sadie pleaded, desperate to explain.

Destiny pursed her lips and shook her head violently.

"Calm down." Sadie forced herself to model the type of tone she wanted the conversation to take despite the way her heart raced. "I understand this is a surprise, but—"

"It's not." Destiny paced into the room before spinning and heading back toward them. "I saw this coming months ago. I knew something was wrong, but damn it, I trusted you."

Sadie followed her into the room. "Honey, calm down. You're blowing this out of proportion. Let's sit down and talk about this like adults. No one broke anyone's trust."

But Destiny wouldn't sit down. She wouldn't look at Sadie, either. Sadie would have thought she hadn't heard her words at all until she said, "Yes, she did. She breaks everyone's trust."

Sadie glanced over her shoulder to Jay, who was still standing in the doorway trying to understand this rapid shift in both focus and topic.

Jay didn't seem nearly as disoriented as she stepped inside and quietly closed the door behind her. Her face had gone pale, but she didn't shrink from the situation as she stood grim and stoic right behind Sadie.

"Don't come in here," Destiny said vehemently. "How can you even stand here after you looked me in the eye and told me you weren't who they said you were? You gave me your word. Is that how you dragged Katia in too?"

"Destiny!" Sadie snapped. "You're out of line."

"Am I?" Destiny's eyes blazed at Jay. "You want to tell her about your long history of broken promises, or should I?"

"I know about Katia," Sadie said firmly.

This seemed to knock some of the wind out of Destiny, who at least stopped pacing even if she didn't reply. Sadie used the break to plow forward as rationally as she could in the moment. "Jay told me everything before we got together. She was up front and open and fair with me."

Destiny snorted.

"I mean it. She's always been calm and kind and trusting, which is much more than you're giving her right now."

"She doesn't deserve your trust."

"Okay." Sadie'd heard enough. "That's it. I won't tolerate you speaking to her this way."

"If you don't want to hear it, then get out."

Sadie's eyes widened as she slowly looked her daughter up and down. "Excuse me?"

"Sade," Jay whispered, "she's got a right to her emotions."

"She doesn't have a right to disrespect you."

"Let her speak her piece."

"I don't need your permission. Either of you. I'm going to have this out," Destiny said resolutely. "I'm not a child, and I won't bite my tongue again. I won't let her do this again."

"She's not doing anything *again*. She didn't do anything in the first place." Sadie pleaded with Destiny to listen. "I understand what you saw was jolting. It's not the way I wanted you to find out, but I'm in love with Jay. I want to be with her. No one tricked me or misled me. She makes me tremendously happy, and I'd hoped that once you understood that, you'd be happy for me too."

Jay brushed Sadie's hand with her own, and Sadie looked up to see some of the color had returned to her face. Sadie felt a flash of relief at knowing the declaration had bolstered Jay, and hopefully laid to rest any of the fears that had resurfaced.

"You can't love her," Destiny said. "You don't even know who she really is. She plays people. She misleads women and uses them. She lies."

Sadie held up a hand to cut her off. Her sympathy for Destiny's position had worn off. "Enough. You're being completely unfair in bringing up things you know nothing about."

Destiny rolled her eyes again.

"I mean it," Sadie snapped. "You've let people you don't even know fill your head with lies instead of taking a hard look at the woman who has worked side by side with you for months. I'm disappointed in you. How can you not know for yourself who she is by now?"

"I thought I did. I gave her the benefit of the doubt, and I let her fool me too, but this"—she waved her hand between the two of them—"proves she's exactly who they said she was, a predator who can't keep a promise. Her word means nothing."

Something about those phrases triggered a memory that washed over Sadie so quickly she had to put a hand on the wall to steady herself from being bowled over. Jay's anguished voice echoed through her ears, calling her back to the first night they'd kissed. *I promised . . . I gave my word.*

Sadie turned slowly from Destiny back to Jay, who still stood so strong and steady beside her. She'd changed so much over the last few months, it was hard now to summon the image of her stalwart features twisted with the agony of that night, but the images had been burned deep into Sadie's consciousness by the fear of causing such torment again. Jay had been wracked with guilt about the kiss that had broken a promise. A promise to herself? Or a promise to someone else?

"You promised." Sadie whispered the words aloud.

Jay nodded slowly. "I did."

"You promised her what? To stay away from me?"

"Yes!" Destiny sounded victorious.

"No." Jay cut back in quietly. "I promised not to do anything to put your heart or your reputation in jeopardy."

"And you think you found some kind of loophole?" Destiny asked disgustedly.

"I know I didn't handle the situation the way you wanted, and I don't expect you to understand how hard I tried to fight these feelings, but I swear I love your mom, and I'd never do anything to put her at risk of being hurt in any way."

"That's bullshit," Destiny said fiercely, and Sadie was still reeling too much to do more than wince at the profanity. "You've already weaseled your way into her heart. She says she loves you."

"And I love her."

"You don't," Destiny said flatly. "If you loved her, you would've put her needs above yours. You wouldn't have put her in a position to lie. You wouldn't have snuck around like a dirty little secret. You wouldn't have exposed her to the possibility of scandals in the press."

"We're not going to get caught by the press," Jay said, but her voice trembled in ways it hadn't earlier. "I've been careful. I'm going to protect her. I meant what I told you. I'd lay down every-thing I have before I let the press get ahold of her."

"Stop!" Sadie shouted. Everything was moving too fast. She could barely keep up, much less process all the new information, but the words being thrown around now were the ones that had raised her ire all her life, and she had to clear a few things up. "You promised her you'd protect me before you even kissed me?"

"Yes," Des said, as if she'd scored a point.

"Not exactly," Jay corrected. "Destiny had some concerns about my feelings for you, and I shared them, so we had a heart to heart."

"When?"

"Madrid."

Another piece of the puzzle snapped into place. "On the court."

"Yes." They responded in unison, but only Destiny seemed happy.

"You two stopped a professional tennis match to talk about your conflicting plans for *my* love life weeks before I had a chance to even consider my feelings on the subject?" Destiny opened her mouth, but with a shake of her head, Sadie cut her off. "And then, without consulting me, the two of you came to some sort of pact about how you would handle situations that hadn't arisen, ones I hadn't even dreamed about, much less consented to?"

"Well . . ." Destiny drew out the word but couldn't seem to find anything to add.

"And you." She wheeled on Jay. "You left me standing alone in that hallway and drowning in my own doubts for a week while you tried to keep some promise you made to *my daughter*."

Jay finally hung her head. "I did."

"Then, when you finally had the decency to include me in part of your story, you left all of this information out of your drawn-out confessional?"

"I did."

"And for over a month you've fed me a story about how you were protecting Des by not going public when really you were protecting yourself from Destiny?"

Jay lifted her eyes once more. "I wanted to protect you both. I still do. She's not wrong to worry about what the press will do to you, to both of you, if this became public."

"See," Destiny said, "even she admits she's put you in danger. She can't keep her promises, and she can't protect you, so she's hiding you. She's lying about you. She's not good enough for you."

Sadie turned slowly back to Destiny. "And that's why you told her to stay away from me?"

"Yes."

"How dare you."

"What?" Destiny asked.

"You are the daughter. I am the mother. What in the last seventeen years of our lives together made you think you had the right to tell me who I could and couldn't associate with?"

233

"Mom—"

"That's right, I am the mom, a mother who has always been up front and honest and forthcoming with you. I taught you to be independent, and I gave you more trust than other parents because I believed in you. Do you have any idea how upsetting it is to find out you didn't think I deserved the same?"

"I tried to tell you about her—"

"You did," Sadie admitted, "but listen to the two people you listed: you and her. What about me? At what point did you stop to consider the fact that decisions about my life are mine to make?"

"I just wanted—"

"That's right. *You* wanted." She was on a roll now. The more she talked, the angrier she got. "You both came to your own agreement based on what you thought was best for me. You both made arrangements for my life without consulting me."

"I'm sorry," Jay said.

"You should be. You made me think you were looking out for Destiny's career."

"I was."

"But you were also keeping secrets from both of us."

Jay hung her head again. "You're right. It wouldn't have changed a thing about how I wanted to handle the situation, but I should have at least told you about the conversation with Des as soon as we kissed."

"You shouldn't have kissed her in the first place."

Sadie whirled back to face Des. "First of all, I kissed her."

Destiny let a little groan escape.

"Second of all, this is why you've been watching us so closely, isn't it? You thought you could just police me quietly or run interference. God, that night in Mallorca, did you even want to hang out with me, or did you just want to run Jay off?"

"No. I mean yes. Both maybe."

Sadie swallowed hard, trying to force down the burn of shame and bile rising up her throat. "Get out."

234

"What?" Jay and Destiny said in unison.

"I am so mad at both of you, I can't even sort out my feelings anymore. I need to be alone."

"Um, it's one o'clock in the morning," Des said.

"And?"

"It's her room," Jay mumbled.

"It was my room first, until I got manipulated out of it. It's my name on the bill, and it's my name that signs the checks. I made all the arrangements, and yet somehow it's the two of you who seem to be making all the decisions around here."

Jay stepped back, clearly recognizing she wasn't going to get anywhere else tonight, but Destiny managed a pathetic, "Where am I supposed to go?"

For the first time in her life, Sadie didn't melt at the mix of emotions in Destiny's voice. Instead, she stood her ground and pointed toward the door. "If you two have my whole life figured out for me, surely you can work that out too."

Jay sat on the bench alongside court number two, bouncing her knees up and down. They called this court the Graveyard of Champions, because so many of the greats had suffered losses here, but she couldn't imagine any one of them had ever endured the type of limbo she found herself in now.

She'd seen Hank enter the players' box, so she suspected Destiny was in the vicinity, but she hadn't actually seen her since she had stormed off last night. Jay had offered Des the empty bed in her room, but that had gone over about as well as anyone with half a brain would expect, and she'd once again returned to her own room to stare at the ceiling alone.

She glanced up at the box once more to see Hank looking disheveled in khakis and a white button-down shirt. Every one of his buttons appeared harassed nearly to the point of popping. He wouldn't meet her eyes, but his expression was grim. More telling, he was alone. Sadie's absence hurt even more than her presence had last night, but at least it made sense. Where had Tad gone? And more importantly, could American military members carry weapons in England?

Jay shook her head and sighed. How had she gone from feeling like a champion to wondering if her doubles partner's father/her girlfriend's ex-lover might have the means to murder her on the court?

"Jay." Heather had climbed down from her tall umpire's chair to speak to her quietly. "You've got three minutes left to warm up or forfeit."

"I'm not allowed to play doubles alone, am I?"

Heather managed a sympathetic grimace.

This was not good. Nothing had been good since yesterday morning when she'd awakened in Sadie's arms. The memory seemed ages old by now, but it really had been only one day ago. Everything else since then had been only blissful steps toward disaster.

"Okay, then. I guess I'm going to have to—"

"Warm up quickly," Heather said, with a nod over Jay's shoulder.

She turned around to see Destiny jog onto the court. Her white skirt ruffled on the breeze she created, and her ponytail bobbed back and forth across her shoulders, but the youthful aspects of her appearance were overpowered by the hard set of her jaw and the spite in her eyes.

"Um, yeah," Jay said slowly. "I guess so."

Heather backed away slowly as Des dropped her bag unceremoniously onto the bench.

"Hey." Jay offered a neutral greeting.

A tiny muscle in Destiny's jaw twitched, but she offered no voluntary response.

"You okay to play?"

Destiny wordlessly unzipped her bag and pulled out a racket, then without a word turned and strode onto the court.

"Fair enough," Jay said. "You serve first."

Destiny joined her at the net for a quick coin toss, then without so much as acknowledging anyone else's presence, strode purposefully to her position at the baseline.

Heather managed to discreetly raise an eyebrow to Jay, who shrugged. "At least we don't have to forfeit."

That had seemed like a win of sorts at the time. An hour later, Jay suspected winning had become a relative term, one she barely understood anymore.

The match had been nothing short of a disaster. A certain amount of tension could have been expected, and certainly in a game in which communication played a central role, she wasn't surprised to find that Destiny's unwillingness to speak to her proved a complicating factor. They'd been there before in the early days of their partnership, and she'd felt somewhat prepared to play amid barely hidden animosity. What she couldn't have anticipated, though, was Destiny's all-out determination to pretend she didn't even exist. Destiny cut her off on the crosscourt, swung rackets dangerously close to her ear, and went up for balls directly over Jay's head.

"Shit." Jay swore and hopped back, trying not to put all her weight on the foot that had just been crushed as Des came down from smashing an overhead spike into the net.

"Game," Heather called from the chair. "Ms. Gabler/Ms. Fradley lead five games to one in the second set."

"Ouch, ouch, ouch." Jay hobbled over to the bench and wrenched off her shoe to relieve some of the pressure from the onset of swelling.

"Do you need a trainer?" Heather asked.

"No," Jay hissed through gritted teeth, as she looked out at Des, who had not left the court. She continued to hop lightly from one foot to the other and take practice swings like a shadow boxer. That's about all Jay seemed to be to Des today, a shadow. "It's not broken."

"Ms. Pierce," Heather said, her voice lower and more personal, "if you need an injury time-out, it's within your right to take a few minutes."

She understood the suggestion. Heather wanted to give her a

chance to pull their shit together, but a ten-minute time-out wasn't nearly enough. Even with an endless number of hours at her disposal, she couldn't conceive of what she'd say to Destiny right now. And she wasn't even sure she should talk to Des about the subject anymore. Wasn't that what had started this whole thing in the first place? She needed to reach Sadie first, but she'd spent all night trying to think of ways to broach the subject with her and hadn't come to any definitive plan. As far as she was concerned, Sadie would be infinitely easier to approach than her daughter.

No, there was no use trying to prolong the misery out there. The ship wouldn't right itself, and Jay was in no position to try to steer. Tired, sad, and now sore, she couldn't think of any viable solution other than submitting to a quick death of their Wimbledon doubles dream.

Slipping her shoe back on and tying it much more loosely than its counterpart, she limped back on court and nodded to Des needlessly. Destiny hadn't made eye contact, and she would have served whether Jay was ready or not. Still, Jay must have been a glutton for punishment, because she couldn't resist another peek over her shoulder at the players' box. Hank sat with his elbows on his knees and his hands folded in front of his mouth as if he intended to pray his way out of this, and next to him sat Tad.

She did a double take. Tad, in Destiny's box, but no Sadie.

She was so surprised she missed Destiny's serve and only jerked back into focus long enough to see a return whiz down her sideline. She felt only a fleeting flash of chagrin at not making a move toward it, before turning fully around to look at Tad again. He wore an olive-green uniform that didn't quite mesh with the emerald chairs, and a stony expression not dissimilar to his daughter's. When had he arrived? And where was Sadie? It felt so wrong that he should be there and Sadie, not. The idea went against all experience and everything she'd come to understand about their parenting roles. Just another confusing twist in a long string of disorienting events.

To her left, the unmistakable pop of a racket colliding with tightly wrought strings drew her back to the moment, but not quickly enough to fend off a return straight at her chest. Instead of shifting to either side for either a forehand or a backhand, she merely flicked her racket upright in a defensive shield and bounced the ball back into the net.

"Love-thirty," Heather called unhelpfully.

She glanced from Tad back to the scoreboard before glancing back to Des, who had already tossed the next serve high into the air. *What the hell.* The quick pitch came too fast even by hurry-up standards, and Jay could barely react to the laser that Gabler sent back, threading the needle between them. To be fair, she might have lunged for it under other circumstances, but her foot still throbbed from the last time she'd gotten too close to Destiny.

She had sort of hoped for a quick end to the misery, but the least she could do was assume the position of an active participant in this beat-down, so she fought the urge to scan the crowd one more time. The person she ached to see clearly wasn't coming, and it was probably for the best. Making Sadie suffer through this train wreck of a match would only have added insult to injury.

She limped toward the net and crouched low, head down, back flat, eyes forward. Then in the same second when she registered the pop of racket to ball, she also felt the searing smack of blunt force between her shoulder blades.

"Son of a bitch," she shouted, but the collective gasp of several hundred spectators drowned out the profanity. She dropped one knee into the grass and bit her lip as tears sprang to her eyes from the sting, but as she saw several sets of sneakers move toward her, she held up a hand.

They all stopped, and she drew a shaky breath, then pushed herself shakily to her feet.

"I'm okay," she muttered, though she wasn't sure who she'd intended to convince. Maybe Heather? Or perhaps herself, but she didn't think anyone believed her. She wasn't okay, and the drill bit to the back didn't even rank in the top five reasons why.

She straightened up and looked around. Hank was on his feet, all the color gone from his face. Tad remained seated, head hung to hide his expression. Sadie wasn't there. Des hated her, and the longer this went on, the more Jay suspected she had good reason to. At least she had tapped into some righteous anger. Jay couldn't even summon that.

She'd broken promises, both spoken and unspoken. She'd risked her entire comeback, put strain on the tightest mother-daughter relationship she'd ever witnessed, and let down the only woman who had ever believed in her enough to make her believe in herself. Worst of all, she didn't have a damn clue what to do about it. She'd wreaked havoc in an ever-expanding circle and had to watch powerlessly as ripples of consequences from her actions expanded ever outward.

Anger laced with helplessness ripped at her as the familiar darkness threatened to overtake her again. She had done all this, and she couldn't even pretend she hadn't seen it coming this time. She'd known all the risks. She'd been the only one who really understood them, and yet she'd still marched them all straight into the flames. A ninety-mile-an-hour blunt force chiropractic adjustment didn't seem nearly strong enough punishment.

Thankfully Destiny didn't seem to agree, or perhaps she just didn't want to press her luck by testing Jay's tolerance for pain, and she hit a more moderate second serve right into the net.

"Game, set, match," Heather called from the chair.

It was over.

Sadie paced her room, still fuming. She shouldn't have watched. She'd vowed to make her absence felt today, and yet she couldn't completely disconnect from the match. She'd watched blow by body blow on the Tennis Channel. She'd nearly turned it off when Des had stepped on Jay, then she'd almost gone to the All England Club when she'd hit Jay in the back. Maybe she would have stormed up there and grounded her if Jay had shown any sign of anger, but it was as if all the fire had gone out of her. She took everything in stride, or at least with a quiet limp. Why

240

didn't she fight for herself? Had she finally decided she wasn't worth all this trouble?

"Damn it," she said, for about the hundredth time in ten hours. This was exactly why she couldn't go to the match. She couldn't trust herself not to cave to her emotions. Things had been so much easier last night when the anger had coursed through her veins like fire. The answers had been clearer then. Jay and Destiny had colluded to try to control her life without even talking to her. It hardly mattered what their intentions were. She didn't need other people messing with her independence. And if either of them had taken the time to consider her feelings at all, they should have known that nothing made her madder faster than someone else telling her how to live her life. But what Jay and Destiny had done was even worse: They'd taken choices away from her without even having the courtesy to tell her.

God, how embarrassing. Her lover and her teenage daughter had discussed her love life without her knowledge. The anger flared again.

It had come and gone so many times she'd lost track. The fire had consumed her through the night, then started to wane as morning broke, but with the sunrise came Tad.

She snorted at the memory. She couldn't think of anyone she'd wanted to see less in that moment, and yet there he'd been with boots and buttons polished. It had taken all of ten seconds to figure out where Destiny had gone when Sadie had thrown her out the night before.

He'd held up two cups of coffee and a bottle of Irish whiskey before saying, "We're close enough to Ireland to have this for breakfast, right?"

The flash of something edgy in his buttoned-up perfection had kept her from throwing him out just long enough for him to continue talking.

"I sent our daughter to work."

"You what?"

"I told her that she had a job to do, and if young men and women can march into war zones all over the globe with wives

241

and kids and bills and pain on their mind, she can damn well go to a tennis match while she was mad at her mom."

She'd narrowed her eyes at him. "Are you going to tell me the same?"

"I wouldn't dare," he'd said with a grin. "There's never been a war zone in the world that scared me as much as you do, Sadie."

She'd actually laughed and opened the door to him.

They hadn't talked about Jay or the fight he surely knew about. She'd merely taken the bottle from him and poured a single shot of whiskey into each cup of coffee.

The memory felt almost surreal now, but then again, so many things felt unreal about the last twenty-four hours. At least Tad had stuck mostly to his prescribed role in her life. He didn't question her as she turned on the Tennis Channel, and he hadn't said a word as they watched the train begin to slide off its rails via flat-screen TV. They sat in amiable silence as the first set spun out of control, and she found herself almost glad to have him there. Maybe it was the current stress of her relationship with Des or the loss of having Jay to talk to, but she started to wonder what it would have been like to have had someone beside her through all the tense parenting moments over the years. She'd always feared someone taking part of her joy, but she'd never considered what it would have been like to share part of her burdens. And yet, when she'd glanced over at him, she hadn't been able to stop the pang of regret that he wasn't someone else.

She'd turned back to the TV and gasped as Destiny swung for a high forehand, centimeters from the back of Jay's skull, but before she'd had a chance to process what had just happened, Tad had stood slowly and said, "I think I'm going to stroll on down to the tennis club now."

She raised an eyebrow.

"You see, I've never gotten to be part of a teenage meltdown." His smile had been slow and wry, causing a twinge of affection to stir in her. "I think it's about time I crossed that off my parenting bucket list. That is, if you don't mind letting me give it a go."

He'd deferred to her, again. He'd offered her the chance to get out of a sticky situation without feeling like she'd surrendered control at all. She'd met his eyes, and her chest had constricted. "You really are the perfect man, you know."

He'd smiled kindly. "I really am, which is why we both should've realized years ago it wasn't a man you were looking for."

"I did," Sadie had said. "I'm sorry."

"Actually, I think I did, too. But, just for the record, I don't have any regrets." And with that he'd closed the door and walked away, leaving her wishing she could say the same.

Over an hour later those regrets and doubts still tumbled around inside her brain, along with a myriad of conflicting emotions. For the first time in Destiny's professional career, Sadie had missed an entire match. For the first time, she'd watched her daughter misbehave without stepping in. For the first time, she'd watched Jay under attack and not rushed to her defense. It wasn't easy, but since the two of them had been so damn in control of her life lately, shouldn't they be able to get themselves out of trouble? The problems they faced today were of their own making, and yet her stomach roiled as the Tennis Channel came back from commercial to the announcers gleefully reporting their intent to cut away from live play as soon as Jay and Destiny's press conference began.

Anger, fear, and the need to nurture collided in her, and suddenly the room felt unbearably small. Or maybe that was her own skin. She didn't want to be the woman Jay and Des had painted her as, someone dependent and vulnerable who only mattered in her relation to them, and yet she didn't want to be nobody. She liked being a tennis mom. She was proud of the relationship she'd built with Jay. And having Tad defer to her on everything still didn't make her want to share parenting duties with him fully. She could add all those things together and still not work out the sum of what they meant for her.

The only thing she knew for sure was that she couldn't stand to stay in a hotel room going around in circles, physically or emotionally, a minute longer.

She slipped on her tennis shoes and headed for the door, grabbing her purse on the way out. She tried to tell herself she'd need her ID and room key to get back in, but even she couldn't ignore the fact that she'd picked up her Wimbledon grounds pass as well.

"If the match was any indication of their level of communication right now, this will certainly be interesting to watch, Mary," one of the announcers said, as the feed on the locker room television switched to pressroom coverage.

"Great, we're live," Jay mumbled as she limped through the door and up to the podium. It wasn't going to be easy to tap dance with the pain still pulsing through her feet and back, but after Destiny's attitude during the match, she figured she'd have to do all the heavy lifting behind the mic as well. Destiny still hadn't spoken a word to her, which, given how much she likely had to say, actually showed a lot of restraint. Jay only hoped she had the same sort of reserve with the reporters.

She crashed into the nearest seat in front of the purple and green backdrop, but Destiny pulled her chair a little farther away before easing into it stiffly. Several reporters adjusted their cameras to get them both in the shot, but they wasted no time in launching the barrage of questions.

"What happened out there?" someone called without waiting to be recognized.

"We lost," Jay said flatly. "Largely due to my lack of focus today."

"Did you two speak to each other once the whole match?"

"No," Destiny said quickly.

"Are you two speaking to each other at all?"

"We're speaking to you, Chuck," Jay cut back in, dodging the little lob to Des. "Forgive us for not doing a song and dance, but we just got our butts kicked. If you want us to hold hands and sing 'Kumbaya,' you might have to give us a few minutes."

"Did she break your foot?" someone else called, but between

244

the throbbing of her arch and the rapid back and forth, she couldn't even tell who.

"No, just a bruise," Jay said. Then before anyone else could push that line of questioning over to Des, she added, "We got tangled up. Our timing was off. It happens."

"What about the time she almost hit you with the racket?"

"Which time?" Another reporter cut in, to nervous laughter.

"I was in the wrong place at the wrong time. My fault."

"Every time?"

"Yes," she said, as emphatically as she could manage. No one was buying what she was selling, of course, mainly because it wasn't true. Even a casual tennis follower would've recognized that Des had crossed into Jay's playing space repeatedly, but at least if she kept talking, Des didn't have to.

"Does your breakdown today have anything to do with what happened yesterday?"

She winced as memories of last night flashed through her mind. Sadie, scared and hurt and angry, her eyes wide, her beautiful face pinched together as realization crowded her features. Jay fought to maintain her composure. The press didn't know any of that. Shaking her head, she said, "I don't know what you mean."

"You beat Destiny in singles, and a day later she's breaking your back with a ninety-mile-an-hour serve."

"Oh." She nearly laughed. The reporters thought Des was mad about the singles match. Twelve hours ago, that was the biggest fear in her life, too. What she wouldn't give to go back to worries that could be kissed away. Even now the fact that Destiny hit her with a serve was a minor concern compared to the ones relating to Sadie. "I'm sure that was just a slip of a sweaty grip," Jay said, as the door in the back of the room opened and someone slipped inside.

The lighting was uneven and the crowd thick, but she would have recognized that silhouette anywhere. She'd traced it in the dark and seen it outlined against her own sheets enough times to burn the memory into her mind. All the room faded as her

245

eyes followed the discreet path Sadie took to a seat in the back. All the pain and uncertainty receded. Sadie was there. She was in the room. She might still be mad, she might not trust her fully, but she'd cared enough to show up. Surely everything else could be overcome.

She glanced over to Destiny, whose jaw had tightened so that every muscle in her neck strained. She'd clearly seen her mother, too.

"So, you're really not going to give us any explanation for why the French Open champions tripped over each other all morning on the way to the biggest upset of the tournament so far?" someone asked with clear annoyance in their voice.

She sighed at the trivial intrusion, then turned her attention reluctantly back to the press conference with the sole intention of ending it quickly. "Look, we're all human. We had a rough morning, and we both made mistakes. It happens. We've had a breakneck pace for the last two months. Normally when one of us is off, the other one can pick up the slack, but today we were both struggling, and it showed."

Someone started to shout another question, but Jay held up a hand to cut them off as she continued saying what she needed to say to the only person who mattered. "I'm sure we'd both like to have a chance to do things differently, but we can't time-travel. We can only move forward, learn from our mistakes, and try to do better next time. Or at least that's what I want to do." She flashed a weak smile in Sadie's general direction, hoping the double meaning of her speech came through before she focused back on the reporters. "I know that doesn't sell newspapers, but it's the truth, okay?"

Several reporters shifted in their seats as silence stretched for the longest few seconds of the press conference so far, only to be broken by a female voice that sent a chill up Jay's spine.

"Destiny," she said coolly, "do you agree with Jay's assessment of what went wrong out there?"

Destiny's jaw tightened.

"She's had a rough day, Haley," Jay cut in, her tone more wary than tired now. "Do we really need to make her rehash every point I've already made?"

"Actually," Haley snapped back, "that question was addressed to Ms. Larsen, because what *you* assert as the so-called truth seems a little suspect to those of us who have followed the game for more than a decade."

Jay's face flamed instantly, and this time she didn't seek Sadie's eyes. She felt a flash of shame at the insinuation she'd been shielded from when she was winning. She should've known the doubts would creep back in the moment the scoreboard turned against her. Still, she hadn't braced herself for the bluntness of the assertion or the disdain with which it was delivered. The woman had stopped just short of calling Jay a liar to her face, and now she had to sit there helplessly while everyone turned to Destiny, waiting to see if she'd defend her.

"Destiny," Haley pressed again, more gently, even though Des wouldn't look at her. "Can you please tell us what you think caused the wide array of mistakes and miscues on the court today?"

A tiny muscle in Destiny's tight jaw twitched, as if she was fighting desperately to keep her mouth shut. Jay held her breath until it nearly hurt. The room sat completely silent.

"No." Then Des rose steadily, leaned over the mic, and said, "If you want any more explanations, you'll have to ask Jay. She's the one who can't control herself or keep her promises, and I'm done covering for her."

Then she stormed out the door.

Silence reigned in the room, or maybe Jay could only hear the whoosh of air leaving her lungs as if it had been forced out by a punch to the gut, because once her breath rushed in, sharp and painful, so did a barrage of questions.

"Jay, what's she talking about?"

"How did she cover for you?"

"What promises?"

"What does she mean 'control yourself'?"

"Jay, Jay, Jay."

They shouted her name over and over and over to the popping rhythm of flashbulbs. She sat frozen in place, squinting against the onslaught of light and noise without actually taking any of it in. The only clear thought she managed to have as the familiar numbness consumed her once more was, *Here we go again.*

Chapter Thirteen

Sadie stared helplessly as Jay folded in on herself. Shoulders forward, back slouched, she rested her elbows on the table and hung her head.

Without thinking, Sadie jumped to her feet, prepared to hurdle every camera to get to her, but a firm hand on her shoulder pushed her back down. She glanced up, ready to take a swing at whoever stood between her and Jay, but Hank only shook his head grimly at her.

"Are you sleeping with Destiny Larsen?" someone called out. Jay shook her head.

"Are you romantically linked in any way?"

"No," Jay rasped into the mic, her eyes still fixed on the table in front of her.

"She's mad at you about something," someone said sharply. "Are you going to tell us what?"

"No," Jay repeated.

"Jay," one of the regular reporters, Chuck maybe, pleaded. "We have to write something."

Sadie's chest constricted. He was offering her a chance, a way to save herself. *Take the lifeline.* She had seen Jay do a verbal bob and weave so many times. Surely she could pull off the move now. Sadie willed her to rise to the occasion, to say something funny or pithy to make this all go away.

Instead Jay sighed and looked up at him, her blue eyes now almost as pale and gray as her skin. "I don't comment publicly on my personal life."

There was a collective gasp, then rustling of paper, and more camera clicks.

"So, you admit the conflict between you and the seventeen-year-old Ms. Larsen stems from personal issues rather than the tennis court?" Haley asked, a glee in her voice Sadie had never heard before.

"No comment."

"Jay," Sadie whispered. "Come on. Fight."

"Are you currently single?" someone shouted from the back.

"No comment."

Sadie winced again. She should've been the one to answer that question. She was the only other person who had any right to, or at least she'd had that right last night. Had she forfeited it when she'd thrown Jay out? Or maybe when she'd stayed home from the match. Or perhaps she'd lost her claim to Jay when she'd refused to defend her during Destiny's punishing play today. Had she gotten here too late? Obviously, she'd arrived too late to stop the wound from being reopened, but couldn't she at least stop the bleeding?

"Do any of the other tennis players know about you and Destiny?"

"Everyone knows we are doubles partners," Jay said.

"Have you had any other romantic relationships with anyone else on the tour?"

Jay shook her head.

"Has any other player spent time with the two of you in social situations?"

"No comment."

No fight, no defense, no blame. Sadie watched helplessly for what felt like an eternity as the reporters battered her with questions and insinuations that no human should have to face. And Jay sat there, hunched over, her beautiful face void of emotion, her voice as flat as her refrain. "No comment."

Sadie finally turned back to Hank, whose complexion now ranged somewhere between green and ash. "Do something, or I will."

He nodded to a woman in a Wimbledon polo with a clipboard standing just to the side of the stage and, as Sadie turned to eye her more carefully, the woman made a swipe with her hand just below her chin in the universal sign for cut them off. Another person in a matching polo, a man this time, sprang from his seat in the front row, blocking Jay from view. "That's all for today, folks."

The press shouted their disapproval, but the man held out his arms as if trying to make his rail-thin frame take up more space. "Our next press conference will be in fifteen minutes featuring our men's quarterfinalist and—"

He didn't even finish before half the reporters sprinted for the door, and the others surged toward the stage, but in the commotion, the first tour official had grabbed Jay by the upper arm and hauled her out of the chair toward a door opposite the one most players used to go back to the locker rooms.

Sadie jumped up and took two steps after them before Hank caught her around the waist.

"You're not allowed back there."

"I'd like to see them stop me." Her voice rose to near panic.

"Sadie," he said tersely, "think before you act."

She shook her head, unable to think about anything other than getting to Jay.

"If you, Destiny Larsen's mother"—he paused to let the title sink in—"go charging back into a restricted area chasing her right now, the press will have a field day. You'll only hurt her more."

She started to shake, her whole body torn with indecision. She couldn't do nothing, but she didn't want to make things worse.

"Go find Des," Hank said quietly.

"Des," Sadie repeated. A new rush of emotions surged in her as three realizations hit her simultaneously. Des had done this. Des was alone. The press would come for her next. The anger at the first realization was tempered by the fear accompanying the other two.

"Find her and keep her away from the reporters. I promise I'll get to Jay."

Sadie squeezed his hand, unable to find any words, as the fear inside her ripped another piece of her heart. She made the choice and headed for the players' area. Both of the people she loved most needed her now, and she could chase only one of them. It had to be Destiny.

Jay could hear Hank shouting all the way down the hall. This side of the building was made for whispered conversations, with stark walls and stone floors that only amplified Hank's booming voice.

"I'm her coach," he bellowed. "Unless she's under arrest, you're going to have to arrest *me* to keep me out of that room."

She tried to smile but didn't have the energy. Instead, she simply put her head down, enjoying the cool glass tabletop against the heat burning up her skin. Her internal temperature ran rapidly between fire and ice, and her teeth chattered even as the flames licked her cheeks, but the discordance in her own body barely registered over the echoes in her mind. Sadie, Destiny, the reporters, Katia, all the voices swirled together in a haunting vortex, and Jay closed her eyes, ready to surrender, until the door swung open so hard it slammed loudly against the wall.

She didn't have enough energy to jump, but her eyes jerked open to see Hank's imposing frame filling most of the doorway.

As soon as she saw the terror on his face, a bit of life surged into her. "Where's Des?" Her voice sounded raspy and raw, but she pushed on. "Is she safe? Did they get to her?"

Hank shook his head. "I sent Sadie back to get her. They are both in the locker room."

Jay blew out a relieved breath as some of the tension left her chest. "Good. Now get them both back to America. Tonight."

"I'm not leaving," Hank said flatly, shutting the door behind him and taking the seat opposite her. "I'm staying with you this time."

The comment hit her square in the gut.

This time.

It was all going to happen again. They both understood what that meant, and he'd chosen her. Emotion clogged her throat, but she shook her head.

"Don't tell me *no*. I've seen this play before, and I'm not going to watch the reruns from the cheap seats. We need to rewrite the ending."

"We're the characters, not the authors," Jay said sadly, "and you have to play your part because you've seen the show before. You know what happens next as well as I do. Sadie and Des are going to need someone to help them."

"And you don't?"

"No one can help me now."

"Bullshit." He smacked his meaty paw on the table. "This is not over."

"Of course it's not. What happened out there was tame compared to what's coming. Sadie and Destiny can't even imagine."

"Sadie and Destiny are adults. Well, Sadie is, and Des is close enough. If she wants to be treated like one, she's going to have to face the consequences of her actions like an adult."

"You don't mean that," Jay said softly. "You're mad and scared."

"Aren't you?"

"Terrified, which is why I understand how people act when they're up against a wall. The urge to lash out can overpower you," Jay said with a shiver. "Des didn't understand what she did. There's no way she could comprehend what a comment like that could really do. She only wanted to protect Sadie. Fucked up as it is, she said what she did because she loves her mom."

Hank eyed her suspiciously. "And what about you? How do you feel about her mom?"

Jay's head fell forward once more as the weight of the question slammed down on her. The emotion ripped at her throat, but she let the feelings flow through her, washing away the numbness she'd clung to, and in its place found reserves she hadn't expected.

"I love her," she said, then managed a small smile. "I love her more than anyone can ever know, and that's what's going to give me the strength to do what I have to do."

"You don't have to do any of it alone," he said softly.

"I appreciate that."

"I'm not only talking about myself. She wanted to come back here. I had to physically restrain her to prevent her from breaking down the door to get to you."

"No." Her heart hammered painfully against her ribs. "You can't let her near me, not here, not now. The press, if they see her back here—"

"I know, I know," he said quickly. "I told her. She understands."

"She doesn't!" Jay hopped up and paced her small cage. "She doesn't have a clue. You have to get her out of here. Her and Des both. Get them as far away as possible."

"I'll tell them, but I want to stay with you."

"They won't go without you. If you really want to help me, you have to protect them."

He stared at her, his barrel chest rising and falling so dramatically it nearly popped the buttons off his white shirt.

"I mean it, Hank. If you love me, get them out of the fire and then don't let them look back. Please."

He sighed reluctantly and rose. "I'll do my best."

She threw her arms around him, and he squeezed her so tightly he nearly cracked her back, but she held him just as fiercely, trying to soak up every ounce of affection and human contact to fuel her fortitude.

"I'm sorry," he whispered.

"Me too." She practically sobbed, then wrenched herself away as she pushed him toward the door. "Go."

He obeyed, staggering out of the room. She slammed the door behind him, then fell back into the chair. There would be tour officials and interviews and formal inquiries, but whatever came her way, at least she'd know Sadie was safe.

Apparently, Jay wasn't the only one Destiny wasn't speaking to. By the time Sadie made it to the locker room, her daughter had already showered and dressed in street clothes. Mindful of Hank's warning not to make a scene publicly, Sadie merely followed as Des headed for the players' entrance without saying a word. As they strode purposefully down a series of corridors, Sadie tried to hold her panic at bay by running through the facts of the situation to figure out where things had gone so terribly wrong.

Obviously, Destiny's comments had been the final blow, and every time she thought of her daughter's actions, anger swelled in her, but then again, her words hadn't been her only bad behavior. She'd acted like a petulant child during the match, too. If Sadie had been there when she'd throttled Jay, Des would've never made it to the press conference in the first place. The thought made her stomach clench. If she had parented the situation sooner, if she had gone to the match, or if she'd talked to Des the night before, maybe there would have been no game meltdown to deal with.

God, she'd thrown them both out. Instead of acting like a mother or a partner, she'd kicked them both out of her room and left them to deal with all the emotions, all the uncertainty, all the fear, alone. They were supposed to be a family. Mere days ago, she had been completely enthralled with the idea of having it all. And now her whole world was fractured, with one half of her heart heading in one direction and the other left behind in peril.

The thought finally made her find her voice. "Wait."

Destiny did not wait. She didn't even slow down. She kept walking as if Sadie hadn't said anything.

"Stop," Sadie said more forcefully. Destiny's feet faltered, but she kept moving forward. She was almost to the door that would lead them to a variety of transportation options, and once she pushed through, they'd be too exposed to stay put. Their only choice would be to leave the grounds quickly, to leave Jay behind.

A fierce, protective instinct rose in her again, this time bolstered by a righteous indignation only a parent could muster. Mistakes or not, she was still the mother in this relationship. "Destiny Marie Larsen, you freeze right this second, or God help me, I'll . . ."

She didn't even know what the end of the threat would have been, because she never got to deliver it as Destiny swung open the heavy metal door, shot through, and slammed it behind her.

Stunned, she stood with her mouth open. For how long, she didn't even know. Nothing made sense anymore. Destiny had pushed boundaries and thrown fits and tested every limit Sadie had set over the last seventeen years, but she had never once dared to disobey a direct order. It was as if the last cord Sadie had attached to any sense of control snapped. She didn't even know who she was, much less what she should do next. Time seemed to stall or race, she couldn't tell which. All she could do was stand there, rigid in her indecision.

"Sadie," someone called from behind her. She didn't move.

"*Sadie.*" The voice called louder this time, but still she couldn't bring herself to respond.

Finally, a familiar hand landed heavily on her shoulder and shook until frozen muscles broke their shell of ice.

"Where's Destiny?"

She finally turned to look up at Hank. "She left."

"What? I told you to keep her—"

"I did. I ordered her to stay here, but she just walked out the door."

He blew out a ragged breath, then scrubbed his face with his hands as if trying to wash away everything that had happened. Then with an eerie calm he said, "Okay, we can do this, but we need to go now."

"But Jay—"

"Is in a meeting with tour officials that's going to last a long time."

"But I have to tell them—"

"Nothing. You don't tell anyone anything. Not the league, not the press, not even the bellman at the hotel." Then before waiting for a response, he swung open the door and said, "Trust me. We have to go *now.*"

She did trust him. Then again, what choice did she have? She couldn't get to Jay. She couldn't stand in the hallway all day. For

256

once in her life, she accepted an order and hopped into the first cab in the front of a line of waiting cars.

"When we get there, you might need to stay in the car," Hank finally said, once they were winding through the streets of Wimbledon.

"Why?"

"Because it's going to be a madhouse."

"What do you mean?" Sadie looked around for danger, but all she saw were the neat and tidy rows of houses surrounded by the hedges and low walls she and Jay had strolled by last week.

"The British press. They don't have to follow the same rules, and Des, she just did the paparazzi equivalent of throwing a steak to a pack of hungry lions."

"But you said Jay was with tour officials. Won't they at least protect her from the reporters?"

"It's not Jay we have to protect now," Hank said, a slight crack in his voice. "Look, it's Des."

As the car turned the corner onto their street, they nearly hit a wall of people. Even with the crowd's collective back to them, she could clearly tell they were mostly reporters from the camera flashes and extendable microphones. And from the tight circle they'd formed, she suspected they'd trapped someone in the middle. Hank's lion comment rushed back to her. He hadn't been talking about Destiny's comment. He'd been talking about her leaving the grounds unattended. Destiny was the hunk of meat they all wanted to tear apart.

Without thinking, she hopped from the car while it was still rolling and sprinted toward the crowd. Her daughter was in there somewhere. Her daughter was getting pushed and jabbed and hounded. Sadie raised her elbows and plowed through. If the reporters were lions, she was a rhinoceros. She would horn or trample or toss whoever she needed to get to her child. She wasn't even aware of who she was hitting, but she must have made her presence and purpose clear, because several people jostled aside to reveal Destiny with her hands over her head and her eyes wide with terror.

"How long have you been sleeping with Jay Pierce?" someone shouted.

"Are you a lesbian, or did she seduce you?"

"How many other tennis players have you been with?"

A man was right next to her ear, shouting questions with his camera flashing inches from her face. Sadie's vision flashed red. "Get away from my daughter!"

She hurled her body toward a reporter, causing him to jump back, and she wedged herself into the space his withdrawal created. Then, wrapping an arm around Des's shoulder, she urged her forward to the door. The reporters in front of them, however, refused to budge. She prepared to lower her head and plow them over, but suddenly Tad emerged from the throng in full dress uniform and beret.

"Clear the way," he barked commandingly. "Stand down!"

Several reporters jumped back, and several others stopped pushing long enough to glance around confusedly. Tad used their disorientation to flank Destiny's other side. At the same moment, Hank came bowling up from behind.

"Stay together," Tad called. "Forward march."

"Hey, that's not the military," someone shouted. "That's just her dad."

But before the press could regroup, their motley guard managed to push Destiny through most of them right up to the hotel door.

A harried-looking bellman motioned them inside and then tried to hold the press at bay while they sprinted across the small lobby.

"Go," Tad ordered. "I'll stay here until you're clear."

"I'll help hold them," Hank offered, skidding to a stop next to Tad.

Sadie barely glanced over her shoulder to see them forming a wall across the doorway as she and Des broke for the stairs to the second floor.

They didn't stop running until they reached Destiny's room and piled inside. Sadie pressed her back against the door, gasping for breath, and Destiny fell onto the bed in a heap. Neither one of them spoke as the realization sank in that nothing was going to be the same for them ever again.

Darkness surrounded her as she slipped out of the unmarked town car. Hank had texted that a few zealous members of the press were camped outside, but they couldn't get to the back door. Jay used the shroud of night to her advantage and slipped along the stone walls, down a driveway, and through a small parking area. Then she caught sight of a sliver of light in the wall. Checking over her shoulder one more time, she pushed through the door Hank had left ajar. The light inside hit her like a flash fire, and she almost shrank away from it. She'd been in the dark for so many hours, both physically and emotionally. Her afternoon had been a long series of interviews with tour officials and publicists, and even lawyers. She sank further into a depression with each one as she repeatedly answered the same question. No, she had not had a romantic relationship of any kind with Destiny Larsen, and each time she watched the doubt play across their faces.

Then when she'd finally been allowed to leave, the press hounded her, relentlessly pushing her back into restricted areas every time she so much as stuck her nose out of the business wing of the building. She had to wait until the grounds of the All England Tennis Club closed and had been cleared of all nonessential personnel before she could accept a ride in a tour-owned car, and even then, she'd had to slip in the back like a cat burglar.

Still, as she padded quietly up to her room, she could at least say she'd accomplished her two primary goals for the afternoon. She'd kept Sadie's name completely out of the conversation, and she'd made certain with tour officials that both the Larsens and Hank would be safely and quietly flown back to the U.S.A. before any sort of formal inquest began. They would, no doubt, both be called in for more questions eventually, and she had no idea what Destiny would say, but she couldn't control anything from this point forward, and she wasn't going to even try. All she could hope for now was to take a long, hot shower and attempt to get some sleep.

Unlocking her room, she leaned onto the door, letting the dead weight of her body swing it open, but before she even had the chance to fall forward, she found herself in the full embrace she hadn't even allowed herself to crave.

Sadie's mouth found hers, and all the exhaustion fled from her body. They kissed breathlessly, passionately, clinging to one another as if neither one of them had the strength required to move on their own. Sadie held her face in her hands, and Jay wrapped both arms around her waist. Air came in painful gasps as she sucked up every minuscule drop of affection she could take.

"I love you," Jay murmured between kisses.

"I love you," Sadie whispered, as she pulled her lips free. "I'm sorry."

"No, I'm sorry," Jay panted, burying her face in the crook of Sadie's neck, trying to surround herself in the comfort of her scent one more time.

"If I had come to the match . . ." Sadie said, kissing her cheek.

"If I hadn't come to your room last night . . ."

"If I had texted you sooner . . ."

"If I'd told you about Destiny's demands sooner . . ." Jay said, then pulled back enough to search Sadie's eyes. "Destiny. Is she okay?"

Tears filled Sadie's eyes, giving Jay the answer she hadn't wanted. "She won't speak to me." Sadie dropped her head to Jay's chest. "She's scared and she's hurting, but she's so damn mad. It doesn't matter if I yell or cry or plead. It's like I'm trying to communicate with a wall. Worse, it's like I'm not even there."

Jay held her tightly. "Does she know you're here?"

"She knows I'm supposed to be packing my stuff." Sadie motioned to her suitcase, fully loaded and standing by the door. "But I don't know if she's even aware I left the room, or if she cares."

"She cares," Jay whispered. "She cares about you more than you understand."

Sadie snorted.

"I mean it," Jay said. "She loves you."

Sadie shook her head. "Where did I go so wrong with her?"

"You didn't."

"What she did to you today—"

"Was a mistake," Jay said emphatically. "She's seventeen."

"She knows better."

"Of course she does, but she shot off her mouth in a moment of extreme pressure. I'd love to say I wouldn't have done the same, but I know what it's like to have the world breathing down your neck at your worst moment. I did worse, and I did it for much longer." Jay kissed Sadie's forehead. "But she's going to face consequences now."

"She's already seen it. The press followed her back here." The fear in Sadie's voice tore at Jay's heart. "They mobbed her. They wouldn't let her in the door. They kept shouting awful things. She looked so small and young, and they all wanted blood."

Jay shivered at the memories and stepped back. "That's why you have to go. You need to get her far away from here, away from me."

"No." Sadie shook her head. "That wasn't the deal. Hank said we were going back to America. I thought he meant all of us."

She stared at her white tennis shoes and swallowed the bile rising in her throat.

"Jay," Sadie said softly, "you are coming back with us."

"I'm staying here. I have to go forward."

"In the tournament? You're going to play your match tomorrow?"

"Yes," Jay replied slowly, not yet having the strength to say the rest.

"But then you'll join us?" Sadie's question was almost a whisper now.

"We can't be seen together." No. That wasn't fair. No more hiding and half-truths. That's what had gotten them here. "We can't be together. It's over."

"Over," Sadie repeated as she inched away from her.

"It's the only way."

"Liar," Sadie said, but didn't manage to put any force behind the word. "You kissed me. You told me you loved me."

"I do, which is why you have to stay away. I am only going to bring more pain to you and Des. What you saw her experience today was just the beginning. I can't do that to her."

"She did that to herself. She made that mess. She needs to clean it up. We can help her, hold a press conference or something, I don't know, but we'll make things right."

Jay shook her head. "This isn't some little parenting lesson, Sadie. Papers all over the world are printing headlines right now. Remember how I told you the press was gearing up for their big show? Well, this is it. The story is already all over the internet."

"Then we have to change the story."

"What could she possibly tell people? That she woke up to find her tennis partner making out with her mother while she slept, and she became so enraged that she resorted to physical violence and veiled accusations of sexual coercion?"

Sadie blanched at the retelling, but she managed to squeak out, "That's the truth."

"No one cares about the truth," Jay said. "They care about villains and victims. One of us is going to be cast in each role either way. And I knew that going in. You have no idea what the public eye can do to you, to Destiny."

"She might have to face consequences. I know it won't be easy."

"They will paint her as a spoiled, mean girl. They will assault her character, they will talk about her as morally unfit, they will look for deficiencies in her upbringing. Come on, Sadie, you know how this story ends. You've lived it before. How many times have you told me you've heard everything there is to hear about black, teenage, single moms?"

Sadie sank onto the edge of the bed, and something cracked inside Jay. The pain on Sadie's face clearly said she was winning this argument, and she hated herself for it, but she would hate herself more if she let all her dire predictions unfold without doing everything in her power to stop it. "And there's the story of you dating your daughter's tennis partner. They'll paint pictures of sordid rendezvous, say you lacked control, that you used your position as a tennis mom to—"

"Stop," Sadie snapped, as she hopped up off the bed. "I'm not going to sit here and listen to any more of this."

"Then you have to leave, because if you stay, if you try to make this go away, you're going to hear all of that and much worse every day for a very long time. The press will pick apart every aspect of your relationship with Destiny. We'll forever be seen as some sort of sordid triangle. We will never be free of it."

"I'm strong." Sadie lifted her chin defiantly. "I've been black my whole life. I've been an unwed mother for seventeen years. Do you have any idea what that does to a person's resolve?"

Jay shook her head.

"I love you. I can take it."

"Maybe you can, but you're not the only one involved here. What about me? What about your daughter?"

Sadie didn't respond as quickly this time.

"You can't have everything here," Jay said softly. "I'm sorry I let us both believe that we could. I should've known all along that, sooner or later, you would be forced to make a choice, and you've told me from day one that your choice will always be Destiny."

"Then it doesn't sound like I really have a choice, do I?" Sadie said, the hard edge back in her voice. "Seems like you've made all the choices for me."

"I won't be the person who comes between you and Destiny," Jay said, her resolve stronger after giving voice to the internal arguments that had filled her head all day. "You might be able to live with that for a while, but the resentment would eventually be too much."

"So, we're back to this? You and Destiny deciding that you know what's best for me?" She shook her head. "I thought I'd made it clear how much I hate other people making choices for me."

"It's not just you, Sadie. It's all of us. I have my pride, too. I'm just as stubborn as you are. I'm not going to be railroaded into letting you make all the decisions because you're the mom. I'm not Tad."

Sadie winced. "What's that supposed to mean?"

"It means everyone has always rolled over when the mama bear growls, but this isn't your arena. It's mine. This is my life and my career, too. I've been through this before, and I'm going to take the lead now."

"By take the lead, you mean hide and lie and run?"

Jay sighed. "If that's how you need to think of it, sure, but I'll do what it takes to survive. You don't have any right to take that away from me because you don't like other people telling you what to do. This is my choice."

"And your choice is to send me away? That's the bottom line, isn't it? You'd rather face everything alone than with me by your side?"

"Yes." Her voice held more volume than anger. "It's going to take every ounce of strength and fortitude I have left in me to survive this hell, and I want you as far away as possible while I do."

Sadie stared at her, eyes wide with hurt, lips parted in shock, as if Jay had just run her through with a knife.

"Sadie," Jay pleaded.

She held up her hand. "You've said enough."

She grabbed the handle of the suitcase and swung it toward the door. "You go ahead and do this your way."

"I'm trying to do the right thing for all of us."

"Letting people run over you is not the same as standing up for what's right. That's not strength, that's cowardice," Sadie said. "You're a coward, Jay."

Jay hung her head. She couldn't argue. Even if she'd had the energy or the desire, she didn't have a defense.

"You made me believe, for the first time in my life, that I could have it all. You made me believe you could give me that," Sadie said, as she swung open the door.

"I'm sorry I'm not the person you fell in love with," Jay said softly.

Sadie shook her head. "Me too."

Then she was gone, and Jay was once again truly alone.

Chapter Fourteen

Sadie quietly pushed open the door to Destiny's room and edged her way past the suitcases standing ready for the departure before adding her own to the mix. In the dim light from streetlamps outside the window, she could easily make out the shape of Destiny's form curled atop the bed. Even with sadness slackening her limbs, she felt the pull of her daughter too much to resist. Easing into a chair beside the bed, Sadie surveyed her smooth face, relaxed in sleep instead of twisted in fear or fury. All the old, familiar emotions welled up in her again. They didn't replace the anger she'd felt earlier, but they certainly complicated it. If there was one capacity every mother possessed, it was the ability to be simultaneously furious and filled with love.

Could that skill extend to Jay, too?

She closed her eyes and hung her head. If her feelings for Destiny were complicated, her feelings for Jay were downright convoluted. Jay had been right, at least about Des. She was still young and naïve. She didn't fully understand the chain of events she'd set in motion, but Jay did. Jay should know better. Jay should have the strength to fight for herself, for them. Of course she was scared, and of course she didn't want to go back to the way things had been before, but shouldn't that be all the more reason to stand up for herself, to tell her own story, to make her own voice heard? Unless of course she didn't think Sadie was worth the effort.

Sadie sighed and hung her head as the fear she'd barely held at bay all day broke through the chaos of other concerns clouding her mind. Tears swam behind her eyelids as the echo of Jay's "no comment" rang through her mind. They spilled over onto her cheeks as she envisioned the blank expression on Jay's face as she'd said she wanted her as far away as possible. No matter what the reason, that still hurt.

All this time, she'd been dreaming of someone to share her life with. The good and the bad, the ups and the downs. Even that morning, when Destiny had been behaving so badly, Sadie had longed to have Jay by her side, to talk to, to hold, to pull strength and comfort from. She hadn't relished the idea of a teenage fit on international TV, but a small part of her had looked forward to sharing the experience with someone she loved for the first time in her life.

"Mom?" a groggy voice asked.

She opened her eyes. Destiny squinted up at her.

"Are you crying?"

"No." Sadie spoke automatically, but then gave herself away by dabbing her eyes with the sleeve of her sweatshirt.

"You are." Destiny sat up. "Where did you go?"

"To get my stuff from our room."

"Our room," Destiny said slowly; then she jumped to her feet as if the phrase had burned a hole through her exhaustion. "You mean Jay's room? You saw her, didn't you?"

"Yes." She didn't see any need to lie.

"I can't believe this." Destiny began to pace like a wild animal in a confined space. "After everything you saw today, after everything we went through, after everything I had to do."

"Everything you *chose* to do," Sadie corrected, without much venom in her voice. "The press attention came from a choice you made. The mob outside the hotel wasn't Jay's doing, but you don't have to worry, no one saw me with her tonight. You won't have to worry about that making the headlines."

Destiny stopped moving and stared at her. "Are you serious?"

"Do I look like I'm joking?"

"You think I'm upset about the press? I just put my whole career in jeopardy to protect you from that woman, and you went back to see her tonight. Do you really think the most upsetting part of that for me is that someone else might have seen you?"

Sadie stared up at her daughter, towering tall and furious over her. For the first time, she didn't see her baby girl through the fierce warrior.

"I thought I made myself clear when I made an ass of myself on a show court of the biggest, most prestigious tennis tournament in the world. There is nothing I care about as much as you, and then you throw all of that away by going back to someone who doesn't deserve you."

Sadie blinked a few times, then tried to open her mouth, but all she could squeak out was, "What?"

"How could you do this?" Destiny raged. "You have been so perfect every day of my life. You think through everything, you have an answer to everything, you handled everything life threw at us."

"I didn't."

"You did!" Destiny shouted. "You are a queen. You deserve someone who will put you on a pedestal, someone who will take care of you, and comfort you, and show you off like a jewel. How could the fiercest woman I've ever known fall for a coward?"

The last word made Sadie wince, not because it was too harsh, but because it was the one she herself had used. Why did it seem so much worse to hear it from someone else?

"Do you even know what she did to Katia?"

The question jolted her back into the moment. "That's unfair."

"Don't feed me some line about Jay's side of that story. I don't care if they were lovers or who seduced who. I only care that Jay lied to the press about them for years, and then when the truth came out, she disappeared. She took no stand. She just moved on to another woman, and another, and another. And where is Katia now? Disgraced? Gone from the game. Gone from the public. Gone." Destiny's voice cracked on the last word, and all the fear behind her anger came pouring out. "You are all I have. I can't do this without you. I can't lose you."

Sadie jumped to her feet and tried to pull Destiny into a hug, but she pushed her away.

"Don't."

"Des, honey, I'm so sorry. I should've told you everything sooner. I had no idea what you were so mad about, but you've got this all wrong. Jay isn't who you think she is."

"She's not who *you* think she is. She's not a good person, and I can't believe you don't see that after today. She's doing the exact same thing she did last time."

"She's not."

"She is!" Destiny shouted. "I gave her a chance to do things differently today. I practically dared her to be honest and upright. Instead she proved herself to be exactly who I feared she was. Can't you see the pattern?"

Sadie shook her head, but she couldn't even form a response before Destiny fired another round of volleys.

"She lied to me, she hid away someone she claims to care about, and she exposed both of us to a firestorm in the press. Even when backed into a corner and asked directly about her relationship status, she refused to acknowledge you publicly. She would rather let them think she seduced me than admit *you* even exist in her life. She took what she wanted from you for as long as she could, and the first time she had to answer for her actions, she ran."

"She's trying to protect me."

Destiny snorted. "She's protecting herself. People stand up for the things they care about, but she treated you like a dirty little secret. If she'd had good intentions, she wouldn't have lied or snuck around."

"You're totally misreading the situation, and I can understand why now. I wish we'd had this conversation months ago."

"Months," Destiny groaned.

"Yes, months ago, before you stepped into something you didn't understand to try to warn off someone who had the power to make me happier than I have ever been."

"You're sitting here crying after sneaking back to see her. She's not making you happy. Even now, even with the press begging her for the story, she won't do the right thing. Does that make you happy?"

"No," Sadie said softly. "Today wasn't her finest moment, but I love her, and she loves me."

"Then where is she?" Destiny said flatly. "Why isn't she holding you while you cry? Why hasn't she told anyone else that she loves you? Because life got complicated? Because she wants the easy road out?"

"Because she wants to save us from a firestorm."

"She had her chance to do that today. She had her chance to do so for months. At any time along the way, she could have told the whole world she really loved you and faced whatever came next with you by her side, but what did she say when push came to shove?"

"No comment." Sadie repeated the phrase that had reverberated through her head all afternoon.

"People fight for what they love," Destiny said resolutely. "Right or wrong, I did what I did today because I'm willing to lose everything I've worked for to protect you. I took a stand. What did Jay do?"

Sadie didn't answer. She didn't want to. Saying the words would make them too real. She couldn't face the picture Destiny had painted so clearly. The months of hiding, Jay's denials at the press conference, the way she'd pushed Sadie away tonight. She didn't add them all up for fear she'd reach the same sum Destiny had. Mercifully, she didn't have to, as they were interrupted by a knock at the door.

Destiny opened it to Hank, who stood in the hallway, suitcase in hand. "I spoke to the tour officials. They are sending a car over right now. We're going to take a private charter to Amsterdam, and then from there we'll fly back to the U.S., but we have to leave now."

Destiny nodded curtly and slipped into her shoes, but Sadie remained frozen in her spot as the tearing sensation inside her reached a painful pitch. Pressing the heel of her palm squarely in

270

the center of her chest, she tried to summon any remaining reserves of fight left in her.

"Mom," Destiny said softly, "we have to go."

She shook her head. She didn't have to do anything. She made her own choices. She wouldn't be pushed around, not even by Destiny.

"Mom." Destiny tried again. "She knows where you are, and she hasn't come after you."

"No," Sadie said sadly. "She won't. She told me to go."

Destiny stood silently for a moment, her eyes shimmering with a mix of anger and sadness that Sadie suspected reflected her own, though maybe in different measure. Then she finally asked gently, "Shouldn't that be all the answer you need?"

Sadie nodded slowly. It wasn't what she needed. Not really, but it should have been, and more importantly, it was all she was going to get, so she picked up her suitcase and did what she had done a million times throughout her life. She chose her daughter over herself.

"Sev-en-teen. Sev-en-teen. Sev-en-teen." The taunts had started midway through the first set. She tried to tell herself that at least this one was rhythmic as opposed to the general boos that had rained down on her from the moment she'd walked onto the court, but the hatred behind this sentiment didn't feel any better simply because it had a beat to it.

She arched up for a serve, but a hiss from someone behind her made her wince, and she sent the ball careening into the net. The spectators roared with approval. In the absence of lions in this modern-day Colosseum, the crowd would have to satisfy its bloodlust via the scoreboard.

Sadly, the score wasn't as lopsided as it should have been. She hadn't expected to win a single game, but as she served to stay in the first match, she'd actually won three of them.

Jay collected a ball from one of the ball girls without even a mumbled thanks, not wanting to be seen conversing with a minor, then glanced across the court to see Peggy Hamilton in place opposite her.

Peggy had the lead, but she hadn't dominated the way Jay'd expected her to, even wanted her to. She'd made more than a reasonable amount of unforced errors, leading Jay to suspect the atmosphere was bothering her, too.

"Well, too damn bad," Jay said under her breath, and tossed the ball high again before sending this attempt long by a solid foot. She wouldn't feel sorry for Peggy. She was about to be a quarter-finalist at Wimbledon via the easiest defeat of her life. She would be cheered and adored today, no matter how badly she played. She would go home in peace and quiet. She wouldn't face a single angry fan or sit through a press conference with a salivating press corps. Most importantly, she would spend her evening with whoever she wanted. Friends, family, a lover, all options would be open to her without even a twinge of fear or guilt.

The crowd was raucous now that Jay's double fault had put her within one point of losing the first set. Her fingers twitched in their eagerness to drop the racket and run, but she tossed the ball high once more and lobbed an easy arcing serve over the net. Peggy sent it back with some speed, but before the ball had even cleared the net, she dropped her racket and grabbed her elbow.

Jay didn't even attempt to make a return as she sprinted toward the net, and the crowd sent up a chaotic mix of cheers and gasps.

"Game and set, Ms. Hamilton," the chair umpire called over the noise in the stands, and Jay waited at the net for Peggy, who walked over more slowly, her racket arm hanging limp by her side.

"What happened?"

Peggy ignored her for a moment, and instead directed her reply to the official sitting above them. "I need a trainer. My elbow, it's a sharp pain."

Jay's stomach roiled. "What are you doing?"

Peggy shook her head as she sat down on the bench.

The crowd picked up their chants of "sev-en-teen" again, and someone very near Jay's back added the name "Destiny" as some sort of twisted harmony.

Or then again, maybe they weren't only using Destiny as a name. Maybe this was her destiny. Hated, despised, distrusted, it all felt so familiar. Maybe she'd been stupid to think there'd ever be anything else for her.

Sadness battled with panic in her core, making it hard to draw a full breath for the two processes both attempting to exert their pressure at once. She clenched her jaw and fought to keep her eyes open, knowing that if she let the darkness close in even for a second, she might not be able to banish it again. All she had to do was stay on the court long enough to lose, and then she'd collect her check and get the hell out of London.

She stood up. They'd rested long enough, and yet she suspected nothing would ever feel restful again. She might as well plow on.

She looked over to Peggy, who met her eyes for one short second, but it was enough to see her own sadness and embarrassment reflected there. More disturbing, though, was a sort of resolve Jay hadn't expected, a subtle glint of madness and mischief.

"What?" Jay mouthed the word more than said it.

Peggy turned her head to the trainer jogging toward her.

"It's my elbow," she said to him, clearly loud enough to be heard by the chair umpire's mic. "I don't think I can keep playing."

The words rattled around in Jay's head as she tried to make sense of them, but as they slowly sank in, she felt as though she might be sinking, too. Dread washed over her, swirling around her like a rush of cold water until it settled right at her throat.

"When does it hurt?" the trainer asked.

"When I bend it," Peggy replied. Flexing the joint a few times, she grimaced to illustrate her point. "It's also starting to swell."

"No," Jay managed to squeak. This couldn't be happening. She had only one set left. She could net every ball if she had to, but she was almost free. She couldn't do this again. Not another match, not another press conference, not another scandal.

"I can give you an ice pack or a topical cream for the swelling. It might get you through the match."

"I think I may need to see a specialist," Peggy said calmly.

"No," Jay managed in a panic-stricken voice, but Peggy and the trainer both studiously ignored her. "God, Peggy, don't do this."

She didn't hear her response, if Peggy even made one. All she could hear over the din of the angry crowd was the rushing of her own pulse. She'd barely had enough strength to face today. How could she face tomorrow, or the next day, or the next? She couldn't do it. Not alone. Another realization struck her as the word *alone* spun through her mind. She wasn't really alone. What she really meant was that she couldn't do it without Sadie.

The stadium spun in a whirl of colors. Green blended with white, and her entire field of vision faded to pale light, but suddenly the chair umpire's voice rang out above all the other noise to declare, "Ms. Hamilton withdraws. Ms. Pierce wins by virtue of a forfeit."

The rage of the crowd couldn't match the storm raging in Jay as she snapped back into the moment. The match was over, and yet nothing was over. She didn't know where she'd find the resolve to step back onto this court, but right now she had to focus on finding the strength to leave it.

She collected her rackets without even seeing them. Bracing herself to walk closer to the screaming spectators, she strode toward the tunnel.

As she approached the corner exit where fans could nearly reach out and touch the players, she felt a body brush against her shoulder and heard Peggy softly say, "Stay beside me."

Jay didn't respond. She couldn't, for the lump of emotion in her throat. She simply walked into the tunnel with Peggy wordlessly by her side.

They silently strode that way down the hall and into the locker room until the door shut behind them. Then, dropping her rackets to the floor with a clatter, Jay swayed.

Peggy caught her and pulled her into a hug.

Judging by the sounds of chairs scraping against the floor and other doors swinging open, several people had quickly left the room, but Jay hardly had the wherewithal to care. Anything they'd think of her weakness didn't compare to what most of them already believed about her, and honestly, she didn't even care about that very much. She didn't have the energy to care about anything other than keeping her head above water, a task that Peggy had just made considerably harder.

She pushed Peggy away and stared at her most recent betrayer.

"What?" Peggy asked, her face turning pink.

"You forfeited."

"My elbow hurts."

Jay snorted.

"I'm serious."

"You could have beat me left-handed today."

"And then what? Get killed in the quarterfinals and risk making things worse?"

"Worse?" Jay exploded. "Do you really think anything could be worse than what I was getting out there today? And now I have to face it again."

"But you have a better chance of moving forward."

"I am never going to move forward from this," Jay shouted. "I barely survived the first time. I can't relive everything. I can't. I can't."

"Hey," Peggy said softly, "this is not last time. I know it feels that way, but you are not the same person. Sadie is not Katia."

"You don't know what this feels like. You don't understand what I have to do."

"You have to fight, Jay. If you run now, you'll never come back."

"I don't want to come back anymore. I was stupid to come back the first time. I made the same mistakes all over again, and now I'm going to face the same punishments."

"Stop." Peggy grabbed her by both arms and shook her. "You have to snap out of that line of thinking. You have to change the story. You can't give in to your old demons. I won't let you."

"You don't have a choice."

"I do," Peggy said forcefully. "I made the wrong one last time. I wasn't a good enough friend to you. I was young and scared about my own reputation, and my mom was controlling so much, whatever, but I'm not the same person I was ten years ago, and neither are you. You are not giving up. Not on tennis, and not on Sadie."

"Sadie's gone. She's on a plane back to America."

"Then call her. Go after her. Convince her you're not who they say you are. She already knows you're not after Des. She can't believe all the other stuff too."

"I made her leave," Jay said flatly. "I told her I didn't want her around anymore."

"You idiot. You two were perfect for each other. You could have fought this. She wanted to stay with you. She could have saved you."

Jay groaned. That's the last thing she wanted to hear. "I don't want her to sacrifice herself or her daughter for me. I'm not worth it."

"You are. God, if I ever see Katia again, I will choke the life out of her with my bare hands for making you think that. You are good and kind and noble. Everyone can see that but you."

"No. The fans, the press, they are always going to see me as a predator, and the only thing keeping me from believing them is that I'm willing to sacrifice everything to protect the people I love. I have to do this, and I have to do it alone."

"You don't. You can push back, tell the truth," Peggy pleaded. "Scream it until you're heard. You don't have to accept someone else's story."

"The story is better than the truth. It's the only way I can live with myself. It's the only way I can salvage any sense of self-respect or make any meaning out of this."

Peggy shook her head sadly. "Then I'm staying with you. You can't push me away. If you insist on spiraling out of control, you'll take me with you." Jay shook her head, but Peggy smiled. "I'm changing my part of the story, and I'm not going away until you're ready to change yours, too."

She hung her head, afraid Peggy would see the gratitude in her eyes. As much as she wanted to have the strength to go on alone, she simply didn't. As much as she wanted to pretend she was a loner, she wasn't. And as much as it hurt to wonder if things could have been different if she'd allowed Sadie to stay beside her, she couldn't stop herself. At least with Peggy here, she could tell herself not everything was the same as it had been before. Maybe she could pull strength from that difference to get through one more match without putting Sadie in any of the danger that came from being associated with her.

"The tennis world continues to be rocked by the recent scandal and insinuations coming out of Wimbledon, as Jay Pierce advanced yesterday by virtue of a forfeit," the announcer said again and again and again. The TV in the executive lounge had been tuned to sports highlights at the top of every hour for the last four hours. Sadie once again looked around for another open spot, but seeing as how the lounge was packed with delayed travelers, they were lucky to have found seats at all. The high-back chairs and circle formation around a small table gave them at least a modicum of privacy and comfort. Giving them up now might require her to stand indefinitely, and since she hadn't slept in two nights, she again chose the torture of reliving Jay's match yesterday. After the commercial break, she'd get to relive her press conference.

She blew out a deep, steadying breath as the announcers went on.

"Pierce took the court to a sea of boos and harassment after suspicious comments from her seventeen-year-old doubles partner suggested inappropriate conduct of a personal nature." The narration paused for viewers to hear the horrific taunts. Sadie ground her teeth to hold back the feeling that she could have stopped it all. Jay could have stopped it all, too.

"After winning the first set, Pierce's opponent and reportedly longtime friend, Peggy Hamilton, began to complain of an elbow

277

injury," the announcer continued. "The two were later seen leaving the All England Tennis Club complex together."

This comment had yet to pass without feeling like needles under her skin. Jay had allowed Peggy to stand by her, to escort her off the court, to stand between her and the press.

"People who follow the sport have pointed to Pierce's reaction to Hamilton's forfeit as a sign there may even have been a fix on."

Sadie glanced up at the screen again in time to see Jay mouth the word *no,* as Peggy turned from the trainer to the chair umpire. Then Jay closed her eyes, and for a moment it looked as though her knees might buckle underneath her.

"No doubt there will be more scrutiny as Pierce faces Jillian Fradley in this afternoon's quarterfinal match. That is, if the match is able to go forward at all. For more on that, let's check in with our weather team, who are currently tracking a line of severe storms moving across Europe."

Sadie sat back, her muscles melting more from lack of control than from any real relaxation.

She had a few minutes' break before she'd be subjected to the replay of Jay's press conference, though in some ways that video was worse than the first. At least when Jay was on the court, all the venom came from the crowd. Under the bright lights of the pressroom, Sadie could clearly see that more of Jay's torment stemmed from internal sources. Then again, Jay wasn't alone in that area.

She glanced across the small table to see Destiny still staring at the television, her complexion now a grayish green, and her eyes darker and more sunken than Sadie had ever seen them.

They hadn't spoken since leaving London. At first Sadie didn't have the strength to keep arguing with her. Then the anger had returned, but she hadn't known who she was madder at, Destiny, Jay, or herself. After she'd calmed down enough to see the signs of her own struggle mirrored in each of their expressions, she wasn't mad at anyone. Now she felt only sadness.

She sighed as the emotion rolled over her again. She was alone. Her daughter was in pain. Complex problems loomed like the clouds on the horizon. This was the time she normally sprang into action. She'd been in millions of hopeless situations throughout the years. She'd been looked down on and underestimated and stereotyped, and every single time she'd used her detractors to fuel her fire. Every time, she'd turned inward and found the strength to prove them wrong. And she'd triumphed by relying on herself instead of other people. She'd never needed anyone else. Until recently, she'd never even wanted anyone else. She'd never understood women who fell apart after a breakup.

A breakup.

The phrase floated through her mind. For the first time in her life, she'd been broken up with. Jay had told her she didn't want her around. She'd been dumped.

For some reason the thought hit her in the chest. She'd always been the one to push people away. She'd always been the one to make the call. She'd always been the one to go it alone.

Alone.

Why did everything keep coming back to that?

"And we're back to the Wide World of Sports, where this week, that wide world focuses on one word: Wimbledon." The TV announcer cut back in after a blissfully mundane commercial break. "And at Wimbledon, all eyes are currently on Jay Pierce, who, I'm sure you all know by now, is refusing to comment on reports that she had an inappropriate relationship with her underage doubles partner."

Sadie couldn't take it anymore. Someone else could have her seat if they wanted it badly enough to sit through the audio torture of that press conference again. Pushing her heavy body out of the chair, she strode purposefully to the opposite side of the room and leaned her forehead on the cool glass of the floor-to-ceiling windows that overlooked the dormant runways.

She could no longer hear the television speakers, but somehow Jay's words still followed her. Without meaning to, without wanting to, Sadie had memorized the chain of questions and answers and no longer had any control over her recall of them.

"I take full responsibility for my actions, both on and off the court," Jay had said.

"So, you admit to wrongdoing with Destiny Larsen?" someone had asked.

"I admit I wasn't the mentor or the tennis partner she wanted or deserved."

"Were the two of you a couple?"

"No."

"Did you ever pursue her romantically?"

"No."

"Are you currently involved with anyone romantically?"

Jay's voice gave only the tiniest waver. "No."

"Are you going to tell us what you did that made Destiny Larsen so mad at you? What promises she says you broke?"

"No," Jay said flatly. "I'll only say the blame lies with me. She is a bright young tennis star and a fierce competitor. She and her entire team deserve the best on every level, and I think we can all agree that's not me."

Sadie had the sudden urge to put her fist through the glass holding her up. The attacks on Jay's character still hurt. The fact that Jay was so quick to protect Destiny bothered her on multiple fronts. One, Destiny didn't deserve that level of loyalty, and two, if anyone was meant to protect her daughter, that was a mother's job. Perhaps most infuriating, though, was the fact that even while under attack, even in her clearly visible pain and humiliation, Jay would rather face everything alone than with Sadie by her side.

"Mom."

The word barely registered through the hurt threatening to swallow her.

"*Mom.*" Destiny tried again, this time laying a hand tentatively on her shoulder.

She turned to look at her without really seeing, but Destiny pushed a thick slip of paper into her hand.

"I rebooked us on a different flight."

The words didn't make sense. The WTA had handled their travel arrangements. Destiny had never been involved in making those decisions. Sadie didn't even know she knew how.

"You got us on a different flight to New York?"

"No," Destiny said, then looked out the window almost sheepishly. "I got us tickets back to London."

This time, as Sadie stared at her daughter, she actually saw her, saw the color return to her cheeks, saw the determination flash in her eyes, saw the grim line of her mouth.

Panic rose in her again, the same way it had the day before when the press had trapped her baby in their vicious circle. She couldn't face that again. She wouldn't. "No."

"I have to," Destiny said, with a flatness to her voice that echoed the numbness she'd heard in Jay's.

"You don't."

"I made a mistake."

"Yes, you did," Sadie admitted, too frightened to feel any pride that Destiny had finally come to that conclusion on her own. "You shouldn't have aired your frustration to the press, but you can't take that back now."

"That's not the mistake I'm talking about."

"What?"

"I made a mistake when I said Jay wasn't good enough for you."

"Oh." Sadie didn't know what else to say.

"I didn't think she was good enough for you. I didn't think she could be the kind of partner you deserved. I didn't think she could love you the way you deserve to be loved. In the past, she has always run when things got hard. She's always hidden. She's never taken a serious stand in her life. I didn't think she was capable."

The words made all the air leave Sadie's lungs.

"I was wrong."

Sadie shook her head. "No, actually, you were right on that count."

"She—well, I think anyway . . ." Destiny acted as if the words were stuck on the roof of her mouth and she had to force them out. "She loves you."

"People fight for what they believe in, for what matters to them."

Destiny looked over her shoulder at the television, and Sadie followed her line of vision to see Jay sitting, tired and broken and still taking a beating. "I think she *is* fighting for you," Destiny said. "She's standing there taking all the fire so that you can get away safely."

Part of Sadie understood that. She realized Jay's intentions were good, but that still left her on the outside looking in. "Maybe, but she made it clear she doesn't want me by her side while she does it."

"Did you know I asked dad once why he didn't ever want to live closer and see my matches and travel with us more?"

Sadie shook her head again, unable to follow yet another twist in topics and tone.

"He told me not everyone can be a tennis mom, and that was lucky for me, because I already had one of those. He said he figured what I needed most, once those needs were met, was for someone to just quietly stand a little farther away and make the world safe enough for you to keep doing your job. He said he loved me as much as you did, but the two of you just loved differently."

Sadie thought of Tad, and the truth of his statement. He did love them in his quietly steady way. She knew it as surely as she knew her own heart. She saw it every time she looked into those blue eyes of his. But, as she remembered the adoration in his eyes, her mind shifted to Jay's, so similar in color and yet so different in the emotions they held. Fire, passion, a desire that had consumed every part of her. Where had it all gone when they'd needed those things most?

"Some people rage, and some stand beside the people they love in the middle of an angry mob, but maybe other people bring the whole mob down on themselves so the people they love have time to catch a flight back home," Des said. Looking out over the rain-soaked runway, she added more quietly, "And some people make mistakes even when they are trying to protect the people they love."

Sadie smiled sadly as some of the pride she'd been unable to summon earlier broke through her pain. She cupped her daughter's face in one hand. "We all make mistakes. I love you—"

"Unconditionally. I know." Des met her eyes. "You always told me that no matter what I did or how mad I made you, you'd never stop loving me."

"It's true."

"Because you're the mom, and Mommy knows things," Des said, a hint of her own smile returning. "But you also told me that when I made a mistake, I needed to learn from it and make it right. I have to go back there to do that."

Sadie stared at her little girl, who looked more like a woman now than she ever had. Destiny wasn't the baby she'd held in the palm of her hand, or the sullen teenager she'd been days ago. She wasn't even the angry child she had been yesterday. Something powerful and profound had shifted in her.

"I'm proud of you for wanting to make amends," Sadie said emphatically, "but I'm not sure it's what Jay wants from us."

Destiny snorted. "Aren't you the woman who screamed at both of us about how decisions about your life aren't someone else's to make?"

Sadie smiled sadly. That seemed like a lifetime ago.

Destiny put a hand on Sadie's shoulder and squeezed before nodding toward the TV. "Look, Jay is up there fighting for us. Maybe that's a mistake. Maybe she'll think me going back there to fight for her is a mistake too. Or maybe she's just never had anyone fight for her, so she doesn't believe she's worth fighting for."

The truth of that statement hit Sadie like a hundred-mile-an-hour serve to the chest. No one had ever fought for Jay before. Everyone had either run or allowed themselves to be pushed away. She stared up at the screen. Jay certainly looked broken, alone, and resigned to her fate. Turning back to her daughter, she saw the same fear and resolve in her eyes. For once, both the women she loved were tugging her in the same direction.

The last piece of Sadie's resolve cracked.

Destiny lifted her chin defiantly. "Whatever flight you decide to take is fine with me, but you raised me to take responsibility for my actions, and to fight for what I believe in. That's why I'm going back to London."

"No," Sadie said resolutely, "that's why *we* are going back to London."

Chapter Fifteen

Something hit the windshield of the traditional London black cab with a *thwap*, and Jay looked up in time to see a tabloid newspaper lying flat across the glass before being unceremoniously brushed away by a quick flick of a windshield wiper blade.

To his credit, their cabbie had been the very picture of stiff upper lip in the face of the crowds trying to get at them, and he didn't so much as twitch at this latest intrusion. Jay wished she had some hint of that British ability to carry on amid an attack, but if not for Peggy sitting next to her, she might have ordered him to turn around and drive her right to Heathrow Airport.

"Hey," Peggy whispered, "look at me, not the headline."

Jay shook her head. "I didn't even notice which one it was."

"Good," Peggy muttered in a way that suggested she had, but Jay couldn't imagine why it would matter. They all said basically the same thing. She was a predator and possibly a pedophile. It didn't matter what catchy title anyone slapped over the accusations. She was once again the poster girl for the religious right's funding campaigns to eradicate gay rights. As if it wasn't bad enough, she had lost Sadie and her own career. Now she'd be used as a cautionary tale aimed at stripping away the rights of lesbians everywhere.

"Deep breaths," Peggy urged, as the cabbie wound slowly down Somerset Road toward the players' entrance of the All

England Tennis Club, and their car once again got hit with a barrage of coffee cups and hurled insults. At least she couldn't distinguish their words from inside the cab. Then again, they wouldn't stay inside the cab.

The driver pulled inside the wrought-iron gate and in front of the players' entrance, leaving them only a few steps to go to reach the sanctity of the buildings surrounding Centre Court.

"Ready?" Peggy asked, as they came to a stop.

The answer was clearly no. She wasn't ready for any of this, and yet at the same time she was as prepared as any person could reasonably be. She'd walked this path a thousand times in both memories and nightmares. She at least knew exactly what to expect. She didn't know if the knowledge she'd gained from previous experience was a blessing or a curse. Still, she nodded resolutely and handed the cab driver a wad of cash more than large enough to cover the extra trouble of transporting them. Then she swung open the door and stepped into the firestorm.

"Dyke," someone screamed, and the crowd erupted.

"Pervert."

"Seventeen."

"Go home."

"Going to hell."

All the words spilled out at once, and yet somehow she managed to hear them all individually as she unfolded her long frame from the car.

"Go," Peggy shouted, scrambling out from behind her.

"Go," Hank yelled from somewhere to her left.

She ducked her head and took two steps before she processed that she had actually heard Hank.

She whirled around to face the spot his voice had come from and was hit with the burst of light from a hundred flashbulbs.

Rubbing her eyes, she heard another voice call, "It's Larsen!"

She blinked away the white spots from her vision in time to see Destiny sprinting toward her with her eyes low and her hands covering her head.

"Destiny, Destiny, Destiny." The crowd clamored for her to

look their way. She refused. "Was Jay your first? Are you a lesbian? Where was your mother when all this was happening?"

Hank came rushing up behind her with Sadie in tow as Peggy found her feet as well. Before she could process what was happening, Jay's shoulder collided with Destiny's as the two of them were encircled and pushed toward the door.

Tour officials joined the throng and herded them through the hallways toward the players' area, and in her mix of confusion and panic, Jay allowed herself to be carried along. Her heart hammered at Sadie's proximity, and not in a good way. She hadn't even begun to think about how she'd protect them this time when they reached the final fork in the hallways where everyone should turn toward the lounge and locker rooms. Destiny came to a halt beside her.

"I have to go to the pressroom," she said abruptly.

Everyone who had been following purposefully behind them piled up in a mass of tripping feet and colliding limbs.

"I've prepared a statement."

Fear, raw animal fear, clawed at Jay's insides as tour officials turned to one another, each one no doubt hoping someone else would make the call. Decisions of this nature probably fell under the job descriptions of people much higher up on the pay scale.

As the silence stretched on, it became shockingly apparent that none of them had the authority to stop her, and the terror became too much for Jay to withstand any longer.

"No," she snapped, causing everyone to stare at her. "Absolutely not."

Destiny lifted her chin defiantly. "I wrote a speech. I'm going to read it to the press."

"Like hell you are. Do you know what I've gone through the last two days trying to protect you? You are not going to throw that all away. I forbid you."

Sadie laughed. The melodic sound cut through the tension like a knife through flesh. All the fear and anger inside Jay welled up and then suddenly dissipated.

"You can't forbid her," Sadie said lightly. "She's a strong young woman raised by a single mom who never took 'no' for an answer. She takes orders about as well as her mother does."

Jay stared at Sadie imploringly, the impulse to push her away and pull her close ripping her apart. "You can't let her do this. Think about her career."

"I did," Sadie said calmly, "and so did she, but then she also thought about her character and came to the conclusion that was more important. I happen to think she's correct."

"I don't," Jay said, then shook her head. "Or I do, but she doesn't have to fall on her sword. There are other ways. I can't allow this."

Destiny ignored her and pushed open the door to the pressroom.

Jay watched her go, then turned back to Hank, Peggy, and Sadie, silently begging one of them to do something.

Sadie only smiled again. "Good luck bossing her around."

"I'm not bossing her around. I'm trying to protect her."

"You can't," Sadie said softly, "but you can support her."

Hank silently swung open the door and nodded for them to enter. Peggy followed, but Jay stayed rooted to her spot. This couldn't be happening. She wasn't strong enough to stand it, but as Sadie finally sighed and went through the door without her, she finally realized she wasn't strong enough to stop it, either.

In the short seconds it had taken Sadie to join her daughter, the room had already erupted into chaos. Reporters who had only moments ago finished grilling the newest women's semifinalist were jumping over chairs to reset their cameras and recorders. They didn't even wait for Destiny to sit down before they began to shout questions.

"Where have you been?"

"Does Jay Pierce know you're here?"

"Have you filed criminal charges?"

"Are you gay?"

"Was your relationship with Jay consensual?"

Des's eyes widened as the gravity of the moment seemed to hit her, and she sought Sadie in the crowd.

Their eyes locked as Sadie stepped forward, just out from behind a camera. She couldn't bring herself to sit for the buzzing of her nerves, and her hands shook so badly she had to clasp them tightly in front of her, but she managed a short nod of encouragement and a half-smile.

The small gestures must have been enough, because Destiny pulled a piece of crumpled paper from her pocket and unfolded it with trembling fingers. She smoothed the creases almost obsessively, then laid it flat on the table before leaning toward the mic.

The room went silent but for the pounding of Sadie's heart and the sound of Destiny clearing her throat.

"I, um . . . I prepared a statement. I wrote it myself, and um, no one else has read it," Destiny started. "I am not going to take questions at this time, but I, uh . . . I wanted to, or needed to, say a few things, before—well, I should have said them sooner."

She and Sadie drew in a shaky breath in unison, but as Des lowered her head to read, Sadie felt a body push close against her shoulder. She would have assumed it was a reporter trying to get closer if not for the scent of salt and sandalwood surrounding her now.

Turning her head slowly, she saw Jay beside her, pale as the lights shining on Destiny, but for the bright blue eyes focused on the front of the room.

"Two days ago, I sat in this room, filled with frustration and anger, and I let my emotions get the better of me. I made a flippant comment meant to sting the woman sitting next to me, and I am ashamed of my pettiness. In that moment, I wanted to lash out, but I hadn't considered the full impact my words would have, or what others would infer from them. I came here today to explain myself, to correct the misconceptions I am responsible for, and to apologize."

No one made any attempt to interrupt as Destiny paused to take another breath.

"First of all, the promises I alluded to Jay breaking were not mine to know about. They were the sole responsibility of two adults in a relationship I was not a party to. I have no intention of butting into their personal life any further by making statements that abuse their right to privacy. I will, however, say I misjudged both parties in my limited understanding of their character and intentions."

"Who are you talking about?" someone shouted, and Jay twitched beside her, but Des didn't break her stride.

"Furthermore, I want to be absolutely clear that, at no point, have Jay Pierce and I been romantically involved, nor has she ever acted inappropriately in any way toward me or even in my presence. Jay has been a kind and patient mentor who attempted to be a friend to me. In my prejudice and poorly executed attempts to protect someone I loved from a threat that didn't exist, I treated her unfairly. I certainly didn't do anything to earn the loyalty she has shown me over the last few days. The hell she has had to endure was of my making. I am the one who deserved everything she faced."

In her peripheral vision, she saw Jay shake her head, but Sadie wordlessly reached for her hand. Intertwining their fingers, she gave a tight squeeze to keep Jay from pulling away.

"I behaved badly at every turn," Destiny said, her voice, which had been so resolute before, now growing thick with emotion. "I was selfish and childish and spiteful. I let down myself, and my coach, and my mother, who raised me to stand up for what's right no matter the cost. I disappointed the fans and misled all of you, however unintentionally. I should never have said the things I did, and the moment I realized how my comments had been misconstrued, I should have immediately issued a correction. Mostly though, I should have trusted Jay. I should have believed she was the person she had shown herself to be, over and over again, and not the person rumors made her out to be."

Destiny looked in their direction, but Sadie knew that this time it wasn't her eyes her daughter sought.

"I am sorry. I know that's not enough for all the pain I caused and the wedge I drove between two people who deserve so much better. I don't know how to fix the trust I broke, but I hope this is a start. I hope everyone I hurt can find a way to forgive me eventually, but in the meantime, I hope that all of you can give Jay the fairness she deserves as she takes the court today. I, for one, will be cheering for her when she does."

With only a slight crack in her last words, she bowed her head, and Sadie's heart nearly burst with pride.

She'd done it. Her daughter had made it through. She'd made a beautiful, genuine, sincere statement all on her own. Surely her words would make things better now.

But no sooner had the thought fluttered through Sadie's mind than the shocked silence in the room erupted into a barrage of questions.

"Why were you mad at Jay?"

"Did Jay pay you to make the statement?"

"Who are you protecting?"

"Did your mother know you were lying?"

"Can anyone else vouch for Jay's relationship status?"

"Have you ever seen Jay with other women?"

Destiny raised her head, her facial expression a mix of exhaustion and disgust, and Sadie clung tightly to Jay's hand.

"Where is Jay now?" someone shouted, and Destiny's eyes flicked once again toward them before staring down at the table.

Hank jumped toward the stage shouting, "No questions. She's not going to take any questions." But it was too late. Several reporters had turned in the direction Destiny had looked.

"There's Jay," one reporter called.

"With the mother," another shouted.

Reporters pushed through seats and tripods trying to get toward them.

"Are you two together?"

"How long have you been an item?"

"Is this what Destiny was mad about?"

"Ms. Larsen, were you sleeping with Jay while acting as Destiny's chaperone?"

"Were you ever married to Destiny's father? Where is he now?"

"How many of Destiny's tennis associates have you dated? Were they both men and women?"

"Who was watching your daughter while you were sleeping with Jay?"

Sadie's face flamed, and she opened her mouth to shout them down, but Jay tugged her back, using their interlocking fingers to secure her grip even as Sadie fought to hold her ground.

Tour officials closed around them once more, forming a barrier between them and the press while Jay's upper body strength won out and Sadie was dragged from the room.

"Let go of me." Jay jerked her arm from the grasp of whatever random tour official had hold of her, then through gritted teeth managed, "Please."

Sadie and Des stumbled to a stop around her as the shouts from the pressroom reverberated down the hall and into the players' lounge.

"Are you okay?" Sadie asked Des.

The girl nodded, but the fear in her eyes said otherwise. "I'm sorry. I didn't know they would turn on you."

"Hush," Sadie soothed, hugging her tightly. "I'm fine. I'm just worried about you."

"But the things they said about you. I didn't know how to respond. I froze."

Regret and shame oozed from Destiny's voice, and Jay felt them filling her as well, only her feelings were compounded by guilt, because she had expected exactly what had happened. She'd screamed her warnings to both of them. Why had they refused to listen?

"Ms. Pierce, you're supposed to take the court for warm-ups in five minutes," the tour official who'd dragged her in there said apologetically.

Jay stared at her as if she'd just spoken a foreign language, and she must have gotten the point because she backed away silently.

Finally, Hank and Peggy pushed through the door as if they'd been the rear guard of some violent retreat.

Jay spun from one to the other, then back to Sadie and Destiny without really seeing them. They were all in the trenches now when it should have just been her. The questions clamored through her brain once more, not the ones directed at her, but the shots aimed at Destiny and more so at Sadie. Even above the disorienting din of overlapping insults and insinuations, she clearly heard the shift away from her own past and into Sadie's. It had taken the jackals only thirty seconds to transition from the predatory lesbian myths to the stereotypes surrounding single mothers.

Frustration exploded inside her, and she whirled to slam a fist into the wall, but Hank caught her arm centimeters before impact.

"Whoa," he said gently. "If you need to hit something, aim for my stomach. It's a lot softer."

She didn't see any humor in the situation as she spun to face Destiny and Sadie. "Damn it, that's what I was trying to protect you from."

"You can't," Sadie said softly.

"I could have." Her voice cracked. "I was doing okay."

Peggy snorted and Jay's shoulders sagged.

"I was doing my best."

"I know." Sadie stepped closer. "You were doing too much."

"I wanted to save you from all of that." She gestured vaguely in the direction of the pressroom. Then, looking back at Des, she said, "I wanted to protect you from going through what I went through."

"You can't," Sadie said again before Des had a chance to respond. "You can't protect her from learning what she needs to learn, any more than you can protect me from loving you. No matter how much you want to throw up walls everywhere, that's not how parenting works, and it's not how love works either. Both of those experiences make you vulnerable."

"I don't want to be vulnerable," Jay said in a fit of honesty. "I

293

can't open myself up anymore, not to attacks or pain or losing you again. There are too many other people involved now. I can't lose control of the situation."

"It's not my strong suit either. I've always done things my own way. I've built my whole sense of self on standing alone and fighting the world single-handedly. And winning. I always came through on my own." Sadie's smile turned sad. "I suppose I'll do it again if I have to."

"You didn't have to. I was prepared to take the fallout for you."

"But that's the thing. I don't want you to do it for me, either. That's even worse because, on top of feeling alone, it makes me feel helpless. At least alone is familiar."

"No, you aren't alone," Jay said pleadingly. "I sent Hank away and I shielded Des and—"

"I want you." Sadie interrupted, cupping Jay's face in her hands. Jay tried to turn away, but Sadie held her. "Look at me, Jay. I want you. I need you. Do you know how hard that is for someone like me to say?"

Jay stared into the deep brown eyes, the ones that had challenged her and comforted her, and stirred her to believe in things she should never have believed were possible. "I'm not strong enough to do this again."

"Then don't. Do something different this time. Let's do something different together," Sadie begged. "You and me and this family we are patching together of people who love and care about each other. Put your faith in us."

The door swung open again, but this time the tour official merely stuck her head inside as if she feared what she might find. "Um, Ms. Pierce. It's time to take the court, or, um, you could forfeit."

Jay sighed. That was what this all boiled down to. She either had to step up or give up. The tearing sensation returned to her chest as two forces warred within her. She could end the fight right now. She looked around at the expectant faces surrounding her. Peggy, who'd stood by her. Hank, who had fought his way back to her. Destiny, who had put her whole career in jeopardy to defend her. And Sadie, who loved her enough to risk the world she'd spent her entire life building.

She could forfeit the match and save some of the pain, but in doing so she'd forfeit any right to their devotion.

Reaching up, she covered Sadie's hand with her own as she nodded slowly.

"Yes?" Sadie asked, tears shimmering in her eyes.

"Yes," Jay whispered, then leaned in and kissed her.

Her lips were as soft as Jay remembered, and the contact every bit as electric, as it sparked a hope in her that she hadn't let herself feel for days. It started in her core and spread through her limbs like a current of energy reanimating fatigued muscles and firing dormant nerve endings back to life. But before she had the chance to fully recharge, someone behind them cleared their throat loudly, and Jay broke away to see the tour official regarding them with confusion.

"I'm sorry," she said sheepishly, her eyebrows raised. "Is that a forfeit on the match or do you want to play?"

"Play!" everyone in the whole room answered in unison.

Chapter Sixteen

"She didn't even get to warm up." Sadie said, sidestepping through the crowd of people surrounding Centre Court to get to Jay's player's box. They hadn't had time to get to their seats before the match began, but even from the bowels of the building, they'd heard the boos echo around the grounds at the start of play. Still, they had to wait for the changeover after the first game before they could sneak in without obstructing anyone's view.

"I don't know," Hank said, a hint of teasing in his voice. "I think that kiss might have had a warming effect."

Sadie's face flushed at the memory and she hoped he was right.

"Yeah," Des said. "Judging by the way she bolted down the tunnel toward the court, I think she's going to be okay."

"She didn't even move that fast when the press was chasing her," Peggy added.

Sadie turned to face her. "I'm so sorry you had to help her through that alone. I should have been there."

Peggy waved her off as they found their chairs. "I should have been there last time. You let me repay a debt. You can have the next one, though."

The players walked back onto the court as Sadie pondered the last statement. There would be another time. They would all face more questions after this match, after the tournament, at the start of the next one, and possibly for the rest of Jay's career. The thought didn't please her, but the idea of being the person by Jay's side through it all did. The two of them together could provide Destiny with all the support and positive influence she would need to come of age through this trial as well. The last few days had not been an ideal environment for forging a family, and yet that's exactly what they'd done.

Down below on the green expanse of grass, Jay strode to the baseline and the boos rang out again. She calmly accepted two tennis balls and bounced them before, under the guise of handing one back to the ball girl, turning to face the crowd. Her blue eyes, luminous even from a distance, scanned the rows until they fell on Sadie. A smile spread slowly across her face, and she nodded.

Then she exploded into action. There was no other way to put it. If there was a tennis move to be made, Jay made it, and did so magnificently. Sadie could almost see an aura of command radiating off her as she sprinted, glided, slid, and swung in the most powerful display of fight and finesse Sadie had yet to see in women's tennis. Camera lenses pointed toward their box to catch every reaction to every epic point, and soon whispers spread through the crowd as people around them noticed their presence. No doubt many of them had already been in the stadium before Destiny's press conference, but word must have been spreading, because as Jay's play continued to improve, so did her reception.

It started with a smattering of applause down the right sideline as one of Jay's serves kissed the line, followed by a more grudging bit of acknowledgment when a drop shot had so much spin it landed on her opponent's side of the net before kicking back over the tape.

By the next changeover, Jay had broken her opponent and held serve, giving her a 2-1 lead, and Sadie estimated more than a quarter of the crowd was openly cheering for her. The break between sets also gave the spectators a chance to pull out their smartphones and read the sports headlines.

Peggy held up her phone to Des. "Your statement to the press is trending on Twitter, and it's the top story on every news site."

Destiny's complexion went a little gray, and Sadie reached across to take her hand.

"We'll get through it," she whispered.

"Yeah." Des forced a smile.

"Hey," Peggy cut back in lightly. "Would now be a bad time to ask if you're still going to play doubles with Jay, because if you're not, I think you and I could—"

"Peggy," Hank warned.

She laughed. "I'm just teasing." Then turning back to Des, she whispered, "Not really."

The little aside made the corners of Destiny's mouth curl up and Sadie's shoulder muscles relax slightly. She didn't really believe Peggy would steal Jay's doubles partner, but she appreciated the confidence boost she'd just given her daughter.

"Hey," Hank whispered, pulling their attention back toward his end of the row. "Have any of you considered the fact that Jay could win this?"

They all turned from one to another, each appearing mildly embarrassed to admit they hadn't.

"She'd be a Wimbledon finalist. That wasn't the plan when she walked in here today," Peggy said. "She just wanted to survive today."

"Me too," Des mumbled, and Sadie silently added a *me three*.

Jay jogged back across the grass once more and quickly sent the first serve careening off the crosscourt sideline. Hank said, "Now might be a good time to reevaluate the plan."

And he was right, as usual. Jay's adrenaline didn't seem to be waning. She got better as the match went on. The crowd's response improved as well, and both Jay and the spectators seemed to feed off each other. Every time the cheers grew, Jay responded by giving them something to cheer about, until they both crescendoed as Jay sent the match point skidding across the baseline at Jill Fradley's feet.

To her credit, Jill smiled brightly as she jogged to the net and threw her arms around Jay. Sadie barely had time to feel even a twinge of jealously that someone else got the first sweaty hug before Jay broke free and sprinted toward their corner of the court. Sadie leaned over the sidewall, laughing as she expected

Jay to run right up to the scoreboard they were sitting over so she'd be able to shout down her congratulations, but as Jay approached, she hurdled the low, green wall around the court. Hair disheveled, skin flushed, she climbed through the crowd until she sprang onto the roof of the press box. Then it was just a small hop down into Sadie's arms.

Either oblivious to the camera lenses or merely unconcerned by them, she wrapped one arm around Sadie's waist, tipped her back slightly, and planted a kiss right on her mouth.

The crowd gasped, and then from the sound of things, many of them cheered. Sadie didn't have the wherewithal to count voices with all the sensory overload she was experiencing. The scent of sweat and sandalwood, the taste of salt on parched lips, the press of hard muscles against her once more, and the crowd of thousands disappeared. For a glorious moment, Jay was there again, and there was only Jay.

Much too soon, Jay eased back, still clutching her tightly and said, "You wanted me to fight for you. How was that for a start?"

She laughed. "A start? Yes, I suppose that was a pretty good one."

Jay made a show of glancing around at all the cameras being thrust into their personal space, and her smile faltered slightly. "There will be more fights ahead. For all of us."

"We're ready," Sadie said, then turned to Hank, Peggy, and Des.

Jay raised an eyebrow toward Des.

"Yeah. Well, I mean, you hurt her and I will not hesitate to hit you with more than a serve, but the rest of it all—" she shrugged and gave a half-smile—"my mom raised a fighter."

Jay reached out to give her a fist bump that must have been captured by every camera in the stadium, because the gesture sent up another round of applause.

"What about me?" Peggy held out her fist. "Can I get my photo taken with the newest Wimbledon semifinalist?"

Jay stuck out her fist again. Then, as if the words had just sunk in, her eyes went wide and she repeated the word "semifinalist."

299

Hank laughed and yanked her into a bear hug. "Yes, semifinalist, and I've already got some video files I want you to look at. Oh and also a new serve drill I want you to try, though I don't know how you're going to top this celebration. You know at Wimbledon it's traditional to jump into the crowd only after you've won the whole damn thing?"

Jay laughed and turned back to meet Sadie's eyes once more as she said, "I won everything that matters."

Epilogue

"You want to sleep with the trophy tonight?" Jay asked Des, as they finally left the ballroom of whatever hotel the WTA had rented for the U.S.A. finalists and winners to celebrate in. And by celebrate, they clearly meant mingle with sponsors, because that's all they'd done for hours. Or maybe days. Jay wasn't certain anymore, not of the date, not of the time, and not of who all she'd spoken to during this endless event. Hell, she only knew which city they were in because the trophy she had crooked under her arm had US Open Doubles Champion inscribed on the big silver cup.

"Yeah," Des said dreamily. "I kind of do. It's becoming a post-tournament tradition."

Jay smiled at the fact that they'd won enough tournaments to build traditions. Two majors in one year with a handful of other minor victories in between. Four out of six of the warm-ups for the US Open alone. Not that she was counting. Except she was totally counting, all the wins she could get. Though, admittedly, her definition of "win" had changed a lot in the two months since Wimbledon.

As if on cue, she felt Sadie's hand slip into her own. The sensation had become a familiar comfort over the months of press conferences and intimate interviews, and even a couple

301

of sessions with a professional biographer. She'd answered more questions about her life in the last few weeks than she'd answered in the three decades leading up to them, and the only way she'd found the fortitude to push on was that every time the urge to run pulsed through her, Sadie's hand, steady and strong, held her rooted right where she needed to be.

"Are we taking this party back to our room?" Sadie asked Hank as he fell in beside them.

"I'm going to bed," Des grumbled, grabbing the trophy from Jay. "And if there are any parties in your room tonight, I don't want to know about them."

Hank snorted.

Jay gave Sadie's hand a little squeeze. The transition from single mom to mom-dating-your-doubles-partner hadn't always gone smoothly, but even amid the awkwardness, Destiny had stuck to her promise to put Sadie's happiness above her own. And as the chaos and scrutiny that had once terrified them gradually became their new normal, Des's wry sense of humor had emerged as a coping skill.

They arrived at the elevator and piled inside before Sadie pushed their button and said, "Well, maybe we'll all have a more subdued celebration over breakfast tomorrow. There's a place down by the—"

"No," everyone else said in unison, and Sadie laughed.

The sound rolled over Jay like the warm water of a long shower after their exhausting three-set match earlier in the day.

"Fine." Sadie chuckled as the elevator door opened. "Everyone can sleep in tomorrow, but you guys are going to have to let me have a party or something at some point, because I'm the proud mom and the proud girlfriend, and that's a lot of proud to contain in one body."

"Goodnight, Sadie," Hank said happily. "I'm not the mom or the girlfriend, but for what it's worth, I'm proud too, and not just about what you guys did on the court. I mean, mostly the court, but the other stuff too."

"Goodnight, Hank," Des said with a quick hug. "We love you, too."

He smiled and wandered off down the hall.

"And goodnight to you," Des said to Jay. "Don't forget we owe Peggy dinner before leaving New York."

"Pretty sure she's not going to let me forget," Jay said. "It's the first thing she said when she hugged me at the net today."

"And that was before she had to stand there and watch all the big bank people hand us that check for $700,000," Des said.

"I hope she orders a filet mignon and washes it down with a bottle of Dom Perignon," Sadie said, almost gleefully. "You can afford it."

"Thanks to you," Jay said, leaning in to kiss her on the cheek.

"No, thanks to your skill." Sadie kissed her back.

"No, thanks to my skill," Des said, then held up the big silver cup in front of her face. "But don't kiss me."

"Okay, I'll kiss her again," Jay said, then planted another dramatic smooch on Sadie's cheek.

Des sighed heavily. "I can't wait until you guys are out of the schmoopy stage."

Sadie ducked around the trophy and kissed her daughter on the temple. "You should see what we're like when you're not around."

Des grimaced and backed away. "And on that note, my room is all the way at the other end of the hall."

"Goodnight, honey."

"Yes," Jay added. "Goodnight, honey."

"Goodnight, Mom," Des called, then added, "goodnight, Not-My-Mom."

Sadie rested her head on Jay's shoulder as they watched her go. "She's doing okay, isn't she?"

"Yeah," Jay said, a little wonderstruck by it all. "I think so."

"Thank you for that."

"You've had a lot more to do with it than I have."

"That's true," Sadie said lightly, "but I don't know how I would have gotten her through the last two months without you."

"You would have found a way."

"Maybe," Sadie said, then kissed her again. "But I'm sure glad I didn't have to do it alone."

Jay turned to face her. "Me too."

"I spent so many years proving I could do it all on my own. It seems silly now, but I can hardly remember why I felt like sharing parts of me with someone else, or sharing her with someone else, would mean there was less love to go around."

Jay nodded thoughtfully. "At least you had her. I wouldn't let myself love anyone. I pushed away every person who even tried to love me for years. I wouldn't even let my friends get close until you came along."

"And now?" Sadie asked hopefully, as she used the key card to open their room.

"And now I have a family. It's an unconventional family, but it's our family. And I love every piece of it."

Sadie opened the door to their room and tugged her inside, but a sudden thought made Jay halt in the door frame. Sadie turned, her eyebrows raised. "What is it?"

"I just realized tennis had the answer for me all along."

"How so?"

"Because no matter what the final score will be, every win gets its start with the same advice. I'd just never listened to it until you came along."

Sadie cocked her head to the side. "What advice?"

Jay smiled and wrapped her arm around her waist. "Love, all."

Acknowledgments

Normally when I write books about exciting subjects far from my own life experiences, I issue a silly disclaimer like, "I am not a tennis star; I just play one in a book." These statements are generally made tongue-in-cheek, as anyone who has seen me repeatedly net backhands at the local parks can verify that I am a long way from the professional tour. However, over the last few years I have been drawn increasingly close to the world of tennis. My son, Jackson, has taken to this sport I had never played, and I have learned to love it through his eyes. I have also learned to love it as a parent who sees the game challenging my child to reach beyond his comfort zone, to grow stronger, to build stamina, and to develop a mental fortitude the likes of which no other sport has demanded of him. I have enjoyed every minute of learning the ins and outs and cultural norms of this new world, even though they have often left me feeling helpless as I sit on the sidelines. I have both thrilled and cringed at the rules about not coaching (or even talking) during matches, leaving the game to be navigated almost solely by those on the court and independent of who's in the stands. In short, I may not be a tennis star, but I have certainly become a tennis mom, and those experiences have helped me tremendously when writing this book. So, thank you to the wide world of the USTA and the small world of Western New York tennis. I would especially like to thank Jane Gens for being the best coach we could ever ask for. In addition, I am grateful to the Chautauqua Tennis Club, the Fredonia High School tennis team, and all the wonderful local players and coaches who have given their time and energy to help bring our family up to speed and give these characters a touch of authenticity. Then a wonderful crew of copy editors and proofreaders including Cara, Rebecca, Ann, Marcie, Caroline, and Susie served as my powerful and last line of defense against the horror of typos in the final draft. I thank them all endlessly!

I also want to thank my Bywater family. As usual, Salem West, Marianne K. Martin, Kelly Smith, and Ann McMan were a joy to work with, despite the fact that I came in a little close to the wire with this one. Special thanks goes, once again, to Ann McMan for the awesome cover that not only speaks to the intensity of my main character, but also showcases a real athlete with a real athletic body.

I am blessed to again have a diverse group of people to lean heavily on when trying to make this book everything I want it to be. Longtime friend and beta reader Barb Dallinger asked some great questions that helped me focus some points about the intricate world of tennis travel instead of just guessing. Toni and Tosh were open and honest with me about tackling details outside of my own life experiences with authenticity. I don't know that I would have written this book without knowing I could trust them to do so. Lynda Sandoval, my editor and awesome friend, offered wonderful insights laced with challenges to not take the easy way out.

I also want to thank the people who contribute to my work in ways that are harder to quantify, but no less important. I have the best writing support group in Georgia Beers, Melissa Brayden, and Nikki Smalls. I am also spurred onward and upward by every reader who has ever bought, read, reviewed, or offered feedback on my work. Writing can be lonely sometimes, but knowing there are people out there waiting for the next book helps keep my head in the game and my butt in the chair.

And speaking of people who keep me going through good times and bad, I am tremendously blessed to share my life with the two best teammates and tennis partners in the world. Jackie, thank you for showing me new ways to find joy every day. This book wouldn't exist if you hadn't given me the chance to be your tennis mom. Susie, I know I bring down your average on the court, but I hope I contribute in other ways, and I pray you always know how much I appreciate your unending love and support, come what may.

Finally, I want to acknowledge that every blessing in my life is born from the love of my creator, redeemer and sanctifier. *Soli Deo Gloria.*

About the Author

Rachel Spangler never set out to be an award-winning author. She was just so poor during her college years that she had to come up with creative ways to entertain herself, and her first novel, *Learning Curve,* was born out of one such attempt. She was sincerely surprised when it was accepted for publication and even more shocked when it won the Golden Crown Literary Award for Debut Author. She also won a Goldie for subsequent novels *Trails Merge* and *Perfect Pairings.* Since writing is more fun than a real job and so much cheaper than therapy, Rachel continued to type away, leading to the publication of *The Long Way Home, LoveLife, Spanish Heart, Does She Love You, Timeless, Heart of the Game, Perfect Pairing, Close to Home, Edge of Glory, In Development,* and *Love All.* She is a three-time Lambda Literary Award Finalist and the 2018 Alice B. Reader Award winner. She plans to continue writing as long as anyone, anywhere, will keep reading.

Rachel and her partner, Susan, are raising their son in Western New York, where during the winter they make the most of the lake-effect snow on local ski slopes. In the summer, they love to travel and watch their beloved St. Louis Cardinals. Regardless of the season, she always makes time for a good romance, whether she's reading it, writing it, or living it.

For more information, visit Rachel online at www.rachelspangler.com or on Facebook, Twitter, or Instagram.

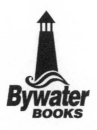

Bywater BOOKS

At Bywater Books we love good books about lesbians just like you do, and we're committed to bringing the best of contemporary lesbian writing to our avid readers. Our editorial team is dedicated to finding and developing outstanding writers who create books you won't want to put down.

We sponsor the Bywater Prize for Fiction to help with this quest. Each prize winner receives $1,000 and publication of their novel. We have already discovered amazing writers like Jill Malone, Sally Bellerose, and Hilary Sloin through the Bywater Prize. Which exciting new writer will we find next?

For more information about Bywater Books and the annual Bywater Prize for Fiction, please visit our website.

www.bywaterbooks.com